A Perfect
Copy

Published 2022
by Poolbeg Press Ltd
123 Grange Hill, Baldoyle,
Dublin 13, Ireland
Email: poolbeg@poolbeg.com

A catalogue record for this book is available from the British Library.

ISBN 978178199-719-2

www.poolbeg.com

A Perfect Copy

Derville Murphy

POOLBEG

About the Author

Derville Murphy practised for many years as an architect and art curator before completing an MPhil, Irish Art History, TCD, and subsequently a PhD on Art and Architecture, UCD. In 2008 she founded art@work Art Consultancy. As an artist, she has exhibited widely, with solo exhibitions in 2005 and 2007 in the RIAI – her paintings are in several public art collections. As an academic she has written articles for journals including the Irish Art Review and Architecture Ireland. Her debut novel, *The Art Collector's Daughter* was published as an eBook in 2020, followed by *If Only She Knew* in 2021. *A Perfect Copy* is her third novel.

For more details about Derville and her work, visit her author's website at www.dervillemurphyauthor.com

Dedicated to Peggy (1923 –2020)
and the Murphy girls

Acknowledgements

This book was inspired by a family secret, not talked about for so many years that it was simply forgotten – my husband's grandfather was Jewish. Knowing this, I tried to imagine what his life would have been like and the events that led to this collective 'forgetting'. At the end of the day, his story wasn't so remarkable. It was the story of thousands of other Jews who, like him, were forced to flee from bigotry and persecution. But, for me, this journey into the past uncovered a new world, a rich tapestry of Jewish life in Eastern Europe during the mid-19th century, and I used this knowledge to weave an entirely fictional story about art, love and obsession.

To gain an understanding of the Jewish history of the period, I researched the subject in as much as I could. For anyone interested in learning more, the primary works I used are acknowledged at the back of the book. In this regard, I am also indebted to respected Jewish heritage expert, Hilary Abrahamson, who kindly read my manuscript and pointed out several significant errors that I had made, for which I am truly grateful. I also wish to thank Liubov Sichkar for her invaluable advice on researching the history of Ukraine and accessing Russian and Ukrainian databases. As always, my thanks are also due to Ele von Monschaw, Paintings Conservator at the National Gallery of Ireland, for her advice on art conservation and painting techniques of the period.

For reading my final draft, and providing structural editing advice, I am indebted to my book-club buddies and beta-readers, Marguerite Hanratty, Yvonne Donnelly, and Mavis Donnelly – and from an art perspective, art historian, Geraldine Canavan. To Patricia O'Reilly, author and inspirational teacher, who also read an early draft, thank you for your valued advice and generous mentoring. Also, many thanks to my writing group, Elaine Banfield, Carol Hayden, Tricia Holbrook, Elizabeth McGillion, Ger and Monica Whelan for reading early chapters and their constant support and encouragement.

Once more the team at Poolbeg have been a joy to work with. In particular, the multi-skilled Paula Campbell, Publisher, for her resilience in these Covid times and making the impossible possible; also, Gaye Shortland, Editor, whose diligent editing skills have greatly enhanced the final product.

Finally, but not least, I would like to thank my daughters Amy and Niamh for 'political-correctness' lessons – my adorable twin grandchildren, Matty and Olive, for giving me so much joy – and my lovely husband Brendan who always supports me in everything I do.

Cast of main characters

Present Day

The Staunton Family
Daisy Staunton
Karen – Daisy's mother

The Tarrant Family
Ben Tarrant
Sally – Ben's eldest sister.
Katrina – Ben's older sister

The 19th Century

The Rabinovitch Family
Bubbe Sadie – grandmother
Abe Rabinovitch
Zipporah – Abe's wife
Rosa – eldest daughter
Lena – daughter
Josef – eldest son
Reubin – son

The Cohen Family
Rabbi Cohen
Bena – the Rabbi's wife
Moishe Cohen – their son

The Taube Family
Bubbe Mim Taube – grandmother
Meyer Taube
Jessica – Meyer's wife
Isaac Taube – their son

This novel describes fictional characters and events.

PART 1

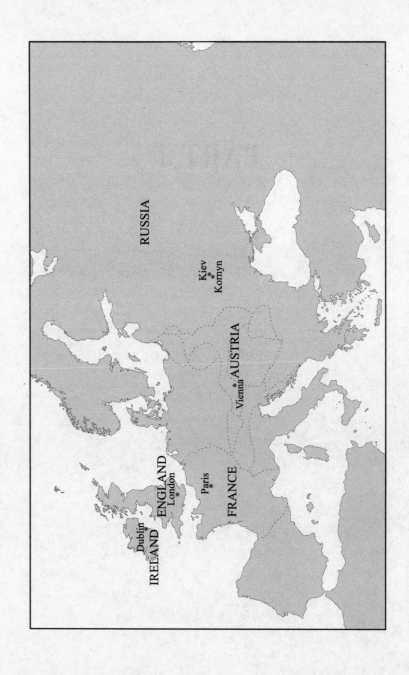

Chapter 1

Dublin
October 2011

Daisy was flustered by the time she arrived in Ballsbridge – she was fifteen minutes late. She had been stuck in a taxi in rush-hour traffic. Although Bellamy's representative at the door had moaned that the economic recession and the wet weather would put off the punters, the room was packed. Here in the cold, elegant, oak-panelled reception room of the Royal Dublin Society, bodies were sitting cheek to jowl. The proceedings had started. At a lectern, on a raised dais, the ebullient auctioneer, flamboyantly dressed in a cream sports jacket, yellow dickey-bow tie and blue shirt, was directing the proceedings at a brisk pace.

Daisy found a seat in the middle of the fifth row from the front, and manoeuvred awkwardly past unyielding legs, bags, and umbrellas. Sitting beside her, a well-upholstered, bald man was holding a wooden bidding paddle with the number seventy-eight on it. He was dressed in country tweeds and smelled strongly of damp dogs. He breathed noisily through his bushy moustache, his bulk forcing her to sit slightly forward. Daisy held on to the catalogue nervously. She had never been to an auction before and tried to concentrate on what was happening. From the corner of her eye, she noticed another latecomer enter – he was tall, brown-haired, thirty-ish, and strongly built. He ambled up to the front, stopped, stood leaning against the wall and opened and closely examined his catalogue.

"What are you interested in?" whispered the earnest-looking lady sitting to the other side of her.

"Oh, I'm selling, not buying."

"How exciting! What number?"

"One hundred and twenty-six."

"Up soon, so. I'll keep my fingers crossed."

"Thanks."

Daisy put one well-manicured hand on top of the other to hide her shaking fingers. Once more distracted, she noticed the tall latecomer leaving the room.

"Mustn't have got what he came for," whispered the earnest lady.

"Lot number twenty-four," said the auctioneer.

As the auction got under way, her damp-dog neighbour, annoyingly, proceeded to give a running commentary.

"Absolute rubbish!" he responded to the Gerard Dillon that she had admired earlier at the pre-sale viewing, and

2

"Crap!" was his comment on the rather elegant oil painting by Louis le Brocquy. It was sold for six figures, after a tense bidding war between two gentlemen, one at the back of the room and one near the front.

Eventually, after twenty minutes or so – during which time her heart was beating like the clappers – the auctioneer said the magic words.

"Now we have lot number one hundred and twenty-six, a beautiful late-nineteenth century portrait of Lady Helen Frome by the well-known Victorian society painter Thomas Rafferty."

The background murmur in the room quietened, as people strained their necks to see the painting.

"A highlight of this season's sales, from one of Ireland's finest artists. The work has only recently come to light."

An assistant had entered the top of the room through a side door, mounted the dais and was whispering into the auctioneer's ear. The man then stepped back to the side of the room, holding a sheaf of papers in his hand.

"So sorry, everyone. It seems we are withdrawing this item. Slight problem with the ... *er*, details. Now then, ladies and gentlemen, lot number one hundred and twenty-seven, new to the market ..."

"Excuse me, miss." A hand fell on Daisy's shoulder.

She looked up – it was the security guard who had been at the door when she came in.

"Could you come with me, please?"

Daisy was confused – why had they stopped the sale?

3

Her heart racing, she clutched her handbag, and pushed awkwardly past the other people seated in the row. Then, with the security guard leading the way, she followed him down the aisle as people stared at her with narrowed, curious eyes. She felt mortified, as if she had done something wrong.

He led her into a room at the far side of the hall, a book-lined office that smelled of dust and beeswax. An officious-looking man, balding with half-glasses, was sitting at a desk. Another man was seated opposite him – the latecomer she had noticed earlier.

"Take a seat, Miss Staunton, if you please. My name is James Lamb, I am a director of Bellamy's."

"What's this all about?" She attempted to sound assured, but her voice sounded small and squeaky – someone else's voice.

"Well, Miss Staunton, there is some confusion," he said kindly. "This gentleman has just brought to our attention the fact that your painting may not be what it seems."

Daisy looked blankly at the young man.

"This is Ben Tarrant," said James Lamb.

The young man nodded at her and smiled perfunctorily.

"You see, he also has a portrait by Rafferty that is identical to yours."

Ben Tarrant passed her a photograph of what appeared to be a perfect copy of her painting. Daisy examined it incredulously.

4

"Could she have had two portraits painted?" she asked in disbelief, her heart sinking.

"It is possible, but unlikely I'm afraid. It is not unheard-of in the past for someone to have several portraits made, at different stages in their life. Usually at auspicious occasions, say an engagement or marriage, or on a special anniversary. But other than portraits of the Royal Family, or important public figures, it is unusual to have two exact copies of the one portrait. The provenance documents you sent us, Miss Staunton, in retrospect, are somewhat vague. You inherited this painting from your grandmother, you say?"

"Yes, she inherited it from her own grandmother, I believe."

Ben frowned. "So, the sitter was a relative?"

"Yes, she was my great-great-grandmother, Lady Helen Frome."

"Well, according to my family the portrait is of my great-great-grandaunt, Lena Tarrant," said Ben, sounding amused.

"How fascinating. Sounds like the basis of an interesting story," said James. "The first names, Helen and Lena, are similar, possibly the same person. Unfortunately, this leaves our auction house with something of a dilemma. To sell the paintings without further research into their provenance would possibly diminish their value for both parties, as there is the risk – if I might say, without meaning to cause offence to either of you – that one of these is a fake."

"So how do we find out which one?" Daisy asked.

"Well, we research the paintings' provenance – try and find out who owned them, and when. See if you have any sale records, any exhibition listings – old photographs, even family letters that might refer to them. And you might also consider getting an expert to look at them both. Professor Johnathan Trimble in Trinity College is an authority on Rafferty. But maybe start with Dr Dermot Nolan, in the National Gallery. He works in the Centre for the Study of Irish Art. He wrote an article about Rafferty for one of our catalogues last year. Maybe, Miss Staunton, if you were to leave your painting with us after the auction and if, Mr Tarrant , you could bring your painting into our offices in Kildare Street over the next day or two, then I can ask Dr Nolan to pop in and have a look at them." He got to his feet. "Now, if you will excuse me. I really must be getting back to the auction. You will have a lot to discuss. Do let me know how you get on."

"We certainly will," said Ben.

James opened the door for them and they left.

Outside, Ben's initial air of confidence seemed to have evaporated, only to be replaced by a bewildered expression.

"Well ... *er*, Daisy, looks like we have a bit of a problem here." He flexed his hands, cracking his knuckles.

She crossed her arms. She got the impression that Ben Tarrant was used to getting his own way.

"How –"

"Why –"

They'd both started to talk at the same time.

He waved his hand, gesturing that she should go ahead.

"I was going to ask you," she said, "if you had any idea how this could have come about? Are they the same person? I know very little about my great-great-grandmother. I'll call her Helen, this 'great-great' business gets wearing."

"I am afraid I'm equally in the dark. But I am anxious to sell the painting. All of this talk of experts sounds expensive." He bit his lip. "I was hoping for a quick sale."

"Me too – it's disappointing," she said with a sigh.

"Maybe if we join forces, collaborate, we might expedite things sooner?"

"Possibly," she said doubtfully. "Do you know anything about art?"

"I did it for my Leaving Cert, got an A."

"Ah, impressive." *Not* – she thought. She tried to place his accent, not Dublin 4 anyway.

"I suppose we could start by talking to that guy he mentioned in the National Gallery?"

"Why not? And maybe go back and talk to our families and see can we make any more sense of this. Do you have a business card?"

"No, sorry, clean out of cards," he said, grinning. "If you give me your number, I'll contact you in a few days and we can arrange to meet up and compare notes."

"OK, here's my card – it's got all my details on it. Just in case you need to email me."

"Thanks." He smiled and put it, without looking, into his jacket pocket.

"And your number?" she persisted.

"As I said, I'll ring you."

They left the building and parted outside. She hailed a taxi and left him standing on the pavement. It had started to rain again. He looked like a wet, brown Siberian bear, she thought, as the taxi pulled away.

***

The taxi stopped about 500 yards down the road from the Royal Dublin Society, at the cottages where she was living. She looked at the water level in the River Dodder – it was high for the second day in a row. She hoped it wasn't going to flood again – they had just finished the repairs after last time, and a musty smell still lingered about the place. She was relieved to find there was no one else there when she got in. Seán was working late and Katy had a date. Daisy guessed this as she looked through the open door to her flatmate's bedroom and saw clothes strewn over the bedroom floor. A pair of discarded tights trailed over the threshold and into the living room. She threw the offending object back into Katy's room and firmly closed the door. In her own room, the smallest of the three, she took off her coat, and changed from her office clothes into a pair of leggings and a big woolly jumper. Then she headed to the kitchen to pour herself a large Pinot-Grigio. She needed a glass of wine before she could face ringing her mother.

"How did you get on, love?" her mother asked eagerly.

"I didn't sell the painting."

"Oh no! Why ever not?"

"You won't believe this, but they withdrew it. There was this guy there who claimed he had a painting that was exactly the same as ours – a perfect copy. So, they thought that one of them could be a fake."

"My goodness, how extraordinary!"

"Yes, it's really disappointing. I mean, why would anyone have two almost identical portraits made? Are you sure there isn't anything more, Mum, that you can tell me about it?"

"Well, other than the fact that it was never hung up, as far as I remember. That was certainly odd. You'd think having a society beauty in the family would be something you would want to impress everyone with. It was in Nana's attic, in her house in Rathmines. I remember seeing it when my father took me up there as a child. He laughed and said that she must have dirtied her bib in some way. I remember thinking then how beautiful she was. In fact, she looks a bit like you, Daisy. It must be where you get your lovely olive-coloured skin from." She started coughing and couldn't seem to stop.

"Are you OK, Mum?"

"I am afraid I've been talking too much, dear," her mother Karen said.

"OK, Mum. Go get a drink of water and get some rest. I'll be over after work tomorrow evening. We can talk more then."

Still spluttering, Karen just about managed to say goodbye. The feeling of panic returned, as Daisy wondered how much time her mother had left. She thought briefly of ringing Fintan and telling him the news, but decided against it – she wasn't in the mood. She checked her phone to see if he had rung earlier. He hadn't. He was probably working late. Her call to London could wait till tomorrow.

***

Ben Tarrant didn't ring her the next day, or the next. Her first impression of his arrogance was obviously spot on. True to type, Daisy thought. He was making her hang around until it suited him to call her. On the third day, she was considering ringing up Bellamy's looking for his details when he at last made contact.

"Hi, Daisy. This is Ben Tarrant. From the auction."

"Hi, Ben."

"I was ringing up –"

"To arrange to meet. Look, I'm in a bit of a rush at the moment – I don't have time to chat. When are you suggesting?"

"How about I see you in the café in the National Gallery for a coffee on Friday? I'm a primary-school teacher, but I can get off early on Fridays. The kids have sports, and I rotate with one of the other guys. Does two o'clock suit?"

"Yes, that's fine. I can make that work."

"See you then so. Bye." He put the phone down abruptly.

No bloody manners at all, she thought, annoyed as she left for her client meeting.

***

Daisy loved the peace of the gallery. The familiar smell of old wood and floor polish instantly made her feel calm as she entered the building from Merrion Square. She walked briskly through the exhibition spaces that showed the 19th century art. She didn't have time to stop today as she usually did. She didn't want to be late. Although she knew she wouldn't be, because she was always early – she hated the stress of being rushed.

In the café, she queued for a cappuccino then found a table near the entrance, opposite the bookshop, so she wouldn't miss him arriving. In contrast to the peace and quiet of the formal gallery spaces, the café was part of a modern extension to the original nineteenth-century building. It was high-ceilinged, white-walled, and had a long flight of steps that led, as if heavenward, to the galleries at the higher level. Today, it was noisy and bustling, full of tourists, as well as the usual colourful, arty clientele.

At quarter past two, when she was debating whether she should leave, she caught sight of him sauntering up the walkway towards her. He was dressed a bit more respectably than at the auction, but not a lot. His brown waxed jacket had seen better days. She looked away so he wouldn't see her looking at him.

"Mind if I join you?" he said with a grin.

"Ah Ben, good to see you again," she said, smiling woodenly, inwardly seething at him for being late.

"Sorry I'm late. The traffic was awful – there are demonstrations up at Dáil Éireann."

"Ah, yes, I'd forgotten about that," she said, relenting. "I'll just grab a coffee."

He returned with a coffee and a generous slice of walnut cake.

"So, have you recovered from the shock?" he asked.

"Just about. My mother was disappointed – it's technically her painting. She was as surprised as we were. When she had a chance to think about it, she suggested that the copy might have been made for the sitter's family. Say, if she was living far away from them, or she had emigrated."

"Yeah, it's a possibility. Want some cake?" He had brought an extra plate for her and two forks. He cut the cake in half and pushed the plate over to her without waiting for her to answer. "My sister has a cake shop in Glasnevin. It's called 'Muffin Top'. She named it after

12

me." He laughed. "I blame her for my sweet tooth. Bet you're like my girlfriend though, permanently on a diet."

Not wanting to be so summarily typecast, she took the cake with a polite smile and, cutting a piece with her fork, took a small bite. She rubbed her watch anxiously. They should get down to business – she had another meeting at four o'clock that she needed to prepare for. "My mother said that she remembered the painting was in my grandparent's attic – they lived in Rathmines," she explained briskly. "My grandfather, Donal O'Reilly, was a civil servant – worked in the Land Commission. He was originally from Kildare from a farming background. My grandmother was English – she was into horses, dressage, and show jumping. That was how they met. Her maiden name was Unwin. Her father was a doctor, I believe, who came from a town just outside Bath. And that's really as much as we know."

"What about the name Frome? That's unusual."

"My mother didn't know exactly where the name came from. So, I looked it up. It's English. The word comes from the Ancient British word '*ffraw*', meaning fine, fair, or brisk. My mother said she was always told that the Unwins were quite well-to-do. They were not too impressed with my grandmother marrying the son of a farmer. But during the war my mother's older brother Edward sent over their young son, Sonny, to stay with my grandmother. My mother was only four or five at the time, so she doesn't really remember him that well, and they kind of lost contact after he went back to England."

13

"Are there any records, family trees, anything like that?"

"No, not really. A few old photographs of my granny and grandad, and a couple of old medical books from my great-grandfather. That's about it."

"So, the Fromes were English?"

"Yes, apparently. And you, how did you get on?"

"Well, it's harder to ask my parents."

"Why?"

"They're both dead." He took another mouthful of his cake.

"Oh, I am so sorry," she said, embarrassed.

"Don't be, they died when I was quite young – in a car accident. My older sister brought me up. To be honest, I was never too interested in my family background. We meet up with the cousins once a year. I've millions of them – Irish Catholics, you know."

She smiled a little tight smile. So, he had guessed she was Church of Ireland.

"I also have relatives in Britain," he continued. "Their name is Taube. My sister keeps in contact with them. I've no interest myself. She tells me it's useful, if only to track what they die of – so that our medical choices are informed ones."

"Ah." She wasn't quite sure if he was joking or not. "I was thinking about a plan of action."

"Yeah?"

"Yes. James Lamb rang me to say that he had contacted Dr Nolan at the National Gallery, and that he has agreed

14

to look at both paintings. He asked Bellamy's to drop them into the gallery. The conditions are better there to examine them. Lamb said that Dr Nolan will let us know when he is ready to meet us – and that maybe we should each write down a family tree. There are a few websites that do this. Ancestry.com looks like a good place to start."

"OK, fine."

"This might take us both a bit of time."

"Well, my girlfriend is on my back about this. We are planning to get married next summer. So, there are bills to be paid."

"Really – congratulations." She rubbed her watch again. "So …"

"As a matter of fact, she's waiting for me outside. We're due to go to a wine-tasting, this afternoon. I'd better be off. " He got up. "Will you make the appointment – or will I?"

"I will," she said.

"Great, let me know when. See you soon."

And he was gone, lumbering off down the crowded walkway towards the exit.

***

"What was she like then?" Julie asked as he got into the passenger seat of her Volkswagen Golf.

"*Ffraw,* she was *ffraw* – fine, fair and brisk."

"You're talking shite, Ben. What did she look like?"

15

"Well, actually, she is very like the woman in the portrait."

"Your great-great-grandaunt?"

"Yeah," he said absentmindedly, as she reversed out of the parking slot onto Merrion Square.

"Is she good-looking?"

"Concentrate on what you're doing, will you!" he said as she just missed a car coming at speed from the other direction. "I suppose she is – fair hair, olive-coloured skin, brown eyes," he continued, once they were safely driving up the side of the square.

"Tall or small?"

"Come on, Julie, I hate when you do this. She's small and fat, and looks like Gollum, and she has a pronounced overbite."

"You're probably related."

"Possibly."

"You better not get too friendly, so."

"No chance of that, she's not my type," he said, turning to smile at her. "Now where's this bloody wine-tasting then?"

***

Ben gently pushed Sally's fat tabby cat off the oak table. The cat hissed, baring its tiny teeth at being disturbed, and then loped off up the steps into the hall. He wrapped his hands around the mug of coffee, sipping it slowly as his sister stirred a pot of curry on the range. Smells of cardamom, ginger, and garlic filled the kitchen, and condensation fogged up the window, hiding the view of her small but lovingly tended garden.

"I don't believe you. This isn't one of your yarns, Ben?"

"Not a word of a lie, Sis."

"And the painting was exactly the same?"

"Yup."

"That's so strange," said Sally, pushing her curly hair from her brown eyes, sweating from the heat of the cooker.

"It's not unheard-of for a copy of a portrait to be made, but it is unusual. The auctioneer hung on to the other woman's painting and asked me to bring ours in. He has arranged for some guy at the National Gallery to examine both of them. But, in the meantime, he also advised us to do some digging into their provenance."

"Provenance, how are you! You are sounding very learned on the subject! You will have to change your name to Gompertz," she said, looking back at him ironically.

"What do you mean?"

"You know, William Gompertz, the arts editor you see on the telly, on the BBC."

"Funny, *ha ha*. But I am going to have to brush up on my art history."

"Well, you did get an A in your Leaving Cert."

"Yes, so I told Frau Ffraw, but she wasn't impressed."

"Frau Ffraw?"

"Daisy Staunton, the owner of the other painting. Her great-great-grandmother's name was 'Frome' from the word '*ffraw*' meaning 'fine, fair, or brisk'. Daisy is a marketing executive, south-sider, bit prim and proper, you know the type."

"I'm sure she's lovely. God love her if she has to deal with a philistine like you."

"Thanks for the vote of confidence."

"You're confident enough," she teased him. "But back to the painting."

"Well, can you tell me any more about it?"

"Not a lot, except that it came from Dad's side of the family. Uncle Paddy told me that his grandfather – our great-grandfather – was a tailor in Dublin. He had a shop in Grafton Street, Antoine's. His first name was Antoine – as you know, that's Irish for Anthony. He did ladies' tailoring for well-to-do women. You could try talking to him."

"I presume he is still living in the flat in Rathgar?"

"Yes, he is. Though he must be a good age now. You know how good he was to me when Mam and Dad died.

All of those years ago, Paddy had lent Sally money, got her a job in the PMPA insurance company which was just starting up at the time. He knew one of the owners. He had also lent her money when Ben went to teacher-training college at St Pat's, towards an allowance.

"I don't know what I would have done without the extra few bob he gave me. You were an expensive little bugger! Doesn't seem much now – but at the time it meant a lot."

Ben got up and, bending down, wrapped his arms around his sister, giving her an affectionate hug.

"Ah, you're a saint, Sally. I know you made sacrifices

18

for Katrina as well, but for me especially. You should have gone to college yourself."

"No, love. Not everyone wants to go to college. I'm quite happy doing what I'm doing." she said, extricating herself from him.

"I hope so. It's not too late, you know."

"No, thanks."

He paused. "This whole situation about the painting is really intriguing me. It's the kind of thing you'd see on one of those television investigations – *Fake or Fortune?* Do you have a minute to look at the painting?"

"Yes, sure," she said, checking her watch and looking at the pot on the stove. She wiped her hands on a towel.

Decorated in the same eclectic mix as the rest of the house, the dining room was filled with a mixture of old and new furniture. The painting was hung on a wall painted a deep cherry-red. It had been in the same place for years, beside an old-fashioned Victorian cabinet that was filled with a selection of familiar, mismatched china that Sal used daily.

They both stood on the far side of the table so that they could get a better view of it.

Ben sipped his coffee as he gazed at the portrait.

"I will miss it when you eventually sell it," said Sal.

Ben squeezed her hand. "It's funny the way that you can look at a painting that you are familiar with – and not really see it. She was very beautiful," he said pensively.

"Yes, she was."

19

The pose, semi-reclining, was conventional. Lena, as Ben had come to think of her, was looking directly at the viewer, her head supported on the palm of her hand. Her long, honey-coloured hair was wrapped in a loose coil around her elegant neck and fell across the exposed area of her breasts. Her skin was luminous – not ivory, but a shade warmer, the colour of buttermilk – hinting at her foreignness. While her elbow was resting on the arm of a chaise longue, her lower body was curled on the couch, allowing the fabric of her blue-silk skirt to fall in shimmering folds to the floor.

"Her beauty even transcends historic ideals, which sometimes don't relate to what we consider beautiful today," said Ben thoughtfully.

"Yes, you're right," agreed Sal, as they both continued to gaze at the image.

"She is so ... alluring – and definitely has a knowing expression in those amber eyes."

"And I love her evening gown. The blue silk sets off the sapphire-and-diamond necklace. Wonder what happened to that?"

"Probably pawned years ago. Looks like it was worth a few bob."

"Do you know," said Sal, "it sends shivers down my spine to think that she was alive all that time ago, and that she is connected to our family – to us."

Probably also to the fair Frau Ffraw, thought Ben. There was a definite resemblance.

Chapter 2

The Centre for the Study of Irish Art was off the main entrance walkway in the National Gallery and up a narrow set of stairs that Daisy hadn't noticed before. Dr Dermot Nolan – a handsome, earnest young man, fair-haired with round, arty tortoiseshell glasses – was wearing a navy linen jacket and jeans. He showed them into a bright, white, roof-lit room, surrounded by low-level bookshelves and standing-height desks intended for referencing. In the centre of the room were their paintings, arranged side by side on easels. Once the introductions were made Dr Nolan pulled three chairs over in front of them and invited them to sit down.

"Well, as you both know, James Lamb rang me last week after the auction and asked me to have a good look at these two works, which I did," said Nolan. "They are very beautiful, and although the Tarrant painting is unsigned, I believe that both are very fine examples of Rafferty's work. The fact that they are identical is most unusual. Do you know anything about the artist?"

"Just what we read on your website," said Daisy, "and in *Painters of Ireland* by Anne Crookshank and the Knight of Glin. I looked it up in the library."

"Good, that's a start," he said, smiling encouragingly at Daisy. "Well, as you now know, Thomas Rafferty was a highly regarded nineteenth-century portrait-painter. His father was an artisan painter of family crests and decorative panels, particularly on carriages, which were the fashion at the time. As a young boy, he showed talent. So when he was twelve, he was sent to the Dublin Society School, in Kildare Street – where Dáil Éireann, the government offices, are now."

"I remember my old art teacher telling me about it," said Ben.

"You studied art – that's great – it will be a help in trying to establish the paintings' history."

Ben gave Daisy a smug grin.

"You were saying, Dr Nolan," said Daisy.

Yes, the Dublin Society School was set up to cultivate the fine arts in Ireland. It was primarily a drawing school of the human figure, landscape, and architecture – but it also taught sculpture. Rafferty did well there, winning several annual prizes and came to the attention of a British artist, living in Ireland, Stephen Catterson Smith. Smith was the leading portrait-painter of the day, and himself the son of a coach painter. Maybe that was why he took an interest in Rafferty. Anyway, when Rafferty was nineteen, Catterson Smith gave him a letter of introduction to go to Paris, to the renowned, neo-classical, portrait and history painter, Jean-Auguste-Dominique Ingres. Although at this stage Ingres was quite old. Apparently, he took a liking to Rafferty, who was by all accounts a handsome and charming young man and gave him a job as one of his studio assistants. Rafferty learned an academic, neo-classical style there. But he must have also absorbed the influences of the younger artists of the day in Paris."

"It must have been an exciting time to be an artist," said Daisy enthusiastically.

"Yes, I am sure it was. There had been a move away from classical ideals. Younger artists were embracing a more naturalistic and expressionistic way of painting, and of course Paris was the centre of the art world. But there would have been a lot of competition for work. So, Rafferty moved to Vienna. For a portrait-artist like Rafferty, you could see the attraction – it offered rich pickings for artists in the court of Franz Joseph I and Empress Elisabeth. In Vienna at that time, Franz Xaver Winterhalter was one of the most successful German portrait-painters of the day – famous for his romantic portraits of the Empress, and indeed of the young Queen Victoria. You may have heard of him?"

Ben nodded knowingly but caught Daisy looking at

him, one eyebrow raised and mouth pursed to the side.

"Although Rafferty never achieved the status of Winterhalter, he did achieve modest success amongst the courtiers and minor dignitaries of Vienna." Nolan took off his glasses and rubbed them with a crisp white handkerchief.

"When did he go there?" asked Daisy.

"Oh, about 1860," replied Nolan. "He stayed there until 1862 when he moved to London. Although, a few years later, it appears he got involved in some scandal and fell out of favour, forcing him to return to Ireland. I'm not sure precisely what the scandal was, but it was referred to in Lady Ellen Fitzherbert's diary in May 1865. I've photocopied the extract for you."

He handed each of them a sheet of paper and read out the text from his own copy.

"'*Rafferty was unavailable to paint Vanessa*' – that's her daughter – '*because of the recent unfortunate scandal in London. They say he is in Brighton, licking his wounds – no one has seen him for months.*'" He put the copy of the letter down carefully, on top of the other documents. "He eventually returned to Dublin, started painting again and was reasonably successful until the turn of the century. He died in 1910. But after that episode he never regained the popularity he had previously enjoyed."

"Was he a bit of a rake, old Rafferty?" asked Ben.

"Maybe you will be able to find out," replied Nolan. "From the way he painted, he certainly liked women –

his portraits from his time in Vienna are quite luscious. We have a file here of details and images of some of his works. You can see how his style developed from this earliest, rather naïve, portrait of his sister in 1853 when he was seventeen, to the polished, if a bit stiff, neo-classical style of this elegant lady, Madame Sophie de Dampierre which he painted during his time in Paris." Nolan passed the two images to Daisy and Ben. "Then there is this portrait painted in Vienna of Countess Alice Von Habsburg, a distant cousin of the Emperor. You can see that by this stage Rafferty has developed a more expressionistic, romantic style. The female figure is almost coquettish."

"Yeah, I see what you mean. She has –"

"Do you have many works by Rafferty?" interrupted Daisy, alarmed at where Ben might be taking this.

"In the gallery no, only these two. Generally, there are probably about twenty or so of his works accounted for, although we know of a lot of his other portraits from historical records. He was fairly prolific. Your painting, or 'paintings', would be a great addition to his oeuvre."

"That's all really interesting," said Daisy. "Can you tell us more about them?"

"There is not much I can tell you, I'm afraid. To the naked eye they look identical. There is some slight difference in the texture of some of the brushwork, but they both look like Rafferty's work. Yours, Daisy, has his distinctive signature. But because yours has no signature,

Ben, and the fact that it is almost identical to Daisy's, there is, understandably, a question mark over provenance. You will probably have to investigate further to establish how the paintings came into the ownership of your respective families. But, also, we probably need to undertake a technical analysis of the two works, to look at them almost forensically, to establish definitively that they are both original works by Rafferty. Or if one of them is a copy."

"A fake, you mean."

"I prefer to say 'a reproduction' but not by Rafferty."

"How would you go about this?"

"Well, we could start by doing some investigative work here, examining them under infra-red and ultraviolet light. This can help us to understand the condition of the paintings, the materials used, and if they are similar. The infra-red photography detects carbon-based materials, such as pencil, charcoal and ink which might show under-drawings that might give us clues. If it is warranted, we could arrange to undertake a paint-analysis using an electron microscope. Also, we might consider having them X-rayed."

"Do you do that here?" asked Ben.

"Good Lord, no. That must be carried out in laboratory conditions. We have, in the past, had them done in hospitals. Do you have any medical connections?"

"My sister Sal knows one of the radiographers in the Bons Secours."

"Great. I can give you a letter from the gallery. I'll give

you a call if I think it's necessary. But this is a private undertaking, just so you know. The gallery couldn't fund it. But, on a personal level, I am happy to carry out the tests here in my own time, and I will help you in any way I can. Obviously, if I incur additional expenses, I will need to pass them on to you. But, other than that, I am really interested in this, and I will help you in any way that I can."

"That's so kind of you," said Daisy warmly.

"My pleasure," he said, looking at her, his eyes twinkling. "You are very like her, you know – she was a beautiful woman."

"Thank you," said Daisy, embarrassed, smiling back at him.

***

Ben was tired – school had been hard going today. Although he loved the kids in St Denis's, the inner-city boy's primary school where he worked as a teacher, it was demanding. But it was where he had always wanted to be – where he believed he could make a difference. Today he'd taken the kids from fifth class down to Fairview Park. Nice day, he'd thought – a bit of fresh air – get the boys to engage with nature. He'd even gone to the trouble of inviting his old school pal Nigel Bolger, a 'twitcher', to talk to them about indigenous birds.

In retrospect, he had to admit, the outing was not one of his better ideas. Two of the lads had robbed a bike.

Some stupid eejit had left his shiny new racer locked to a metal stake supporting a young tree – and guess what? The lads lifted the bike, the stake, and the tree and ran off with them. He had left Nigel in control of the class while he dealt with the Guards who had been called by an ould wan who saw the whole thing happen.

By the time he'd finished with the Guards and returned to Nigel, the rest of the class had disappeared. Nigel was left with just two lads, Billy Fagan and Connor 'Lofty' O'Leary, as the other lads cruelly called him – his dad kept pigeons.

Ben suspected that Lofty, who had really bad eyesight and peered through thick lenses, had seen nothing all afternoon but sky.

"Listen, Nige, we'd better call it a day."

"No problem, Ben. A lot of them went home – they said they had loads of homework. They said they'd see you tomorrow," said Nigel apologetically.

"I bet they did. OK, Connor and Billy, say thanks to Nigel – you may as well head off too."

"Sort it out with the Guards?" asked Nigel, as the two boys scuttled off.

"Yeah, sort of. I'll have to call in to the kids' parents tonight and get them to make the lads return the bike. If they do, the Guards won't press charges."

"Will you be in trouble with this?"

"It's not good. I'll have to ring the principal and give her the heads-up."

"How will she take it?"

"Like she takes everything," Ben said with a rueful smile. "She'll give me a bollocking in that disappointed voice of hers. One that she seems to keep specially for me. And I'll be on playground duty for the next five years – at least."

"She sounds like a tough one."

"Yeah, one of the other teachers has started calling her Annie Atlas. She's taller than both of us – and I'm tall. She must be about six foot six. And she works out. She's fit – but not in a good way – in a 'you-are-a-total-excuse-for-a-man', kind of way."

Nigel laughed. "Fancy a pint?"

"Love to, mate, but I'd better get to those parents before the little feckers sell the bike on to someone else. And I promised to call in to my sister later – she wanted to talk to me about something. Next time, Nige. Listen, thanks for today, I really appreciated it."

"No problem, Ben. I really enjoyed it – especially seeing the little egret. But I've got a splitting headache now – the kids are full on. I always thought your job was a doddle – all those afternoons off, and endless summer holidays. Maybe being a photocopier salesman wasn't such a bad career choice after all."

"You said it, Nige."

***

Later that evening, he sank back into Sally's comfortable armchair in the living room. He always felt relaxed in his sister's house. After she had split up with her husband Fergal, Ben had moved in with her for a few years to help her with the mortgage repayments. He had only reluctantly moved into the apartment in East Wall when he started sleeping with Julie. Not that Sally would have minded. Hard to believe that was three years ago. But it was Julie's ultimatum last Christmas that she would dump him if he didn't make a commitment that had resulted in their finally getting engaged. And after spending two weeks over the Christmas holidays thinking about it – mulling over his future – he had taken a deep breath and taken the plunge. At thirty-three, he reasoned, if he wanted a family, then it was probably time to settle down. Looking back, it hadn't been easy. Julie had been ecstatic at first, choosing the ring, telling everyone their news. Then they started trying to save, spending less time in the pub and fancy restaurants, and more time together. Although their sex life had never been better, it also meant that they spent a lot of time talking about the wedding, and this had taken its toll on them both. In fact, they never seemed to talk about anything else. He felt she had become obsessive about it – and she thought that he wasn't interested enough.

Being a designer, she wanted everything to conform to her own aesthetic. She described this as pared-back and understated. But it seemed to Ben that nothing was simple or straightforward. She was treating the whole thing as if it were one of her trendy interior-design projects. He would rather have had something modest, just a church ceremony and a small reception in a local hotel for family and friends. He supposed, though, that most men felt like that.

"Suck it up," Nige had advised him when he broached the subject. "Isn't she drop-dead gorgeous? I'd give her whatever she wants."

He had smirked. Which had surprised Ben. He thought Nige only got excited about little egrets.

He glanced around the familiar living room and sipped his beer. In contrast to Julie's minimalism, he preferred his sister's eclectic style. The walls painted deep cherry-red, together with the cream curtains and beige carpet, made the room feel warm even on the coldest days. She had chosen things to display because they were interesting, or attractive, usually things she found rummaging at a market, or in a second-hand shop. Sally certainly had a good eye for colour and style. A slender glass vase with stems of contorted willow sat on the mantelpiece together with a collection of Buddhas of various makes and sizes. Overall, the decor was quirky, but it was also comfortable and cosy.

He thought how Julie talked disparagingly about Sally's house. Julie was the daughter of an unmarried mother who had struggled to make ends meet living in a council flat in the inner city, but becoming an interior designer had given her confidence and was fundamental to her sense of self-worth. She favoured cold modernist interiors, all stainless steel and shades of grey. Ben shuddered at the thought of having to live in one of those places where you had to take your shoes off as soon as you came in the door. He'd get used to it, he supposed. He swallowed another mouthful of cool beer from the tin. Sally was in the kitchen making him tea.

He was beginning to calm down and feel the stress of the day melt away. Regaling Sally with this afternoon's disastrous events, followed by a description of the visit to the kids' belligerent parents, had also helped. Now that he could see the funny side, it didn't seem so bad. And, although he knew he should ring the principal tonight, he decided to throw caution to the wind and face it all tomorrow.

"Garden's looking well, Sal," he said, looking out at the illuminated planted patio with its large clay pots filled with ferns, bowls of cyclamen and winter pansies, as she returned with their tea and two slices of buttered banana bread.

"Yes, it's really taken shape this year. I must say it's such a pleasure to look at when I come home in the evenings after spending all day in the café."

"Business OK?"

"You know I'm not in it for the money. I made the rent this month and enough to get by."

When Ben and his sister Katrina had eventually moved out to go their separate ways, Sal had taken early retirement from the insurance company, and taken a lease on premises near where she lived. It was just up the road from the Botanic Gardens. It had always been her dream to run a cake shop. She had always loved baking. As kids, she provided a constant supply – her cupcakes were legendary on Stella Avenue, in Glasnevin, where their parents had rented a house. Sally was also well able for the general wheeling and dealing involved in operating a small business. But, most of all, he knew she loved meeting people and hearing their stories.

"Actually," she said then, "that's what I wanted to talk to you about – money."

"Oh? You need a loan? No probs. How much?"

"What I need, I am afraid, Ben, is even above your pay grade."

"What is it?" he said, suddenly concerned.

"Well, it's Fergal."

"Jesus, what hole did he climb out of? You haven't seen him for years!" he exclaimed, eyes glinting angrily.

"No, I haven't, but he rang me yesterday. To cut a long story short and, believe me, it was a long story, it always is with Fergal – he wants me to pay him half of the value of the house, or if I don't have the money, to sell it."

"He can't ask you to do that!"

"Apparently he thinks he can."

Sally and Fergal had been married for six mostly unhappy years, before she had finally turfed him out after her mam and dad died. Their dying was a kind of wake-up call for her – making her realise what was important in life. When she and Fergal had initially bought the house, they had taken out a joint mortgage, and both of their names were on the title deeds.

"I suppose I should have formalised things after he left. I had planned to, but I just never got around to it. He has never looked for a divorce, and I have never met anyone since that I was prepared to take a risk on. I am painfully aware of how foolish this sounds, but I just got through my life at that time as best I could. It wasn't easy, I was only twenty-six, I had to mind you lot. Katrina was only fifteen and you were only eighteen."

"When he was drunk, did he ever hit you, Sal?" Ben asked gently.

"Yes, many times." She lowered her head so he couldn't see the tears in her eyes.

"Poor Sal," he said, moving over to where she sat on the couch and putting his arm around her. "Look, don't worry, we'll sort this out. He can't just walk back into your life now and expect to be handed half of the money for the house. You paid the mortgage for the last twenty-five years since he left, that has to be worth something. One of my mates, Cormac, is a solicitor. I'll have a word with him and see what we can do."

"Oh, Ben, I hardly slept a wink last night worrying about it. I couldn't bear to lose this house – my home." Tears filled her eyes and, as she picked up the china cup of tea from the small table beside her, he noticed her hands were shaking.

***

By the time he had finished school, Ben's head was pounding. But at least it was Friday. The conversation with Sal the week before was still on his mind. He had made an appointment for himself and Sal to see his friend Cormac, the solicitor. Unfortunately, he couldn't meet them till next week. Hopefully, he would tell them that Fergal, the bastard, hadn't a leg to stand on.

Julie hadn't helped his peace of mind either – she had been banging on about presents for the bridesmaids. He was to buy each of the four women a piece of jewellery. A gold chain and pendant by an up-and-coming jewellery designer in Temple Bar. Christ, he didn't even like most of them. He would have to talk to her – again. Really, this was all getting out of hand. He knew this was important for Julie, but it was a complete waste of money.

Although they were saving for the wedding, at least they weren't starting from scratch. He had always enjoyed relative financial peace of mind because of a family legacy a few years ago. His bachelor-uncle Tommy, on his mother's side, had left him his flat in Fairview, and Ben still had the proceeds of its sale after his uncle's debts had been cleared. The money had paid the deposit on the new apartment in East Wall. He had hoped that one day it would also go towards buying a house. But no. Julie had insisted on spending a large portion of his money on this bloody wedding. Although, in fairness, her mother had also contributed. But that wasn't the point. It wasn't just the money – all of this was in really bad taste. He couldn't reconcile the poverty that he saw every day at school with these notions that Julie had of a sanitised, privileged life – someone else's idea of a life. After they got engaged, he had suggested to her that she organise everything herself – bad move. She had sulked for a week. Eventually, he had given in and tried to help with the arrangements, feigning enthusiasm as best he could.

But the main reason for his headache was that today had been one of those days at school. Mozzy McManus, although only ten, was built like a brick shithouse and had beaten the shite out of an older boy, Danny Moran. As a result, and because of the incident with the bikes, Ben had spent an hour with the principal as she delivered an excruciatingly tedious lecture to him on class discipline.

The last thing he wanted to do was visit his Uncle Paddy, but he knew that to cancel the appointment would have disappointed the old man who had sounded delighted to hear from him.

It was after four o'clock before Ben finally arrived in Rathgar Road. The Victorian terraced house had seen better days, displaying the seedy signs of multiple occupancy. He noticed that a blue sweatshirt had been hung out to dry from one of the upper windows. The lawn, if you could call it that, was full of weeds and cigarette butts. Ben went down the steps to the half basement and rang the doorbell.

His uncle answered promptly and ushered him into the hall.

"Ben, lovely to see you! It's been a while. Come in, come in – welcome! I have everything ready to make tea."

Ben lowered his head as he entered the low-ceilinged living area. Uncle Paddy invited him to sit on an old-fashioned easy chair, then busied himself in the adjoining kitchen. He returned with a chinoiserie tray, on it were a china teapot, cups and saucers and a plate of digestive biscuits.

Ben thought the old man was looking remarkably well for his age. Uncle Paddy was stooped but seemed fit – his skin was sallow, finely lined, and his head still had a thin covering of fine white hair.

Paddy poured the tea.

"There you go, Ben. Milk, sugar?"

"Thanks."

"Would you like a biscuit?"

"Thanks, Paddy," said Ben, taking one out of politeness.

Ben awkwardly held the china cup and saucer, balanced on his knee, and attempted to nibble the biscuit. He eventually gave up and carefully put them down on a nest of tables near his chair, then stood up and took off his jacket. The flat was warm and stuffy, with a musty, old-man's smell, although everything was immaculately tidy.

He proceeded to tell Paddy the story about the painting and why he was now, after all these years, suddenly interested in their family's history.

"Is there anything you can tell me about your grandfather, my great-grandfather, Antoine Tarrant?" he asked.

"Well, my father – your grandfather – trained as a tailor with him, in his shop on Grafton Street, you know. But he never took to it. Just hated sitting down at a machine all day. He left to work for the China Showrooms. And, when I was a teenager, he got me in there as a travelling salesman. In those days, in the 1960s, it was considered quite a glamorous job. Touring the country in my Ford Cortina was a great way to meet the ladies, let me tell you. There weren't many Irishwomen could resist a piece of china. I used to have boxes of tea-pot seconds I would give them, in the boot of my car." He chuckled, amused at the memory.

"And where exactly was your grandfather's shop?" Ben tried to focus the old man.

"Ah yes, number eighty-five, where Clarke's shoe shop is now, just opposite the junction at Duke Street. It's the first floor on the right as you are heading up Grafton Street. I can see it now: the name was written in gold on the black door at street level, and on the first floor was the reception – off that was the salon where the models showed off the garments to the customers. In those days wealthy ladies still bought a number of outfits for the season. They would come up from the country, stay in the Central Hotel, or the Shelbourne – and go the theatre, or the concert hall. You know, make an occasion of it.

Visiting him was strictly by appointment. He did prêt-à-porter and made-to-measure. Clothes were terribly expensive to buy then, and after the war the selection was limited, you know. There wasn't the number of shops there is now – Brown Thomas, Switzers, and McBirney's were the main ones. Most people had their clothes made by a dressmaker, or a tailor. And Antoine was trained as a tailor."

"Antoine's parents – do you know anything about them?"

"Now you're testing the old grey-matter. No, I don't know a lot about them. Except that he was a merchant, in grain, wheat, I think. I remember my father saying they were Austrian – they lived in Vienna. Antoine was born there, but moved to England, then on to Ireland as a young man."

"Really? How extraordinary! Why on earth didn't Dad mention this? He was always a man of few words, but I would have thought that the fact that his grandfather was Austrian would have been a conversation piece! Did Mam know?"

Paddy shrugged his shoulders.

"No idea. I can't remember ever discussing it with them."

Ben, rubbed his forehead, trying to take it all in.

"Any idea when Antoine moved to Ireland?"

"Afraid not, Ben. I was never interested in that sort of thing. I know we have cousins in England. I remember this guy coming over to Dublin. Must be twenty years ago now, from London, said he was some sort of relation – funny name. What was it, Troy, Taffe? No, it was Taube. He told me he had done work on a family tree. He asked me for details of the family, who married who – who had what children. I promised I'd get back to him. But I never did. God forgive me! I think I have his address written down somewhere. Dora used to send him a Christmas card every year."

Paddy got up and shuffled out to the hall to the telephone. He returned with an indexed address book. "Here it is." He gave the open book to Ben who copied the name 'Alex Taube', the Croydon address and a telephone number onto the back of an old business card and put it in his wallet.

"I don't suppose you have any family papers, old letters, anything like that."

"Good Lord, no," said Paddy. "I got rid of all the old rubbish we had collected over the years when we moved here from the house in Terenure, just before Dora died." His rheumy eyes filled with tears.

Ben leaned over and took Paddy's bony hand in his.

"I miss her every day, you know, Ben. Even though it's been twelve years now."

"She was a lovely woman, Uncle Paddy."

"She was that. So, in answer to your question, I've no papers – only memories," he said with a wan smile. "The only thing we kept from my parents' things was the cloth."

"Oh?"

"Yes, a tablecloth. It came from Vienna, I believe. Dora used it at special family occasions – always at Christmas. It was an heirloom, she said. She was very proud of it. Would you like to see it? It's in the hot press."

"Yeah, please," said Ben, more out of politeness than any real interest.

Paddy returned a few minutes later and handed Ben a folded linen tablecloth. "Take it. I've no use for it. You'll be getting it when I'm gone anyway. Maybe your fiancé would like it?"

Ben didn't think so but smiled.

"Thank you, Paddy, that's very kind of you. I'll treasure it."

***

The following morning, Ben called in to Sal's cake shop on Botanic Avenue.

"Keep an eye on things for fifteen minutes, will you, Gráinne," said Sal, "while I have coffee with my brother."

The pretty, green-haired student with multiple nose-rings smiled at them.

They sat at the window overlooking the tree-lined edge of Griffith Park and sipped the coffees that Sal had made them. She'd also buttered Ben a scone – it was fresh from the oven.

"So, they were originally from Vienna, how interesting. When was that, did he say?"

"He didn't know. But I reckon it must have been around the 1880s. He gave me the name of a family relation in London, by the name of Taube, who had done some work on the family tree and suggested I write to him. Hopefully he's still alive! But he also gave me a present – he suggested I give it to Julie actually. But I am pretty sure she would have no interest in it. I thought that you might like it. As Paddy said, it's an heirloom." He took the folded cloth out of a plastic carrier bag.

"Hang on!" Sal jumped up and removed the cups to the counter, then wiped and dried the table.

Ben carefully handed the folded linen to his sister.

"Oh, Ben, are you sure?"

"Absolutely. Julie would just stuff it at the back of a cupboard, and it would never see the light of day again."

Sal felt the fabric, rubbing it gently between her fingers. It was light and feathery, the colour of old parchment and there was some embroidery on it. "Will we lay it out?"

"Yeah, why not?"

She carefully unfolded the cloth. The border was decorated with interlaced, stylised, flowers in a geometric pattern. The outlines were embroidered in blue and filled in with tiny cross-stitches in white silk thread. Single flower motifs were scattered across it. There were a few stains on the linen, and a careful darn in matching cotton on one corner where the cloth had been torn.

"It's beautiful, Ben. It looks very old."

42

"Yes, it certainly does."

"The embroidery looks a little crude by today's standards. We are used to the precision of this kind of thing being done by machines. And, if I'm not mistaken, it looks like different people worked on it. You can tell by the unevenness in quality. Look, here the stitches are neat and precise – but these are less so. You could just imagine on long winter evenings, when there was no electricity, a group of women sitting together sewing, making this cloth for some young girl's trousseau. Just think, Ben, that this was made by members of our family over a hundred years ago. I wonder what kind of women they were. If this cloth could talk, I wonder what stories it would tell?"

Chapter 3

Kornyn, Kiev Province
The Jewish Pale of Settlement
1853

The four candles created halos around the faces of the women, so that they looked like icons of medieval saints that the Catholics bought in the market. Rosa hoped the shadows they cast didn't make her nose look longer than it already was. Surreptitiously, she wiped her brow with the tips of her fingers. Isaac's presence unnerved her. He was helping her younger brother Reubin, a poor student, with mathematics. The boys sat at the table on the two chairs, while the women sat on boxes in front of the stove. She had caught Isaac looking over at her several times, as she tried to concentrate on her stitches.

Since her marriage had been arranged with Isaac – almost two months ago – her mama Zipporah, her grandmother Bubbe Sadie, her sister Lena and herself had filled the hours before bedtime embroidering the linen cloth. It felt so soft in her hands – the finest linen in all of

Zhytomyr. Now draped between their knees, Rosa thought the cloth, and the slow act of sewing, created a mystical membrane between them, a spiritual web connecting their minds and bodies. And when it was finished, in the years to come, she would look at it and be reminded of these evenings when all the people she loved most in the world were safely cocooned together here in this room. By then, the Lord willing, she would be sewing another cloth and telling her own children her grandmother's outrageous tales and passing on her mother's wise advice.

Rosa shivered – a premonition maybe – she sensed that she should savour this precious moment before everything changed forever.

Now, in late summer, the cloth was covered with interlaced flowers made from skeins of white and blue silk thread that Mama had bought from the drapery shop in town. Initially, Mama had laid the fabric out on the table and drawn the pattern with dressmaker's chalk. The girls followed her lines with tiny chain stitches that their grandmother had taught them to make when they were little. Sometimes, if they were not concentrating, if the stitching wasn't neat enough, Bubbe would chide them for being careless and make them do it again. Ironically, this usually happened when she distracted them with her stories.

As they sewed, the old woman told them her own salacious versions of biblical tales, or regaled them with her memories, stories of times past when they didn't have the comforts that they had now. With watery brown eyes, tea-stained teeth and skin as wrinkled and brown as a walnut, she would describe the early days of her marriage: long hard winters when the water in the well froze for months, and they had to melt snow to make tea – and when the ice on the river was so thick they couldn't cut a hole to wash the sheets. It was so cold that if they didn't leave the doors open to let the warm air from the stove circulate, then even the contents of the chamber pots would be frozen. Bubbe Sadie described how they would wear the same clothes for weeks on end, and wrap sackcloth around their bodies, and bandages around their feet, for extra warmth. Those years the price of wheat would go through the roof, and often they had no bread. They only had enough money to buy flour for challah on Shabbos by selling their precious eggs. And for weeks they lived on barley broth and borscht, made from potatoes and beetroot. There wasn't the luxury of plums or peaches then, and sardines were as rare to be had as hens' teeth. In those years, the old woman laughed, even the Russian women were skinny.

"Tell us the Bible story about Jacob and the ugly sister," Lena demanded.

"Again! Are you not fed up with that old story?"

"No, no – please, Bubbe!"

"I'll just get Isaac some tea, Mama," said Reubin, rising from the table.

"I'll get it for you, son – you continue with your studies."

Mama rose to make tea for the two boys, and Rosa and Lena stopped sewing to listen to their grandmother's story – as the familiar smell of burning apple-wood chips from the samovar heating the water for the tea wafted around the room.

"Jacob and Esau were twin brothers, the sons of Isaac and Rebekah. Because Esau was his father's favourite, Jacob tried to trick his father into agreeing to make him, Jacob, his heir. When Esau discovered his brother's deceit, he threatened to kill him, and Jacob was forced to flee to a land far away to live among his mother's people."

The old woman had lost some of her teeth, and to compensate spoke slowly, articulating every sentence with exaggerated facial expressions. Together with her dancing, gnarled and nut-brown hands, the effect was hypnotic.

"After many days and nights travelling, Jacob arrived at his Uncle Laban's homeland where he met Laban's daughter, his beautiful cousin Rachel."

"And what did she look like?" Lena asked excitedly, although she had heard the story many times before.

"She was pretty, with the fairest hair, and eyes the colour of amber."

"Like me," said Lena, laughing.

"*Tchst, bubbala!* You want our guest to see how vain you are?" said Bubbe Sadie.

"He knows I am joking."

Isaac, sitting back in the chair listening, was watching their faces. He smiled but said nothing.

47

"Go on, Bubbe," said Rosa, looking indulgently at her younger sister.

"Jacob was so struck by her beauty that he asked Laban for his daughter's hand in marriage. Now Laban had two daughters – Rachel had an older sister, Leah, who was not so beautiful."

"Say it, Bubbe Sadie – she was ugly!"

"Beauty comes in many guises, Lena. But it is said that one of her eyes was straight and true, but the other seemed to be constantly looking over her shoulder!" The girls laughed as the old woman theatrically crossed her own rheumy eyes for effect. "Leah was also the eldest daughter and, as tradition demands, she should marry first. Because he had no money, Jacob offered to work for Laban for seven years if he would let him marry Rachel. Laban, who was as cunning as a fox, agreed to let Jacob stay. After seven long years had elapsed, Jacob went to his uncle and demanded his daughter Rachel's hand in marriage. So Laban arranged a magnificent feast for Jacob, and all the men gathered in his honour. Eventually, after much eating and drinking, when darkness fell, Laban took his daughter, heavily veiled, to Jacob, and they lay together as man and wife. But the next morning Jacob realised it was Leah, the older, uglier sister, that he'd had relations with! He was furious. He rushed to confront Laban, claiming that he had tricked him. But his wily uncle told him that he, Jacob, chose to stay – and that he, Laban, had made no firm promise. 'What kind of a father would agree to a marriage that would shame his eldest daughter?' he said angrily. So, Jacob, after lying with Leah, was forced to take her as his wife. But, as time passed, he was still besotted with Rachel's beauty and eventually he went, once more, to Laban and begged him, 'What must I give you to take Rachel also as a wife?' And the devious Laban said, 'If you work for me for another seven years, I will also give you my youngest daughter.' So that's what Jacob had to do, until finally he was allowed marry Rachel – and then the two women and Jacob lived unhappily ever after."

"Then what happened?" asked Lena.

"That is another story, for another evening. You want to exhaust an old woman telling stories?"

"How did Jacob not see that he was sleeping with the wrong woman – was he blind?" Asked Rosa.

"Blind drunk after the feast laid on by Laban," said Lena as she clapped her hands in delight. "Poor Jacob!"

"Poor Leah," said Rosa sadly.

"Well, that wouldn't happen anymore, daughters," said Mama as she returned with glasses in silver holders filled with steaming tea for the two boys. "That is why we have the veiling ceremony, where the groom veils his bride himself so that he can be sure he is marrying the right woman!" She passed around a plate of kichels, the cinnamon biscuits she served to visitors. "Enough, Bubbe, don't let Tata hear you twisting sacred stories. Back to your sewing, or that cloth will never be finished."

***

Rosa was stirring the plum jam in the deep brass preserving pot over the wood-burning stove. A comforting, end-of-summer smell of ginger and cinnamon pervaded the kitchen. Her arm was aching – it was hard work. She had asked Lena earlier to take over, to give her a rest.

"I just have to finish peeling these," Lena had said.

That was five minutes ago.

Typical, thought Rosa. She turned to try and catch Lena's eye, but her younger sister continued to ignore her. Seated at the table with a basin of potatoes, Lena was dressed in a faded brown dress, an old black woollen jacket knitted by Bubbe, and a blue linen scarf that tied back her hair. With her pale skin, light-brown hair, and amber-coloured eyes, Rosa thought she looked like the *Girl with a Pearl Earring* – the painting by Vermeer she had seen in a hand-coloured reproduction in Bena Cohen's art book. No wonder she was so spoiled. She certainly stood out from the other Jewish women in Kornyn. Although the two sisters were alike, Rosa looked more like her mother and had a longer nose. She knew she was pretty enough, but the boys in the town didn't look at her with doe-eyes full of longing – the way they looked at her sister. According to Mama, Rosa's distinguishing feature was her hair, which was a shade darker than Lena's and

50

inclined to be wavy – that and her small feet. Although Rosa was never quite sure what the benefits were of having small feet.

Rosa tried not to be envious of Lena, but sometimes it was difficult. Her sister's attitude didn't help. She was so sure of herself. Although two years younger than Rosa, with her superior education she felt entitled to treat Rosa as an equal.

Lena, like Rosa and the other young girls, had attended classes organised by Rabbi Cohen's wife to learn to read and write in Yiddish. Bena Cohen came from a wealthy Odessa family and had been educated at home by a governess. Not only did she teach the younger girls, but she held classes in the afternoon at her home for older girls who wished to learn Russian and French. It had taken a while to overcome Tata's initial reluctance. Not because of the money – they had little enough, but he knew the rabbi would come to some arrangement with him – it was more the principle of whether education was wasted on a girl. Mama, like most women of her generation, couldn't read or write. She used a wooden frame to count the rubles she made from the jam and schnapps. But she told Tata that she wanted more than the narrow confines of her own life for her daughters. She thought education would ensure a better marriage for the girls. Rosa hadn't wanted to go. She preferred to be at home making things with Mama, rather than being stuck all day in Bena Cohen's schoolroom. But Lena was clever, sociable, and above all persistent. So, despite Bubbe's dire warnings that no man would want a woman who was cleverer than him for a wife, eventually Tata, who liked to think that he was an enlightened man, had succumbed to the concerted pressure and agreed. Lena was always able to twist him around her little finger to get what she wanted.

Rosa knew Tata hated confrontation of any kind. He was a rabbinical scholar and spent most of his days in quiet contemplation, praying and studying the Talmud – or drinking tea with the other learned men in the synagogue while debating interpretations of holy texts. He didn't concern himself with ordinary things, like putting food on the table for his four children – that was for Mama to figure out. He expected her to be a dutiful wife and provide a good Jewish home for their family.

Sometimes Rosa wondered how Mama managed to survive on the few rubles Papa received from the Rabbi, and from his own students – the young men who came to the house in the evenings to learn Hebrew and study for their Bar Mitzvahs. But Mama was an industrious woman, a good cook, and her own mother, Bubbe Sadie, had taught her the skills to be a good needlewoman. Tata often said proudly that Mama could make a silk purse out of a cow's ear. Mama also made Shabbos candles, plum jam, elderflower wine, peach schnapps, cinnamon cookies, and with Bubbe's help, embroidered shawls and tichels, the scarves married Jewish women wore to cover their shorn hair.

Every Wednesday the boys would gather Mama's weekly produce and bring it to Reb Nudelman's yard, ready to sell in the town's market and the fairs held on Christian holy days.

She told the Russian bureaucrats that the wine and schnapps were potions used in Jewish sacred ceremonies. "They don't understand our language, or our ways," said Mama. "You could tell them anything and they would believe it." Her business was no threat to the local tavern keepers who turned a blind eye. Like other market towns in the area, the Polish magnate who owned the town, a scion of the house of Krushynsky, leased the taverns to the Jews who ensured that taxes were paid to the Tsar. Tata said, no one else could be trusted not to drink the profits, certainly not the Polish Catholics.

Except for Shabbos, Mama worked from sunrise to sunset. Every morning she rose at dawn, got water from the well and cleaned the dark earth floor until it was as smooth as Russian black marble – so that you could walk over it in your bare feet without feeling the sharp edge of even the smallest pebble on your skin. And before the girls had even risen from their beds, every surface in the house was scrubbed down, the stoves cleaned, and the table was set.

As Rosa stirred the jam, she was feeling apprehensive. The calm before the storm. Her sister Lena was in one of those moods – like a pecking hen, relentlessly heckling their mother.

"Don't you ever wish, Mama, you understood Hebrew, could read the Talmud, and know what the men are talking about?"

Her mother, Zipporah, was sitting on a chair with a large enamel bowl in her lap, stoning plums.

"*Oy vey*, Lena, don't let your father hear you," she said. "Why must you question everything? It's not for women to read the sacred texts. That is for fathers and husbands. Anyway, don't you learn French and Russian, is that not enough? Learning is all very well, Lena, but you also need to know how to make plum jam and pickled cabbage. These things are far more useful to a girl than learning Hebrew. That is, if you don't want your new family to starve!"

Lena visibly recoiled.

"What new family?"

"Your father has good news – he is going to speak to you later when he comes home from evening prayers."

"Mama, tell me now!"

"And bring bad luck on the family! I promised. Your father will tell you himself. Now why don't the two of you go out to the yard and pick more plums. My bowl is empty. I'll stir the jam." Mama gently pushed Rosa aside and turned her long back on them, stirring the jam vigorously.

Lena knew she was wasting her time – she would get no more information from her mother. She knew she had probably already said more than she intended.

***

At the back of their modest two-storey, red-bricked house was a yard where the hens were kept, and behind that again a small orchard with six fruit trees – apples, pears, peaches, and plums – and a line of tall elder bushes. Mama's plum jam was much sought after amongst the Jewish community in Kornyn. At the end of every summer the plums would ripen, and it was the sisters' job to pick them before they fell – so that they were just ripe enough to eat – and not too soft for the jam.

Rosa carried the basket, and her sister dragged the Grim Reaper – the name they used for the wooden pole with a two-pronged fork attached which Reubin had devised to pick plums just out of reach.

"Rosa, what on earth was she talking about? My 'new family'? I am only sixteen – I am too young to get married."

"You might think you are too young, but you are not really. Aren't lots of your friends betrothed?"

"But Mama always said that eighteen was time enough for all of that. You are eighteen."

"That's true, but I heard Mama and Tata arguing last night in loud whispers after we had gone to bed, and you were asleep. But I couldn't hear what they were saying."

"I wonder who it can be? Anyway, I don't want to get married, not for a few years."

"There are advantages," said Rosa dreamily.

"Like what?"

"Well, you can have nice things – be somebody in the community. And just imagine having your own tiny babies, Lena."

"*Feh!* I can't stand children, I prefer dogs – well, some dogs."

As if on cue, the neighbour's mangy dog that the sisters had nicknamed Bercovich started barking.

"Lena!" Rosa was shocked. "What else is there in life but to be a mother and have children?"

"You make us sound like breeding heifers, Rosa. I suppose marriage might give us a few more luxuries than we are used to – but that's all. It's pitiful that we are so poor. Why can't Tata be like other men and have a trade that Jews are allowed, like a tavern keeper, or a merchant – something that earns more than the pittance he gets at shul."

"You don't mean that, Lena. I know you are annoyed that Mama won't tell you the news. But you'll hear soon enough."

Lena sighed and threw one, then another, bruised plum over the garden fence and into the garden next door. Bercovich howled then barked frantically. Lena grinned as Rosa made a disproving face at her but said nothing. Her sister had a hard, ruthless edge that Rosa could never understand. She had been like that since she was a little girl. It was something Rosa didn't like to dwell on.

After a few minutes Lena asked, changing the subject, "How are you getting on with Isaac's family? His mother is such a bad-tempered old bitch."

Rosa had met Jessica Taube several times at this stage and did not disagree.

"Hopefully, when I get to know her better, she won't be too bad," Rosa said charitably. "At least, I get on really well with his grandmother, Bubbe Mim. She's always so kind to me when I bring over Mama's jam. I hope the rest of Isaac's family like me."

"What could they possibly not like?" retorted Lena, eyebrows raised.

"Oh, I'm not as pretty as you, and don't have your witty tongue."

"You have other gifts, Rosa. You are better wife material than me. As well as having those incredibly small feet!" She laughed heartily.

That was the thing about Lena – she could make a rabbi laugh – it was hard to be cross with her for too long.

***

Lena was like a coiled spring by the time Tata's long, stooped figure could be seen turning the corner into their tree-lined street. She was sitting on a low wall waiting to ambush him. He was dressed in the long black coat and the somewhat shapeless black hat he wore to the synagogue – his straggly grey beard and pigtails hanging down in front of him.

Rosa watched from the front window as the two of them approached the house.

Lena was gesticulating excitedly to Tata. In response, he raised the palms of his hands heavenward and then joined them together, indicating he was still praying as he walked, head lowered, along the dusty street. But when they eventually entered the kitchen he turned to her, his purple-lidded brown eyes twinkling with excitement behind his spectacles.

"After dinner, Lena. When we have eaten the food that the good Lord has provided, and your mama has prepared, then we will discuss family matters."

After Tata blessed the food, they all ate without speaking until not a morsel of the herrings and barley stew was left on a plate. Throughout the meal Reubin and Josef made faces at Lena when Tata wasn't looking.

Finally, with fingertips touching, looking down his long nose over gold-rimmed spectacles, Tata spoke to them all.

"As your mother hinted at earlier – she can never keep a secret for long," he looked affectionately at Zipporah, "I have made a wonderful match for Lena." He sighed, bursting with pride. "After lengthy discussions, Lena is to be betrothed to …"

He paused for effect, looking around the table.

Lena's face was white as a sheet.

"Rabbi Cohen's son!"

"*Moishe Cohen!*" said Lena, aghast.

"Moishe Cohen, no less!" said Tata, smiling and nodding enthusiastically.

"Tata, you cannot be serious!" said Lena.

Tata looked confused at this reaction. Reubin and Josef's mouths were wide open in disbelief. Mama shuffled nervously in her chair.

"But he is old, Tata! He already has a family!"

"Moishe is not old, daughter – he is in his prime, twenty-six years of age, a young man."

"But I am too young to be married."

"You are sixteen, of marriageable age, and you will marry Moishe."

"But I don't want children," she said defiantly, turning to her mother.

"*Lena!*" said Mama shocked.

"Not everyone is meant to be a mother!" Lena glared angrily at her.

"So, the eggs think they are smarter than the chickens?" Zipporah retorted, looking at her daughter with annoyance. "It is our duty, daughter, to have children and multiply and spread the word of the Lord."

Rosa was shocked but remained silent. She wondered where her sister's anger came from. No good ever came from railing against the way of things.

"You won't have a choice, daughter. You will have a ready-made family, and with good luck, a brood of your own healthy children to follow," said Zipporah. "He is a kind man, Lena, and everyone says what a good father he is to his children."

"Remember how Moishe's first wife died two years

ago," Mama explained to them all solemnly, "giving birth to a stillborn baby. He has two other children: a boy, Samuil, who is now seven and a little girl, Perle, three years old."

"But Tata –"

Tata put his hand up to interrupt her. "It is a great privilege for our family to be connected to theirs. As you know, the Cohens come from a long line of rabbinical scholars."

They were also Tata's employers, thought Rosa. It would have been hard for him to turn down this 'honour'. The Cohens lived in a double-fronted stone house facing onto the tree-lined town square near the wooden synagogue. Lena would have to work, like Mama did, but it would be considered a privilege to look after Moishe's family while her husband devoted his life to study and prayer. The alliance also had the advantage of enhancing their own family's prestige. It would possibly lead to Tata being given more responsibilities with better terms at the synagogue. And the fact that Moishe was older, in Tata's eyes was probably seen as a benefit for his wilful daughter.

"Enough, Lena. I realise this might have come as a shock to you. But you are no longer a girl, you are a young woman, and this marriage is a gift from the Lord – a more advantageous match than I could ever have dreamed of for you. Now, no more talk about this. Can a father not enjoy an evening's peace with his family after a day spent carrying out his religious duties?"

"Don't forget, Abe," said Zipporah, putting her hand on her husband's arm. "You promised that this evening you would help Josef and Reubin with their mathematics."

"Ah yes, how could I forget! But am I not the luckiest man in Kornyn, two daughters betrothed to be married? God is good, Zipporah, we shall grow old in peace, with the happy sound of grandchildren at our feet."

"Lena, help Rosa clear the table," said Mama, looking anxiously at her daughter.

Lena rose, hands trembling, and took the mismatched china plates to the bucket, then lifting it with both hands walked slowly out to the pump in the back yard. Rosa followed her.

"*Oy vey, Rosa, what am I going to do?*" she wailed, once they were out of earshot. "I won't marry Moishe Cohen." She sobbed, tears running down her beautiful face.

"Lena, little sister, although they cannot force you against your will, I don't see how you cannot marry him."

***

Over the next few days, regardless of how many times she cried and wheedled, Tata stood firm. For a man of many words, he simply refused to engage with her on the matter. Her marriage was his duty to arrange – end of story. Lena was devastated. Their older brother Reubin who was fourteen, at Lena's urging had tried to intercede on her behalf, but Tata was adamant that the marriage would be a good one. Rosa suspected that Mama too had misgivings but knew that if Lena rejected Moishe's offer she would shock their community and bring disgrace to the family. There was also the matter of the dowry. It had been a struggle for Tata to save for Rosa's dowry. The Cohens, Tata's employers, were willing to accept a modest sum for Lena because of Moishe's situation. Mama had told Lena in no uncertain terms that, despite her beauty, if she didn't marry Moishe, she would end up an old maid – a fate most young girls considered worse than death. There would be no other offers.

Mama kept telling Lena that Moishe was a kind man, and at the end of the day kindness was a more important quality than a handsome face. But as images of her beautiful sister sharing a marriage bed with Moishe crept into Rosa's mind, she shuddered. She knew this aspect of the marriage would not be easy, and she felt sorry for her sister. At twenty-six, Moishe Cohen should have been in his prime, but instead he looked much older. He was very tall and thin, and his long beard already had premature streaks of grey. Hopefully, as Mama kept saying, he would be kind to Lena.

Rosa knew that a life of drudgery like Mama's was not the future Lena had imagined. Hidden under her sister's feather mattress were romantic novels that she had borrowed from the girls she met in Bena Cohen's.

With all her learning, Rosa thought, you'd think she would have realised that the lives of the aristocratic Russian heroines within those pages were far removed from the reality of poor Jewish girls. In real life, this offer of marriage was the happy ending – a great honour, for Lena and for the Rabinovitch family.

Over the next few days, Mama never lost an opportunity to reassure her younger daughter. And every evening, as Lena helped Mama prepare dinner, they had different versions of the same conversation. This evening was no different.

"Mama, please listen to me!" Lena pleaded. "I don't want to marry him!"

"*Want* – is it? You should be grateful – your father has made a great match for you."

"But – he's too old for me!"

"Ten years' difference. It's not so bad," her mother replied reassuringly. "And he's used to the ways of women. So sad his first wife dying. A good and pious woman by all accounts. The midwife said the baby hadn't moved for weeks. It's a blessing at least that the other two are half reared. To raise another woman's baby takes a special gift, Lena." Zipporah looked sceptically at her daughter.

If the Cohens knew what they were letting themselves in for, Rosa thought apprehensively.

"Anyway, you have six months to look forward to your wedding. Meanwhile our new year, Rosh Hashanah, is only three weeks away and Rosa's wedding will be upon us all before we know it."

"Rosa's so lucky. At least her husband will be a young man."

"But not such a good prospect, though I suppose he will be a lawyer – eventually." Zipporah smiled knowingly at Rosa. "But you," she turned once more to Lena, "will be marrying into Jewish royalty. Just think, Lena, a scholar from the distinguished Cohen line!"

"I can't see the advantage, Mama. I'll just have two jobs to do, bringing in an income as well as raising a family. Whereas Rosa won't be pickling cabbage – she will have servants, she won't even have to peel a potato! She will have fine costumes, live in her own house, and maybe even get to travel."

"Lena, no more! I won't have you talking like that. Maybe it was a mistake allowing you to go to Bena Cohen's school after all. A head full of nonsense, that's all you have gained."

Chapter 4

In the room behind the kitchen Rosa, lying in her narrow bed, looked sympathetically over at her sister. Still shuddering, Lena had eventually fallen asleep and was now snoring gently beside her.

Rosa pulled the soft, woollen, crocheted blankets around her chin. This was her secret time. A time she closed her eyes and allowed her mind to fill with thoughts of Isaac. In contrast to Moishe, he was young and handsome. He had shaved off his payot and his beard was short, dark and smooth – not long and wiry like Moishe's and Tata's.

Rosa knew of the physical dimension to marriage. Mama had told her that it was her duty to engage in acts of intimacy with her husband. But she had also said that sometimes it could be enjoyable for a woman. And Rosa did not doubt her – she knew how it all worked. It was hard not to, living in such close quarters. Her parents' bedroom was just above the kitchen and late at night she and Lena could hear the creaking of floorboards, and their muffled groans of pleasure. Everyone in the house did. However, Rosa was apprehensive about doing it – 'the act'.

Her friends whispered that the first time it hurt, that you bled, but that it was usually fine after that. And when she felt the fluttering feelings of desire stirred by her own probing fingers, she looked forward to lying with him, imagining his strong arms holding her close. Her only fear was that somehow she would disappoint him.

The marriage agreement had happened quickly and unexpectedly. Isaac's father, Meyer Taube, a Kornyn grain exporter, had moved with his family to Vienna the year before. However, two months ago he had visited the Rabinovitchs's house to drink tea with Tata. He told Tata that he had hired a shadchan to find a suitable bride for his son Isaac, and that the matchmaker had come up with a few names including Rosa's. He said he was in town on business, visiting his brother Kazimir who ran a tavern on the other side of the town square. So, he was taking the opportunity to see Rosa – to check her out as a potential bride for his son. Meyer's mother Mim Taube had sung her praises and told him tales of her good works in the community. After he had met her, to everyone's surprise, he had immediately suggested the betrothal of the young couple. Tata told Rosa that Meyer Taube had been extremely impressed with her modesty and selflessness and felt that he need look no further.

Although Rosa was delighted at her good fortune, she had also been surprised at the Taubes' offer. Because, regardless of Bubbe Mim's kind words, she knew that Meyer Taube could have any girl in town he liked for his son. Possibly this was a strategic move to preserve his own comfort. Maybe he thought, because she was good and kind, she would put up with his wife Jessica's bad temper, and not cause endless rows.

Rosa's brother, Reubin, had also suggested that Meyer Taube wanted to marry into a devout family as a kind of spiritual insurance policy, because he had neglected his own religious duties. Whatever Meyer Taube's reason, Reubin was surprised that Tata had agreed to the match. But Rosa suspected that he had been persuaded by Mama who saw it as a great opportunity for her eldest daughter and had persuaded Tata, despite his reservations, to accept the proposal. Mama reassured her husband that Isaac was a good Jewish boy – hadn't Tata taught him himself? And despite his misgivings, a few weeks later the Taube family had travelled back from Vienna for an extended holiday in Kornyn. But the real purpose of their visit was to meet Rosa's family and finally agree the marriage conditions suggested by the shadchan.

The Taube's old family home was next to their warehouse at the top of the street, with one side facing onto the town square. It was one of the finest houses in

Kornyn. On the street side, it had five windows on the front and an ornate timber porch painted pale blue. But on the market side it had a series of wooden kiosks at ground level with wooden shutters that were opened on market and fair days where the Taubes would buy wheat and barley grains from local farmers. When Meyer had left with his family to start a new life in Vienna – his mother, Bubbe Mim, had refused to go – and Isaac had stayed behind with the stubborn old woman to wind up his father's business in the town.

So that the young couple could meet up and see if they were amenable to the match, Tata had invited Meyer, his mother Mim, wife Jessica, and Isaac to visit. Rosa remembered how Zipporah had spent the week before the visit cleaning, scrubbing, and mending all their clothes. Spicy smells of cinnamon kichels and plum tart filled the house. And on the dresser was a jug of tall-stemmed, yellow sunflowers freshly picked from the yard. Everything was perfect.

As her handsome Isaac had entered the room, Rosa had felt her heart beating in excited anticipation. But Jessica Taube had bent her head as she came through their door. It was then Rosa realised that all her mother's effort had been in vain. Jessica Taube had no need to stoop – she was not a tall woman. But the weight of her humiliation in agreeing to this match was obvious to all – and with this realisation, Rosa's heart had sunk.

"*Shalom*, my friends, come in, come in. Welcome to our

humble home." Tata had stood, arms outstretched – his gentle face illuminated with kindness.

Rosa had winced at his use of the word 'humble,' because she saw through the Taubes' eyes that their house was indeed humble. The visitors seemed to fill the room. Especially Meyer Taube, who was a big bear of a man, his curly brown hair nearly reaching the low wooden ceiling. On his first visit Rosa had instantly warmed to him. He had a bushy, short beard, and smiling brown eyes. Although he had the reputation of being a tough businessman, Rosa felt that he was also kind and caring.

Conversely, her prospective mother-in-law, Jessica, skinny-hipped and lipped, had lived up to her reputation. Her long face was framed in an ornate, highly decorated straw hat, with black and white feathers and ribbons – and a wig, made from the lustrous black hair of a much younger woman. Rosa had thought Mama's black embroidered tichel that she made herself, worn over her shorn hair, showed off her classical features and was much more elegant.

Rosa had felt proud of her brothers and sister. They were washed and clean, hair shining, and dressed in their good clothes, normally worn only to the synagogue. After formal introductions, the visitors were invited by Tata to sit down on chairs that they had borrowed from neighbours, while Mama had fussed over the two old ladies, making sure they were settled closest to the stove. Mama had enquired solicitously about how the Taubes were settling back into their old home – while Rosa, using silver glass-holders that Mama had borrowed from Bena Cohen for the occasion, had served tea from the teapot on top of the china samovar. Lena had passed around the tart and cookies on small, mismatched china plates. But, as Rosa sat back sipping her tea, she had been mortified to notice that Jessica Taube – holding her tea in one hand – kept lifting her skirt from the floor, even though it was as clean as a whistle. Rosa had been dismayed at the woman's disdain – she had heard that there were wooden floors in the Taube's house. But when her eyes had caught Bubbe Mim's, who was chatting to her own grandmother, and the two old ladies beamed at her, Rosa's heart had filled with confidence that everything would be alright.

Tata, never short of a few words, had kept the conversation going. He asked Meyer about the difficulties of trading in Vienna. Tata was puzzled as to how Meyer Taube, a Jew, could live, let alone work there. But Meyer had shrugged his big-bear shoulders and smiled.

"There is a lot more tolerance in Vienna. Many of the leading doctors and lawyers are Jews. We are accepted – and if there are difficulties there are always ways around these things. Money talks. As well as prayers, of course."

Tata had not seemed overly impressed but nodded politely.

Rosa remembered how nervous she had felt when Mama theatrically, not forgetting the purpose of this social event, had suggested they all go out to see the orchard.

"Yes, yes. We should let the young couple introduce

themselves to one another," Tata had said, smiling benevolently.

Rosa had bowed her head modestly and crossed her hands on her knees so that no one would see them shaking.

When they all finally left, leaving the door ajar, Isaac, who seemed to realise how nervous she was, smiled encouragingly at her. He had an earthy, sweet smell, she noticed – it must be from working with wheat.

"Would you like to live in Vienna?" he had asked gently. His hands were resting on his knees, and she noticed, unusually, that he had long fingers and clean unbroken nails.

"Yes, of course, it sounds wonderful. I believe the streets are paved with stone and the buildings are covered in gold."

"Not all of them but, yes, it is magnificent." He had smiled indulgently. "It is quite different from Kornyn. But will you miss your family?"

"Of course, but I will also enjoy getting to know my new family."

Isaac had raised one eyebrow and smiled when she said that. She wondered was he laughing at her – did he suspect how terrified she really was of the prospect?

"Bubbe Mim tells me you are the kindest girl in Kornyn. She was the one who insisted that we were well matched. As you can see, there is really no need for the matchmaker in our family."

71

"Since your family left, I often visit your grandmother," she had told him. "I thought she might have been lonely. Usually, I go in the afternoons when you are at the warehouse. I bring her jam, schnapps, and drink tea with her to keep her company. She also says nice things about you. She is very proud of you."

Isaac had smiled and nodded his head in acknowledgement.

"Just one thing. I feel I must warn you," he then said earnestly. "We are not as devout as your family. In Vienna – despite what my father says – being Jewish makes life difficult."

"But I can still practise my faith and keep a kosher house?"

"Yes, of course," he had said quickly.

A bit too quickly, Rosa thought afterwards.

He didn't touch her – it wasn't allowed. But his eyes had devoured her, and she felt those familiar tingling sensations of desire wash over her again.

"I think we will get along very well," he had said quietly.

"Yes. Yes, we shall," Rosa had replied, her eyes telling him in one glance what her lips could never utter.

***

After the introduction, a period of Shidduch, or arranged meetings, had started. A kind of organised bumping-into-

72

one-another. Mama would send Lena and Rosa over to the Taubes with some pears, or hot pastries she had just made for Bubbe Mim. Usually, the sisters were sent in the evenings when Mama knew that Isaac was sure to be there. Isaac also started coming over to the Rabinovichs once a week to help Reubin with mathematics and to get to know the family.

On these occasions, Rosa had been shy and embarrassed. She was not sure what to talk to him about, he seemed so clever and worldly wise. She was grateful for her brothers' tomfoolery and Lena's ability to chatter to a chair. She knew Isaac well enough to say hello when she saw him around town and over the years, she had noticed him growing into a handsome young man. But, in reality, he was a stranger to her.

The previous time he had called over, she remembered vaguely that Lena had chattered away, gossip mostly, bits of news that she would have picked up at Bena Cohen's school. But Rosa was consumed with shyness. As Lena talked, it was her that he was looking at, while she tried, and mostly succeeded, in keeping her eyes averted. When Rosa eventually built up enough courage to participate in the conversation, she asked him about his studies. And he answered her questions with a kindness and consideration that she found reassuring. He seemed a sensible young man and, unlike her brothers who rarely took her questions seriously, Isaac appeared to value her opinion. But despite, or maybe because of her attraction to him, she found these arranged meetings stressful.

The problem with living in a small town was that she also kept meeting him unexpectedly. So that lately she felt permanently on edge, never fully able to relax. Like the other day when she and Mama had met him with Bubbe Mim in the street near Shklovsky's, the kosher grocery shop. Mama had chatted to Mim Taube, about the weather, the cost of flour, and taxes on kosher meat – while she had stood by filled with embarrassment. She couldn't even look at him, and had kept her head lowered, only stealing a glance as he headed towards the shop. But as his grandmother opened the door, he stood back and caught her eyes. She felt her cheeks flush as she remembered how he had returned her gaze smiling, but coolly appraising at the same time.

**

It had been a long, tedious afternoon, Rosa was bored cleaning knives, a job that she hated. Through the window, she could see Mama outside gossiping with the neighbours. The others would not be home for at least an hour from school. On an impulse, she put aside her chores and sneaked into Mama's bedroom and peeped into the cupboard where her wedding dress was kept. Mama's friend, Babtsy Kaplan, had made the dress. Rosa recalled how the dressmaker had measured her in her home, a mud-walled, thatched cottage at the edge of town. Rosa had been so excited at the prospect of seeing it finished that the suspense had been almost unbearable. But when she had finally finished, Rosa had not been disappointed. It was exquisite – made from the finest white cotton and trimmed with beautiful, filigree lace brought in by one of the traders from the market in Kiev. Now, the dress was wrapped in cotton sheets to protect it from the smuts emanating from the stoves that seemed to get everywhere in the house. Although she could not see it, Rosa was reassured by the knowledge of its presence.

Rosa closed the cupboard, moving to the end of her parent's bed, lifting the carved lid of the wooden chest. Rosa's great-grandfather had made it all those years ago for Bubbe's own wedding. Breathing in the scent of lavender, she felt the layers of crisp, white linen: three chemises, two pairs of drawers, and two petticoats, one red and one black, that the women in her family had sewed with her – for her – over the past few months. They were still working on the cloth, the most beautiful and intricate piece of all.

Rosa smiled as she thought of those long evenings laughing and telling tales of times gone by, and her heart was filled with sadness at the thought of how much she would miss them all.

She glanced at the old red biscuit-tin where her father kept the money he had saved for her dowry. After the young couple were married, they would move to Vienna and live with the Taube family while Isaac would start his legal studies at the university. Rosa dreaded leaving her family – but she also knew she had to go – wanted to go. It was a great opportunity for her to get away from Kornyn. Because life was always going to be difficult here for her family – as it was for all the Jews. Although they cohabited in relative peace with their neighbours, the Poles and Slavs, the Jews were second-class citizens. On the face of it, they ran everything. However, a shadow permanently hung over the Jewish community. Rosa could never understand how her peaceful and industrious people were so despised. Tata said it was the fact that the Slavs and Poles didn't understand Jewish customs and ways, and that people always feared others who were not like themselves.

Coming up to the Christian celebration of Easter, this hatred was palpable. Even though the Jews became quieter, kept their heads down as they walked through the streets, the jibes became louder, nastier, and more insulting. They claimed that the 'yids' murdered young Christian boys to use their blood in their sacrifice for Pesach, the feast of Passover. And despite explanations to the contrary, the taunts continued.

The older people still remembered the anti-Jewish riots in Odessa thirty years ago – when Jewish women were raped, and fourteen men were dragged from their homes and beaten to death.

As Rosa grew up, she learned to turn the other cheek when the other children goaded and spat at her. But once she heard whispers of these atrocities, she too shared her people's feelings of apprehension as the holy days approached.

All things considered, although Rosa knew that it would be a wrench to leave her family, she was excited about her marriage and the prospects of going to Vienna. She had heard of the material luxuries in the city's markets and shops, and that there were all manner of public concerts and entertainments. Tata had also told her about the magnificent churches and palaces, the finest in the land. But more importantly for Rosa, it was a place where Jews could live in peace, where, instead of being despised, they were respected and admired for their culture and learning. What a place to live!

Despite her excitement, which hit her at unexpected times during the day – as she was peeling potatoes or washing dishes – she thought of how much she was going to miss her family. And she would try to hide from Mama the tears of sadness that welled up in her eyes. But, of course, they could visit – and even, the Lord willing, eventually they too could move to Vienna.

***

Rosa never minded distributing the food on the evening before Shabbos. It was a tradition in the community to make sure everyone had something nice to eat for the celebrations the following day. And she had grown fond of her 'ducklings', as Lena scathingly called them. At this stage, it was seven o'clock and she had already visited three households. Because Isaac's family were home, at least she didn't have to visit Mim Taube. She would see them tomorrow.

Meyer Taube had invited the Rabinovichs for Shabbos dinner. Rosa shuddered at the thought. The prospect of this formal visit to his home and talking to Isaac in front of his mother and father was terrifying. She wondered whether, when she was married and living in Vienna, she would find his mother less intimidating. In a year's time, would she be making cinnamon kichels and challah bread with Jessica Taube and taking them to deserving neighbours. Maybe they were all too rich in the city, and she wouldn't need to.

Rosa's last call was to Bena Cohen, with just the bottle of Mama's schnapps remaining in her basket.

She reached their stone house on the edge of the square beside the wooden synagogue. No one ever used their front door with its ornate Mezuzah, the small decorative wooden case that held miniature sacred text from the Torah, signifying to the world that this was a Jewish household. Instead, she walked around the house and knocked gently on the back door which was promptly opened by Bena who ushered her into their large kitchen.

"Rosa, you brought Zipporah's schnapps! You are too good to me! She knows how I like a sip of it in the evenings.

Join us! Come, sit with the children. I am nearly finished making soup. I got a beef tongue from the butcher. Your timing is perfect – I have just made tea this minute."

"Thank you, Mrs Cohen. That would be lovely, although I can't stay long. I promised Mama I would be back before nightfall." Rosa sat down at the table.

Samuil, a small, serious boy, and little Perle were sitting at the table, both drawing on slates with chalk.

"What are you drawing, Samuil? Is it a dog?" Rosa asked.

"No, a horse."

"Ah, silly me," she said kindly. "And what's Perle doing?"

"She can't draw, Wosa," Samuil said with a lisp. "She's only a baby."

Bena smiled affectionately at her grandson. Then turned her attention to Rosa.

"And what of our wonderful news. I believe we are to be related by marriage, Rosa – the Rabbi and your father have made a match. Imagine, your sister and my son!" She beckoned Rosa to join her at the stove where she was stirring the soup, out of earshot of the children. "Although Lena comes to my school, and she is always very diligent in her studies. I feel that I don't know her quite as well as I know you. She is very pretty, and clever, but does she like children?" She looked over anxiously at her grandchildren playing quietly.

"My sister, as you know, is much cleverer than I," Rosa

said cautiously. "And yes, she is good with children. She has the gift of making them laugh."

"That's good, children like to laugh. But there will be crying too – plenty of it, believe me. Babies, that's all they are, to lose their mother so young. Samuil still has nightmares, poor little man. My poor Moishe is only beginning to get over it. But the Lord knows, a man needs a wife. Anyway, I will have a chance to meet her and judge her character for myself. Jessica Taube has invited us to share Shabbos dinner with you all tomorrow so that Lena can meet Moishe before their betrothal is announced to the community."

Rosa didn't like to say that Reubin had already heard whispers about it in the market. And that on hearing this, Lena had told Rosa that she felt a noose was tightening around her neck.

"And we will finally get a chance to celebrate your own engagement properly. You are blessed by the Lord, Rosa. Isaac Taube is a fine young man. The Rabbi speaks highly of him. He was a good student, good to his Bubbe Mim, and even – Lord bless him – to his mama. Not always easy!" The jowls on her chin jiggled as she threw her head back and laughed.

Although Bena Cohen enjoyed the privileges of her wealthy and cultured background, she was unaffected in her demeanour and the antithesis of her husband. Whereas he was a serious, spiritual man, weighed down with the worries of the world, his wife took life's challenges lightly, and nothing seemed to dim her good humour.

Bena stopped laughing as they heard the latch lifting on the door.

"Well, how are all of the preparations going, is the dress made?" Bena said, changing the subject abruptly.

"Marriage is a serious business, Mama – don't let the Rabbi hear you talking about such frivolous things," said Moishe entering, smiling at the two women.

"Look who is here, children – Tata!" said Bena.

Tall and thin, Moishe Cohen had inherited the physical appearance of his father, but the good nature of his mother. As he entered the room, the two children jumped up from the table and ran to him, wrapping their arms around him.

Poor mites, thought Rosa, and for Moishe too she felt sympathy. She remembered his wife as being a gentle woman. Although older than Rosa, she always had a kind word and a warm smile for her when she had called to the Cohens' house. On those occasions, she was usually cooking at the stove, or mending clothes.

"Son, sit down – drink tea with us."

Moishe sat down beside Rosa. His mother fussed over him and brought him tea as the children vied for his attention, until eventually he took both children on his lap, little Perle sucking her thumb and Samuil sitting on the other knee with his arm around his father's neck.

"Give your Tata some peace, children, he has only walked in the door," said Bena.

But the children ignored their grandmother and Moishe seemed to enjoy their attention.

"Rosa has bought me Zipporah's schnapps – hopefully, it will help me sleep tonight."

"It makes her snore," said Moishe to Rosa, straight-faced but with laughing eyes.

"What a thing for a son to say! Snore? Me? It is the Rabbi's snores that rattle the house," she retorted good-naturedly.

"And how are you, Rosa? Soon to be married, I believe?" Moishe asked.

"Yes, the Lord willing," said Rosa shyly. "And you too, Moishe. Tata told us you are to marry Lena. We are to be brother and sister."

"That will be my blessing, and if your sister is as half as good a woman as you are, then I will be a lucky man indeed."

Chapter 5

Dublin
November 2011

The Kilkenny design shop was busy. They were sitting at the window of the first-floor café with steaming cups of coffee, overlooking the grounds of Trinity College. In the distance Ben could see guys playing rugby. He shivered at the thought of it. The temperature had dropped suddenly.

"Met Éireann are forecasting more snow," he told Daisy.

"I hope they're wrong," said Daisy, sipping her coffee as Ben buttered his fruit scone. "The city grinds to a standstill at even a flutter of snow."

"Don't talk to me. The last time it snowed, the school playground was like an ice-skating rink. The teachers had to wear socks over their shoes so they wouldn't end up falling on their arses. And the older boys built an enormous snowman in the priest's garden."

"Oh, that was nice," said Daisy, smiling.

"Not really. Guess where they put the carrot?"

Daisy burst out laughing. "The school can't be that bad!"

"No, it's not. I love the little feckers," he said, smiling. She looked pretty when she laughed, he thought to himself.

"Anyway, down to business," said Daisy. "You have some things to show me."

"Yes." He opened his battered leather briefcase and took out a plastic bag containing the tablecloth that Paddy had given him. He held it out to Daisy. "Have a look at this."

"Hang on, just let me get rid of these." She moved her cup and plate out of the way and turned to the side as she took the cloth from the bag. "Gosh, it looks incredibly old. The linen is like fine parchment. It's very beautiful, just look at the detail. You so rarely see anything like this – you forget how exquisite hand-sewn work is. Did your uncle tell you anything about it – where it came from?"

"No, other than it has been in the family for years. He remembered his granny saying it was an heirloom."

She carefully folded it up and put it back in the bag. Ben leant over and retrieved a second object out of the briefcase. He handed her a small pencil portrait set in an oval mount in a simple wooden frame.

"This was in my mam's house. My sister Sal gave it to me recently, thought it might give us some clues. We don't know who he is."

"A handsome man," she said, inspecting it closely.

"Do you think he looks like me?" he said, grinning.

"No, not really."

"What about the nose?" He turned his head in profile.

"Well, maybe a bit," she conceded graciously. She looked at the back and laid it down on the table. "There's writing on it – what script is that?"

"I don't know. I called in to Dermot Nolan, to ask him about it. He said the drawing was of interest, rather than of any real artistic value – probably a sketch done by a street artist. The kind of thing people got as souvenirs when they were on holidays, or to give to a loved one. He thought the writing could be Russian, but he wasn't sure."

"And you have no clue who this man could be?"

"No, I am hoping to find out. I am planning to go to London to visit a relation of mine, Alex Taube, some sort of cousin. He's done some research on the family and my Uncle Paddy tells me he has made a family tree. I'll take a Ryan Air special. Flights are dirt cheap at the moment."

"Really? I wrote to that cousin of my mother's – you know, the evacuee I was telling you about from the Frome side, Sunny Unwin. In fact, I have arranged to meet him next time I'm in London. I go over there quite a bit – my boyfriend works there."

"Oh, you're seeing someone?"

"Well, as I said, he lives in London. He was promoted in the bank where he works, and he moved there about six months ago."

"That must be difficult for you," he said kindly.

She bit her lip, pulling it to the side. He'd noticed the last time he met her that she did this when she was anxious. She looked well today, he thought. Not in her formal work clothes, she was wearing a leather jacket and jeans with high-heeled boots that made her look taller. Her hair was gathered on the top of her head. The style suited her, it emphasised her fine bone structure – and it occurred to him once again how much she looked like the woman in the portraits.

"Well, Daisy, much as I am enjoying talking to you, I have an appointment with a solicitor in Merrion Square. So, I'll have to love you and leave you."

"Actually, I have things to do too," she said awkwardly.

He stood up and put on his jacket. "How about we co-ordinate our trip to London. Two heads are better than one, and all of that. I know you will be tied up with ...?"

"Fintan," she said.

"But," Ben continued, "we could chat on the plane on the way over and come up with a plan. Dermot Nolan hasn't completed his initial investigation yet. He said he will be another week or two. Meanwhile, we are supposed to be concentrating on establishing a provenance. Oh God! I am late as usual. I'd better be off, Daisy. I'll organise the flights if you like. You give me the dates. I'm due some leave in school because I attended a course during the summer."

"Oh, on what?"

"Maintaining discipline. The principal sent me." He grinned sheepishly. "Anyway, you give me the dates and I'll book the flights."

"No, it's alright. I can ..."

"No problem, I'll do it. That's settled then."

***

Ben was ten minutes late when he reached the solicitor's office, a Georgian building on Merrion Square, even though it was just across the road from the National Gallery. A secretary showed him into a bright airy room with high, stuccoed ceilings and an ornate marble fireplace.

Sal was already with Cormac by the time he arrived. She was dressed up for the occasion in a skirt and boots with a smart woollen coat that he had never seen before. Ben nodded at Sal and approached Cormac to shake his hand.

"Cormac, thanks for seeing us."

"No problem, Ben."

Although the same age as Ben, the solicitor looked older, prematurely balding with a round, fresh, face and thick glasses.

"Sal." Ben kissed his sister on the cheek and sat down beside her.

"Sally has just been explaining the situation to me."

"Right," said Ben. "He can't do this, can he?"

"Well, as I was telling Sally, first things first – she should start divorce proceedings. Better late than never."

Cormac turned to Sal. "As I said, it's important to separate Fergal and yourself legally and financially. The process will consider both of your situations, assets, savings, pensions and the like. Otherwise, you are leaving the door open for future claims, and possibly denying yourself any benefits you might be due, such as a share of his pension. But from what you say, Sally, he has more liabilities than assets. However, if his name is on the deeds of the house then he does have an equity in it. A share if you like."

"What exactly is he entitled to?" said Sal, sounding crestfallen.

"To calculate what his equity might be, you would begin by subtracting the property's liabilities – such as the balance due on the mortgage – from its current market value. But it's more complicated than that. His share of the balance depends on a lot of other things as well. Such as whether he contributed to the deposit, or the mortgage repayments, and for how long. Also, how much you have spent in the intervening years in maintaining the house to preserve, or enhance, its value. In a situation like this, financial records are important. The solicitor who acted for you at the time of the purchase would have kept records but usually only for seven years. The deeds themselves are held by the lending institution, the bank in this case. So, your own records are important, Sally, bank statements and the like."

"Well, I wouldn't say they were good but, yes, I do have records."

"So, from what you are saying, Cormac, we will have to pay him back what he contributed," said Ben.

"Yes,"

"That's all?" said Sally.

"Your husband would also be entitled to an equitable share of the benefit of his investment. On a simplistic level, this is a fair percentage of the increase in value of the house when you bought it and what it is worth now."

"But that could be a lot of money," said Sally in alarm.

"Unfortunately, yes." Cormac looked over the top of his thick glasses, his expression grim. "Those houses are going for good money. In fact, I recently represented a purchaser of one just up the road. From what Ben has told me, and the rough figures he gave me, I'd say that could amount to anything up to twenty thousand euro, Obviously that's a ball-park until we see the detailed numbers."

"So would Sally have to sell the house?" asked Ben.

"If it is the only means she has of paying him, then I am afraid the courts could order her to do so."

Ben looked at his sister. She was white as a sheet. He leaned over and grasped her hand in his. "We will get the money, somehow," he said reassuringly.

"I read in the paper recently that you were selling a painting by Thomas Rafferty at auction, and someone turned up with an exact copy," said Cormac.

"Yeah, 'fraid so. Experts think one of them might be a fake."

"Let's hope then it's not yours," Cormac responded.

***

Outside they stood on the pavement, going over what Cormac had told them.

"Look, Ben, I just want to make one thing clear. I don't want any of your money from Uncle Tommy. Nor do I want the money from the painting. That's yours, Mam specifically left it to you. At the time, I got their savings which I needed badly."

"Which you spent on us, Sis." Ben put his arm protectively around his older sister.

"I can probably get a loan from the Credit Union. From what Julie told me about her plans the last time I met her, you will need every penny you have."

Ben suspected that his sister felt Julie was completely over the top with the wedding. But she would never say so. He didn't disagree with that view. But it was more complicated than that. Julie's sense of style was her armour, her identity, it gave her confidence – and the wedding was an opportunity to be seen as an equal with many of her better-off workmates. This, together with the mother and daughter's desire to impress friends and family, meant that the whole thing was unusually significant for them both. He had tried once to explain this to Sal. He wasn't sure though, that his self-sufficient, frugal, and occasionally self-righteous sister had really understood.

Ben, took a cigarette from a packet in his jacket pocket and with a flick of a disposable lighter, lit it, inhaling deeply.

"I thought you had given those up!" Sal scolded.

"I had, but it's hard to kick the habit."

"Look, Ben don't worry, I can sort this out myself – really. You have enough on your plate as it is." Sal stood up straight, her expression worried but determined.

"Jesus, the bastard! I am so sorry, Sal – you don't deserve this." Ben took the cigarette from his mouth and threw it on the ground, stamping it out angrily.

"You're right," she said with resignation. "But I'll just have to deal with it."

She reached up to him and kissed him on the cheek. He stood fuming, hands in his pockets, as he watched her walk down Merrion Square towards Westmoreland Street to get the bus home.

***

Later that evening, just after seven, Julie picked him up from his apartment in East Wall. They hadn't been out to a restaurant for ages and, to keep her happy, Ben had reluctantly agreed. Leinster and Munster were on Sky Sports at eight o'clock. He would have liked nothing better than to collapse on the sofa, have a few cans of beer and watch the rugby match. Unfortunately, she had other plans for him – she wanted to discuss the reception. He really wasn't in the mood. But he had promised to be more engaged with the arrangements after the last blow-out between them at the wine-tasting. He had suggested to her, half-jokingly, that they should ask the hotel whether they could buy a few crates at Lidl's and bring them to the venue.

To meet in the Italian in Fairview wouldn't do either. Instead, she'd insisted on driving into town to Grand Canal Dock.

After initially berating his choice of jumper and jeans as looking scruffy, she had kept him amused on the drive across the city with tales of a difficult client that day at the interior design studio in Sandyford where she worked. A successful businesswoman had wanted a dedicated bathroom in her apartment, fitted out in Italian marble, for her Yorkshire terrier. Julie jokingly referred to it as the 'pooch douche'. She described how the woman had insisted that the little dog was involved in selecting the finishes, looking to see if the dog was happy with each of the choices. Julie was witty and observant but, despite her banter, he knew she would have been kind and gone out of her way to help the woman.

He had met Julie at a disco at the teacher's club in Parnell Square a few years ago. She was there with one of her friends who worked at his school. Compared to the other women he had dated since leaving college, she was so glamorous. He didn't think that he had a hope in hell with her. But his mates had egged him on, and to his amazement she had agreed to dance with him – for the whole night. They had discovered that they had similar tastes in cinema and music, though sport was beyond her. She was easy company. On their second date, walking home late at night, he had been touched by the fact that she had been inconsolable at the sight of a young fox run over by a car. But he had also learned quickly that she was fiercely independent and would not let him get away with anything, unlike his sisters, who had always fussed over him. But not Julie. On the occasions he stayed in her flat in Clontarf, she had insisted that he do his share of the chores. It was this combination of softness and her spiky attitude that had attracted him to her in the first place.

It was quiet enough when they got to Grand Canal Dock – the home of Dublin's Google offices, frequented by the young and affluent. It was still too early for theatre goers and the night-time punters. Despite his initial reluctance at the unnecessary drive into town, Ben still felt a buzz of excitement when he arrived at Dublin's trendy urban quarter. The sculptural installation, criss-crossed, red columns of neon light reflecting in the deep black waters of the dock, was theatrical – it provided a focus for the area's funky modern architecture. The pièce de résistance was the new Grand Canal Theatre. With its strong geometric shapes of colliding planes of glass, designed by 'starchitect' Daniel Libeskind, Ben thought it looked like something you would see on a futuristic film set – not in downtown Dublin.

Julie had booked a restaurant near the theatre – one of those trendy wine bars she admired that were always draughty, with exposed concrete slabs and visible wiring, that invariably had high uncomfortable stools.

Between admiring her long legs in her skinny black jeans and listening to her stories, by the time they had reached the restaurant his mood had mellowed, and he had almost forgotten about the rugby.

She was looking gorgeous. And when they had arrived, he had noticed, with satisfaction, the admiring glances of the other guys in the restaurant.

Julie pushed her blonde fringe from her eyes as she looked at the menu. "I think I'll just have a starter," she said dismissively.

"We drove all this way just for a starter! Well, one of us had better give the chef something to do. I'll have a burger."

"Ben, please, this is a vegetarian restaurant."

He threw his eyes up to heaven. "Alright, a pizza."

After they had ordered, he drank his beer, and she sipped a Diet Coke.

"So, what is about the reception that you wanted to discuss so urgently?" he asked.

"The food at the reception."

He looked at her in disbelief. "I thought we had agreed on the menu at Tinakilly House."

"It's just ... Sally has offered to do the catering. She rang me this afternoon – she wants to do it as a wedding

94

present." Julie looked uncomfortable, ill at ease.

"Oh, that's a lot to take on. Although it would be no problem to her. She did it before for a friend of hers – she did a great job. That's really kind of her!"

"Yes, but that is not what I want. I don't want some kind of 'home-made production', as if we couldn't afford a proper reception. And we would have to rethink the location. Our choice of venues would be limited. She really wants to do this for us – well, for you really."

"We would certainly save a shedload of money," he said hopefully.

"Well, it's just … that's not what I want. I have put so much effort into all the arrangements. She can't do as good a job as a professional. I don't want to offend her, Ben, but I just want things to be perfect for us." Julie smiled coyly as she stroked his thigh under the table.

He pushed her hand off. "Look, OK, I get it." Though he thought she was being foolish to turn down Sal's offer. "She probably just wants to be involved – to help us. How about you let her do part of it – say, make the desserts?"

"Homemade chocolate biscuit cake?"

"Yeah, whatever you want."

"No," she said firmly. "That's so naff."

"Now you're being ridiculous!"

Julie's lip quivered. "You always seem to take her side, Ben."

"It's not a matter of sides, Julie. It's just a meal."

"That's just it. To me it isn't just a meal, it's part of the most important day of our lives, and I want everything to be perfect." Her eyes welled with tears, and the tip of her nose started to turn red.

"I'm sorry, Julie, of course you do." He relented, taking her hand. "It's just been a long day. I'll have a word with Sal. I'm sure she'll understand." He leant forward and, taking both of her hands in his, said tentatively, "Julie there is also something important that I wanted to ask you."

"What?"

"You know I told you Sal's husband Fergal turned up out of the blue looking for money. Well, we visited Cormac this afternoon – you know, the solicitor – he was at the engagement party."

Julie was listening attentively. "Yes."

"Well, it seems that Sal will have to stump up twenty grand, at least, to get rid of Fergal."

"And?" Julie said warily.

"I may have to lend her some money."

"How much?"

"Maybe – ten grand."

"What?" Julie said in disbelief. "That explains her offer to do the food."

"No," said Ben sharply. "She has refused to take money from me. I'll have to insist."

"So where are you going to get the money from?"

"Well, things still look uncertain about the portrait. There is no guarantee that I am going to get the twenty grand that I had hoped. If it's a copy it will only be worth

96

a fraction of that. I have to help Sal, which goes without saying. So, I was going to give her some of the money I inherited from Uncle Tommy and maybe we could look again at the costs for the wedding? The last reckoning we did was about eighteen for the day – including the reception – and five grand for the honeymoon. Say we postponed going abroad till next year and just went somewhere in Ireland and cut back on some of the other costs."

She looked at him aghast and stood up.

"I don't believe it. There you go again, putting her first ahead of me," she said furiously. She leant down, fumbled with her bag and then threw a tenner on the table. "I've had enough, Ben – what I want seems to be pretty low on your priorities. What's the point in being engaged! Here's your bloody ring – why don't you give it to your sister? You can find your own bloody way home!"

He watched in disbelief as she threw the ring onto the table and stormed out of the restaurant.

He sat there stunned for a few minutes then called for the bill, knowing he should go after her. The waiter approached and he went through the motions of paying by credit card, then drained the rest of his can. He really didn't have the bandwidth to deal with Julie this evening. And momentarily the thought occurred to him that if he legged it to the bus stop in Westmoreland Street, he'd just about make it back for half-time to watch the rugby. But as he picked up the diamond engagement ring from the table, he realised that wasn't going to happen – he had to deal with this.

He rushed to the door and looked down the road to where she had parked the car. But at this stage she was long gone. The snow that was forecast earlier had started to fall, dissolving instantly into the mirror of black water, and lying like white gauze across the hard surfaces of the docks.

Chapter 6

Daisy had arranged to meet Ben in the departures lounge. She found flying stressful enough and the thought of hanging around for him would only have added to her anxiety. It had been a good call on her part – he had arrived just as they were about to board.

As the plane took off, she closed her eyes, crossing her arms, hoping that he wouldn't see how nervous she was. But once they reached cruising height and the plane was making the wide arc to face the direction of the Irish sea, she relaxed.

"Such a beautiful, clear winter sky – it's a great morning to fly," he said, looking out of the window, apparently oblivious to her anxiety.

"A glass of white wine, please," she asked the flight attendant who was standing beside her with the trolley.

"Anything for you, sir?"

"Just coffee, please."

After the woman moved on, Ben turned to Daisy. "You're starting early."

"I just hate flying – the wine calms my nerves. These short hops are the worst. They can be very bumpy."

"Well, you can hold my hand, if it makes you feel better," he said, eyes twinkling.

"Thanks, I'll bear that in mind," she said sardonically, taking a gulp of the wine.

"So, tell me about this guy you are seeing, *er* ...?"

"Fintan."

"Yeah, Fintan. What does he do in London?"

"I told you – he's an investment banker, he works in the city."

"How exciting," said Ben, one eyebrow slightly raised.

"It's not really. He works hard – always doing overtime. Bankers are so demanding – they seem to think they own their staff."

"Do I sense a touch of bitterness there?" Ben asked.

"Well, obviously I am not thrilled he's in London, and I'm in Dublin," she said emphatically.

"How long have you been going out?"

"Oh, for years – since we both left school."

"Not long so," he replied dryly.

"Long enough," she said with a smile. "I will be thirty on my next birthday."

"Ah, the biological clock is ticking," he said, grinning – goading her.

"Absolutely not! If you must know – not that it's any of your business – we have decided not to have children."

"That's a big decision," he said seriously.

"Yes, it was. You know – there are advantages in having children – and there are advantages in not having children. We both love our jobs, are ambitious, and we want to do well. We want to travel, and kids are such a big commitment – they tie you down."

"Bit like dogs really," said Ben flippantly. "But I admire your certainty." He looked out of the window – his neck craned to get full advantage of the sun-blushed colours of the early-morning sky.

Daisy had no wish to look out of the window herself. But, as the wine worked its magic, she began to mellow. She was conscious of his bulk sitting beside her and was aware of his subtle spicy scent.

"So, tell me about your job," he asked. "Where do you work? You're in marketing, right?"

"I work for a small marketing firm based in Leeson Street. It's been very successful and has won loads of industry awards. The work is varied, and we have a few really interesting clients."

"What sort of products?" he asked politely.

She got the impression he wasn't really interested.

"I work more with people than products. I specialise in motivational change."

"You get people to change their mind in order to make them buy or do something that someone else wants."

"I wouldn't put it as crudely as that, but yes. Right now, I am working on a campaign for the Health Board to encourage women to report domestic abuse."

"Oh, I thought it would be all about selling fast cars and cigarettes."

She felt that she had gone up in his estimation – not that she cared what he thought. She was also aware that she was feeling lightheaded.

"What are your plans today then?" she asked, trying to sound more focused than she really was.

"Well, today I am heading to the Victoria and Albert Museum to their textile department to see can I date the tablecloth that I showed you, and tomorrow I'm hoping to meet the English cousin, Alex Taube."

"Where does he live?"

"Croydon, just outside London. I can get a train there from Victoria Station. So, what about ... Sunny Onions?" he asked, smiling provocatively.

"Unwin. It's Sonny Unwin," she said, exasperated but faintly amused. "I am meeting him tomorrow afternoon in Knightsbridge."

"Sorry, once I have a name in my head, I find it hard to shake." He looked at her quizzically.

Did he suspect, she wondered, that she was just a bit tipsy.

"Why don't we meet up for a drink tomorrow evening, swap information?" he asked.

"Well, no – if you don't mind. I just want to spend the

short time I have with Fintan."

"We could meet early, say six o'clock, have a catch-up and then you can head off to meet him. It's just, I'm flying home on Sunday. I've got school on Monday, and your flight isn't till Monday evening, if I remember rightly."

"OK, let's do that, I won't be able to stay long though."

***

The ten-fifteen Saturday-morning train from Victoria to Croydon was quiet enough as shoppers travelled in trains going in the opposite direction towards the city centre. He sat back as the train barrelled through the seemingly endless urban sprawl of the city and sipped his takeaway Cappuccino wondering what Alex Taube would be like. The old man had been enthusiastic when he had talked to him a few days ago on the phone and had promised to dig out the family tree for his visit.

Ben was pinning his hopes on learning something from the old man, and that this trip to London, which had cost him a few bob, was not going to be a complete waste of time.

Julie was still not speaking to him. She had suggested they take a break for a few weeks to consider what was important in their relationship. Reluctantly he had agreed – and the diamond ring was still sitting in his desk at home. At least he hadn't had to justify the cost of this trip to her.

103

Yesterday, after booking into his hotel, he had visited the Victoria and Albert Museum. He thought he might find similar examples of his cloth in their textile department. The visit had been disappointing. There had been a whole glass display-case of cloths of all shapes and sizes. But he hadn't learned a whole lot, other than the embroidery, which was rather crude, was similar to other pieces, described as folk art, from all over Europe. Decorating linen cloths in neat cross-stitch was something that women in the past seemed to do. He had hoped to talk to someone, but no one was available. He was annoyed with himself for not thinking ahead and making an appointment with the textile conservator, a Dr Perry. At least, the attendant had promised that Dr Perry would look at his photographs of the detailed embroidery and get back to him.

Later, after a few hours spent aimlessly wandering around Oxford Street, he had returned to the hotel near Oxford Circus where he had a few beers at the bar, caught up on the highlights of the day's sports, and went to bed early.

This morning, relaxed after a good night's sleep, he was looking forward to meeting Alex Taube.

Leaving the station in Croydon, he hailed a taxi to the leafy suburb where Alex lived with his wife Belle. The detached house, of generous proportions, was red-bricked and plastered above ground-floor level with imitation Tudor-style timbering. He smiled to himself –

Julie would hate this. They had been looking at houses a few months previously – just looking. It had been her choice, the wedding or the house first, and she had chosen the wedding. He remembered how the estate agent had proudly described a tiny terrace house in Dublin's suburb of Castleknock as in the "two-door style".

"Delighted to see you, young man," said Alex Taube, answering the somewhat alarming melodic chimes of the doorbell. "Come in, come in!"

Ben guessed that his uncle was in his early eighties, a few years younger than Paddy. He was completely bald and had wide hips and a soft belly that hung over the top of his trousers. There was a vague family resemblance to Paddy in that he had similar brown eyes and sallow skin.

"Good to meet you too, sir."

"None of that 'sir' business, Ben. I'm originally from the East End, a cockney boy."

"You have done well so," said Ben, looking around the spacious house, as Alex showed him into the plush living room.

"I have that, I must admit. This is my current wife, Belle."

"Oh, don't mind him, my love. Same old corny jokes." Belle was a small, spritely woman with short straight grey hair fixed back with a jewelled clip, and dressed in a neat pale-green, twin-set and matching tweed skirt.

"The old ones are the best, I always say," retorted Alex, unabashed.

"Let me take your coat, Ben," said Belle. "Now sit down, make yourself comfy. Would you like tea, my love, or coffee?"

"Tea would be lovely, thank you, Belle," he said sinking into a sea of cushions on the velour-covered couch.

She left the room to make the tea.

"I got my papers out after you phoned. Although I must admit it's been a few years since I've looked at them. Your Uncle Paddy promised to come back to me, but he never did. So, I might have the names of the current generation, but not their dates. Let's see now ..." He unfolded a family tree that he had drawn in blue Biro. "So, you are Tom's boy."

"Yes, I have two older sisters, Sally and Katrina."

"You must be spoiled rotten!" the old man exclaimed. "And your mum and dad died in a car crash if I remember. Incredibly sad. I was so sorry to hear that."

"Yes, it was. But it was a long time ago. If they had been around, then maybe I would have known more about our family. Why is it that when we get around to ask these things, it is already too late?" Ben leant forward, his hands clasped. "As I told you on the phone, the reason I wanted to talk to you now is that I am selling a painting that belonged to my great-grandfather Antoine Tarrant."

"Anton – his name was Anton – German for Anthony."

"Oh. He must have changed it. Antoine would be the

106

Irish form. Well, I was always told the painting was of my great-great-grandaunt, Lena Tarrant. But I discovered recently that there is another painting in existence that is almost exactly the same. It is owned by a Dublin woman, Daisy Staunton, who claims her painting is of her great-great-grandmother, Helen Frome. The gallery advised us to check out the provenance. So, I was trying to find out about the family – and see can I shed any light on the two portraits."

"Well, I can't tell you anything about the paintings. It's the first I've heard of them. But I can tell you what I know about the family. From the records here, you can see that Anton's father was Isaac Tarrant. He was married to Rosa Rabinovitch – and his father Meyer Tarrant, your great-great-great-grandfather, was a brother of my great-great-grandfather, Kazimir Taube."

"If they were brothers, then how come they had different names?" asked Ben, looking puzzled.

"They were four-by-two's," said Belle, coming back from the kitchen. She was carrying a tray covered in a white linen cloth, with gold-rimmed china teacups, with a plate of chocolate digestive biscuits.

"Sorry?" said Ben.

"Not very subtle, Belle," Alex said, smiling affectionately at his wife. He turned to Ben. "Four by two – rhyming slang for 'Jew'. Belle is one too – a Jew. Our family was originally Jewish."

"Really?" Ben was stunned.

"Yes, we still are. But Meyer changed his name, from Taube to Tarrant. Old Kazimir stuck with Taube."

"Why would they change their name?"

"Lots of reasons in those days. To escape conscription was a common one. Or simply to have an easier life – be done with the constant persecution. Although for some it made no difference what they were called, they were still made to suffer."

The old man's rheumy eyes filled with tears and his wife, head bent, fidgeted with her spoon. A poignant sadness descended. Nobody spoke for several seconds, as they were each reminded of the appalling atrocities that befell the Jewish people under the Nazi regime.

"I am lost for words, Alex," said Ben. "I didn't expect this. I often wondered about our family's colouring, but I thought that we must have had some Mediterranean blood. And there are a lot of Spanish-looking people in the west of Ireland, maybe because of trading with Spaniards over the centuries."

"No, you've Jewish blood," Alex said, nodding his head, the smile slowly returning to his eyes. "Have a biscuit, son. I only get these when we have visitors."

Alex handed him the plate and Ben took two.

"So, what do you know about the family back then?" Ben asked.

"Not a lot really. My father told me that Meyer and his brother Kazimir were originally Polish. Kazimir, my great-great-grandfather was a tavern keeper, he moved to London in the 1880s. Your great-great-great-grandfather, Meyer, was a merchant, a trader if you like, who moved with his son Isaac to live in Vienna in the early 1860s. Anton, Isaac's son, ended up working for a tailor in London where he married an Irish girl, and after a few years in the 1890s they both moved back to Ireland. I believe it's all online now, on these genealogy websites. You could try those – unfortunately, I never got the hang of computers."

"Do you have any old photographs of them?"

"I have a few, mostly of my family, but here's one I dug out that you might be interested in. You can have it – it may be a help in your search. I think it's of Isaac. It's a studio shot taken of him as a young man in Vienna."

He showed Ben the photograph. Isaac was in his thirties, he guessed. He had dark hair, was clean-shaven and dressed smartly in a black coat, with a paler waistcoat and an ornate tie with a jewelled pin. Ben thought that he didn't look particularly Jewish.

Ben took a photograph out of his pocket of the sketch that Sal had given him. "My sister gave me this sketch – it came from my granny's house. Do you think this could be him?"

They compared the two images.

"It could be, I suppose. Hard to tell though."

Ben took another photograph out of his coat pocket.

"This is some writing on the back of the sketch – mean anything to you?"

109

The old man reached for black-framed glasses.

"*Mm*, yes. It's in Yiddish. It says, *Isaac Taube aged eighteen, Kiev, 1860.*"

"It's him so!" said Ben. "And his wife was Rosa. But there's no sign of a Helen or a Lena in this tree."

"No, not that I know of. Strange that. I mean having the name Tarrant she must be one of your family."

"What about records, or family mementos?"

"Nothing, I'm afraid." Alex took off the glasses. "Anything of value we probably sold long ago," he joked.

"Your family," Ben asked tentatively, "did they suffer during the Holocaust?"

"We were here when it happened. We escaped the Shoah, the genocide – thank the Lord. We were the lucky ones. I was only nine years old. But we suffered. The knowledge of the atrocities weighed heavily on us all. Still does. It was only afterwards, when information from survivors started to trickle out of the camps, that my parents discovered the extent of the evils perpetrated by those monsters. Then there was an overwhelming guilt that they had not been able to save those who perished."

The old man seemed to crumple into his chair, head lowered, tears trembling on his pink-lidded eyelashes. He went into a trance again, but only briefly this time. Then drawing on some hidden inner strength, he seemed to pull himself out of a past that only he could see. He wiped his eyes with big-knuckled hands and smiled slowly, nodding, looking at Ben, once more engaged with his visitor.

"Well, Ben, it was lovely to meet you, but we had better call it a day." He added, making a valiant attempt to rally round. "Belle gets tired, you know. Not as much life in the old girl as there used to be!"

Belle smiled and winked at Ben.

"Well, it was lovely to meet you both, and thank you so much for your hospitality," said Ben, shaking the old man's hand.

Alex didn't get up. He looked exhausted.

"Do ring us, and let us know how you get on," he said as Belle showed Ben to the door.

***

He had arrived early, at the Italian wine-bar at St Christopher's Place. He had arranged to meet Daisy at six. He was sipping a glass of white wine, contemplating what he had learned that afternoon, when he saw her walking across the square towards the restaurant. Her fair hair was loose and lying on her shoulders, rather than tied back as it had been on previous occasions. She was wearing a long, dark-green, woollen coat, a short black skirt, and high black boots. Frau Frome, he thought, had a bohemian chic that he hadn't noticed before.

"Hi," she greeted him, smiling, as she entered the bright modern restaurant and sat down at the table. "This place looks good."

"Yeah, I did some homework, it got good reviews. I've

ordered Pinot Grigio, I noticed yesterday that you liked it. I hope that's OK?"

"Perfect."

He poured her a glass of wine.

"You're looking well. Have a good day?" he said.

"Thank you." Her eyes sparkled in response to the compliment, "And yes, my day was fruitful."

"Oh, that sounds promising. So, is it fake or fortune?" he smiled.

"You first – how did you get on?"

Ben took a slug of his wine then fiddled with the stem of the glass.

"Well, I think. I am still a bit flabbergasted, shocked if I am honest, by what my cousin Alex told me."

"What?"

"It appears that my family were Jewish."

"Really? That explains the dark, brooding good looks."

He was slightly taken back – up to this she had been reserved, even formal towards him.

"I didn't think you'd noticed," he responded flippantly.

"And how do you feel about that – being of Jewish descent?"

"I'm not sure. I haven't had time to process it yet. A bit sad, maybe, that my family were in a position that they had to change who they were. They were originally called Taube, it seems. I suppose Tarrant is an improvement." He smiled. "It's also made me question who I am – who

I thought I was. As I said, I'll have to think about it."

She paused and appeared to carefully consider what she would say.

"I suppose now you will have to bear some of the weight of Jewish history on your shoulders – something that previously you thought wasn't anything to do with you."

He looked at her, surprised. "Yes, that's more or less how I feel."

"And what did you learn about them?"

"The man I visited today was Alex Taube. My great-great-great-grandfather and his great-great-grandfather were brothers, Kazimir and Meyer Taube. Meyer, who was married to a woman called Jessica, changed his name to Tarrant. Which makes Alex a cousin, several times removed. I can never work these things out. Meyer Taube's son was Isaac. They were both traders. They lived in Vienna, towards the end of the nineteenth century. Isaac's wife was Rosa Rabinovitch. Alex didn't know anything about a Lena Tarrant. And he had never heard of the paintings."

"But that's great! With those names and rough dates, we should be able to find details of them on the census records, on one of the genealogy websites."

"He also made me a copy of the family tree." Ben took the folded sheet of cartridge paper that Alex had given him from his pocket. He unfolded it and handed it to her.

"It's in Biro – what a lovely thing, with its wobbly

lines," she said, as she examined it closely. "The time taken to do this, and the emotion attached to it, are so much more meaningful than a spreadsheet."

"Yes, I suppose that's true. But what's on it doesn't mean a lot to me at this stage. I showed Alex a photo of the pencil sketch and we compared it to some old photographs he had of Isaac. He also translated the writing on the back which is actually Yiddish, and this confirmed that the sketch was Isaac Taube and made in 1852 in Kiev when he was eighteen."

"Well, that's amazing progress, Ben! It's something definite to work on. And how about the visit to the Victoria and Albert Museum yesterday?"

"Not as successful, unfortunately. I had hoped at least to pin down the date and location of where the tablecloth was made. A Dr Perry rang me this afternoon, she told me it was mid-nineteenth century probably from Eastern Europe, possibly Polish, but she couldn't be entirely sure."

"Oh, at least that's something."

Daisy handed the family tree back to Ben, and he carefully refolded the piece of paper and put it back into his coat pocket.

"So how about you? How was Sunny Onions?" he asked grinning.

"Grand," she said, smiling. "He is living in a home in Knightsbridge. A nice place, as these places go. You will be pleased to hear that although my meeting wasn't as revelatory as yours, I also made good progress. I think I

114

have traced the identity of the woman in my portrait."

"Really!"

"Sonny's grandmother was Georgina Frome, the daughter of Helen and George Frome. Our Lady Helen." Daisy's eyes were wide with barely contained excitement. "As far as Sonny knew, they lived in London in Cavendish Square."

"Very posh."

"Yes, must have been. He also showed me this."

Daisy handed Ben a faded sepia-tinted Victorian photograph in a cardboard mount. It was of a woman in a dark satin dress, holding a single rose. She was standing beside what looked like a studio mock-up of a section of a classical temple, with a bower of roses draped across a low balustrade. The woman was unsmiling, as photographs of the period often were, but beautiful. She had fair hair, dressed in ornate, plaited coils on either side of her face. The dress was full skirted with an off-the shoulder neckline edged with lace. She looked as though she was dressed to attend a formal social event.

"It's her!" Ben said excitedly.

"Yes, it's her alright. But do you notice something else?"

Ben scanned the photograph and shrugged. "No."

"Look at what she's wearing around her neck – it's the same blue-sapphire and diamond pendant as the one in the painting. Sunny says he remembers his grandmother wearing it at Christmas."

"Does he still have it?"

"No, he thinks his grandmother must have sold it. He certainly doesn't remember his mother wearing it. Anyway, we don't need it – this photograph is enough proof of its existence."

Ben examined the yellow-tinted, fading photo. There was a photographer's mark, '*Farnham and Co, Marble Arch*' embossed on the back of the cardboard mount. '*Helen 1870*' was written faintly in pencil.

Just then Daisy's phone rang, and she took it from her handbag.

"Fintan, hang on a second." She rose from the table. "Sorry, Ben, I'll just take this outside. I'll be back in a minute."

He watched her outside the restaurant, her back to him. She raised her left hand in a gesture signifying annoyance. He guessed the news wasn't good.

"Everything OK?" he asked when she returned to her seat looking flustered.

"Typical! He can't meet me this evening till much later. He has to entertain clients from Brussels."

"Oh, that's too bad. You're stuck with me, so."

She was biting her lip anxiously. "It's just so bloody annoying. I only get to see him once a month. You'd think his bloody boss would be a bit more understanding."

"The boss sounds like an arsehole all right. Look, you must be hungry – why don't you join me for dinner. Unless you want to go somewhere else?"

"Thanks, Ben, that would be lovely," she said gratefully. But he could sense her despondence.

After they had finished their meal – she'd had pasta and he had a burger – he ordered a second bottle of wine.

"Daisy, one thing that has intrigued me is, why are you selling the painting?"

"I could ask you the same thing."

"Well, to be honest," he replied, "I would keep it if I could. I suspect my sisters are disappointed. It has hung in Sal's dining room for as long as I can remember. She's almost part of the family. It was my fiancée's suggestion to sell it. It is a bit large and old-fashioned for most houses, and we needed the money. I think I told you we're getting married next year. Julie is planning the wedding. As you know, these things are expensive."

"How exciting – where is it being held?"

"Tinakilly House."

"Ah, lovely location. Will you be buying a house?"

"No, not immediately. I live in an apartment in East Wall that I bought a few years ago. Julie rents an apartment in Clontarf. We will rent out my place and find a larger apartment in Clontarf until we can afford to buy there. She wants to get the kids' names down for the local schools."

"Oh, you have children," she said, surprised.

"No, but we will, hopefully. Julie's big into planning ahead." He grinned.

"Ah, wise move."

He thought about what she had said the day before,

about not having children. But this time he thought he detected a note of sadness in her voice.

"But to get back to my question, why are *you* selling the portrait?"

"It's complicated. I actually don't need the money right now. But my mother has cancer, a form of leukaemia. It's progressing slowly. I want to be able to pay for her care in the future, to keep her in her own house – rather than putting her into a nursing home. The painting is hers. She won't let me waste my own money, wants me to keep that for when Fintan and I eventually buy a house together."

"I'm sorry to hear that about your mother."

"Thank you. It's one of the reasons I haven't moved over here to London."

"That's understandable. You should treasure the time you have left with her."

"Fintan thinks I should put her in a home," she said abruptly.

"Oh." He frowned. "That must be difficult for you. For you both."

He noticed she had a little bruise under her lip where she had been biting it.

"Tell me about yourself," she said, changing the subject. "Your school is in the inner city, so you told me."

"Yes, it is. I try to beat an education into the little divils whether they like it or not."

"I don't buy that for a minute," she said gently.

"No, you are right, I love my job. I love the kids, and I love working in that part of the city. There is a real sense of community. Everyone knows everyone else's business, but they also watch each other's backs. A kid gets sick, and someone organises a fundraiser. Someone's mother is not able to cope – and the other mothers rally round. But it's hard for many of them. In many instances, the parents struggle to make ends meet. There's high unemployment, drug abuse, petty crime. I admire the women most – they are usually the ones holding things together. They are so proud and protective of their kids." He didn't want to bang on about school. Julie had more than once asked him was there anything else that he could talk about. "Enough about me. You were saying, you're working on a campaign highlighting domestic abuse?"

"Yes, it's a tricky one. How to get people not to turn a blind eye when they see it happening, without putting the lives of these women, or men, at greater risk. So, what does Julie do?"

"She works at an interior-design studio in Sandyford."

"Oh, that's interesting."

"Yeah, she loves it. Keeps me amused with all the stories about the customers and their wacky requirements." He paused, looked down at the table. "Actually ..." he said sheepishly, "she broke off our engagement last week."

"Oh Ben, I am so sorry to hear that!" She looked genuinely upset.

119

"It was over the reception," he said flippantly.

"Really?"

"Yes, my sister offered to do the catering."

"How kind of her! That's a big undertaking. But you said she was in that line of business."

"Yeah, she runs a coffee shop."

"So, what was the problem?"

"You tell me. Julie just wants everything to be perfect."

She put her hand on top of his. "It doesn't sound too serious," she said encouragingly. "I'm sure you can work something out, and she'll come around."

"Daisy, sorry to have stood you up. I left as soon as I could."

A tall, thin guy was standing at the table. He was dressed in a long trench coat over a smart casual jacket with a white open-collared shirt and jeans.

Daisy looked up guiltily and removed her hand abruptly from Ben's. "Oh Fintan! You managed to escape. This is Ben. I told you about him."

"Ah Ben, nice to meet you. Well, I can't impose on you to entertain my girlfriend any more than I have already."

"Not at all, I really enjoyed it," said Ben.

"I'm afraid we have to be at Simon's for drinks in half an hour," said Fintan in a business-like manner.

"Oh, you didn't tell me," said Daisy.

"No, it was last-minute."

"Could Ben come too?"

"Sorry, I am afraid that's not possible." He smiled

insincerely. "It's a work thing."

Ben thought to himself, he's not a bit sorry.

"Ben, thanks for looking after me," said Daisy, smiling gratefully at him as she stood up.

"It has been my pleasure."

"Good luck with Julie! I'll ring you when I get back to Dublin." She put on her coat and reached into her bag, looking for her purse.

"This one's on me," said Ben. "You can get me back – the next time," he said provocatively, making eye contact with Fintan.

Fintan eyed him warily.

"Great, if you're sure, thanks a million. Safe flight home," said Daisy.

Ben stood up as she left. Fintan put his arm possessively around her as Ben watched them head across the square towards the taxi rank.

What an arsehole, thought Ben.

~~~~~

Chapter 7

Kornyn
1853

Looking at her family, who had just come from evening prayers at the synagogue, Rosa was proud of the effort they had made for her. Tata was wearing his good coat and Mama was wearing her black Shabbos dress. Even the boys were dressed in respectable clothes. Although Rosa felt her stomach sink as she glanced at Lena. Her sister's pale cheeks were flushed, and her hair fell loose around her shoulders like a golden veil. Rosa noticed that her navy costume, an old one of Mama's, was tight around her chest – her sister was really filling out. Already she was taller than Rosa, almost the same height as Zipporah.

Rosa reminded herself that she too looked well. Bubbe had made her a new costume for the occasion in a dark green barathea cloth, cut to flatter her waist, and the skirt was fuller than she normally wore. Mama had got the cloth from a Jewish trader she knew from the market, and she and Bubbe had examined pattern books in the drapery in Kiev to see the latest fashions in St Petersburg. Bubbe had made her a simple lace collar to finish it off and given Rosa tiny pearl buttons which she had carefully sewn down the costume's pleated front.

As the Rabinovitch family were ushered into the Taube's main room, the Cohens were already there. Rabbi Cohen and Bena beamed at them as they came in while Moishe stood looking uncomfortable with little Perle in his arms and Samuil seemingly glued to his side.

Rosa caught her breath at the sight of the table set for Shabbos dinner. Silver candlesticks glistened and glasses sparkled on the white, cloth-covered table laden with food. She nudged Lena to stop her gawping, and they both had to make an effort to walk softly so that their boots didn't clatter off the wooden floor.

"Welcome, welcome!" Meyer gushed, making a great show of greeting them all. His warmth and good spirits were infectious, and everyone relaxed a little.

"What a fine spread Jessica has for us this evening," said Bena Cohen.

"Indeed, it certainly is," said Zipporah politely.

"I supervised every bit of its preparation myself," Jessica told Zipporah in her clipped voice. Zipporah gave her one of her tight little smiles, as she explained how she had hired Polish women to clean for the visit, and a Jewish widow, Havel, to prepare kosher food.

Realising how nervous Rosa was feeling, Zipporah smiled at her daughter encouragingly.

The large table almost filled the room, and everyone sat down immediately. Meyer Taube sat at the head of the table, Tata on one side and Jessica Taube on the other. The Rabbi, a kindly but serious man, whose face Lena once said cruelly would curdle milk, sat at the other end with the children either side of him next to Zipporah and their grandmother. Rosa sat opposite Isaac and Lena opposite the Cohen's son Moishe. But tonight, there was no sign of the easy good nature she had witnessed in Moishe the previous evening. He looked unimpressed at Lena who was chattering away to her brother Reubin and was rudely ignoring him and, more importantly, as good manners would suggest, his mother Bena who was seated beside her.

Fortunately, Meyer nodded to his wife to start the ceremonial meal and quietness descended. Jessica Taube lit the candles, passing her hands over them, then covering her eyes she said the blessing. They all joined in as the Rabbi lead the traditional song "Shalom Aleichem" – "Peace Be Upon You", welcoming the two Shabbos angels into the house. The Rabbi then gave the Kiddush blessing over the wine and another over the plaited challah bread which was then shared amongst them.

The meal had several courses and was more elaborate than Rosa was used to: gefilte fish, soup, then a baked chicken dish and kugel followed by several delicious tarts and pies. Jessica Taube had certainly set out to impress.

As the dishes were passed around the table, Rosa had a chance to observe Isaac. The contrast was marked between Isaac and his father. Whereas Meyer Taube was loud and brash, his son was quieter, self-contained – although from the way he answered any questions asked of him, he was not lacking in confidence. When they had finished eating, Jessica Taube poured tea from a silver teapot which sat on top of the most ornate silver samovar that Rosa had ever seen. She handed round blue glasses in silver holders – all matching – and no doubt not borrowed from their neighbours as Mama had done.

"I hear Tsar Nicholas is still stirring up problems in the Holy Land," said Tata to Meyer Taube who was sitting at one end of the head.

"Yes, he seems determined to do battle with the Ottomans," replied Meyer. "There are fears of conscription. Enlisting officers are becoming more expensive to bribe, and you know how fond they are of Jewish boys." Meyer looked grimly at Isaac. They both knew that the authorities deliberately went after Jews. Politically they were easier targets. "So, I am considering changing our family's name. There is a man, who knows a man, in Kiev who can get fake papers – for a price."

Tata sat back in his chair, shocked.

"That is a drastic action" said Rabbi Cohen. "Your name is your birth-right, it is a testament to who you are, where you came from."

"Well, there is precedent in the Talmud," said Meyer, keeping the tone light, "though I should tell you! It is said 'Four things annul the decree that seals a person's fate namely: alms, prayer, change of name, and change of deeds'. As you know, my Rebbe, if Isaac is enlisted, he could spend twenty-five years fighting in various parts of the empire for causes that concern only the Tsar. He would have to forgo the opportunity of a university education. And Abe's daughter could be a widow before her time." He looked over at Rosa who bowed her head so they could not see her alarm at his words. "And, of course, he would be unable to practise as a Jew. They would force him to eat food that is not kosher or starve. And as for observing the Sabbath!" Meyer theatrically threw his hands up in the air.

The Rabbi looked uncomfortable and was about to say something but Isaac, to prevent an argument, said quickly, "What my father says makes sense." Pulling his shoulders back, he looked Tata squarely in the eye. "Some of my friends have already taken drastic measures to avoid conscription – a few have self-mutilated, cut off their fingers or toes, or had all of their teeth removed. I have even heard of a young man who got his father to put a burning rod in his eye. So – all considering – a name does not seem to be such a big price to pay."

"The Lord help us all!" said Tata.

"I am afraid, Abe, our people can no longer leave it up to the Lord – we must save ourselves." Meyer looked apologetically at the Rabbi. "There is an army regiment stationed in Zhytomyr – it will be coming here next, I believe. I was going to ask if we could move the wedding forward so we can return early to Vienna? Isaac will be safer there. He is starting university next month. He applied using his new name."

"And what is that?"

"Tarrant. English, I believe."

Tata nodded slowly – Rosa held her breath as everyone around the table waited for Tata to reply. Eventually he said with resignation.

"Rosa Tarrant, it has a good sound to it."

The Rabbi, his face thunderous, got up and left the table.

***

It was still warm as Rosa walked to the end of their street. She passed the brick plant along the perimeter of the sun-bleached wheat field – then through the scrubland with the wooden watermill painted white and black, to the edge of the Irpin river. It was a well-worn path. Every week the sisters took the sheets to the washing place – they were too big to wash in the metal bath that they used for the rest of the laundry. Mama had asked Lena to help her, but her sister still hadn't returned from her friend Sarah's house where she had spent the afternoon. "She is studying," said Mama, throwing her eyes up to heaven.

The basket was heavy for one person to carry, and

Rosa stopped several times along the way to rest her aching arms. But, if the truth be told, she liked the solitude of this walk. Once she got to the river's edge, she breathed in the smell of the place, the air heavy with the sweet-balsamic scent of the pine and spruce trees, and the musky smell of moss.

At home, it was always so busy, people coming and going, her brothers fooling around, and in the evenings Lena's discontent constantly ringing in her ears. But here at the edge of the river all was quiet – peaceful. Nothing but the rippling rush of river water coursing towards the Dnieper River, and onward to the Black Sea. These calming sounds were only briefly interrupted by a screech of gulls squawking querulously as they flew across the water towards the denser trees on the opposite riverbank.

The sky seemed to be bigger outside the town, bluer anyway, with white, pillowy clouds moving across it at a pace in the breeze. Even a preying kestrel hovering over the water's surface seemed to falter in its attempts to maintain its position. A good washing day, Mama had said earlier – she would hang the sheets out that evening so that they would be dry later the following day.

Rosa would miss Kornyn, this small town nestled into the curve of the river, where she knew every street, every building and most of the inhabitants – in the Jewish community anyway.

When she got to the place where the women did their washing – where the river widened, it was shallower there – she sat down on a familiar flat rock. She took off her boots and rolled up the waistband of her skirt, so it reached only to her knees – then hefting the sheets out of the basket, she waded into the cold water where it formed a natural pool at the river's edge. She walked slowly, feeling the hard round pebbles of the riverbed on the soles of her feet. Mama had given her a bar of soap made from candle tallow and unfurling the sheet with the flow of the water she scrubbed any stains she could see. Mama never referred to these stains, where they came from, but Lena often joked to her sister that they were the traces of unborn Rabinovichs. Rosa shuddered at the thought. She would have to face all of this sooner than she expected. After Meyer Taube's announcement at the Shabbos dinner of their imminent departure, it had been agreed that the wedding was to take place in a fortnight.

Rosa wrung out the sheets and folded them as best she could, returning them to the basket. But as she did, she was startled by sound of someone approaching along the river path coming from the woods. It was a Russian soldier. He was of mid-height, dark with flat, Slavic features, his beardless face red from the sun. As he got nearer, she could see his skin was sweaty. He looked agitated. Rosa was alarmed at the sight of him and assumed he was lost. He gesticulated, speaking to her in Russian.

"I am sorry, sir, I don't speak Russian," she said nervously in Yiddish.

A leering smile spread over his face as he pointed to

129

her skirt, rolled up, her skinny white legs still wet. Frightened, she tugged at the waistband, trying to pull her skirt down to cover herself.

He said something to her, then suddenly lurched forward and yanked at her skirt – then again, till the cotton material ripped and she was standing only in her shift. As he brutally pulled her towards him, she screamed, but there was no sound. She could see the whites of his eyes, his dilated pupils, his breath was sour and the bristles coarse on his chin. His hand grabbed her roughly between her legs. She started screaming. This time she could hear the sound. He pulled her to the ground, the full weight of his body on top of her, pinning her arms over her head with one hand, while tugging to open his breeches with the other.

Through the blood-red haze of terror a shadow fell over her as another man forcefully pulled him off.

"You filthy Russian bastard!" a voice said in Yiddish.

It was Isaac. Her Isaac.

He had a knife under the man's throat. He held the soldier to the ground.

"Go, you bastard! Never let me see you in this town again unless you want to be buried here!"

The soldier got up and fled, fumbling with his flies as he hobbled away along the edge of the river. He stopped when he got about thirty yards away and raised his fist at them, his face purple and contorted with rage, shouting in Russian.

130

Rosa, shaking like a leaf, stood up. Isaac gave her the torn skirt and she pulled it up over her legs, struggling to keep her balance as she did so.

"Are you alright, did he hurt you?"

"Yes," she said, still terrified.

"Did he ...?"

"No, no! You came just in time."

He put his arm around her to comfort her, as tears spilled down her face – shaking, she clung to him.

"Come, Rosa. We must act quickly. He could return with more soldiers, they are camped further up the river, not far from here. The fact that I, a Jew, challenged him will not go unaccounted for. Then neither of us will be safe. I will take you to my mother."

She held the torn skirt to her, and he carried the basket as they walked quickly back along the path towards the town. Just as they could see the gate to the laneway, she tugged at his arm.

"Stop, for a minute, Isaac."

She looked up into his eyes. But his eyes avoided hers, accentuating the mortification she felt at her predicament.

"Thank you, Isaac, you saved me. But how did you know I was here?"

"When I arrived to give the boys their lessons, Zipporah asked me to come down and help you carry the basket home – wet sheets are heavier than dry ones."

"Mama. *Oy vey*, how can I tell Mama what happened! And Tata ..."

"My mother will know what to do. She will help you – get you cleaned up."

***

Jessica Taube's lips were set in a thin line as she brought Rosa a basin of water. Isaac was waiting downstairs with Meyer Taube who was there when they came in. The older woman handed her a cloth and some lavender-infused soap, not the watery tallow soap Mama used, but real soap. Rosa wished that her prospective mother-in-law would leave her – allow her some privacy. Instead, she sat there, sewing Rosa's ripped skirt, lifting her head every few seconds to watch as Rosa washed the mud and grime from her legs.

"Did he enter you?"

"No," Rosa said, embarrassed by the older woman's directness. "Isaac arrived just in time."

"*Hmm*," said Jessica. She gave her back the hastily mended skirt.

"You must tell your mother what happened but say nothing to anyone else. Do you hear me, Rosa?"

Rosa was still in a trance – she could not make sense of it all. She knew it was a terrible thing, but why was Jessica Taube being so cold to her?

"Isaac was so brave – he pulled the soldier off me – he saved me."

"I hope my son doesn't live to regret this."

132

"What do you mean?" Rosa said weakly.

"They won't leave it like this. For a yid to beat up a soldier. One way or another, girl, we will all pay for this."

Isaac walked her home, carrying the washing basket. But she insisted that he leave her at the door. In the kitchen, Bubbe Sadie was sitting in a chair crocheting, and her mother was busy stirring a pot on the stove for dinner – she turned as her daughter entered. Lena was sitting at the table peeling beetroots and her hands were bloodied purple with the juice. At the sight of Lena's hands, Rosa fainted.

"Rosa, Rosa, babushka! "

As Rosa recovered, Mama, kneeling on the floor, cradled her in her arms. Rosa smelled the warm, comforting smell of her, and eventually pulled herself up off the floor. Lena helped her onto the seat.

"Are you ill? Tell me what is wrong, Rosa. Tell me!"

~∽~

Chapter 8

For the next few days Rosa did not set a foot outside the door. Rosa had told Mama everything, who in turn told Tata. Eventually, because Rosa was so distraught, Mama had no choice but to tell her sister and brothers. They were horrified at what had happened but, to protect Rosa's honour, sworn to secrecy.

The house was full of whispers as everyone tiptoed around her, and Mama made her constant cups of tea. After the fourth day she managed to sleep through the night without the nightmares where she relived every minute of the attack. Then, on the morning after Shabbos, when she was sitting quietly with Mama in the kitchen, Tata and Reubin had come home in great agitation from shul. They had seen soldiers in the town square and Tata was worried there would be retribution for the soldier's humiliation at Isaac's hands. And, apart from this new complication, there was also the ever-constant fear that the boys would be targets for conscription.

Mama was like a cat on a griddle, everyone was nervous. Tata had arranged with Rabbi Cohen for Reubin, Josef and Isaac to hide in the synagogue for a few days, while the soldiers were in town. The Rabbi had built a secret room underneath the floor of the prayer hall, just big enough for six people, intended as a safe place for his own family. But, in this instance, without anyone saying, it was understood that there was no need for Moishe Cohen to hide – he looked too feeble to interest the Russian officers. Meyer Taube and Tata agreed that if the soldiers called to their houses, they would say that the young men had gone for a few weeks to study with Rabbi Twerski, of the well-known Hasidic dynasty, at the Rabbinical court in Talne.

Fortunately, by all accounts, that night the soldiers were only interested in getting drunk in the town's taverns. But at dawn the next morning in driving rain, tired and mean from the effects of the drink the night before, the soldiers called to every house in the town looking for young men over fourteen years of age. They rounded up about fifty boys: Slavs, Polish Catholics, and twenty-four Jews, and took them off crammed into three cattle carts. Some of the Jewish boys hadn't even made their Bar Mitzvahs. Tata told Mama and Rosa how their hysterical mothers had run along the rutted road outside of the town beside the carts. Soaked and muddied like drowning river rats, and yowling like dying animals, they clutched onto clothing, or anything else they could grab hold of. While the soldiers, brutally, fended them off with the butts of their rifles.

"Like lambs to the slaughter," Mama had said.

Later that morning when Rosa had ventured out to the market with Mama, the town was in mourning and she could feel the weight of despair hanging in the air, as women wailed in the streets, clutching one another, stunned by the magnitude of their tragic loss.

The Rabinovichs and the Taubes had said nothing to anyone else about Reubin, Josef and Isaac hiding. Rabbi Cohen could not hide every Jewish boy. Instead, they publicly praised the Lord that their sons had been lucky enough to be out of town. It was on occasions like this that the Rabbi offered Tata his protection – a luxury that no amount of money could buy.

***

In the midst of the tragic events of those dramatic few days, everyone appeared to have forgotten about Rosa. But that evening Tata was unusually morose and withdrawn. His shoulders slumped and he moved around the kitchen as though it was a great effort.

"Husband, a terrible, terrible thing has happened, I don't know how, but the Lord will give mothers the strength to go on. He always does, no matter how big the sacrifice."

"It is not the lost boys, Zipporah, although it is an inconceivable tragedy to have lost so many." Tata looked over at Rosa, and there were tears in his rheumy eyes.

"What is it then? What is wrong?" asked Zipporah.

Josef and Reubin, noticing the alarm in their mother's voice, stopped arguing to look at Tata.

"I have something to tell you all. I met Meyer Taube today."

"And?" said Mama.

"There is no easy way to say this, my dear." He looked at Rosa.

"What Tata? What is wrong?" said Rosa.

"Isaac will not marry you. He wishes to withdraw from the arrangement."

"But why? Why, Tata?" said Rosa stunned.

"Because of what happened at the river. He says you are ... You are damaged goods, Rosa."

"But nothing happened, Tata, I promise. Isaac *knows* this – nothing happened."

"Meyer says his son cannot be sure. If he marries you now, and you should conceive, in nine months' time he will wonder if the child is his, or another man's."

"No, no, I don't believe it! I am going to see Isaac – talk to him. There must be a misunderstanding."

"I am sorry, my child," he said gently. "I am afraid there is no misunderstanding. Mama, take Rosa to our room."

Mama, as shocked as Rosa, helped her distraught

137

daughter stumble up the stairs to their room. The rest of the family sat stunned, until the silence was broken by the sound above of Rosa wailing.

***

The old woman, Mim Taube, small and stooped, was in the process of making starch from potatoes. The Slav servant had helped her with the heavy work of bashing the potatoes, and now she was reducing the sieved liquid to a gloopy syrup.

"Bubbe, you know you don't have to do that," said Isaac. "We can get widow Havel to make it, or we can buy some starch in Shklovsky's."

"You think money grows on trees? While the Lord gives me strength, I will work. Anyway, it helps to get rid of my anger. For such a thing to happen to Rosa, such a good girl."

"You think I did the wrong thing – breaking off the engagement?"

"No, no. It is not you I blame. It is that Russian animal who attacked her. No, Isaac, your father was right to advise you as he did. You cannot marry her now. She would bring her shame with her. It would follow our family and bring us bad luck."

"What will happen to her?"

"Damaged goods, who will take her?" The old woman shrugged. "Her family will look after her. The Rabinovichs are good people. She won't starve. Now go up to

138

Shklovsky's. As you are so keen to throw your father's hard-earned money away, you can buy me more potatoes."

***

Over the next few days, Isaac carried out his daily routine: morning prayers at shul, then sorting out the outstanding accounts at the warehouse with his father. But he felt an unbearable sadness hanging over him at what had come to pass. He knew that his parents were right, and that it was too big a risk to marry Rosa. Although she had said she wasn't raped, how could he be sure that he had arrived in time? For the first few days after it happened, images of her haunted his mind. Sweet, gentle Rosa. He knew he had let her down, that he was being a coward. A braver man would have ignored the lot of them and taken his chances. But, as the days passed and the family's departure for Vienna got closer, he felt the black cloud slowly start to lift and excitement build at the prospect of starting university. And, after a while, the admonishing voices in his head lessened – until finally he convinced himself that it had been merely an arrangement of convenience for both sets of parents. And although they had been betrothed, he had not really known Rosa. How could he? Apart from that time at the river, they had met only in the company of others. Still, he had stopped giving Reubin lessons. In fact, he avoided meeting the Rabinovichs as much as possible.

Until one afternoon about a week later, as Isaac crossed the main square, he saw Lena Rabinovitch leaving the apothecary's shop. There was no way of avoiding her.

"Isaac," she said haughtily, "it is surprising that you dare show your face after what you did to my sister."

He gripped her arm and squeezed it tightly.

"We are not supposed to talk about what happened to your sister – for Rosa's sake. If we are to protect her good name, then no one must know."

"You think no one knows? Then you are a fool. Even the dogs in the street know that you have broken off the engagement."

"Yes, but the other thing. Look, let me carry your basket, it's heavy, and we can talk privately."

"I should want to talk to you?" She shrugged, holding onto her basket.

"How is she? How is Rosa?"

He grabbed her arm and walked beside her.

"She's alright. She cries a lot. But she'll get over it."

Isaac's heart sank at her words.

"How are the rest of the family, Reubin, Josef?"

"Fine. You want me to make small talk with you after you ruined my sister's life?"

"Look, Lena, how can any of this be my fault? Maybe we were never meant for one another. Maybe the Lord had other plans for us both."

Lena stopped and looked at him strangely, and the anger suddenly seemed to drain from her face. She really was very beautiful, he thought – Rosa's little sister.

***

The following day was August the nineteenth, the feast of the Saviour, a Christian holiday and one of the town's fair days. Isaac was sitting in the shade of a chestnut tree drinking tea outside Gulko's, a kosher bakery, and eating one of their cinnamon pastries. Looking across the square he imagined it looked like a scene from biblical times. Kornyn was bustling with farm workers from surrounding towns and villages who had come to buy at the market, or simply to enjoy the spectacle of the day. Dogs ran between people's legs looking for scraps of food, and small children who had escaped from the clutches of their parents shrieked simply for the joy of it. The doors of the wooden and stone stalls in the arcade that lined one side of the square were thrown open and filled to the gills with grain, chickens, leather goods, cured meats and cheeses. Sometimes all these things were together in the one stall. Traders who lived on the square were hanging out of open windows or standing at their street doors. Others operating from purpose-made kiosks, or from the back of a cart, noisily bartered their wares.

"*You think I am a rich man?*" shouted a disgruntled, punter.

"*On my life, the Tsarina herself would not sniff at this silk!*" shouted a small, fat Jewish woman to a sneering, well-costumed Polish lady.

Isaac smiled at the sight of her. She had wrapped swathes of assorted fabric around her middle like a rainbow sari, so that she looked like a giant colourful bauble. She could hardly move and was sweating profusely from the heat.

Isaac was tired. He wanted to go home and put his feet up. He had been sitting here for over an hour waiting for his father who was in his Uncle Kazimir's tavern attempting to close a deal with a visiting grain merchant. Then coming through the crowds, he saw Lena with one of her friends, Sarah. He stood up as they passed and greeted them, not expecting Lena to engage with him. He had been unsettled by their meeting yesterday. He was already in the process of sitting down again when she stopped. He straightened up.

She looked at him disdainfully.

"Isaac, you are still here. I thought you were leaving town."

"We are leaving for Vienna soon," he said, sounding brusquer than he intended to disguise his unease. "One week, maybe two at the most. As soon as my father has completed the sale of the warehouse. The buyer, a merchant, is coming from Kiev to meet him tomorrow."

"So soon," she said. "You go ahead, Sarah, I will catch up with you."

Her friend, who had long teeth that sat on her lower lip, looked at her with one black eyebrow arched, and theatrically bid them both goodbye.

Lena looked down at the ground, then raised her eyes to Isaac, moving a little closer.

"I will miss you, Isaac," she whispered.

"Miss me? What do you mean?" he said, surprised.

"Yes, I will miss you. You probably never realised this, but I have grown very fond of you." She smiled provocatively at him.

He looked at her, not quite sure if she was teasing him, or why she was acting like this.

"How is Moishe?" he said nervously.

"I will not marry Moishe. Tata knows it, and the Rabbi knows it! They cannot make me marry someone to whom I do not wish to be married. It says so in the Talmud. No matter how much it suits them both."

"No, of course, that would be very wrong."

"So, you see, Isaac, we are both in the same situation." She put one hand on his arm, and as she did so it was as if a sweet, searing pain coursed like a knife through his body.

***

After that, he made a point of being in the square, drinking tea in Gulko's every afternoon as she made her way home with Sarah from Bena Cohen's. He watched to see her as she came through the white plastered archway at the side of the house. After formal greetings, Sarah walked with them so as not to attract attention, but her friend entered a trance as soon as he appeared. Isaac thought she was like the 'see-no-evil, hear-no-evil, speak-no-evil' brass monkeys, that they sold in the market. Effectively Lena and himself were alone.

But the guilt he suffered was wearing him down. The last few mornings, after his prayers, he vowed not to go to meet her again. He told himself he was betraying Rosa. He felt he was playing with fire. But Rosa had never stirred his desire as Lena did. Lena was different and he was drawn to her like a moth to a flame. He suspected that deep down he did not even like her. But she was so beautiful, and sensuous – the feelings she evoked made him quiver with desire – and at night in his narrow, childhood bed he could not sleep from the want of her.

"You must offer to marry me instead," she had said that afternoon after Sarah had bid them goodbye.

He had immediately recoiled at the suggestion.

But she pressed into him, firmly, so that he could feel the fullness of her breasts through his shirt.

He pushed her away. "Lena," he said, shocked. "Someone might see."

"Oh, I just tripped. Silly me," she said, and she leaned over and picked up an imaginary coin from the dusty street.

***

It hadn't been as difficult to arrange as he had expected. When he suggested the plan, his father had been shocked initially. Abe Rabinovitch and Meyer Taube had agreed, after the incident at the river, to say that it was Rosa who was having second thoughts. But with the girl going around like a wraith, looking like she had lost the will to live – and with the very real possibility that she could be with child, a *mamzer* – Meyer knew they would have to come up with another story.

"*Hmm*, Lena," said Meyer. "She's very attractive, has a shapely figure, I must admit," he had said knowingly.

"Lena!" Bubbe Mim had screeched that night at dinner, aghast, as Isaac knew she would be. "That girl is trouble, too full of herself – she will lead you a dog's life! You think you will have a minute's peace? And how could you do this to Rosa – has the child not suffered enough?"

Jessica Taube, who had been chewing chicken, had almost choked on it. "Trash, that's all they are. I don't know why you are so fixated on aligning us with that family. Are there not enough Jewish girls in Vienna from wealthy families who would be a more suitable match? Is my son to do your penance on earth?"

"Mama, I want this. I want Lena for my wife," said Isaac with determination.

"What about Moishe Cohen? Is she not already betrothed to Moishe?" asked Jessica.

"She will not marry him, and they cannot make her," said Isaac.

"Another scandal," said Jessica, throwing her eyes up to heaven.

Mim and Isaac looked at Meyer simultaneously. The

solution to this situation was obvious.

"Maybe I should talk to the Rabbi," said Meyer, looking at his son.

***

It was hot and sticky in Kornyn. The apothecary said it was over ninety-five degrees, and everyone seemed to walk around more slowly than usual. The tragedy of the abduction still weighed heavily on the townspeople. But the young boys who had managed to escape, reckless in the knowledge of their freedom, swam in the river to cool down. The girls, pretending to concentrate on the washing, watched them from a distance while wading deeper than they normally would into the cold water. The heaviness in the air made everyone bad-tempered: wives nagged husbands, women discarded their expensive wigs and wore cotton scarves wrapped loosely around their shorn heads. No one could sleep – kept awake by the crying of sweaty babies thrumming through thin wooden walls. And in the forests on either side of the river, wolves could be heard howling in the distance.

Rosa had been pickling the olives that Mrs Blumkin from two doors up had given Mama in exchange for their plums. Papa, Reubin and Josef were at shul and Lena was at Sarah's house. Mama had been in a bad mood all afternoon. Rosa had been sitting in the kitchen mooning over the portrait of Isaac, a pencil sketch made on a visit to Odessa that he had given her when they had first met as a keepsake. Zipporah had snapped at Rosa, unfairly she thought, when she had failed to bring in the boys' shirts from the line after a sudden torrential shower. Feeling guilty at her outburst, Zipporah had suggested that Rosa take advantage of the privacy provided by the men's absence, and that she wash using cool water from the pump in the yard. Her mother helped her fill jugs and carry the water into the metal bath they used for the purpose. Afterwards, she had fussed over her and helped Rosa dry herself like she was a child. She promised to take her to the mikvah pool in the bathhouse where Jewish women immersed for purification after they bled or gave birth, once Rosa's niddah was over. Importantly, it would serve as a signal to the other Jewish woman in the town that Rosa was not pregnant.

Rosa suspected this was the cause of her mother's bad temper. Because Rosa's niddah, which was usually as regular as clockwork, had not started. Every morning Rosa prayed that the blood would come, but so far not a drop – nothing. Even Mama was beginning to look at her strangely, and she had questioned her again in detail about what had happened at the river.

Rosa had never felt so lost, and lonely. She wondered how an act, over which she had no control, could have turned her life upside down. And to make things worse Isaac, her saviour, had cast her away like a leper. Consumed with grief, she hadn't wanted to leave the house. She felt ashamed of what had happened and humiliated that Isaac had seen her like that. But most of all she was broken-hearted that he had ended their betrothal – because she loved him. That day at the river when he had looked at her with such kindness and concern, she knew then that he was meant for her. Since then, she felt as if she had been hollowed out inside, and all that was left was an empty space filled with bitter despair. If only her monthlies would come, then she could prove beyond any doubt that nothing had happened with the soldier.

***

At the other side of the shtetl, the men were leaving shul after the afternoons' spiritual debate lead by Rabbi Cohen. The recent shower had not served to relieve the oppressive atmosphere. As Abe walked towards the door, the Rabbi called him.

"Abe, wait!" said Rabbi Cohen, "I need to speak to you."

"Of course, my Rebbe."

"Come, sit with me – my wife will make us tea."

The Jewish shul was a small wooden structure built by the men of the town some ten years previously and was already too small for the town's needs. Beside it, the Rabbi's house was much more substantial, a stone house, that had been built by the Jewish community for their spiritual leader.

Rabbi Cohen was well respected in Kornyn, and people flocked from the surrounding countryside to get advice from him: a barren wife, a disrespectful son, a father who gambled – the usual trials of family life. For such a holy man, and belied by his sorrowful face, he was blessed with a pragmatic nature. He would nod his head sympathetically as if he had personal experience of the petitioners' dilemma, and this made it easier for them to accept whatever advice he gave.

The Rabbi took Abe out to the private courtyard at the back of the house.

Bena Cohen, as if primed for their arrival, brought out two glasses of tea, and served it to the men as they sat under the shade of the courtyard's bountiful, gnarled apple tree. They sipped their tea companionably. Abe waited for the Rabbi to tell him what was on his mind, not wanting to interrupt the solace of the moment, which was only broken by the sound of crickets and trickling water leaking from the pump.

"How is Rosa after her terrible ordeal?"

"Oh, my Rebbe, not good. The child doesn't eat, she won't leave the house. We have tried to keep the matter private. The Taubes' prescience in not talking about what happened has helped. But her refusing to go outdoors is causing tongues to wag. Somehow people have heard that the engagement is off. Isaac even went so far as to say it was Rosa who didn't want the marriage to go ahead. But her actions are not supporting that claim."

"The Lord has certainly sent you a trial to bear, Abe. But I understand that it isn't the only cloud on the horizon. What about your daughter, Lena? I believe ... she is not too pleased with the prospect of marrying my son, Moishe."

"Oh, don't pay any attention to that, my Rebbe." said Abe brusquely. "That's only natural modesty, fuelled by a young girl's reluctance to grow up and take on the duties of a woman."

"I believe it is more than that, Abe. She has told Sarah – whose parents rightly told me – that she has said categorically that she will not marry Moishe."

Abe covered his eyes with his hands, afraid to look at the Rabbi. "God knows, I have tried, my Rebbe, I won't lie to you – she is proving very stubborn. How can she not see what an honour this is for our family? I thought I could make her change her mind."

The Rabbi nodded slowly and bowed his head, saying nothing for a while. Eventually he sat up straight and tapped his knees with both hands.

"So, we have a reluctant bridegroom, and a reluctant bride."

"Yes, Lord save us," said Abe in desperation.

"And you can swear to me on your life that the girl is still ... intact."

"I swear, my Rebbe, on my life, that she is still a virgin."

"Then maybe, Abe, we have misinterpreted the wishes of the Lord – and we are matching the wrong couple."

***

The wedding was small. Rosa thought her lovely white

cotton dress with the embroidered lace looked a bit tight. She didn't know how she was going to get through the day's celebrations. Mama had given her water laced with vodka which she sipped, breathing in slowly, the alcohol making her light-headed. She was sitting in Bena Cohen's drawing room surrounded by the women from her and Isaac's family. They had been telling stories, singing songs, chattering away. Apart from the odd pitying glance thrown in her direction, the women seemed oblivious to her inner turmoil. Opposite her, sitting on the bridal chair, and studiously avoiding her, Lena was like the cat who had got the cream. Mama was on one side of her and Jessica Taube on the other.

Eventually, the two women stood to break the plate together, symbolising the seriousness of the couple's commitment – what was broken could not be put back together. As the sounds of clapping and greetings died down, Rosa heard the men entering the courtyard and opening the latch on the door. They were coming for the Badeken, the veiling ceremony. She held her breath. She prayed that it had been a bad dream – that somehow she had imagined it all, and that he was really coming for her.

Isaac entered the room, followed by Meyer Taube, Tata, Rabi Cohen, and her brothers Reubin and Josef. Rosa closed her eyes, desperately hoping, praying. But as everyone cheered, she opened them only to see Isaac place the veil over the one he had chosen – over Lena.

Later, the women joined the men for the Chuppah, the

wedding ceremony, which had been set up in the synagogue. After he had signed the Ketubah, the marriage contract, Lena had walked seven times around Isaac who was now also dressed in white. Then Lena stood beside him under the huppah, the wedding canopy. The ceremony was about to begin. Rosa was shaking uncontrollably. She breathed in deeply, trying to steel herself to bear witness to what was yet to come: the betrothal blessings, the reading of the marriage contract then the ring ceremony, followed by the seven blessings. But as Isaac stood there with her sister under the canopy Rosa thought of Bubbe's story and she wanted to scream at him – *don't do it, Isaac!* Because only then did she finally accept that Isaac was going to marry the wrong sister. As Isaac looked longingly at Lena's veiled face a black void engulfed Rosa and she thought: *she will never – ever – as long as she lives, love you as I do.*

Rosa fainted.

A few minutes later, as Rosa lay reviving on a cold stone floor, she saw the blurred faces of women standing around her. They had dragged her into the kitchen so as not to disrupt the ceremony. She struggled to her feet with help from two of the women. In the other room she heard the breaking of glass, and the cries of *"Mazal tov!"* She could also smell roast chicken, mingled with the sweet and sour smell of her own vomit.

"She is definitely with child," said somebody.

Rosa fainted again.

PART 2

◈◈◈

Chapter 9

Vienna, Austria
November 1861

"Frau Tarrant, how nice to meet you."

Thomas Rafferty felt his heart beating in his chest, as he bent to kiss her hand, breathing in her light, spicy scent. Freesia, he thought, with sandalwood undertones.

"May I take your cloak and bonnet?"

"No, thank you. I don't believe we will be staying that long."

He gestured towards the chaise longue.

"Take a seat, please. May I get you tea, or lemonade?"

"Nothing, thank you."

She was breathtakingly beautiful. Eyes like a young deer, amber-brown and liquid, with dark, straight brows and full, slightly pouting lips. Her hair fair – her skin the colour of buttermilk.

She kept her head tilted to one side as she spoke, facing the window, towards the light. So that when she turned, the scar that ran down one side of her face came as a shock.

"Ale maybe?" he said, to cover his confusion.

"Please, that would be perfect."

He got up and approached the table at the side of the room where he kept a pitcher of ale.

"We should wait for your husband."

"Certainly. As you wish."

They sat in silence for a few minutes, giving him a chance to study her further. Underneath her heavy wool cloak which she untied, she was expensively dressed in a light grey-silk costume with black lace trimmings. Her matching black hat had long black and white feathers that framed one side of her face. At her neck she wore a large purple glass brooch. The colour matched the shaded tones of her skin. His heart palpitated in excitement.

She folded her hands over her long legs – he had noticed as she entered the room they were perfectly proportioned with her upper body. As she breathed, her breasts swelled under the grey silk, although little flesh was bare.

Thomas breathed in deeply to calm himself.

"Will he be long, do you think?"

"No, he is just using your facilities." She blushed slightly, bringing the colour of rose madder to her skin.

Like a bruised peach, he thought. He noticed an inflection of an accent he couldn't quite place.

The door opened and Isaac Tarrant walked in. Thomas noted he was taller than himself, broad-shouldered, good figure, with dark-brown hair and clean shaven. He seemed confident and assured.

"Rafferty, good to meet you. Apologies for the delay. Nature called, and my carriage had gone – didn't want to leave Frau Tarrant standing about."

They shook hands. Tarrant's were soft and smooth, like a woman's. Thomas was conscious of the oil paint beneath his nails.

"So, what do you think? Can you do her justice? I assured her you could leave out the scar."

"Barely noticeable," Thomas said, his amiable face confused, not wanting to embarrass her.

She looked away, unsmiling, towards the window.

"Sorry, Herr Tarrant, my manners. Please take a seat."

He sat down on the chaise longue near his wife.

"Price?" he asked.

"Oh, let's discuss that another time." Thomas brushed his hands nervously through sandy-coloured slightly dishevelled hair.

"No, I'd rather agree upfront," Isaac Tarrant replied brusquely. "Full portrait, in a costume which I will select – all the trimmings. It's for our salon – we are refurbishing at the moment."

"Well, that would require say ten or twelve sittings of about an hour and a half. It would be one hundred gulden."

"Call it eighty and we have a deal."

"*Hm.*" Thomas coughed into his fist. "That's my standard fee, Herr Tarrant."

"One hundred is a scandalous amount. Let's say ninety."

Thomas noticed her hands clench although her face was still turned away.

"Fine, Herr Tarrant."

"Good man." Isaac Tarrant stood up abruptly and shook Rafferty's hand.

Frau Tarrant also rose, holding out her hand. Rafferty again kissed the finely boned knuckles, savouring her smell.

Hat in hand, Isaac Tarrant raised his elbow and she, barely touching his arm, allowed him to lead her out of the room.

"The first appointment?" Thomas asked.

Tarrant turned as he reached the door.

"Oh, let's say next week. Wednesdays are good for me. I'll drop her around about nine o'clock in the morning and send my carriage to collect her at ten-thirty."

When they had gone Thomas sat back in his chair and inhaled the remnants of her perfume deep into his lungs. She was the most beautiful creature he had ever seen.

***

Thomas rubbed circles in the frosted windows to look out onto the narrow street, his arms bracing his chest for warmth as the heat from the stove struggled to take the chill off the room. Outside it was freezing. For days, bitter northern winds had driven snow across the city. At least the wind had dropped. Now, snow was falling gently, but persistently, in swathes of crystal flakes. The street sweepers had struggled to keep the pathways clear, and piles of snow-covered ash-mounds and horse-dung formed dirty banks at the sides of the road. This morning, another virgin layer filled the carriage ruts running down the cobbled street. There were still few carriages to be seen.

He watched as the grocer's boys struggled with handcarts piled high with boxes of all shapes and sizes as they made their morning deliveries. The figures, as if mummified, were wrapped up in layers of clothes, woollen scarves and hats, their wooden clogs bound with sackcloth.

When he had arrived that morning in the studio, Berthe, the young girl from the parish, had left a bucket of chopped wood and two pitchers of water, drawn from the sink in the communal scullery in the basement. She had swept the floor as he had asked. He had spent the last hour tidying up, organising things. He had sorted tubes of paint into wooden boxes and cleaned his brushes which were now neatly arranged in old metal cocoa-tins, sorted according to size and type.

For the portrait, he had ordered prepared canvas from the colour-man. He usually gave his canvases a coat of paint himself to add depth to the colours he would lay over. The base colour varied, depending on the subject matter. He thought of her buttermilk skin and imagined a mixture of Prussian blue and vermilion providing a perfect foil. The canvas was large; he usually preferred to paint on a smaller scale, but this was a full-length portrait.

However, he was far from starting to paint. Today he would sketch her, immerse himself in her. So that through the act of drawing, representing her image would become as much instinctual as reflective. How would he pose her, he wondered? Standing upright seemed so unnatural, unnecessarily stiff like a cabinet photograph. If only she could be prone, lounging, naked on the chaise longue, he fantasised. But he knew that was impossible.

She arrived on time, accompanied by her husband's grandmother, an old crone, Mim, who she summarily introduced. After taking their bonnets, furs and capes and hanging them on the coat stand, he offered them refreshments. This time she asked for tea, and he busied himself preparing it, pouring water he had heated on the stove into a heavy ceramic teapot. He took two china cups with odd saucers that he had picked up at the market and surreptitiously wiped the single silver spoon. He brought the cups of steaming liquid to them on the shiny japanned tray that his Irish mother had given him as a present for his new business venture.

"I am afraid I have no sugar, Frau Tarrant."

"I don't take sugar," she said. "On principle. I don't agree with slavery."

"No, neither do I," he said enthusiastically. "Agree with slavery, I mean."

"Although we are all slaves in one way or another," she said in a matter-of-fact manner.

"Indeed," he said, not sure how to respond. So far, his experience with wealthy women had taught him to tread warily. There was a fine line between friendliness and overfamiliarity that you crossed at your peril – as he had learnt previously to his cost.

"Today, Frau Tarrant, I thought, if it were alright with you, we could do a few poses. I would like to sketch you, to try to establish a suitable arrangement. Do you have any articles you wish to be included, family jewellery, or a pet perhaps?"

"I seldom wear jewellery, only if ..." She lowered her gaze and didn't finish the sentence.

He was afraid he had embarrassed her in some way, but he couldn't think why.

"And I don't have any pets. I had a small dog, a pug, Moshi, but he died." Her amber eyes welled up with tears. Raw umber with flecks of yellow ochre, he thought.

They discussed the weather, the fact that she was looking forward to the spring, the first snowdrops and being able to ride her horse in the Prater, the park outside the city walls.

The old crone sat in a chair near the stove watching the proceedings as they tried various poses for Frau Tarrant's comfort. Eventually they decided she would stand beside the table, one hand resting on its edge supporting her. At a later stage, he told her, he would

161

draw a decorative classical balustrade, and set the scene in a park.

Once she was settled and comfortable, he drew quick sketches, discarding each on the floor as soon as he was finished to start another. Until he was surrounded by sheaves of flimsy, white butter-paper.

Eventually she said, "Monsieur Tarrant, may I rest for a while?", and she stood up, arched her back, and stretched out her arms, as graceful as a swan-ballerina. He realised that the pose he had spent nearly an hour trying to capture simply wasn't going to work.

"Do you think that you could persuade your husband to let me paint you reclining?"

"Oh, he wouldn't approve. I know without asking."

"You obviously have difficulties with your back," he suggested, guessing wildly.

"Yes. Yes, I do."

"Well, then maybe if you suggest that reclining would be easier."

"I'll try, Monsieur Rafferty, but I am afraid I cannot promise."

***

At the next appointment, as well as the crone, her husband came with her. He complained that his wife had found the previous week's pose difficult – it had strained her back. She had been in pain for several days and had been unable to carry out her normal duties. When her husband had said this, Helena caught Thomas's eye briefly. So quickly, he thought afterwards, that he might have imagined her implication of collusion. However, Herr Tarrant had reluctantly agreed that because of his wife's back problems, the pose could be prone. Provided, of course, that it was decorous, and the normal considerations of modesty expected of a lady of her class and position were adhered to.

From then on, they fell into an easy routine.

She had brought an evening gown with her in sapphire-blue silk with black antique lace. Sleeveless, the neck of the dress was off the shoulder but stopped short of revealing any cleavage.

Thomas had borrowed a modesty screen from his landlady Frau Lipsky, which he had placed at one end of the studio. The crone sat on an upholstered chair near the window so that she could supervise proceedings.

"I am afraid, Frau Tarrant, you will have to remove your hooped petticoat."

"Yes, of course. I understood that would be necessary." She seemed unperturbed.

"I will leave you to disrobe in peace. I need cigarettes. I'll just slip out, but I will be back in five minutes."

Thomas went to a tobacconist across the street. He had started smoking while working in Paris, an expensive habit that he only indulged in when he was feeling stressed, like today.

When he returned, she was sitting primly on the edge of the chaise longue.

"Did you bring jewellery?"

"Yes, my husband wants me to wear these."

She had a leather case in her hand that she opened to show him. A necklace and matching earrings of sapphires and diamonds.

"They are magnificent, Frau Tarrant. Your husband must love you very much."

"He didn't buy them for me. A client gave them to him to pay off a debt. He said I could wear them for the portrait," she said, without showing emotion.

"Ah," he said, unsure how to respond.

"Could you help me fix the clasp, please? It is awkward."

She held the jewels to her neck, and he stood behind her and closed the clasp.

"There! You look like an empress, fit for the Hapsburg court," he said, attempting his most charming smile.

"Thank you. How do you want me?" she asked, eyebrows arched and head slightly bowed.

"Well, maybe if you recline on the chaise longue and find a position that you are comfortable with," he said slightly nervously, his previous confidence waning.

She reclined on her side facing him, her head resting on the palm of her hand, her elbow resting on the side of the upholstered arm of the couch.

"Maybe straighten your back a little, and if you could lift your chin."

He approached her and, hardly tipping the soft flesh under her chin, he rotated her head slightly. He stood back. "Perfect." Then he arranged the skirt of the blue silk so that it fell in shimmering folds to the floor, smoothing it at the top of her thigh and fleetingly feeling the warm flesh underneath.

He returned to the easel, his fingers trembling, and started to sketch until his mind entered the familiar creative trance. Using charcoal, he sketched out the figure on the Prussian blue-and-crimson background – unconscious of the movement of his hands, his desire channelled into creating her form on canvas – until he was satisfied that the proportions were right. Then using pure Prussian blue that he squeezed onto his palette, he started to outline the contours of her body and how it moulded itself into the couch.

"Do you mind if I don't make small talk?" she asked in a clipped voice with that funny accent she had.

"No, of course not, Frau Tarrant. We can be quiet if you like."

"No, I hate silence. You must tell me about yourself. You are English?"

"No, Irish."

"Is that not part of England?"

"Well, we don't like to think so. We are as different as Austrians are to Hungarians."

"That different?" She smiled.

"And you, do I detect a slight accent? You are not

originally from Austria."

"No, we are Russian, West of Kiev."

"Ah, yes, that region was originally part of Poland – a good Catholic country like Ireland."

"I am not a Catholic. We are Jews."

"Yes, of course." He was annoyed with himself for potentially embarrassing her.

She looked at the crone who glared back.

"You want to interrogate my granddaughter-in-law, or you want to paint her? Your time is up, Herr Rafferty," Mim said brusquely.

"So soon," he said in anguish. He put down the brush carefully and, using a rag doused with white spirits he cleaned his hands. Then he walked over to her and assisted her as she got up stiffly from the couch.

"I look forward to seeing you next week, Frau Tarrant," he said formally, bowing his head slightly. "I will leave you to change. I need to go and get more supplies anyway."

She reached into her reticule and pulled out a delicate, lace-trimmed handkerchief. She sniffed slightly and held out her hand to him to kiss and, as he took her hand, she pressed a small piece of paper into his palm. Her eyes met his directly, commanding him not to comment.

When he got out in the street, he looked at the scrap of paper. On it she had written:

Get rid of my duenna, so we can speak privately.

***

After Thomas had returned from his visit to the colour-man, he was still feeling elated. What did this mean? Why did she need to speak to him privately? He stood at the canvas, inspecting the morning's work.

He examined the preliminary painting – the alignment and proportion of the limbs. It was imperative to get the armature of the portrait correct at the beginning. With the cold eye of a surgeon, he had imagined her body without flesh – calling on his academic knowledge of the skeletal form. He found this act of layering paint a physical manifestation of his mental process. It was like one of Strauss's symphonies, with a slow metronomic start – building slowly, until it reached a crescendo of feeling that rippled through his body and made him feel as if it was going to explode.

From now on, he could imagine her unclothed, the focus of his desire – which the clothed body would ultimately allude to – reflected light on skin, the cadence of the colour of her curves' secret places. Only then could he capture the fall of cold silk on warm flesh. If only he could see her naked!

He lit another cigarette, inhaling deeply the comforting fumes. Since she had first come to his studio, two weeks ago, he hadn't been able to get her out of his mind. It wasn't just her beauty, which admittedly was remarkable, it was some extra quality about her that he couldn't quite put his finger on. She was tantalising him, that was for sure. He was finding it hard to work, thinking about her. Maybe it was knowing she was unattainable – she would have no interest in a lowly painter like him. Although, he thought with satisfaction, that was changing. He was slowly gaining a reputation as a portraitist within Viennese social circles. He had even been invited to a salon at the Rothschilds' last week. But he had yet to gain the social standing of Friedrich von Amerling, court painter to the Emperor and the fashionable portraitist of the day. He was still an Irish nobody.

After her last visit, he had tried to temper this absurd, almost debilitating, infatuation by engaging in a dalliance with the easy-going Frau Estella Baumann, the wife of a louche Austrian minor-aristocrat whom he had met at Frau Schwartz's Wednesday afternoon salon. But fulfilling his physical needs had not extinguished his desire for Helena. Like a love-sick calf, he thought of her constantly. He had not been smitten like this since his youth, when he had a brief, although immensely pleasurable, affair with a singing teacher several years older than himself while painting a portrait in a draughty castle in the Scottish Highlands. Remembering that time, he recognised what he was experiencing now – alternating feelings of painful longing – then of profound loss, waiting endlessly for the week to pass until she returned once more.

The note she had pressed into his hand had confused him. Maybe she was feeling the same way about him – although, he had not sensed her desire. If anything, he was not entirely sure if she even liked him. She had talked today – asked him questions really – about himself, where he came from. She hadn't given much away about herself. But then the crone was always watching. If only he could distract the crone in some way. Bloody woman, it had cost him fifty kreuzer a day to pay for her ale on the last two visits.

She was as bad as his landlady Frau Lipsky whose behaviour he was finding increasingly annoying. Most days, on some flimsy pretext, she dropped into his studio, and she too would spend at least an hour wasting his time and drinking his ale while she gossiped about the other tenants. He inhaled deeply on the cigarette then stubbed it into a saucer encrusted with dried-out varnish. Maybe that was the answer – he would talk to his Jewish landlady.

***

That evening, dressed in a clean linen shirt, sack jacket, and trousers that had no paint spatters, he descended the steps to his landlady's basement apartment. Frau Lipsky lived in two rooms behind the scullery and the communal laundry area. She was sitting near the stove wrapped in a large, colourful woollen blanket, wearing fingerless gloves, knitting. A glass of schnapps was on a table beside her. He could smell the herrings she had eaten earlier lingering in the warm smoky air.

"Herr Rafferty," said the landlady. "What a nice

surprise. Things are good with you? Fine ladies in fine carriages means good fees? I hardly see you anymore."

She spoke quickly in Viennese German. Although he was fluent in both French and German, he struggled sometimes to understand her precise meaning with this local dialect. His frown signalled to her to slow down.

"So, to what do I owe this pleasure?" she asked suspiciously.

Feygele Lipsky was a large, bosomy woman with a red wig, an unusual choice for a Jewess, and bulging brown eyes. She was Austrian and, as far as landladies go, was a pleasant and reasonable woman. Until you couldn't pay your rent, then these qualities evaporated, and she became a virulent wasp letting you know in no uncertain terms that your belongings would be turfed out in the gutter unless you produced what was owed.

"I am in a bit of a pickle," he said, giving her the full benefit of his Irish charm and boyish smile. "I was wondering if you would be able to help me out?"

"I'm not interested in sob-stories about money. No pay – no stay. You know the rules, Irish!"

He raised both palms in an open gesture.

"No, Frau Lipsky, it is woman trouble, not money trouble. Lady trouble to be more precise."

"Ah, you want advice, you have come to the right place. I am an expert in affairs of the heart. Three husbands, in ten years. I outlived them all. And still, I have men who –"

"It is the lady in the carriage," he said, cutting her off, not interested in hearing about her love life."

"*Oy vey!* You aim high, Irish! But she is trouble, that one. I can tell just by looking at her. I never trust women with big feet!"

He looked at her with a bewildered expression. "To be honest, I never noticed her feet. She is incredibly beautiful, and the gentlest soul you could meet. I am trying to paint her. And to paint her, I need to know her."

Frau Lipsky's eyebrows were raised ironically into two black semicircles of disbelief, her chin disappearing into the rolls of fat in her neck.

"Not in the biblical sense!" he said, feigning dismay. "I need to understand her personality. But every visit, Frau Tarrant brings her husband's grandmother as a duenna, an old crone who sits in the corner of the room like a tiresome Tyrolean troll. My creative spirit wilts under her spell." He held his palms open dramatically in a pleading gesture.

"You want to play hanky-panky," she retorted, unimpressed.

"No, I want to paint her!"

"So, what can I do?"

"I want you to distract the crone. She likes ale, and no doubt is fond of cards. Aren't all old women?"

"You think I have nothing better to do than play cards and drink ale with an old woman, so you can play hanky-panky with a woman with big feet?"

171

He suspected that cards and ale were exactly what she did every afternoon, but he repeated patiently. "I only want to paint her. I would make it worth your while."

"How worth my while?"

"Say, a half a florin per visit."

"One."

"Fine, one florin per visit."

"Where are they from, the family?"

"From the town of Kornyn, near Kiev."

"*Hmm*," said Frau Lipsky with pursed lips and a conspiratorial expression. "Leave it with me, Irish. Now you will have a glass of schnapps with me, or maybe vodka."

"That would be delightful, Frau Lipsky," he said in resignation. It seemed that he would have to listen to stories of her past love life after all.

***

The following week, shortly after Frau Tarrant and her duenna arrived in the studio, Frau Lipsky knocked on the door and entered unceremoniously.

"Sorry to interrupt you, Herr Rafferty!" She nodded at the ladies. "I was wondering if your guests would like any refreshments – some ale, maybe some schnapps – it is heavy today."

"You are so kind, Frau Lipsky. Ladies, let me introduce my landlady, Frau Lipsky," he said in German.

Both Helena and Mim looked disdainfully at the

flamboyant red-haired Jewish woman. She was wearing a colourful crocheted shawl draped over her large bosom and a long maroon costume that was noticeably dusty and had seen better days. Helena stayed reclining on the couch and Mim didn't even bother getting up.

"You are very kind but no, thank you. Herr Rafferty has ale," said Mim in a thin, clipped voice.

"Oh goodness," he said, hands dramatically to head. "I am afraid I don't! I completely forgot to get some. I do have lemonade though."

Mim looked at him with barely concealed contempt.

"Herr Rafferty tells me you are from Kornyn, Frau Tarrant," said Frau Lipsky in Yiddish.

"Yes, that is so," Mim replied primly.

Thomas was nodding his head encouragingly, although he didn't understand a word they were saying.

"My second cousin, Rebecka, married a man from Kornyn. Berl Kunis, you know him? He's the apothecary. Right now, things are not so good for him, I believe?"

"Berl Kunis? I don't believe you?" said Mim, suddenly animated. "I have known Berl since he was a small boy, wearing his sister's dresses and wooden shoes. Long before he became a successful businessman, let me tell you."

"He's done well."

"And Rebecka is your cousin, Frau Lipsky?"

"Second – on my mother's side."

"Well, it's a small world!"

"Tarrant, this name, the Russians gave it to you?"

"No, no, it was Taube. We changed it to save my grandson Isaac from the Happers, the conscription agents for the Tsar's army."

"*Ahem.*" Thomas coughed politely into his hand, to remind Frau Lipsky of her mission, as the two women appeared to be getting carried away

"Frau Tarrant you cannot sit in that rackety old chair, in this draughty studio. Your daughter-in-law will be safe with Irish. He's a Catholic – sexually repressed, if you ask me. Come sit in front of my stove – we will drink ale, schnapps maybe, and play cards. And I have apfelstrudel. I will tell you what has happened to poor Berl since you have left. You wouldn't believe that life could be so cruel."

"I had heard whispers, Frau Lipsky. Well, if it is alright with you, Helena?" Her small, stooped figure had gained a youthful verve and, without waiting for her charge to answer, like a whippet in heat she was already halfway across the room.

The silence hung heavy on the air after they had left. Thomas wondered if she could hear his heart pounding in his chest.

"I have you to myself – at last," he said nervously, with a smile.

He moved over nearer to her, where she had remained prone on the couch. Her pupils were dilated and her moistened lips slightly parted.

"I wanted to be able speak privately to you," she said.

174

"About anything in particular?" he said breathlessly.

"I feel that there is some chemistry between us."

"I feel it too – if only you knew how much. I cannot sleep, thinking of you." He knelt down beside her and grasped her hand in his.

"I wanted to be able to talk to you," she said, eyes downcast. "You know, really talk. I don't have many friends in this city, and I am – lonely – sometimes." She looked at him, her eyes filled with tears. "You seem so kind and sympathetic." She gave him a funny lopsided smile. "Maybe we could be friends. I need a friend." She touched the scar on her cheek with the tips of her fingers.

"Your cheek?" he said hesitantly.

"My husband ... it was an accident. But I don't wish to talk about it. Just kiss me."

He leaned forward and kissed her gently on the lips, his fingers barely touching her skin. Then he grew braver and pulled her closer to him.

***

On every subsequent visit, after they had arrived and exchanged greetings, he would go to the tobacconist across the road to buy cigarettes, smoking one slowly on the way back, giving Helena time to undress, remove her hooped petticoat, and arrange her pose. The sound of the front door opening on his return was the signal for Frau Lipsky to collect Mim. Then they had forty-five minutes before Frau Lipsky returned with the old woman, who was at that stage sated with gossip, and inebriated from the schnapps.

As Thomas painted Helena, they talked. He told her how he was from Dublin, the capital city of Ireland, the third largest city in the British Empire. How his father painted panels on carriages for the gentry, and how he had taught him how to paint. He explained that when he was eighteen, with his father's blessing and a letter of introduction from his patron, he had travelled to Paris and worked in the studios of Ingres. From there he had come to Vienna in the hope of making his fortune and reputation by obtaining commissions as a result of the impending building boom on the Ringstrasse.

He asked her questions about herself, her family, her childhood growing up in Kornyn. She described the small market town nestled in the curve of the Irpin River – how her family were devout Jews, her father a rabbinical scholar who worked with the local rabbi – and how her mother produced fancy goods for the market to supplement her husband's meagre wages.

As she talked, sometimes he would leave down his brush and just watch her, mesmerised by the feline languor she exuded. He had never met a woman before who was so completely at ease with her body. He could not resist the urge to repeatedly go over to her – to touch her – to fuss with the fabric of her dress, to pull the silk lower to expose more of her cleavage. Then aroused, to slip his hand in under the cold fabric to cup her warm breast. Several times he had lifted the layers of her silk skirt to her waist, gently parting her thighs, her left leg still hanging over the edge of the coach. Then through the open seams of her drawers, he tentatively allowed his fingers to explore the hidden velvety flesh. During these times, it was as if she held her breath, startled but motionless. He knew she was aroused, by the moistness of her. But forty-five minutes was not enough, if he was to seduce her, and make sufficient progress with the painting so that the crone would not be suspicious.

"If only I could see you naked," he said to her.

"You know it is not possible – not advisable," she warned, touching her cheek.

They had kissed passionately. He had developed an intimacy with her body in his probing, but they had not made love. For her, it was a step too far. For him, it was torture.

"How can I show you how much I love you, clothed, uncovering only bits of you at a time. You are killing me, Helena."

"It is simply too great a risk – my husband's grandmother could return at any minute."

When she had gone, he took out sheets of cartridge paper and drew her naked body, imagining all of the places of her that he had explored. One afternoon, in a creative frenzy fuelled by sexual frustration, he started painting her on a second canvas. He painted for hours as

177

if possessed by a devil until the daylight was long gone, the stove had grown cold, and the smell of cheap oil from his lamp was making him queasy. He realised he had not eaten since noon. Eventually he fell asleep on the chaise longue, clutching a cushion to his face, her freesia and sandalwood scent still lingering on the brocade fabric.

Chapter 10

Not far from Rafferty's studio, on the more fashionable Spiegelgasse, the Tarrant family had just finished a celebratory birthday breakfast. They were gathered in a ground-floor reception room that the previous owner had used as his office. It had been temporarily converted into a dining room for family meals while the first-floor rooms were being refurbished.

Franz the butler had cleared the plates of half-eaten caramelised pancakes with plum compote that Helena had asked the cook to make for the occasion. Today was Isaac's birthday. He was twenty-seven years of age.

"What has become of us?" moaned Bubbe Mim. "Reading a psalm at shul or donating to charity is the way to celebrate birthdays – not eating fancy pancakes!"

"How did the session with Rafferty go yesterday?" Isaac asked his wife, ignoring his grandmother.

"I am finding it more comfortable, certainly."

"And your back?"

"Better."

"Good. I look forward to an improvement in your – demeanour." He looked archly at her then rested the delicate gold-rimmed china cup on the saucer.

"More tea, please, Marie," Isaac's father Meyer said in pidgin French. He articulated every syllable as he spoke – gesticulating with his large, hairy, well-manicured hands – as the German maid also spoke only elementary French.

"*Bien sur*, Herr Tarrant," replied the maid, dressed in a crisp white apron and lace cap, as she took his cup over to the samovar.

"And how are the decorations for the salon, Helena? Will it be finished on time?" Meyer asked his daughter-in-law.

"The builder tells me that the granite for the alterations to the windows was delayed with the bad weather. Some of the roads were impassable. But he received word yesterday from the supplier that it will be here by next Tuesday at the latest."

"It has been one thing after another," Isaac said testily, "first the lead pipes, and now the granite. I should fire that idiot and get someone who knows what he is doing. Our family have been trading across Europe for centuries without all the palaver that this fellow seems to encounter."

"The weather is hardly his fault," said Helena calmly.

"These things can usually be dealt with to ensure your goods get priority as soon as conditions improve. The skill is in negotiating tariffs and knowing when to grease the wheels of local administrators," Isaac retorted.

"Bribing, you mean."

"Yes, when necessary. I don't know why you are so sanctimonious. Who do you think pays your bills?" Isaac said, annoyed.

"Can you two not at least be civil? You call this a birthday?" said Mim in exasperation.

"Sorry, Bubbe – I mean Grandmother," Isaac apologised. He turned with exaggerated civility to address his wife. "What will you do today, Helena?"

"Lieutenant Lewinsky has kindly offered to accompany me to a friend of his, Frau Winkelman. She is showing me the work of a cabinetmaker that we might be interested in."

Isaac's eyebrows rose briefly in alarm.

"Only the best, *ahuva*," said Meyer. "Just make sure you are getting good value."

But before Meyer could launch into the inevitable lecture, Mim interrupted quickly. "Oh, by the way, I received a letter from Kazimir yesterday."

"Really, what news from the shtetl?" Isaac asked, trying to lighten the mood. Putting his knife and fork down on his plate, he turned respectfully to his grandmother.

"Oh, he was badmouthing the Tsar, as usual. Freeing the serfs while the Jews still cannot own land or travel

181

freely? What justice is there in that? Some things never change. He also despairs with the Russians clamping down on the Jewish tavern keepers, trying to control the price of vodka with exorbitant taxes on Polish-owned inns and taverns, and lowering the prices at Russian ones."

"Any news of my family?" Helena said with studied disinterest.

"After the expensive education that your poor father paid for, you have forgotten how to write?" said Mim.

"I do write, when I can, but with all of this ..." She waved her hand wearily, implying the effort of it all. "I haven't written for a while."

Mim's mouth screwed up like she had sucked on a lemon. "Your sister is struggling, I believe. The boy, Samuil, he must be fifteen by now, he would have made his Bar Mitzvah. Well, he caught scarlet fever last spring, and his asthma has worsened as a result. But the big news is – you will be pleased to hear," Mim looked slyly at Helena, "they got permission to travel and are taking the new train from Lviv and coming to Vienna!"

"Here, to us?" Helena said, alarmed.

"No. They didn't ask for that – too proud. They are staying with Rabbi Shulman near the synagogue."

"Why are they coming to Vienna?" Isaac asked in concern, putting down his linen napkin.

"Well, it seems that the young man's condition is extremely debilitating. Berl Kunis, the apothecary in

Kornyn – you know, I told you he is married to a cousin of the artist's landlady?"

"Yes, yes, go on."

"Well, he told Moishe and Rosa of Doctor Straus here in Vienna who specialises in lung diseases. Moishe's father, the Rabbi, will pay, presumably."

"This will be awkward for us," Isaac said, looking in alarm at his mother.

"It certainly will," said Jessica. "Presumably, we will not have to socialise with them. They can hardly expect us to act as tour guides."

"No – obviously not," he replied. "But they will wish to visit Helena."

Helena touched the scar on her face nervously.

"I can see them here, in the breakfast room," she said. "I will explain to them that we have the builders in, and that we are not in a position to entertain."

"Well, you must manage it as best you can. We do not wish to be inhospitable to them," Isaac responded. Then turning to his mother, he said earnestly, "Mama, will you make sure they have everything they need?"

"Son, you owe them nothing!"

"No, Mama, but they are good people. We have enough. However, you are right of course. I must consider my business, my clients. We cannot undo all our hard work to get accepted here. In fact, I met Herr Lieberman yesterday, Papa. I told him about the portrait. He is a great fan of Rafferty's work. Once the salon is finished, he promised that he and his wife will accept our invitation to dinner, to see the finished painting."

"Now that is a complete waste of money if you ask me," Meyer retorted. "Begging your pardon, Helena, no offence intended, but could we not have just put another mirror up there?"

"Beauty is a much-admired commodity in Vienna, Tata." Isaac glanced briefly at his wife. "Especially when it is transposed into a covetable object."

"Well, it is certainly a mark of your success, Isaac, that you can afford such a thing. We have certainly come a long way from Kornyn," said Jessica proudly.

"But there was no need for all of the name-changing," interrupted Bubbe Mim. "There is no shortage of successful Jews here in Vienna."

"Yes, Bubbe, but at least we got here – safely," said Isaac.

"*Hmm*," she said, unconvinced. "I wonder what your sister is like now, Helena? How long is it since we have seen them – eight years, I think? Rosa was such a lovely girl, so beautiful." She looked directly at Helena, "Beautiful on the inside."

Helena threw a look of pure hatred at the old woman.

"Grandmother, there is no need for that," Isaac rebuked her.

"I have things to do before I meet the lieutenant this morning. Excuse me." Helena rose from the table.

"Helena," Isaac stopped her, "I should like to be

involved in commissioning any furniture. We do have a budget for these works. I must say, I was alarmed at the escalating costs of Venetian glassware," he said archly, but with a smile on his face. "I received a bill last week that would have fed your family in Kornyn for six months."

"You may have changed your name, your religion, and your profession, husband – but inside you are still ... the son of a shtetl street trader," Helena retorted angrily. "No offence intended to you, Tata."

Meyer looked annoyed, and about to reprimand her. But his wife glared at him to say nothing.

Isaac's face, on the other hand was impassive.

When she was angry, he thought, the scar was a livid red. His stomach lurched at the sight of it. What would Rosa make of them all?

***

As Isaac was leaving the house to head to his office, Lieutenant Lewinsky, resplendent in a long grey military coat with brass buttons, was being shown in by the footman. The gilded ormolu clock in the breakfast room chimed. It was ten o'clock and the builders were working on the first floor.

"Morning, Lieutenant. Early for you, I would have thought," said Isaac, putting on his hat.

"Indeed, Herr Tarrant, but your wife was very keen to see cabinets made for good friends of mine, the

Winkelmans. I must say they are quite exquisite, mahogany inlaid with ash."

The lieutenant had removed his helmet and ruffled his fine blonde hair. He was fresh-faced from the cold.

"Well, don't let her spend all my money, Lieutenant. Or there will be hell to pay."

The lieutenant's pupils dilated like a startled rabbit at his words, and Isaac could see he was unsure how to respond. Lifting his hat, and bowing with a sardonic smile, Isaac left the house, as the sound of banging and hammering started on the upper floor.

Really the lieutenant was a pathetic excuse for a man, Isaac thought. He didn't know what Helena saw in him. Still, he was useful, at least he entertained her, relieving him of a lot of the social duties that he found tiresome. She couldn't come to much harm with Lewinsky either, Isaac chuckled to himself. But best to keep the lieutenant unsure of him. Afraid even.

His mood started to lift. He was glad to get out of the house – the constant noise drove him mad. No wonder his mother and grandmother had been complaining. The sooner the builders were finished the better. Really, he should have rented somewhere else while the work was going on. However, it would have been a complete waste of money as currently you couldn't escape the sounds of construction anywhere in the city.

Vienna was like a giant building site – carts trundled through the narrow streets filled with building materials of every description. Dust was everywhere. And when it settled on newly fallen snow, it was churned about by foot and wheel so that it looked like the frothy chocolate milk served in the city's numerous coffee houses.

This morning, servants were out washing grimy windows and brushing steps with vigour. He nodded at several acquaintances he passed – Jewish businessmen, like himself, swaddled in heavy black coats and fine fur hats. Isaac pulled up his mink-lined collar against the chill north wind and headed south towards his office on Wendelstadt, in the city's ever-expanding suburbs. Circumventing the walls of the Hofburg Palace, he walked through the park. On one side were the gilded railings of the Hofgarten, the private palace garden – and on the other, the public Volksgarten with its ornamental plants and shrubs. Both were still covered with a blanket of snow.

At a brisk pace, snow crunching underfoot, he passed under the monumental arched Burgtor – the gate where the city wall had been partially breached by Napoleon's invading army fifty years before. Now, in less turbulent times, the young Emperor Franz Josef had ordered the pulling down of the old, eight-metre-high medieval city walls, together with the defensive walls and ditches in front of them. In recent years, this open land had been used as ceremonial parade grounds, and by market traders. Now it was to be redeveloped.

Isaac crossed the temporary access road linking the medieval city with the suburbs, across the deep chasm where the walls had been demolished. He looked down on the site now occupied by hundreds of wooden builders' huts and iron fencing. Momentarily overcome by the putrid smell of human and animal detritus churned up by the excavations, he placed a white handkerchief over his mouth.

Franz Josef had promised that the new development, known as the Ringstrasse, would outshine Haussmann's magnificent boulevards in Paris. Isaac and his father had seen the plans in the City Hall, which showed a grand boulevard flanked with magnificent buildings that would circle the old city – and included new government buildings, a palace, a theatre, opera house and public parks. Since the proposals had been announced, the elite of Vienna had been scrambling for sites to build palatial homes there – especially the wealthier Jews. One day, Isaac thought, he would have a house there too.

Isaac thought with some satisfaction how well things had gone for them since their move from Kornyn. Their timing had been fortuitous. Vienna had enjoyed peace and prosperity since the uprising in 1848 and subsequent liberal reforms. Although, for the first three years after they arrived, the Crimean war had been challenging. It had forced the Tarrants to trade overland to avoid the military action on the Black Sea. But since then, things had steadily improved. As a result, their business was now outperforming their wildest expectations – trade had boomed. They bought grain grown in the rich, black soil of Ukraine from the farmers and middlemen in the shtetls, a business Meyer knew inside out. And from warehouses in Odessa their ships crossed the Black Sea, sailing up the Danube to distribute it to Vienna and from there on by train to destinations all over central Europe. On the return journey they brought back whatever cargo they could sell on at a profit. Although not in the same league as the wealthy Ephrussi family, grain traders turned international bankers, the Tarrants were doing very well.

He and his father made a formidable team. Once Isaac finished university, he had used his legal skills to help Meyer develop the business. He had persuaded him to diversify, to cash in on the building boom in the city and trade in marble. Russian red was well priced, but not as fashionable as the whiter Italian marbles from Carrara. Gilders were also busy. He could never get over the amount of gold in this city – if you stood still for long enough in Vienna somebody would gild you. He smiled to himself at the thought.

For the Tarrants, the building frenzy had presented other opportunities. This rush to be part of the new Ringstrasse development meant that some of the older buildings, such as their new home, were available to rent for a reduced price.

It had been an excellent idea to move to Spiegelgasse, a symbol of their success. Unfortunately, this had not been acknowledged by the snobbish matrons of Viennese society. Although here the Jews were tolerated, the Tarrants were still considered *parvenu*. His mother didn't help – her French was poor, despite his offering to hire a private tutor for her, and French was the language of the social elite of the city. As for his grandmother, she was a lost cause – but at least she had a smattering of German. At home, they generally spoke Russian amongst themselves, occasionally Yiddish when no one else was around. Helena, like himself, thanks to her education, spoke French well. She had only the slightest of accents. But once they refurbished their house, hopefully they could start to entertain on a grander scale.

But his heart sank as he thought that these plans would have to wait. Before then, he had other problems to face. He had been shocked when he had heard the news at breakfast of Rosa and Moishe's impending visit. And familiar feelings of guilt and sadness returned at memories of her.

Rosa, Rosa, why was I not braver, he thought sadly. Why did I not stand up to them all? Instead, I allowed that witch to enchant me and fill me with desire that she never intended to fulfil. What kind of a woman is she not to want to be a mother? But, he thought sadly, he could not lay the blame entirely at his wife's door. He too had failed in aspects of their marriage. He knew, as a good Jewish husband, that it was his duty to pleasure and cherish his wife. He must try harder, then maybe they might find a way. He should not have riled her this morning, he thought guiltily. In fairness, Helena was no better, or worse, than most of the women he knew. And he had to admit she was beautiful – and desirable.

She had also been right about the house – and the portrait. As she had anticipated, Herr Lieberman had been impressed. He had been almost frothing at the mouth in anticipation of seeing the finished painting. Maybe the eccentric old man was right – Isaac had been amused when he had told him recently that to gain pleasure from objectified beauty was less complicated than dealing with the real thing. Certainly, less expensive. To have Lieberman as a partner, one of the city's wealthiest bankers, would pay the bills of Helena's expensive modiste for a long time to come. Yes, he thought with a pride mixed with sadness, Rosa would certainly be amazed at the transformation of their fortunes since they had left Kornyn.

~~~~~

Chapter 11

Rosa, Moishe and Samuil stood on Spiegelgasse, looking across the street at the townhouse, one up from the corner of Gluckgasse. Rosa's feet were cold and wet – her leather boots had split with all the walking on the hard cobbled streets.

"That cannot be it," she said, looking in horror at Moishe.

The townhouse was four storeys high, finished in cream plaster coursed to look like stone. The window surrounds were highly decorated and painted white. And over the arched wooden entrance door, at first-floor level, there was a balcony with ornate black railings where a builder's hoist had been temporarily set up. A workman in a shabby coat was in the process of carefully lowering a large bucket of rubble to another man waiting on the street below, his arms theatrically outstretched as if he was going to catch it.

"I think it is, my dear. What a handsome residence. It looks like they are refurbishing." said Moishe without enthusiasm.

"I hope it isn't a bad time to call – Lena did say three o'clock."

"How many families live here, Tata?" the boy asked in amazement.

"Just the one, I believe, Samuil," replied his father.

"They must be as rich as the Romanovs," said his son.

"Indeed, they must," said Moishe. "Come on, let's get this over with."

As they approached the entrance, the workman shouted to his colleague on the first floor, and he moved aside from the landed bucket. The skinny wretch, his skin darkened from the sun, nodded briefly, obviously unimpressed by the shabby visitors.

"There's no mezuzah on the door," whispered Rosa.

Moishe looked at her with raised eyebrows. As if to say, what did you expect? He lifted the heavy brass knocker. The door was opened almost immediately by a uniformed footman who took their coats. Then he showed the trio into a dining room fitted out with an oval-shaped table and fine, gilded damask-covered chairs. Although the room was modest in size, a glass chandelier hung from the ceiling, and a large, ornately framed mirror was on the far wall.

Rosa, looking nervously around the room, stood beside a chair.

"Sit down, Rosa – it is expected," said Moishe gently. "You too, Samuil."

Rosa reluctantly did as he suggested, trying to hide her split boots under the voluminous skirt of her well-worn black Shabbos dress. The hem was wet and dirty from the snow. She suddenly noticed how worn Moishe's good jacket looked. He was standing, still wearing his black Biber hat. His beard and long side-curls were now almost entirely grey. Seeing her anxious expression, he smiled at her with his soft brown eyes, and she breathed in slowly, trying to calm herself.

Rosa was dreading this meeting and had not slept a wink the previous evening thinking about it. She had never forgiven her sister. It had taken her a long time to swallow the shame of what had happened. Moishe had helped, of course – he had explained to her over and over again, how it had been the Lord's will, and that her future was intended to be with him. Moishe was a good man – a gentle man.

Rosa felt herself inhale sharply as Lena entered the room. She stood up awkwardly as her sister – like a beautiful painted doll wearing dress-up clothes, her hair uncovered and lighter than Rosa remembered – seemed to glide across the polished stone floor to greet her. She was wearing a fitted rose-coloured velvet costume trimmed with satin ribbon, with a soft, antique-lace collar, modestly pinned at the breast with an amethyst brooch set in gold. But, as Lena approached her, the light caught the side of her sister's face. Despite the application of face paint and powder, Rosa was shocked to see a scar, about five centimetres long that ran down the middle of her cheek.

"Lena!"

"Helena. It's Helena now, Rosa. It's better, more appropriate for here. And how are you, and Moishe – you both look so well. And this must be Samuil – I wouldn't have recognised you – quite the young man."

"What happened to your face?" asked Rosa, ignoring her greeting.

"It was an accident," Helena said dismissively, obviously not wishing to discuss it further. "And Samuil, I believe you are sick – you poor thing!"

Samuil, embarrassed with the sudden attention, coughed, nervously covering his mouth. Helena moved back slightly, as though afraid she would catch something.

"Samuil has asthma, Lena – it's not contagious," said Rosa sharply.

"Well, I'm afraid, this is the wrong city to visit for someone with asthma with all of the building works going on. And as you can see, we are doing work here ourselves. I must apologise for the dust. The house is in a mess at the moment, we are decorating the salon. You wouldn't believe how shabby it was when we moved in. Anyway, do sit down – please. How lovely to see you, after all this time. I must apologise for my mother-in-law,

Jessica, not being here to meet you, she is out visiting, and Bubbe Mim is in Berdichev. She went with Meyer to visit her sister – he had business there. We call her 'Grandmother' now, it's the Viennese way. So, I am afraid it is just me." She paused, smiling at Rosa.

But Rosa knew by the way her pupils had contracted that she was putting on a show for them – underneath it all, Rosa sensed Lena was just as nervous as she was.

"And how are the boys?" Helena asked.

"Well – as you know Josef and Reubin are now living in Odessa," Rosa said tentatively. "They found work in the docklands area, loading and unloading the grain-ships. Last month they wrote that they were working on one of Isaac's ships that had arrived from Constantinople."

"What a coincidence. If only I had known," Helena said flippantly. "And where are they staying?"

"With a Jewish widow. They are already involved with the community. Although, Tata is not happy. He is worried about anti-Jewish riots." Rosa shivered. "We pray that they stay safe."

"And Mama and Tata?"

"Oh, they are both well, they sent their love. At this stage, they are over Bubbe Sadie's death. She never really recovered after the bad cold she caught at Yom Kippur. She was dead by the time the snow had melted."

"Yes, Mama told me in her letter. I was so sorry not to have been able to visit and to support her while she sat shiva. But it wasn't possible with the roads at that time of year. At least now there is the train." Helena's eyes glistened and she wiped a tear from her eye at the thought of the old woman.

"No one expected you would," replied her sister without much sympathy.

"You plan to attend Herr Doctor Strauss?" said Helena, brittle and bright as she turned to Moishe.

"Yes, Berl Kunis, the apothecary, recommended him."

"The doctor has a good reputation, I believe. Will you be here for long?"

"As long as it takes to sort this young man out," Moishe said, smiling at his son.

Moishe and Helena chatted for several minutes about friends and neighbours in Kornyn, till they had exhausted their list of shared acquaintances.

During this superficial exchange, Rosa's anger built up inside her, conscious that what had happened between her and her sister had not been acknowledged. Thinking about it, she felt the colour rise in her face and neck until she felt her head and heart were both going to explode.

Then unable to contain these overwhelming emotions, she exclaimed, "I did *not* have a child. I was *never* pregnant!"

Samuil looked at her, alarmed.

"But you do have children, dear," Moishe said gently, looking over at her, then at his son, with a concerned look on his face.

"Yes, of course, Samuil and Perle, and I love them as if they had been my own." She breathed out slowly,

197

almost a sigh of relief. There, she had said it.

"The Lord saved you, Rosa," said Helena, looking uncomfortable. "I am glad to see you are so happy and content. Moishe obviously looks after you very well."

This was not the answer that Rosa wanted. She looked apprehensively at Moishe. His eyes pleaded with her to say no more. The heavy silence that ensued was filled with the muffled sounds of a builder banging upstairs.

"Oh, look at the time. My maid, Gretta, will be wondering where I am. She's German – such a treasure. You must come over again and visit, but now unfortunately I must go. The stuccadore is due to call – he has designs for the plasterwork for me to approve, but maybe ..."

Sounds of the front door opening distracted her.

"*Rosa! Moishe!*" Isaac burst into the room. "How wonderful to see you both – and this must be Samuil. How tall you are!" Isaac, hatless and clean-shaven, was elegantly dressed in a long dark-grey coat and a white shirt with an ornate pale-grey silk cravat.

Rosa felt she could not breathe, that she would faint. He strode across the room and took her trembling hand in his and kissed her fingers, not taking his eyes off her face.

"Rosa, you look well. I hope life has been good to you?"

"Yes, yes, it has. Thank you, Isaac," she said, lost for words.

"You are home early, Isaac," said Helena, obviously disconcerted by his entrance.

"Well, I couldn't miss seeing our family from Kornyn. And now that you are here, hopefully we will all be able to spend some time together."

Helena's face fell, and Rosa's heart soared.

Chapter 12

Rosa had been up since six, to make sure they were all washed and dressed to attend morning prayers with Rabbi Shulman.

He lived in the top-floor apartment of one of the two five-storey houses built in front of the old Stadttempel, the city's synagogue. When they had arrived, Rabbi Shulman had explained to Moishe and Rosa that when it was built only Catholic churches could be seen from the streets – other religions' buildings had to be hidden from public view. But, despite having no visible exterior, on the inside the synagogue was the most magnificent building that Rosa had ever seen.

The first morning she had attended morning prayers, she had stood in awe as she surveyed the spectacular view from the two-tiered women's gallery. She could see waves of shtreimel hats and kippahs. The men wearing prayer shawls, with phylacteries – the small leather cubes containing tiny rolls of parchment inscribed with verses from the Torah – strapped to their arms and heads. While overhead a magnificent dome with a central lantern light cast a transcendent glow over the proceedings. Overcome by its beauty, looking up at the dome, Rosa imagined this was what heaven was like. Here at the Stadttempel she could feel her people's history in her bones – in sharp contrast to the humble, wooden structure in Kornyn.

The Rabbi's apartment on the other hand, despite its palatial interiors, felt suffocating. It was awkward living there. Rabbi Shulman was elderly and set in his ways – and although he had treated them with nothing but kindness, Rosa was feeling more anxious with their situation by the day. She could not even help in the kitchen, as the Viennese Jewish widow who looked after the Rabbi insisted on treating Rosa like a visitor, making her feel even more beholden.

They had been in Vienna for a month at this stage, and she had visited the house on Spiegelgasse several times. After their first awkward meeting, Moishe and Samuil had escorted her to the house but had declined to go in.

Rosa suspected that Helena, as she insisted on being called, carefully orchestrated these visits. They were unnecessarily formal occasions, arranged during the afternoon when Isaac and Meyer were still at the office. Bubbe Mim and Jessica were usually present, and the women drank tea from beautiful china cups and picked at a selection of dainty cakes. As Helena and Jessica boasted about the comfort of their new lives, Rosa listened politely while inwardly seething. Sensing this, the kindly Bubbe Mim would routinely attempt to turn the conversation to reminisce with Rosa about Kornyn, and the people they knew there. However, Helena or Jessica invariably changed the subject. As a result, Rosa had not been able to have a private conversation with her sister. Although she relished the thought of unleashing her anger at Lena, she had become resigned to the situation, and accepted that it would not be in her best interests to do so – and that maybe it was just as well that Lena had put those defences in place.

During the time they had spent in Vienna, Rosa and Samuil had also attended several consultations with Doctor Strauss.

The Austrian doctor was not what Rosa had initially imagined. She had expected some worthy gentleman, quiet and unassuming. Instead, he was a rather debonair character who wore outrageous clothes. Rosa wondered how she would ever take such a man seriously. But the doctor seemed to know what he was talking about and had conducted several examinations of Samuil, using his listening tube, or stethoscope as he called it. He had also taken detailed notes of Samuil's diet, exercise, and personal habits.

In between visits to Doctor Strauss and the Tarrants, while Moishe was with the Rabbi, Rosa's days had been spent with Samuil. In the morning, once prayers were over, they would usually visit one of the city's sights. But after an hour, or two, at the most, Samuil's cough became persistent. His wheezing was so alarming that they were forced to sit down somewhere, and drink tea which they bought from a street vendor. Once he had recovered sufficiently, they would return to the apartment to spend a long afternoon in the drawing room. Rosa crocheted and Samuil looked at the Rabbi's books. These were mostly theological texts written in Hebrew, and Samuil quickly became bored. So, she usually ended up playing cards with him. As a result of their time spent together, she had become closer to the boy.

Samuil had made his Bar Mitzvah two years ago, and he was now fifteen. He was still at that awkward transitional stage when a boy changes into a man. His chin was covered with fine dark hairs – a "baby beard" he, self-deprecatingly, called it. He was tall for his age, not as tall as his father, but she guessed that one day he would be. Rosa felt there was a lovely quality of innocence, together with a sharp intelligence, about him. Often when Moishe was being particularly obtuse – not understanding that ordinary folk's lives were not centred on the Lord – Samuil would catch her eyes and they would share a moment of amusement, a conspiracy of silent laughter against the unworldly Moishe. The boy also had a wicked sense of humour, and he would mimic Doctor Strauss, repeating in heavily accented Yiddish something he had said, and they would both end up doubled over with laughter.

***

They had been in Vienna longer than they had initially intended, and at this stage Rosa knew that Moishe was anxious to get home. Today she was making her way with Samuil to the doctor's rooms near the General Hospital on the far side of Schotten Thor on Alser Gasse. They were both unusually quiet. Their appointment with the consultant was at ten o'clock and he was to give his summation of the results of the tests he had carried out over the previous week's visits.

"Will I need surgery do you think, Rosa?" the boy asked nervously.

"No, I shouldn't think so. I am not sure what he is going to suggest, possibly a combination of drugs and exercises. Anyway, don't worry – I suspect it will be nothing too onerous."

Samuil, a head taller than her, was wearing one of his father's old jackets that she had adjusted for him.

"It would be wonderful to know that I had a future," he said shyly.

"What do you mean? Of course you have a future. Your whole life is in front of you."

"Do I really, Rosa? The way I am, can you see me being able to work, to marry and have children?"

"Of course, Samuil! A handsome boy like you – any girl would be honoured to be your wife."

"Honour? Like you honour Tata?"

"Samuil, I don't know what you are implying," she said, annoyed, her eyes flashing in anger. She stopped to look up at him. "Your Tata and I are devoted."

"I understood, you know, what you meant, the day we arrived," he said sheepishly. "When you said to Aunt Helena that you weren't pregnant after she left. My friends told me what happened to you with the Russian soldier, down at the lake – how you were betrothed to Uncle Isaac, and that he abandoned you and took your sister instead."

"Samuil, that was a long time ago." She lowered her eyes, embarrassed that he knew of her humiliation.

"I don't want a pity-match with any girl. I want to know love – in the spiritual – and the physical sense."

"Samuil, you should speak to your father about this." His honesty and vulnerability shocked her, cutting her like a knife.

"You know that's not possible," he replied, his eyes downcast. "Tata is not concerned with earthly pleasure, only divine reward."

"You are wrong, Samuil, he would understand," she said, hearing her own uncertainty.

"Anyway, whatever happens today with the doctor, Rosa, I have really enjoyed these weeks here." He changed the subject artfully, skilfully making the point that he was no longer a child. "This visit is an experience

I will never forget. The city is amazing. Although I had seen drawings of the palaces, nothing prepares you for the grandeur of the place. So much stone and stucco."

"And gold," she said, smiling. And, although she was grateful to him for not embarrassing her further, her heart went out to him.

"Tata says that it's a gilded cage for its citizens," he said enthusiastically, "except it isn't, is it? It's not a cage. Quite the opposite – you feel free here. Very few people have spat at me or called me names. But what I have really enjoyed is spending time with you, Rosa."

She squeezed his arm as he started a fit of coughing before she knocked on the door of the doctor's rooms.

Dr Strauss had a florid complexion, thick moustaches, and was prematurely bald. Today he was wearing a pair of yellow-tartan, patterned trousers and a brown fashionably cut, sack coat. Rosa's eyes were drawn to the ornate gold watch which was dangling on a chain from his breast pocket.

"Let's have a listen to your chest today, young man." He opened the drawer of his desk and drew out the familiar stethoscope. Maybe you would take off your jacket and shirt for me."

Samuil undressed, handing Rosa his clothes, then sat in the chair to one side as the doctor inserted the ivory earpieces – these were connected by a woven tube to a narrow wooden cylinder which he placed against Samuil's chest.

"Now just breathe in and out slowly for me," the doctor said. "And again," as he moved the head of the instrument to the other side.

Rosa looked at the protruding ribs in his painfully narrow chest and thought of their earlier conversation. And her heart heaved with pity for the boy. How she loved him and, yes, almost as if he were her own.

Once the doctor had finished his examination, he returned to his seat, and Samuil put on his shirt and jacket.

"Well, Frau Cohen and Herr Cohen, I have finished my observations. As your local apothecary, Berl Kunis, correctly surmised, Samuil has asthma. A disease known about since Egyptian times. But it was the Roman doctor, Hippocrates, who gave it its name – asthma – the gasping disease. The good news is that you won't die from it. Not if you live a life of moderation and avoid undue physical excess. Are you a good scholar, Samuil? I suspect you are. I would strongly advise you to follow your father's line of work and avoid any unnecessary physical activity. There are also other things that you can do to alleviate your condition. Diet is important, although some foods may act as a trigger for your symptoms, and you can try to identify these. But you must eat well, fresh food. Eat as much beef as you can. Eggs too are beneficial."

"Is there a cure, Doctor?" Rosa asked.

"A period spent in my clinic in Neulengbach should bring about a marked improvement. It is situated on the edges of the Vienna Woods on the foothills of the Alps.

The air there is purer, away from the putrid air of this city. I could educate Samuil in managing his condition. In the clinic, I can give him a course of treatment that I am developing, using antispasmodics and nervous depressants. I use morphine, chloroform, and asthma cigarettes. I can also control his diet – kosher, of course – to see which foods exacerbate his symptoms and supervise an exercise regime. And of course, the mountain air has its own healing qualities. It won't be a complete cure, but Samuil should at least be able to enjoy a normal life. If his father's calling didn't suit, he could work at something not too strenuous. Like in a shop, or a counting house. He would be a new man," he added patronisingly, "able to chase after any young girl he chose."

Samuil started coughing profusely.

"But there is another aspect to this disease … Maybe you would wait in the reception, Samuil, while I have a discussion with your stepmother."

"I'd rather stay, Doctor," said Samuil calmly.

"Samuil, maybe it would be better if you do what the doctor suggests," Rosa said, smiling kindly at him.

He got up, and rather sulkily left the room.

"*Hmm*, Frau Cohen," Doctor Strauss said once the door was closed. He leant forward, his elbows on his desk and his hands joined so that his soft white fingertips were touching. "There is another aspect to this disease. It is also considered to be an emotional disorder. Triggered by extreme nervous reactions. In Samuil's case, I can't help noticing how attached he is to you. In my experience, for a young man to be attached to his mother, or in his case stepmother, is not a healthy situation. Underlying repressed feelings of sexual desire can lead to physical and mental frustration – and if these are ongoing, they can lead to serious nervous and physical disorder, such as asthma. So, for this reason also, a period away from you and the family would also do Samuil the world of good."

Rosa sat back in her chair, shocked.

"You are mistaken, Doctor. Because there is only ten years difference in our age, we are more like brother and elder sister. Anyway," she said boldly, "is it not common for young boys to be infatuated by older women?"

"Not to this extent, Mrs Cohen, where his physical health is being affected."

"I am not sure what to say, Doctor Strauss, except that I am alarmed at your diagnosis." She paused, trying to make sense of what he said. "Your clinic, how long would he have to stay for any definite improvement?"

"Three months minimum."

"And the cost? She asked anxiously.

"Fifty gulden a month. That includes full board, of course." Seeing her alarm, he added, "I could accept instalments – say, spread over a year. As it happens, I have a place coming up in a few weeks' time."

"I will have to discuss this with my husband," she said, trying to sound as though his proposal was a possibility, although inside her heart was sinking.

"Of course," he said bowing his head. "I appreciate it is a lot of money. But you will find that the results are remarkable."

She rose to go. "Thank you, Doctor Strauss."

"Maybe you will let my receptionist Frau Frankel know of your decision, after you have talked to Herr Cohen," he said as he opened the door for her.

As Samuil got up to follow her, she avoided looking him in the eye.

"Well, what was so important that he couldn't talk about it in front of me," he said once they were outside.

"Oh, Samuil, I don't know where to start."

He put his hand on her arm and pulled her to face him.

She eventually said, looking at him shyly, "He was making the point that you need ... to be given some independence, and he is recommending you go to his clinic for three months, a sanatorium of sorts in the Alps."

"I would have to leave you, and Tata," he said in alarm.

"It would only be for three months," she said reassuringly. "He thinks that he can improve your condition immeasurably. That you would – provided you follow his regime – be able to lead a normal life."

The boy looked stunned, but she could see hope in his eyes.

"But these things are expensive. How could we possibly afford it?"

"I will have to talk to your father."

Samuil started wheezing again, gasping for breath.

"Can we sit down for a while, Rosa?"

She opened her purse and found her last few coins.

"No, I am tired too – let's take a cab."

***

That evening she had pulled Rabbi Shulman to one side and asked him to show Samuil his collection of fossils that he kept in a wooden cabinet of curiosities in his study. She told him she wanted time to talk privately to Moishe about the doctor's recommendations.

Moishe had listened attentively, his brown eyes tender and understanding as she told him the prognosis and explained about the various triggers for his son's disease. She also told him about the clinic, and the cost of the three-month programme.

"*Oy vey*, such a lot of money!" he said, horrified. "More than the Rabbi pays me in a year."

She then went on to explain the doctor's hypothesis that Samuil's attachment to her was a root cause of his condition and that a period of separation under the circumstances would also be beneficial.

"*That is preposterous!*" shouted Moishe.

In all the years of their marriage, she had never seen him so angry.

"The boy is as innocent as a lamb! That he should have such thoughts is beyond belief."

"Moishe, he is no longer a boy. He is a man. In the

211

Lord's eyes he is a grown man and should be married by now. Maybe the doctor has a point."

"Then we will get him a wife," Moishe said grimly.

"Well, it is not that easy. Samuil is concerned himself, about his condition. He ..." She paused, trying to find the right words. "He is not sure that he could be a husband, the way he is now."

"You have talked to him about this?" he said, aghast.

"Yes, Moishe. I am supposed to be his mother."

He lowered his head, unable to look her in the eye.

"And us? You have talked to him about us?"

"No, Moishe," she said, horrified. "How could you think that of me? I would never dream of discussing our relationship with anyone else."

He looked relieved, then took both her hands in his. "The Lord sent you to me, Rosa." He smiled, his eyes shining with tears of love. "Tomorrow I will talk to Rabbi Shulman, ask his advice."

"No, please don't, Moishe. This decision we make ourselves," she said determinedly.

He looked surprised. It was unusual for her to question his decisions in this way.

"You think our son should go to the clinic?"

"Yes. I want him to have the life he deserves. To be able to work and to have a wife – and children of his own. The doctor has promised me all of this is possible."

"Well. We will see what we can do. The good Lord will show us a way."

"No, Moishe, we cannot wait for providence, we must act now. The doctor has a place in three weeks' time. We wouldn't want to lose this opportunity. I can go to Lena, to Isaac, and ask to borrow the money."

Moishe threw his head back suddenly, his teeth bared, and his nostrils flared in anger.

"*No, under no circumstances. I forbid it.*"

"Moishe, she is my sister!"

"She is the devil! And her husband is not much better. He abandoned you, Rosa, he threw you aside as if you were a wounded animal."

"But Moishe," she pleaded, trying to calm him down, "as you said the Lord looked after me. I – we both – got the better bargain."

"Listen to me, Rosa, I absolutely forbid you to ask your sister, or her husband, for money. As I said, I will talk to the Rabbi, he will know what to do. I will also write to my father and ask for a loan. Now, I do not want to talk about this further."

Chapter 13

It was a cold, bright morning with a clear blue sky and the sun cast long shadows on the narrow, cobbled streets around Stadttempel and the Jewish quarter, so that some of them were almost in darkness. This was Rosa's first time to venture out alone in the city – it was not considered appropriate for respectable Jewish women to be seen unaccompanied in public. But her annoyance with Moishe, for once, gave her the courage to be rebellious.

Samuil, overtired after the previous day's exertions, was resting in the apartment, and Moishe was spending the day in quiet contemplation. Following her discussion with her husband, after prevaricating for a few days, he had eventually talked to Rabbi Shulman. Rosa knew that this had been hard for him. Moishe was a proud man who rarely asked for help, usually confident that either the Lord, or he himself, could provide. But for the boy's sake, and Rosa's, he had talked to the Rabbi.

Rabbi Shulman knew Doctor Strauss, a respected member of their community, and he had heard of the good work the doctor was doing. But after deliberating on Moishe's dilemma, the Rabbi suggested that Samuil was not the responsibility of the good people of Vienna. He was sure that the Jewish community in Kornyn would be delighted to help raise funds for such a virtuous boy. He advised Moishe to write to his father, Rabbi Cohen, who would do whatever was necessary.

Rosa knew by Moishe's reaction following this meeting that he was disappointed with the Rabbi's response. All around him Moishe could see the obvious wealth of the Jews in Vienna. Of course, there were many who were living in dire poverty in damp basements and attics throughout the city. But in the synagogue, on Shabbos, when everyone was dressed in their finery, finding money for the collective good did not seem to be a problem.

So Moishe, reluctantly, had written to his father. But Rosa could tell he was not quite as confident as Rabbi Shulman that his father could help. Kornyn was a small market town and, although the Jewish congregation was sizable, the wealth of the few successful merchants was not enough to mitigate the overall poverty of the majority living there. As a result, his father constantly struggled with insufficient funds to run the synagogue and support his family. Although Isaac's mother's family had been relatively well off, in recent years their haulage business had suffered badly with the development of the railroads and now they too had money worries of their own.

Unsurprisingly, Rabbi Cohen had written back explaining that, although it broke his heart to tell him this, he was not in a position to lend him money. He regretted also to tell him that in a recent storm the roof had blown off the wooden synagogue, and he himself had needed to borrow money from local merchants to get it fixed. He requested that the family return to Kornyn as soon as possible. He needed Moishe's support, as he was too old at this stage to supervise the workmen himself. Together they would pray to the Lord to intercede on Samuil's behalf.

When Moishe had told Rosa this, and of his intention to travel home as soon as he could to help his father, she had been furious with him for not putting Samuil's needs first. Her frosty demeanour had let him know that in no uncertain terms.

So when her sister had sent an invitation to meet in a coffee house near Stephansplatz, Rosa had accepted without first, as she normally would, asking Moishe's permission.

Rosa had been nervous initially when she left the apartment. The fact that she knew so little German didn't help either – for this she normally relied on Samuil. However, her mood lifted as she entered Stephansplatz, and she gazed appreciatively at the cathedral's main entrance. The bright sunshine illuminated the Giant's doorway and twin Heathen Towers and cast the sculptured details of the medieval facade into sharp relief. But her apprehension returned as she crossed the plaza towards Kärntner Strasse and she was heckled by a toothless crone who shoved apples at her, speaking in a tongue she had never heard. The woman was blue with the cold even though she was encased in multiple layers of rags.

Rosa thought about the sharp contrasts between the conspicuous wealth of some Viennese citizens compared to the abject poverty of others. But despite this blatant inequality, this trip to Vienna had shown her another world outside the narrow confines of her home in Kornyn – a new and glamorous world full of possibilities. This was the life she should have had. Rosa felt bitterness rise in her throat, and not for the first time during this visit. She should have had Lena's pampered life of servants and fine clothes, with nothing to worry about other than selecting wallpaper for the salon, or a ladder in her silk stocking. And Isaac, of course. She should have had Isaac.

The few times they had met, she had sensed he was still attracted to her. She herself had certainly felt a desire rise that she had considered long dormant. Rosa had tried to quell these thoughts, pleasant to ponder but futile to dwell on – she had her own life now.

At least, unlike her sister, who seemed to be despised by Isaac's family, Rosa was surrounded by people who loved her. Rosa had grown to love Moishe's family. She missed them and, of course, she missed Mama and Tata.

Thinking about home in this bustling city, she suddenly felt alone. But if she was honest with herself, apart from seeing her family, she was dreading going back to Kornyn. The perpetual grind and hardship of their daily lives was difficult to bear.

Although she still helped her mother to make goods for the market, the income was a pittance, hardly worth the effort involved. The truth was she felt an emptiness in her life, particularly since she had not been blessed with children of her own. Perle was a young woman now and busy with her friends and school – she no longer depended on her stepmother so much. And Rosa's parents, who were still relatively young and in good health, also seemed to have managed well enough without her over the last few weeks. If only she had an occupation.

Rosa pulled the woollen collar of her coat around her neck as she entered Kärntner Strasse. It was cold, and coffee-coloured snow accumulated on street corners and in building alcoves. But the stone streets here in the main shopping area had been swept clean. The people were cleaner too, she thought, smiling to herself. Military men were dressed in brass-buttoned greatcoats over blue trousers with polished black boots. The officers were distinguished by their feathered helmets and steel ceremonial swords which glistened in the sun. How sombre the Jews looked in contrast. Particularly when compared to the Hungarian visitors from across the border – the women in full skirts, with oriental-style brocade waistcoats, and brightly coloured woollen jackets.

Normally with Samuil, she would make a joke about the vanity and pomp of the people she passed. However, today she longed to be a part of their glamorous world. She pulled her threadbare coat around her, but it had little warmth. She had never been so painfully aware of her shabbiness, her poverty. At only twenty-five she felt like an old woman.

Rosa glanced longingly at the shop windows filled with luxuries she could only dream of owning: sumptuous fur coats, purses, valises, and boots of the finest leather.

Despite dawdling, she was still early by the time she reached Kaffeehaus Herzog, where she had agreed to meet her sister, and waited for her at the door not liking to go in alone.

As she lingered, she stood gazing in the window of a hat shop beside the café, filled with fabulous creations of feathered, jewelled, and ribboned hats. Bonnets of the palest straw were decorated with silk roses so real looking that she imagined you could almost smell them. She examined with interest how the hats were constructed, and decorated with nets, and gauzes studded with tiny, jewelled stars. If only she could make hats like these – they were like works of art, each a masterpiece in its own right.

It was no wonder that women were so enthralled with hats. Even the poorest Jewish woman had a special scarf, or a modest hat for special occasions. Rosa's fingers reassuringly felt her own colourful tichel that she had embroidered and decorated with felt and magenta-coloured silk flowers. When your hair was shorn, she mused, a hat helped hide the nakedness of your lost femininity.

Helena was late, almost twenty minutes, but Rosa didn't notice. She stared at the hats, and as she did so an idea begin to form in her mind – a crazy idea. She breathed in the crisp air and arched her back. No, she was not an old woman – she wasn't going to give up just yet.

Eventually a smart black carriage pulled up, and the driver, wearing distinctive black-and-gold braided livery, jumped down from his seat to help Helena onto the street.

"Why didn't you go in, Rosa – get us a good table beside a window?" said Helena, exasperated, after she had summarily dismissed Gretta her maid, telling her to go to the fancy goods shop and buy her ribbon.

When they were seated in the bustling salon, Helena took off her gloves and lay them carefully on the table.

"Bubbe Mim not with you today?" asked Rosa.

"No, she had a migraine. Too much schnapps more like," said Helena waspishly, smiling at her sister.

"So why the summons?" asked Rosa archly.

"I knew you saw the doctor last week and I hadn't heard from you. I wondered when you were going home. Thought we should at least meet before you did." She spoke dispassionately, but then seemed to suddenly notice that her sister was looking unusually animated. "You look well today, Rosa, there is a bloom on your cheeks. I hope you haven't been using rouge. Tata would not approve."

"No, of course not. It's the wind – it is so cold and dry today."

"So how did you get on with Doctor Strauss? Did I ask you before – is he any relation to the musician?"

"You did, and no he's not. The only organs he's interested in are human ones."

"And his diagnosis?"

"Well, he feels that it might be a combination of things. That is why we are still here. Doctor Strauss considers that his condition could be physical, an intolerance to certain foods, or pollen. Or it could be a physical reaction to his emotional state."

"Oh, that sounds mysterious," Helena said eagerly. "How can it be emotional?"

"Well, the Doctor is concerned that he may be overly attached to me."

"To you! But you are his mother."

"Yes, I am his mother. Although I think he considers me to be more like a big sister. He can remember his real mother quite well – he was six when she died. As I am sure you will recall," Rosa said bitterly.

"Look let's not dig all that up again, or I'll leave. I already told you, Rosa. I made the best of a bad situation. Isaac was never going to marry you after what happened."

"Maybe he would have once he realised that I wasn't pregnant. If you hadn't stolen him from me."

Helena got abruptly to her feet. "Look, Rosa, I am sorry if life hasn't worked out for you. You could have waited and married someone else."

"Who would have had me? My life is ... fine, most of the time. Lena, please sit down. I have been thinking. Maybe you could help me. It might ease your conscience."

"My conscience is not bothering me, sister!" she snapped, then moderating her tone, said, "Look, Rosa, I find this raking over the past tiresome. You cannot continue to blame me for what happened. Surely you must accept some responsibility for the choices you made."

"Please sit down, Lena – sorry, Helena. I need your help," Rosa said through gritted teeth, refusing to react to her sister's harsh words.

Helena, eyebrows raised, bowed her head slightly and then sat down.

Rosa told her sister of her dilemma, how she wanted Samuil to be able to attend Doctor Strauss's clinic and that she would like to stay in Vienna for a while. She admitted that being in Vienna had made her see that another life was possible for her. And that she dreaded returning to Kornyn.

"Do you love Moishe?"

"Yes, in a way," said Rosa, not meeting her sister's eyes and fidgeting with her purse.

"Does he love you?"

"Yes, I think so."

"Is he cruel to you? Does he beat you?"

"No," said Rosa, looking at her sister's cheek so that Helena's hand flew up, almost involuntarily, to touch it. "I don't love him as a wife should," Rosa added quickly, looking from her sister's scar directly into her eyes. "And you and Isaac. It has worked out?"

"Isaac and I understand one another."

"You love him?" Rosa asked, eyes flashing.

"He loves me. Although he does not always show it. Rosa, you need to leave this bitterness behind you. You have a good husband, you know. Not the most attractive of men – I realise it must be trying – the physical side anyway?" She raised her eyebrows and paused, inviting Rosa to share her confidences.

Rosa shrugged, as if it were of no importance and indicating she had no intention of discussing this aspect of her relationship.

"Some days are harder than others. But my new family are a great comfort – Samuil and Perle love me – and Rabbi Cohen and his wife treat me like a daughter. But I worry about our future. When the Rabbi dies, Moishe will not take over."

"Isn't that what usually happens in rabbinical families?"

"Moishe is not a leader of men. The Rabbi has a nephew who has recently joined the community. He is more persuasive than Moishe, more learned – younger anyway. He is the person that people will look to. Moishe has already accepted this. He says he can just about cope

223

with his own worries without taking on the rest of the world's. He will continue to help to organise things. But we will lose the house. We could only afford to rent something very basic. It would be the final indignity," she said, her knuckles white.

"Leave him, you are still attractive. In fact, Isaac was only saying yesterday that now you have put on a bit of weight – you were always so scrawny – you are the image of me. You could find someone else. Leave Moishe, come to Vienna, eventually he will divorce you."

"You make everything sound so simple, Lena. You always did. I could not hurt Moishe. But I have been thinking: my life in Kornyn would be so much better, easier anyway, if I was able to do something useful. But I have no education, and I speak only a little German, and Russian. If I could earn some money for the children, I could give them a start in the world. A bit like our own mother. But the things she makes, jam and schnapps, are now in ready supply at the market. I need to learn to make something different."

"Well, you always had beautiful hands for sewing, as well, of course, as your amazing feet."

Rosa, with a wan smile looked down sadly at her split leather boots.

"My feet are covered in chilblains now, not so lovely to look at anymore. But my hands are still good." She splayed out her long supple fingers. "And yes, I was thinking along those lines."

"So how could I possibly help?" Helena said dismissively.

"Well, I would like to work for a milliner, be an apprentice if you like. There are no milliners in Kornyn, everyone makes their own hats, or gets them made in Kiev which is such a long way away. I could also make tichels for Jewish women. Maybe eventually I could even open my own shop."

"Would you, Rosa, really? It would be terribly degrading having to kowtow to all of those demanding rich women."

"Like you, Lena," she couldn't resist saying.

"*Moi*, I am always a pleasure to deal with."

"That's what they tell you, sister. When you are gone, they probably call you a vixen and a painted hussy."

"I doubt it, they are too fond of my money. Anyway, fascinating as your dreams are, Rosa, what has all of this to do with me?"

"Oh, you could give me an introduction to one of your milliners – get them to take me on."

"You are joking, sister. I would be a laughingstock amongst all my rich friends. I can just hear them saying – did you know her sister works in a hat shop? Anyway, Isaac would not hear of it."

"No one need know, Rosa. We don't need to tell anyone."

"Where would you live?"

"With you."

"Absolutely not. As you know, we have the builders in – we have no spare space."

"I can sleep in the attic, in a servant's room. All I need is a bed. I would only work in the mornings. In the afternoons I could make myself useful – mend your clothes – act as your duenna when you go out. Don't you normally have to take Bubbe Mim everywhere with you? If you lend me some of your old clothes, I would be more presentable. You could tell everyone that I am a paid companion."

"*Mm*," said Helena, toying with the idea. "I suppose I could get rid of that bloody old crone going everywhere with me. She stinks of drink, had you noticed?"

"No, I hadn't noticed. But yes, you would be free of her. I would also be discreet." Rosa looked at her sister from under arched brows. "Would I have to pay you?"

"Well yes, you would need to lend me one-hundred and fifty gulden for Samuil's medical bills, and you would probably have to pay the milliner. If you dress me, I can live on very little. Think of it as a loan. I promise I would pay you back every florin, eventually."

"That is a lot of money, Rosa, even for us," Helena said in disbelief. "I would have to ask Isaac and I very much doubt that he would agree to it."

"He might be glad to help me. I mean, the family."

"*Hmm*," Helena said, her brain obviously working overtime. "Let me think about it and I'll talk to him. I'll get back to you as soon as I can, and I'll give you my answer. But, sister, don't get your hopes up. It all sounds very fanciful to me. For how long do you propose to stay in Vienna?"

"Just for three months, enough to complete a basic training with a milliner and for Samuil to complete his course in the clinic."

Helena bent her head to one side and gave her sister a quizzical stare. "Moishe will never agree to this."

"Oh, he will, Lena – leave Moishe to me."

***

As Rosa walked back to Stadttempel, she felt elated. It wasn't just the rush that the strong coffee and sweet sugary cakes had given her. She was delighted with the prospect of her plan. After her initial shock, Lena had been surprisingly receptive. At least, she hadn't dismissed the idea out of hand. Her sister probably did feel bad on some level for what had happened. And Rosa felt sure that Isaac would want to help her. There certainly did not seem to be any shortage of money – and what she was suggesting was a loan – he would be repaid in full. It was, in all, a practical solution.

But what surprised her was that her sister hadn't balked too much at the prospect of her living in her home for a while. She did not seem to be concerned that Isaac still had feelings for her, that he might still be attracted to her. Rosa mentally scolded herself at her self-delusion. Look at me, a black scraggy crow, amongst fabulous peacocks – who would be bothered looking at me? Even Moishe isn't interested in me, she thought sadly.

***

The following evening Rosa stood by the window, holding the note from her sister that her servant had just delivered, breathing in slowly to calm herself. She had been pacing around the room, waiting for Moishe to return from evening prayers. It was dusk, and she watched as a manservant lit an oil lamp in the drawing room of the apartment block opposite. Somewhere on the narrow street, someone was playing Mozart on a harpsichord, the intensity of the music heightening her feelings of anxiety. There was an openness about this city that was unnerving sometimes. It was as if its citizens welcomed the envious gaze of others. Unlike the shuttered windows of Kornyn.

The door opened, and Moishe entered the room. He immediately walked over to the window to close the shutters.

"Rosa, you want to let all of the heat out?" he said in exasperation.

"Sorry, Moishe, I wasn't thinking."

"We don't want Rabbi Shulman to think that we are taking advantage of his generosity."

"Well, I wanted to talk to you about that, Moishe."

"Look Rosa, I know you are upset. But we must face facts – we cannot afford to let Samuil go to the clinic. We simply don't have the money – not now anyway. But if we save, maybe in a few years' time we might look at it again."

"So, you would sacrifice Samuil's life for your pride?"

"That's harsh, Rosa. And not fair. I simply don't wish to be beholden to a man who treated you so appallingly."

"Moishe." She took his hands in hers. He looked miserable. "Moishe, the money we need for Samuil is only part of our problems. Since your cousin Ephraim arrived and established himself in the synagogue, our circumstances have changed. If anything were to happen now to your father, and one day it will – we would be homeless."

"Do you think that I have not thought about that, Rosa? I have thought about nothing else since my cousin arrived. And it is all the more reason to accept that we cannot afford this treatment for Samuil. But I don't want you to worry. When the time comes, I will get a job as a counter or a scribe, for one of the local merchants."

"Moishe, there are enough educated young boys now from the Russian schools who can do that for a pittance. Scribes are not valued the way they once were, things have moved on."

"Well, I could work for a grain merchant, or a tannery."

"Really –"

"Don't worry, Rosa, the Lord will answer our prayers and show us a way," he said firmly, as if to close the subject.

"No, Moishe, I am done with waiting for the Lord to show us the way. Kornyn is full of people waiting for the Lord to show them the way – and in a hundred years' time, they will still be waiting! Being here in Vienna has shown me – you make your own destiny."

"Rosa, the Lord –"

"I still believe – don't worry, husband. But the Lord has shown me another way. I have decided on a plan."

"You, wife, have decided on a plan!" Angry and humiliated, his veins were standing out on his neck.

"I intend to stay here in Vienna while Samuil is in the clinic."

"And how do you propose we pay for that?"

"Hear me out, please. I will spend the time he is in Neulengbach to learn a craft that I can use to help support our family in Kornyn. I am a good needlewoman, and the clothes and hats that I make for myself have always been admired. I will enlist the help of one of the milliners here in Vienna to teach me the secrets of the trade – to show me how to create fashionable hats, and scarves."

"Someone will do that out of the kindness of their hearts, no doubt?"

"My sister has offered to make an introduction for me in Tissot's hat shop on Kärntner Strasse. I would work for free. I noticed that Frau Kauffman struggles with some of the Jewish women who speak neither German nor French." She waved her sister's note in her hand. "Lena will let me stay with her for three months."

"What? No, Rosa – no! Absolutely not. I forbid it." He banged his fist on the sideboard, so that a Dresden ornamental figure of a crinolined lady wobbled noisily but did not fall.

"Let me finish, Moishe. And Isaac has agreed to lend me the money for Samuil."

"Rosa, what devil has possessed you? You have deliberately gone against my wishes and discussed this matter with your sister!"

Moishe's eyes bulged with fury, and she could see the blue veins throbbing at his temples. He grabbed Rosa's wrist and held it tightly. He was hurting her. In all the years of their marriage, she had never seen him so angry.

"You will not do this, Rosa – I forbid it. We are going home tomorrow. This depraved city is obviously having a detrimental influence on you."

"Let me go, Moishe!"

He released her abruptly, and she rubbed her wrist, red with the marks of his fingers.

"Very well, Moishe. I had hoped it would not come to this. I will apply for a get," she said calmly.

"A get – a divorce, are you mad? On what grounds?"

"That I was forced to marry you against my will, which as you know is forbidden in the Talmud. Maybe that is the reason that the Lord has not blessed our union with children –"

His anger suddenly deflated, and his eyes filled with tears. "I am sorry, Rosa. I have not been able to give you

231

your own children. But you have Samuil and Perle. I thought you were happy – that we were happy. Please Rosa, I love you," his voice shuddered, "don't leave me."

"You have been a good husband, Moishe," she said kindly to him, hating to see him so upset, "but this is important to me, and to *our* son Samuil. I will only return to Kornyn if we can have some quality of life. I am not prepared to sit back and accept the inevitability of our declining prospects any longer."

He sat down on the chair and put his hands on his knees.

"So, you will stay with the wife-beater?"

"I don't believe he beat her. She never said that."

He took out a large, crumpled linen handkerchief and dried his wet eyes.

"How do I know you will come back to me? That you won't stay in Vienna."

"It is February now – I will be back with Samuil by the summer."

He rose and took her hands in his.

"Do you promise me, Rosa?"

"Yes, Moishe, I promise."

He nodded, slowly rose and head bent left the room.

Rosa sat down in a chair and closed her eyes. She was shaking and felt spent with the emotion of it all. The sounds of Mozart could still be heard in the distance.

Chapter 14

Dublin
2011

It was Saturday afternoon. In Sal's kitchen Ben was drinking coffee waiting for Julie and Daisy to arrive. His sister was showing him a box of assorted silver items belonging to the family that she had brought down from the attic.

Ben examined a pair of small silver cups. The engraving on them was of tall, narrow, pitched-roof houses and stylised leaves.

"The decoration and shape look a bit odd. Not like anything that I have seen before in antique shops. They look foreign alright."

He replaced them in the box and picked up an ornate silver holder.

"This originally held a glass cup, I have been told," said Sal. "They were used in Eastern Europe for drinking tea."

"What about this?" asked Ben, eyes alight, lifting a delicately engraved silver egg. "Is it a Fabergé?"

"No, I am afraid not. I took it into Adams, the auctioneer's, a few years ago to get it valued. They said it's a cheap Victorian imitation. It's actually an egg cup – look, it unscrews."

"Isn't it amazing to think that these things were everyday objects belonging to someone in our family more than a hundred years ago? Do you know, Sal, sometimes I think, if I just closed my eyes, that when I open them I would be back there – in Vienna in 1860 in a coffee house discussing the day's events, sipping coffee, and eating Sachertorte."

"There had to be cake there somewhere," Sal quipped.

"Seriously, since I found out about the family connection, I have been reading up about Vienna. Jews were tolerated there and free to practise their faith. In fact, they seemed to have been at the centre of cultural life: music, theatre, and the opera. You see, under the Hapsburgs, Vienna enjoyed relative prosperity. It must have been an exciting time to live there. The Austrian Emperor, Franz Joseph, was undertaking major redevelopment. Do you remember him from Leaving Cert History? He knocked down the old medieval city walls to build the Ringstrasse."

His sister had been listening attentively to him. But he thought she looked tired, with dark shadows under her eyes.

"Thanks for having Daisy over, Sal," he said, changing the subject. "I thought you might enjoy meeting her – and Julie is certainly dying to meet her."

Julie was coming from work and had told him she would probably get a taxi.

"Well, I'm glad Julie has finally let you out of the naughty corner and you are on speaking terms again."

"Until the next time," said Ben sheepishly. He had turned down Sal's offer to do the catering at the reception, telling her that he would much rather that she was able to enjoy his big day, and not be fretting about the food. His sister had accepted this, although they both knew the real reason that Ben had declined to take up her offer.

"How did you get on with 'Frau Frome' in London?"

"Actually, we got on really well. She's good craic."

"Is there a bit of the old-green-eye on Julie's part with the amount of time you are spending with Daisy?"

"Possibly – no need though. Daisy's going out with this guy – Irish – a banker – he works in London. Too cool to change a tyre. You know the type, all designer stubble and no substance."

"What people find attractive in others never ceases to amaze me."

"Like me and Julie, do you mean?" he said, teasing her.

"I didn't say that. You know I'm very fond of Julie."

That confirmed it. When women used that expression, 'fond', they usually meant the opposite. But then, he thought, would anyone ever be good enough for Sal's younger brother?

"The family originally being Jewish," Sal said, changing the subject, "certainly explains our dark colouring and sallow skin. I was thinking about it since you told me, and it makes sense. I remember Daddy had some funny little sayings. One of them was, 'You are kibitzing me'. And another was, "You want to sit shiva for me?" – if we were driving him mad. And then there was a strong Jewish community where they were living in Harold's Cross. But they were both practising Catholics. Granny was a Brady – Granddad must have converted when they got married. But it's strange that no one ever spoke about it. Particularly as they were still in touch with the Taubes in England."

"They were different times, Sal."

"Yes, I suppose so. I do remember Daddy telling me that the Free State Government was no supporter of the Jewish cause. De Valera had to deliberately ignore the advice of his cabinet after the war, when he agreed to take orphaned Jewish children into Ireland. By all accounts, there was a strong undercurrent of antisemitism around in Ireland in those days."

"It will take a bit of getting used to," said Ben. "But in a way it also makes looking into our past more intriguing, trying to imagine the kind of lives they had. Any more word from that bastard of an ex-husband of yours?"

"No, all is quiet on the western front. The solicitor has

instigated divorce proceedings. But he suggested that I make a once-off, fair offer in relation to the house to speed things up."

"How much?"

"Twenty-five thousand."

"*Jesus!*"

"'Jesus' is right, Ben."

He now realised that she had been putting on a brave face, as he caught the desperation in her voice.

"Have you been to the Credit Union?"

She pushed her curly black hair out of her eyes, and he could see beads of sweat on her forehead.

"They will only lend me fifteen."

"Right," said Ben, elbows on the table and his head bent, his long fingers rubbing his temples, hesitating only for a second.

"I'll give you the other ten."

"How can you? The wedding –"

He put his hand up.

"Julie will understand. I'll explain to her that your home is on the line here. We will just have to cut back. Lots of scope, *huh*?"

"Ben, I hate taking this from you, but I have been racking my brains to think of how I can raise the money. I will pay you back, every penny. But it will take me time … a few years maybe."

"No need to worry, Sal. I can never pay you back for all you have done for me. Isn't this what family are for?"

Before Sal could answer, the doorbell rang. The two women had arrived on the doorstep at the same time and had made their own introductions. Julie was wearing her working clothes, dressed stylishly all in black, a short skirt and top under a long cream woollen coat. Daisy was casually clad in leather jacket and jeans.

"So, Julie, what do you think about marrying into a Jewish family," said Sal, grinning.

They were all sitting around the kitchen table drinking tea and coffee and eating from a selection of Sal's cakes.

"Maybe we should consider a Jewish wedding ceremony? Sal could make the traditional canopy," said Ben.

Julie's face dropped, horrified.

"Joking, Julie."

"Nothing would surprise me!" she retaliated.

"How are the arrangements going?" asked Sal.

"Well, thank you. The hotel was on to me this morning. We need to pay the deposit by the end of the week. That's not a problem, is it?" said Julie looking, one eyebrow raised, at Ben.

"No, not at all," he said assuredly.

"Have you bought your dress?" enquired Daisy politely.

"Yes, it was the first thing I got. I can't tell you too much in front of Ben though – spoil the surprise. I found it in London in a wedding boutique off Regent Street – it's beautiful."

"I'm sure you will look stunning," Daisy said, smiling.

"Of course she will," said Ben.

"More tea, Daisy?" asked Sal.

"Please."

"So, tell us, Daisy," said Sal excitedly, "are you and Ben any closer to getting to the bottom of the mystery of the two portraits?"

"Yes, hopefully. We have proved that my painting is of Helen Frome, my great-great-grandmother. We think that Lena and Helen are the same person. But we still don't know why in Ben's portrait she is called Lena Tarrant. She may have been married twice. That is the most obvious answer, but we haven't been able to formally establish this."

"Does this mean you two are related – like cousins?" said Julie, sounding pleased.

"Possibly," said Ben, raising an eyebrow quizzically at Daisy. "But the thing is, our great-great-grandmother, who was married to Isaac Tarrant – Antoine's father – was called Rosa. I reckon they married in Vienna in 1860s. Unfortunately, there are no census records in Vienna at that time. Marriage certification was recorded by the religious communities, in this case the Jewish community. This is the photograph that Alex Taube gave me of Isaac. He was working as a trader – an importer-exporter in Vienna at the turn of the century." Ben passed around the old sepia-coloured photograph and they each examined it in turn.

"I definitely think you have a look of him, Ben. Something around the eyes," said Sal.

"A handsome devil, you mean," said Ben, laughing.

"So where to next?" asked Sal. "Vienna?"

"Is that really necessary?" said Daisy. "Surely it is all online these days."

"Well, a lot of the birth and marriage records within the Jewish community are still just scanned documents – in Hebrew."

"Oh, you will have to go, so!" said Sal enthusiastically.

"Won't it be awfully expensive? Surely there is another way to find this out?" Julie said, looking coldly at Ben.

"Well, it's certainly something to think about," said Ben vaguely, avoiding her gaze.

***

Ben rubbed his eyes – his phone was ringing. He put one hand out to get the phone from his bedside locker, remembering the row the night before and why he was alone, and Julie was not in the bed beside him.

"Yeah," he said sleepily.

"It's Sal, sorry to ring so early. It's just after you left last night, Fergal arrived at the house. He was drunk, he was threatening me, he wanted money. He only left when I told him I would call the Guards."

"Jesus, Sal! Are you alright?" Ben sat bolt upright in bed.

"Yes, yes, I am, but I was terrified. He was aggressive and started shouting at me."

"Did he touch you!"

"No, but I think he had taken something. He was as high as a kite. The pupils of his eyes were dilated. His solicitor had been talking to him about the offer. All he could focus on was the money, and how he needs cash urgently to pay off debts. What should I do, Ben – go to the Guards?"

"Yes, absolutely. I'll come around, and we can go down together to the station. Jesus, I'll kill the bloody bastard!"

***

"Obviously, not a lot happening crime-wise in Glasnevin on a Sunday morning," Ben whispered to Sal, trying to lift her spirits as they entered the Garda station.

The garda, an older man with a purple, whiskey nose, slid back the glass screen. He had been reading the Sunday papers.

Sal explained to him what had happened, her voice shaky. And as she filled in the form that the garda gave her, Ben could see her hand trembling slightly.

"You say you are starting divorce proceedings with this man?"

"Yes."

"And that he has been aggressive, physically assaulting you in the past."

"Yes, but that was many years ago. We have not been

in contact. I know it sounds foolish, but just the memory of it terrifies me."

"That's understandable, Ms Tarrant. Look, we will make a house-call to him tonight. Give him an unofficial warning. Unfortunately, though, in this instance you invited him in, and he didn't actually physically assault you. And although verbal assault is not acceptable either, it would be harder to make a charge stick. So, my advice to you is to get that solicitor of yours to contact his, and tell him not to call to the house. If he does, don't let him in, and report it to us immediately. In this way we can build up a record of harassment. Do you live alone?"

"Yes."

"Do have an alarm?"

"No."

"Well, maybe think of getting one," he said kindly. "And one of those security cameras, that don't need to be wired-up."

***

The following morning, as Ben walked to School, along the Tolka river path at the edge of Fairview Park, he rang Cormac. He told him about Fergal's harassment.

"How frightening for Sal. *Mm* ... as it happens, Fergal's solicitor Dave O'Reilly is a pal of mine – we both went to UCD together. He told me – off the record – that Fergal has been dealing in the hard stuff and liberally sampling his own product. It appears that he is in hock to a well-known, and rather nasty, North-side dealer. Dave believes that Fergal is not basically a bad man. But he has a short fuse and a serious enough drug problem. Look, Ben, we could handle this in two ways. We could argue through the courts and try to reduce the sum of money owed to him, which could take up to a year if we are lucky. Or, as I have already suggested to Sal, we could agree a sum of money upfront that settles his claim on the house, conditional on the fact that there is an uncontested divorce. From what you have told me, your sister is not going to have a minute's peace until he gets his money."

"If settling up-front will stop him from harassing her then, yes, let's do that. Could you talk to his solicitor today? I'll talk to Sal."

"Yes, of course. But Sal will need to instruct me formally."

"Thanks, mate."

Ben ended the call.

"*Bastard!*" he said, violently kicking an empty Coke can down the road.

"Temper, sir!" said a familiar voice.

Ben glared as Billy Fagan and Lofty O'Leary ran down the road ahead of him, both laughing hysterically. He looked at his watch. "Shit!" He was late. He could see an image of Annie Atlas waiting for him, hands on sculpted hips at the school gate. What's more he was going to have to tell Julie that he didn't have the money to put his share of the deposit down on the hotel.

"Shit," he said again.

243

Chapter 15

Vienna
March 1862

He checked his pocket watch. It was past the hour. She was late. Thomas smoothed his wavy hair – he had washed and bathed this morning in preparation for her visit. "Next time," she had said, "maybe." He prayed she was not teasing him. He checked the stove. He had lit it an hour ago – the room was warm. The stove had been an early investment. An artist could get away with a certain degree of shabby chic in the room's decor, but warmth was essential. Taking a key, which he kept in a small china jug on the shelf near the stove, he walked over to the bureau and unlocked it. It was filled with bills mostly, but it was also where he kept his money. He opened the wooden lid of a cask, took out the notes and counted them. It was a deeply satisfying feeling knowing that for once he had more money than he knew what to do with.

Isaac Tarrant had called the previous day with half of the agreed fee for his wife's portrait. If only he knew that he would have painted her for nothing. He had also been paid for a full-length portrait of Countess Alice Von Hapsburg, a distant cousin of the Emperor and a member of court circles. Thomas was pleased with the formal portrait, it had turned out well, and he thought with satisfaction that it would enhance his reputation in the city.

He heard the street door opening below and Frau Lipsky's voice greeting Helena.

Seconds later she arrived, slightly breathless after climbing the stairs. But instead of the crone, a young attractive woman was in attendance.

"Thomas, I know you will be desperately disappointed not to meet Frau Tarrant this week. But I brought someone else instead, Frau Cohen – my new companion."

"It is a pleasure to meet you, Frau Cohen," he said, bowing his head slightly, confused, not quite sure of her status, and whether to kiss her hand, or if she was merely a servant.

"I am pleased to meet you too," said the woman demurely in halting French.

He looked at her with a puzzled expression on his face. "You are very alike, you know. Except for the colour of the hair and something around the eyes – but the resemblance is remarkable."

"Really? Oh you know, they say we Jewish women all look the same," said Helena flippantly. "Her features are

245

a little coarser than mine, and her figure fuller – unfashionably so, unfortunately."

Thomas looked at Helena, shocked.

"Oh, don't worry, she can't understand a word we are saying. She doesn't speak French, and hardly any German – only Russian and Yiddish. I taught her basic introductions, but that's all."

"Oh! Still, it doesn't seem right to –"

Helena turned to Rosa and spoke to her in Yiddish. Rosa nodded, smiled at Thomas, and turned to leave the studio.

"I have sent her to buy me some buttons. You can stay while I undress. If you really want to," she said, her reddened lips pouting provocatively as she started to take off her cloak.

Thomas could not believe that the moment that he had dreamt about for so long had been thrust upon him so suddenly. So that now he felt totally unprepared.

He stood breathlessly behind her and, as she lifted her hair coiled loosely at her neck, with fumbling fingers he undid the tiny mother-of-pearl buttons that ran down the back of her dress. Gently he pushed the satin bodice off her shoulders to reveal her buttermilk skin. Then pushing against the back of her skirt so that the front rose like the prow of a ship, he undid the straps of her horsehair petticoat and watched as it fell to the floor. Opening the laces of her corset, he loosened the unwieldy garment. Until, unable to contain himself any longer, he cupped her breasts under her cotton camisole, while kissing her passionately on the neck. But suddenly, through the haze of his desire, he heard the street door opening, and Frau Lipsky's coarse voice rising from below. Footsteps climbed the wooden stairs, heading towards them.

"Oh, she's back already," Helena said, in what he suspected was feigned disappointment. She picked up her discarded clothes and moved swiftly behind the chinoiserie screen.

Thomas turned away and moved behind his easel to collect himself but, as he lifted his wooden palette, his hands were shaking so much he had to put it down again.

"Ah, Frau Cohen! You are returned."

When the hour was up, Rosa moved behind the screen and helped Helena change back into her costume and they left shortly afterwards, promising to return the following week.

After they had left, Thomas sat down on his chair and looked at the portrait. He stared at it for some time then went over to a stack on canvases at the far side of the studio and pulled out the other portrait of her. Well, although not as much as he had hoped, at least he had made progress. If only he could see her completely naked.

***

Tissot's hat shop on Kärntner Strasse was quiet today. Frau Kauffman had gone to get supplies from the

247

haberdashery and was also calling into the fancy goods shop. The Empress Elisabeth, affectionately known as Sisi to the Viennese, had recently worn a hat with peacock feathers. As a result, it was now impossible to get them anywhere in the city. Rosa placed the hat she had just finished in the window. In the backroom young Dora was making felt, stirring a large pot with old wool from discarded jumpers. She had helped her mix a beautiful yellow ochre dye that morning.

Rosa straightened her costume, one of Lena's discarded outfits from last season. She had let it out slightly and now it fitted perfectly. She smoothed back her hair. Although it was still quite short, she had bought a wig of ringlets made from human hair that she attached to the top of her head. She knew it suited her. Frau Kauffman had insisted. It was non-negotiable. She was simply not going to employ a Jewish woman in a cheap wig or a scarf to work as a modiste in her hat shop. "I have my reputation to consider," she had said.

Rosa had been there for ten weeks at this stage and had loved every minute of it. Frau Kauffman, a tough woman, small and wiry, was the epitome of elegance. Her nickname amongst the ladies and courtiers who attended her shop was Birdie – because of her small, pursed mouth and overlapping two front teeth – and her hands which she fluttered like birds' wings to great dramatic effect. Her success was due to her eagle eye for fashion trends. She seemed to know what was happening in Paris before anyone else did. She was also an able dealer and understood instinctively what to say to the women who came into her shop. Frau Kauffman would identify what aspect of a woman's appearance that she felt self-conscious about. Because no matter how beautiful they were, there was always a perceived flaw. And in the most tactful way possible, she would suggest that this or that hat would eradicate it. To a woman with multiple chins, she would tell her that ribbons flatter the face and add definition to the profile. Or the added height of this straw bonnet could only be worn by a woman with a classically aquiline nose.

The only difficulty encountered by Rosa working at Tissot's was language. Yiddish wasn't enough, although in one way it was one of her attractions for Frau Kauffman. She needed someone who could talk to her rich Jewish customers. Some of the older ladies like Rosa only spoke Yiddish. So, Rosa had to learn French and improve her German. But even in such a short space of time she had learnt enough to get by. Frau Kauffman didn't let her near the important customers anyway.

Rosa checked her watch – she wanted to post a letter to Samuil that she had written the previous evening.

"I'm just going to post some letters, Dora. I will be back in a few minutes." She put on her hat, last week's window model simplified for her use and, buttoning up her coat, left the shop.

Mondays were always quiet on Kärntner Strasse. As

she walked to the post office, she thought about how much things had changed in the last ten weeks. Samuil was doing well at the clinic, thank the Lord. Doctor Strauss was pleased with his progress. The boy had written and told her he was hill-walking, and the fresh country air was helping enormously with his energy levels and breathing. The good doctor had also identified that Samuil's condition reacted to nuts of any kind and red wine. She smiled at this – poor Samuil would have to give up drinking wine before he had even started to enjoy it. But, she thought, it was a small price to pay if this improved the quality of his life. He had also learned to play the flute and had discovered he had an aptitude for it. Not only did he love music, but the doctor claimed that the act of playing helped him to control his breathing. Samuil wrote that he was looking forward so much to seeing her and playing for her. He hoped to be back in Vienna by early summer.

The second letter was to Doctor Strauss. Isaac had paid the doctor's fees as agreed. But Rosa had been upset to receive an additional bill from the clinic for a course of bloodletting, an essential part of his treatment. Apparently, it was not covered in the initial amount that they had discussed. She didn't want to have to ask Isaac for more money – not after what had happened the previous week. Her cheeks flushed and her heart raced at the memory of it.

Lena had been late home that evening. She was at the

opera with Lieutenant Lewinsky, a rather dashing military man, one of the most constant of Helena's coterie of hangers-on and admirers. Isaac had been at his club and had returned early a little worse for wear. He had found Rosa in the drawing room, reading a book in front of the fire. She had told him that she was just about to retire for the evening, however he had insisted that she have a nightcap with him. But as he handed her a glass of wine with one hand, his other hand had gently stroked her cheek.

"Do you remember in your kitchen in Kornyn, Rosa, the evening you were all embroidering the cloth and Bubbe Mim told the story about Jacob and the ugly sister?"

"Yes," she had said breathlessly. How could she forget? He was so close to her she could smell the wine on his breath.

"Maybe, Bubbe Mim had second sight and it was a forewarning. Maybe I married the wrong sister after all," he said.

And the feelings that had never left her returned to consume her. From then on, every one of her senses was alert, every moment one of conflicting emotions. Of wanting him, wishing to avoid him, and agonising over when would she see him again, be near him, touch him. She knew this was wrong. But she simply could not help herself. She was also embarrassed, knowing that he was aware of her response, her obvious attraction to him.

"Mrs Cohen, how nice to see you. And looking so well if I might be so bold. Must be the spring air."

It was the Irishman, the artist.

"Herr Rafferty, lovely to see you too," she said in halting French. "I am just on my way to the post office to post a letter to my stepson Samuil – he's in a clinic in Neulengbach."

"Oh, I am also on my way there, to buy stamps. To the post office that is, not Neulengbach. May I accompany you?"

He was so kind and sympathetic, with his smiley blue eyes, and lilting Irish accent. She talked easily to him, was glad of the distraction. She told him about Samuil, the clinic and Doctor Strauss.

"As it happens, I know the doctor well. We often play cards together at my club. His grandmother came from Wicklow – Kilmacanogue, I believe. It's not far from Dublin where I come from. Although, I think he cheats."

"Sorry?"

"At cards, I think he sometimes cheats at cards. But don't tell him I said that."

***

They met again a few days later when Rafferty came into the shop looking for a hat.

"Ah, Frau Cohen, maybe you can help me."

Frau Kauffman took one look at Rafferty and, unimpressed, busied herself with rearranging the display of riding hats on the side counter.

"Of course – what can I do for you, Herr Rafferty?"

"I am looking for a hat for one of my models, something decorative with feathers and lace, maybe even a stuffed bird – they are all the rage, I believe."

"Certainly, Herr Rafferty. Do you often supply hats to your models?"

"Yes, I do. A dashing hat can often embellish a woman's natural beauty and provide a focal point to demonstrate the artist's talents. As a matter of fact, young Dora who works here sometimes models for me. Did she tell you?"

"No, I don't believe she did."

"Frau Kauffman doesn't pay very well, by all accounts," he whispered.

Rosa nervously glanced sideways at Frau Kauffman who was busy with a customer who had just entered the shop.

"As it happens, I am currently looking for a new model. Unfortunately, Dora is not ... suitable for what I have in mind. So, if you hear of any young women who would like to earn some extra cash, let me know."

"How much do you pay, Herr Rafferty?"

"A florin an hour?"

"Really? Well, I'll bear it in mind. Now were you thinking of a particular type of flower, or feathers, for this creation?"

***

"When you came to me first," said Thomas, "you told me you needed a friend. I saw you at the opera last week, with a rather dashing lieutenant. Is he a … friend?"

"Lieutenant Lewinsky?" said Helena, artfully. "Well, he's more of a companion. He's useful – like a puppy. He takes me places. All my husband wants to do is sit in his study and read his incredibly boring books about fossils and ancient monuments. He has no interest in parties, or going to the theatre, or concert halls. But the lieutenant is not a real friend, like you are. I can't talk to him the same way I talk to you. Partly because he's such an awful gossip, but also – to be honest – he's a bit dim. Sorry, Thomas, may I have a break?"

"Of course. Let me get you a glass of ale. Do you know, I am finding it difficult to finish this portrait?"

"Why?"

"Well, I feel that it is not quite right. I haven't managed to fully capture your *duende*."

"*Duende* – what on earth does that mean?"

"Animal attraction and magnetism – the fact that you are so desirable – your feline qualities."

"You're saying I'm like a cat?" She arched her back provocatively.

"Yes, in the way you move and preen."

"That's a very cheeky thing to say, Irish, about a respectable matron."

"It's not that I don't respect you. I do. I just want to capture how much I respect you – want you!"

"Well, that doesn't sound very respectful to me. You must show me some of your drawings of your other models. I want to see what the competition is like."

He handed her a glass of ale and she sipped it, looking at him provocatively, head tilted, from under black eyelashes.

"Well, I have just finished a portrait of Countess Alice Von Hapsburg, a cousin of the Emperor's. Do you know her?"

"I know of her, certainly," said Helena vaguely.

"Unfortunately, it was delivered to the Countess yesterday. But you have no need to worry, she was nowhere near as beautiful as you. It was a challenge to portray her to her liking. Her eyes bulged – a bit like a pug dog, if I'm honest."

Helena laughed, "You are only saying that to make me feel better, Irish. You must have other paintings?"

"Well, the rest are mostly boring old military men and city officials. But I have done a new watercolour, I was hunting with the von Leidings last weekend in their lodge in Kirchengasse."

She put down the ale on a side table, and he handed her his open sketch book.

"This is very pretty. I love it. I love the way you have captured the light and shadows on the snow on the mountains. I almost feel healthy looking at it." She handed him back the drawing and moved to the window so that the light caught her face in profile – the good side.

"I don't think you realise how much visiting you, our friendship, cheers me up, Irish."

"And why do you need cheering up, my darling?"

She turned, touching her the scar on her cheek with the tips of her fingers, in that absentminded way she had, and gave him one of her endearing lopsided smiles.

"My husband."

"Is he cruel to you?"

"Yes, he is. He does not respect me the way that you do. He scolds me in front of his mother, and the crone, and he treats me like a child. And you would not believe how miserly he is with money."

"It's hard to believe," he said adoringly, "that he does not worship at your feet."

"Yes, it is. And what is even more annoying, he has started comparing me, unfavourably, I might add to my ... companion, Mrs Cohen. Rosa this, and Rosa that. I am sick of her. I can't wait for her to leave. After everything I have done for her."

"Mrs Cohen seems like such a nice lady," Thomas said tentatively. "I often meet her on her lunch break from the hat shop. I am usually out for a stroll at that time."

"Oh, she never said!" said Helena peevishly. "Well, she will be gone in a few weeks – thank goodness – back to Kornyn where she belongs to that stick-insect of a husband of hers."

***

256

"So, Helena, what are your plans today?" Isaac asked.

They had all just finished breakfast and the servant was clearing the plates from the table.

"I have an appointment with a Doctor Müller today."

Isaac was wiping his mouth carefully with a linen napkin – he placed it down carefully on the table.

"Oh, anything we should worry about?" His face was impassive, but Rosa noticed that his knuckles were clenched on the table.

"No, nothing serious. Routine, I think he called it, a woman's issue."

"Well, it certainly sounds like something we don't want to discuss at the breakfast table," Isaac's mother retorted.

Rosa looked anxiously at her sister.

"Well, let me know how you get on," said Isaac, looking at her with concern.

"Of course. Anyway, that's this afternoon. This morning I'm looking at a marble statue, by the late Antonio Canova, the famous Italian sculptor. It's of Apollo and would look perfect in the alcove in the hall."

"Canova? Oh for the Lord's sake, Lena!"

"Well, we have to put something in it. There is no point creating a plastered alcove if it's empty."

"Maybe you could put a vase of flowers there?" Rosa said, trying to be helpful.

"Yes," said Isaac, "flowers would be perfect. The bills for the builders' work are now double the initial estimate. We will have to cut our cloth to suit our measure." His voice clipped, he was trying to control his temper. "Helena, we have a whole lifetime ahead of us for buying expensive art works."

"Thanks so much for the sisterly support." Helena looked furiously at her sister.

"Ma'am?"

A liveried footman handed Rosa a letter.

"This was just delivered for you. It's marked urgent."

"Thank you, Franz," said Rosa, concerned.

She opened the letter and read it in alarm.

"It's from Doctor Strauss. It seems there has been an outbreak of tuberculosis at the clinic. Samuil was not in contact with the other patients and is at absolutely no risk but, just to be on the safe side, he wants me to collect him immediately and bring him home."

"Well, you can't bring him here," said Jessica sharply, "not with –"

"Of course you must bring him here. I'm sure we can find room," Isaac said, interrupting his mother as he looked solicitously at Rosa.

"Thank you, Isaac," said Rosa, flustered. "I don't know how I can ever repay you for all you have done for our family. I must find out about transport."

"No need," said Isaac. "I will take you in my carriage. As it happens, I have business in Pressbaum which is quite near there. I hadn't planned to go till next week, but I can bring my trip forward."

"Oh, there is no need to change your plans for me."

"Actually, it suits me. We will have to leave tomorrow morning at eight. Can you be ready?"

"Yes, of course. I just have to tell Frau Kauffman."

"Not like your sister then, who needs at least a week to pack to go anywhere."

Helena's eyes flashed furiously from her husband to her sister. She looked as though she was going to say something but then decided not to.

***

Rosa was in her bedroom at the small dressing table brushing her short hair, which to her delight had grown out curly. Her hands were trembling at the thought of spending two whole days with Isaac. She had refixed her hairpiece when the door was opened abruptly by Helena.

"Do you think I don't see what you are doing," she said, flushed and angry, the scar a red gash on her cheek. "Making cow's eyes at my husband, after all I have done for you."

"Lena, I don't know what you are talking about," Rosa said apprehensively.

"Do you think I'm stupid? I have noticed the way that you blush and simper every time he enters a room – your nervous little laugh. 'What do you think about this, Isaac? Or that, Isaac?' I won't have it. I want you to leave. Go back to Kornyn, and take your snivelling, snorting son with you. I want you both gone. Do you understand me?"

"Perfectly," said Rosa, her eyes filling with tears.

Chapter 16

"Are you sure you are warm enough?"

"Yes, perfectly." Rosa smiled at him.

She was wrapped in a blanket of rabbit furs with warm bricks at her feet. They had left the city just after dawn. Although it was freezing outside, here in the carriage she felt cocooned and protected. With gloved fingers she rubbed circles on the misted windows so that she could see the sun rise over the city. Passing through the Ringstrasse site works, they drove through the outskirts, where tall chimneys spewed black smoke into the air over the ramshackle wooden huts and mud cabins of the factory workers. Here lines of men, women and children trudged along the rutted road towards the beckoning call of the morning bells. The bedraggled figures were wrapped up in heavy bulky coats, their faces almost hidden with hats pulled around their ears and swathed in woollen scarves.

Once outside the city limits, the carriage headed west. Eventually they skirted the parklands of Schönbrunn, the vast neo-classical summer palace where the Emperor Franz Josef reputedly spent most of his time with Empress Elisabeth – then onward through heavily wooded countryside towards Eichgraben. Trees soared on either side of the track, occasionally clearing as they drove by a farm or a small holding. But mainly they passed under pine canopies feathered with the down of recently fallen snow. On the lower, sheltered branches of deciduous trees, to her delight she noticed buds of leaves. And on the ground, the green shoots of snowdrops and wild garlic poked through the snow.

Spring was coming – it was a sign, she thought, that things would get better. She thought of how she would bring Samuil back to Kornyn, to Moishe and Perle, and how different things would be. She would have to leave most of her newly acquired clothes behind, maybe just keep one or two costumes for special occasions. And of course, resume covering her hair – she stroked a short stray curl at the side of her head sadly. As she smoothed her navy wool costume, one of Lena's cast-offs, she thought how Moishe wouldn't recognise her – hopefully in a good way. She felt unusually content.

Today was such a lovely experience, almost an adventure. She felt like a grand duchess riding in this fine horse-drawn carriage through the countryside. For once she was not looking after someone else's needs. She couldn't remember being this idle for a long time.

Initially, she had been apprehensive about accepting Isaac's offer, but she didn't really have a choice. To travel on commercial coaches would have been expensive – it would take several days, with at least one night at an inn. This way, at no cost, she could travel there directly, and they could stay overnight at Doctor Strauss's clinic. They would all be back before nightfall the following day. Because of the snow, it was still too risky to travel once it got dark.

She knew her sister was furious. Helena had tried to persuade Isaac to send her with his grandmother instead. Bubbe Mim – not wanting to be helpful – had refused point blank. She had even tried to cajole Jessica to go with Rosa, but there was no way she was going to sit in a draughty carriage for two days just to please her daughter-in-law. So, in the end Helena reluctantly had to accept the situation.

Rosa hadn't had the opportunity to talk with Isaac in any detail since the evening they had shared the nightcap together. Polite chit-chat was all they had engaged in subsequently. If the truth were known, she still found him intimidating. But in the last few months she had grown in confidence with all that she had achieved. From what he had said to her that night, she knew he still had feelings for her. And although she also felt attracted to him, she knew in her heart that it was just a romantic indulgence – a dream of what might have been. But on one level her sister was right, she was finding it hard to hide her desire for him. Even now her pulse was racing with his proximity. She breathed in and out slowly, hoping he wouldn't notice. She had probably imagined, she scolded herself, that he also felt this way.

From the start of their journey, Isaac had been a perfect gentleman, solicitous about her comfort. He had made her feel completely at ease. They chatted away for the first half an hour or so – then they snoozed – and then started talking again a few hours later, mostly social gossip and politics. Her asking questions, him explaining. They were still two hours away from Eichgraben.

"Was it hard, this move to Vienna? Your success has made it look so easy," Rosa enquired.

"Well, it's certainly not for the faint-hearted. Building the business has been slow. We still have contacts along our old trading routes. But the development of the railways has changed everything. That and the relative peace in Europe. Since the Congress of Vienna, the city has prospered – trade has boomed. Now Vienna is perfectly placed between the East and West to serve both markets. Marble, furs and grain from Russia mostly – silks, spices and coffee from the far east – and manufactured goods from England."

"A long way from Taube's Grain Store in Kornyn," she said, smiling. "Why did you not practise as a lawyer? Wasn't that what you trained as?"

"Because we would all have starved. It has taken me time to assimilate, as they call it – to become more like the Viennese."

"But that has meant abandoning your religion, your people," she said self-righteously, instinctively mouthing Moishe's words.

"No, Rosa. Although I am not as devout as I should be, I have not changed my faith. But I have abandoned the old ways – the belief that a life of prayer can raise us from poverty or protect us from whichever conquering power herds us like sheep into ghettos."

"But is that not the Lord's will? Should we not wait until the Messiah comes to free us?"

"Your grandfather died waiting, and his father before him, and his father before him again," Isaac said, one eyebrow lifted. "No, Rosa we need to become citizens of the world if we are to flourish as a people. I may have changed my dress, but I have not given up my religion, or my traditions. But people fear what they do not understand. Jewish customs are so foreign to them that we must adopt their ways and show them that we are the same as they are."

"But has it worked? Since I started working at Tissot's, I see that Jews, no matter how well dressed they are in the latest fashions, are still second-class citizens."

"Unfortunately, that is the case. In fact, despite adopting Viennese fashions, only last week I was shocked that a client of mine knew that I was Jewish."

"Indeed." said Rosa, thinking how smart he looked in his sable fur overcoat, underneath which she could see a crisp, white linen shirt and a blue satin cravat.

"After all these years with tutors, I speak German and French with only the slightest accent. So I have been told." He smiled self-deprecatingly. "And I only observe Jewish customs behind closed doors. But they still know. There is something about us – maybe we are too austere for the Viennese, not baroque enough." He smiled. Then he turned from her and looked out of the window. "Ennoblement, or high-ranking public office is, for the most part, denied to us here," he said wistfully. "How we look and sound is important if we wish to succeed in society. However, becoming part of the cultural elite does provide Jews an entrée. As you will have gathered by now, most business introductions are made in the social salons run by wealthy Viennese matrons – many of whom are Jewish. So, it is important to be invited to these soirées, to mingle with the rich and influential. Your sister comes into her own in these social gatherings. I hate them – dread going to them. But she is in her element, everyone buzzing around her like moths to a flame."

"She was always witty and charming," said Rosa wistfully.

"Yes, indeed she is that," he replied in a matter-of-fact manner.

"And beautiful."

"That too."

The carriage jolted, and violently lurched to one side, throwing them both forcibly across their seats.

"What the hell?" said Isaac.

"Sorry, Herr Tarrant." The driver had jumped down from his perch and was knocking on the window. "I think we have broken a wheel."

"Oh, Lord no. Can you fix it?" Isaac asked in exasperation, then turned to Rosa. "Sorry, Rosa. Look, I had better get out and see what has happened. Wrap up warm and hopefully we can sort this out quickly."

Thirty minutes or so later, Rosa was freezing, any heat left in the bricks dissipated. She could see her breath misting in the air. In the distance, the plaintive sound of a lone wolf's howl made her shiver, and she pulled the furs up around her.

"I am sorry about this, Rosa," said Isaac, opening the door. "I am afraid we are going to have to stay overnight in an inn. It's not only the wheel, but the axel is also broken. We tried to affect a makeshift repair without success. So, we will have to get a wheelwright to look at it. Karl is going to take one of the horses and ride into Pressbaum which is about two miles from here. Hopefully, we can get rooms at an inn there for the night and this will be sorted by the morning."

Three hours or so later, Karl returned laden down with supplies and looking glum – it was already dark.

"Bad news, Herr Tarrant – there was a market on in Pressbaum today and the wheelwright is pissed as a newt. He is unable to dress himself, let alone change a wheel. But his wife has promised that he will be here without fail at daybreak. Unfortunately, there are no

266

rooms to be had anywhere in the town. There's a rough crowd about with drunkards spilling from the taverns. I don't think you would want to go there, sir. I took the liberty of bringing you some supplies – some food and vodka."

"Oh Lord, there is nothing for it. Rosa, I am terribly sorry, we are going to have to set up a camp here and sleep in the carriage."

Karl lit a fire at the side of the road in the shelter of some trees and prepared a meal of bread and cheese and cured meats which Isaac and Rosa devoured. As they ate, the driver sat respectfully some distance away from them, giving them privacy.

When Rosa had finished eating, Isaac opened a bottle of vodka and poured generous amounts into two small silver travelling cups.

"These are quaint," said Rosa, examining the cups.

He smiled. "They are from home – the tall houses in the engraving remind me of Kornyn. Helena won't have them in the house, so I keep them here in the carriage. Glad you like them. Drink up! The vodka will warm you."

"I'll sleep beside the fire, sir, if that's alright," said Karl.

"Won't you freeze to death?"

"No, sir," he said with a laugh. "I was in the Russian army. We are used to sleeping outside. I have a tent, and blankets."

"Good. But don't stray too far away, Karl, we might need you."

"You have your gun, sir?"

"Of course," said Isaac. "Now, Rosa, we'd best do the same and have an early night. See can we get some sleep."

Rosa closed her eyes, but the alcohol, instead of making her feel sleepy, seemed to heighten her senses so that every nerve in her body was tingling. She was painfully conscious of Isaac's proximity. His spicy scent mingled with the musty smell of the fur blankets. In the distance the howling of the wolves had got louder. She wrapped her arms around herself protectively.

"Don't worry about them," he said.

She opened her eyes – he was looking intently at her. "Contrary to popular belief, wolves tend to stay away from humans, unless of course they are provoked. Try to get some rest. It will be a long day tomorrow."

She closed her eyes again and, after several minutes, she heard the steady sound of his breathing, indicating he was asleep. The wolves' howling continued relentlessly and seemed to be getting closer. She opened the curtain on the carriage window and peeped out nervously, staring blindly into the blackness of the forest.

"It's alright, really," he said, opening his eyes. "You are quite safe here with me."

He moved the rugs with some difficulty and sat beside her, searching for her gloved hands. But as she turned to look at him, he kissed her gently, tentatively on the lips.

"I have been waiting to do that for a long time, Rosa." Then he kissed her again, hungrily this time.

Under her furs, through the layers of wool and silk,

his hand slipped under the top of her bodice and caressed her breast and, aroused, she guided his hands, as he lifted her skirt and the layers of her petticoats.

They made love, tenderly at first, then with increasing passion until they both lay back exhausted.

"I have wanted you ever since you arrived in Vienna," he said, his arm around her, stroking her cheek with his finger. "I have always regretted abandoning you, Rosa. I was young and weak – I should have stood up to all of them and protected you."

"But Lena – I thought you loved her."

"I wanted her, I am ashamed to say – but love, no – never. She has a heart of stone, your sister. Shortly after we were married, she refused to be intimate with me. She doesn't want children. Our marriage is purely one of convenience."

"How could she refuse you? You could talk to the Rabbi, make her see sense."

"And expose my affairs to the ridicule of the world? No. I live in hope. I have tried everything. Your sister tells me that she refuses to be any man's chattel," he said bitterly. "I even gave her an allowance so that she has some independence. Although I still, somehow, end up paying all her bills."

"Her face, Isaac. What happened to her face?"

"Oh that. She fell off her horse riding in the Prater – split her cheek on a rock. But typically makes such a deal of it. It's as if she wants people to think that I did it. Although, I am sorely tempted to, sometimes. But it's not in my nature to hit a woman. And you, Rosa – are you happy?"

She looked away from him. "I am not sure we were put on this earth to be happy. Moishe is a good man," she said guiltily, "a kind man – and Samuil and Perle bring me happiness. As you know, I haven't been blessed with my own children. In Kornyn they whisper that I have been touched by evil spirits, and I am cursed to be barren. But it is not that … Moishe ..." She paused, looking down, her eyes wet with tears. "I suppose in the beginning I dreaded lying with him. He obviously knew that I only did it out of duty. And then later, when I was more comfortable with him – and I had my own needs – well, he seemed to have given up. We do lie together very occasionally, but I rarely enjoy it. Not like this."

He took her face in his hands and kissed her gently on the mouth. "Poor Moishe – poor you," he said lovingly.

***

Memories of the carriage journey home passed in a blur. Samuil, unusually chatty, told them of his time spent in Eichgraben. His face had a healthy glow from the sun, and Rosa noticed that he had put on weight. Isaac and he discussed the joys of hill-walking and got involved in a heated discussion about the evils of slavery and the civil war raging in America.

As she held Samuil's arm, she was proud of her

stepson's confident and assured manner, and his ability to hold his own in conversation with Isaac. She was also pleased that Isaac saw how much Samuil adored her. She caught Samuil looking quizzically at her once or twice and sensed that he noticed he had another competitor for her affections, and she suspected that he was aware of the frisson between Isaac and herself.

When they arrived back in Spiegelgasse, Isaac left Rosa and Samuil, telling them he had business to attend to.

"You seem to be getting on very well with Isaac," Samuil said sheepishly.

"Yes, he has been good to me – to us, Samuil. It was extremely kind of him to collect you from the clinic."

"Don't like him too much, will you?" he said, eyes down and fiddling with his gloves.

"I don't know what you are talking about. Maybe you have TB after all, and it has muddled your head." She squeezed his arm affectionately.

Later that evening Rosa and Samuil had dinner with Bubbe Mim and Jessica. Isaac had not returned, and Rosa was relieved to find that Helena was out for the evening at the opera with Lieutenant Lewinsky. Samuil regaled them with all with his tales of Doctor Strauss and his time spent at the clinic. And after several glasses of schnapps even Jessica was in good form. But it had been a long day and after a few games of cards they all retired early.

***

271

In her single bed, in the maid's room that her sister had assigned her on the top floor of the house, she heard them returning. The horse's hooves, and the scrape of the carriage wheels on the cobbled street outside. Helena came home first, then Isaac sometime later. Rosa guessed it was after midnight when she heard the creaking sounds of steps on the wooden stairs up to the servants' quarters. She watched as the handle of her door turned – and there he was, standing before her bed in his stockinged feet, his shirt open. Filled with a heady mix of fear and desire, she held her breath as he approached her, lifted the sheets, and pressed his body down on top of hers in the narrow bed. Then kneeling between her parted limbs, he caressed her, tracing her body's curves and hollows with his fingers, tasting the darker coloured skin around her nipples, and kissing the velvety soft skin on her inner thigh.

Just before dawn as the sounds of birdsong could be heard through the attic window, Isaac untangled himself from her. She opened her eyes, but he put a finger to her lips before she could speak.

"I must go, Rosa."

He descended the stairs to the floor below and walked along the corridor to his room. As he gently closed the door, he did not see the figure in the shadows shrink back into the alcove, hidden out of sight.

***

After an unusually quiet breakfast during which only the necessary formalities had been uttered, Helena wiped her mouth delicately with a linen napkin.

"Now that Samuil is finished at the clinic, my sister is returning to Kornyn."

Lena's words took Rosa by surprise. She hadn't expected to be dismissed quite so soon.

"Oh, I thought your contract with Madame Kauffman ran until the end of May," said Isaac. "Do you not have several weeks to go?"

"Yes, but –" said Lena

"Rosa can talk for herself, surely," interjected Isaac.

Jessica looked quizzically at her son, then at Rosa. Even Bubbe Mim seemed alert to the tension in the room.

"Oh, Rosa! So soon? You promised me you would take me to see the Prater!" cried Samuil.

"Well, we have been here long enough. I don't want to impose on your aunt and uncle's generosity any more than I have already."

"*Bubbala*, stay just a few more weeks," said Bubbe Mim. "Who will play cards with me in the evenings?"

"Yes, but Rosa must get back to her husband. I'm sure he misses her terribly," said Helena acerbically.

"There is also the matter of the contract with Madame Kauffman which I entered into on Rosa's behalf," said Isaac.

"Oh, don't mind old Birdie," his wife replied. "I can sort her out."

"But, my dear," Isaac said coldly, "I don't wish you to

sort her out. Rosa will finish her training as agreed. Until then, I insist that she stays with us." He paused, then continued, choosing his words carefully. "And how did you get on with Lieutenant Lewinsky last night at the opera, my dear? Did he admire the emerald brooch I, apparently, bought you?"

Helena shot her husband a look of barely concealed hatred and got up, throwing her napkin on the table, and left the room.

"So, Rosa, no more foolish talk of you leaving," Isaac said, his eyes smiling and mischievous.

"Very well, Isaac. That is very generous of you," Rosa said quietly, lowering her eyes so the others could not see her relief.

She did not see the arched but satisfied look that passed between Bubbe Mim and her grandson Isaac.

***

Helena had cancelled her appointment with her modiste that morning, she was in such a rage. She was incandescent with fury. How could Isaac treat her this way? With her sister! Did he think she was a fool – that she would put up with such treatment? They had an understanding, she and Isaac. Or she thought they did. They had their difficulties – didn't everyone? But to be intimate with her sister was unforgivable. She couldn't put up with it – wouldn't put up with it!

She could feel the bile rising in her throat at the thought of having to kowtow to Rosa, and her in-laws' spiteful delight at her humiliation, knowing that her sister was sleeping with Isaac. How long before everyone else in Vienna knew as well, before the whispers started, and the looks of pity appeared as she came into a room? No, she simply couldn't bear it. The blackguard! And, as for Rosa, she was nothing more than a scheming bitch!

Helena paced around the room thinking of her options. Really, they were limited. She could not rely on the support of Jessica or Mim – they would be only too pleased at her downfall. She had heard of *ménage à trois* where people learned to live within these unorthodox relationships. But not her. She looked out of the window and thought about what she would do. Eventually, after thirty minutes or so, she scribbled a note and then rang the bell for a servant.

***

Lieutenant Karol Lewinsky was used to being hastily summoned by young ladies requiring urgent attendance. But this morning it really didn't suit him. The brandy at the officer's club the previous night had been flowing a little too freely, and his head was throbbing. Still, he admired and was fond of the beautiful Frau Tarrant. He didn't wish to disappoint. It was what was expected of him. He had to admit he had enjoyed her witty and entertaining company, as he whiled away his time in

Vienna. He had been stationed here for the past six months after he had received an injury to his right hand during training exercises. But he was nearing the end of his commission, and his father had been nagging him to return to the encumbered family estate and take up duties running the few remaining vineyards that they hadn't sold off to pay their ever-increasing debt.

Helena had asked him to meet her here on the Prater. She hadn't wanted him to call at the house for some reason. He pulled the collar of his greatcoat around his neck. As he sat on the cold stone surround to the fountain, his mare who was tied to a tree was whinnying and skittish. He watched Helena's carriage approaching. The park was quiet that morning, with only the odd intrepid horse rider willing to face the biting north wind.

"Good morning, Frau Tarrant – and Gretta," he said tipping his helmet at Helena's German maid.

The footman jumped down from the back of the carriage and opened the doors for Helena as she and her companion stepped out of the carriage, both wrapped up in heavy woollen cloaks.

As they strolled along the footpath, Gretta hovered a little way behind.

"So, what is your predicament that is so urgent? How can I help?"

"Something has happened. Isaac ..."

She stroked her cheek – the scar was unusually pronounced today, he thought. Must be the cold.

"It is almost too painful to talk about it," she continued, tears filling her eyes. "But I needed to tell you as soon as possible how much danger you are in."

"Me?" He looked confused. His brain still sluggish after the brandy. "Why?"

"Well, my husband has got it into his head that we are intimate. He has become increasingly suspicious of how close we have become over the last few weeks. He is insanely jealous."

"You told him, of course … you assured him that our relationship is purely platonic."

"I tried to tell him, but he would not believe me. He was like a wild beast, consumed with rage. He hit me … and said he was going to find you and kill you!"

"My God, Helena. Are you alright?"

He put his arm around her, turning her to face him. She lowered her head, refusing to meet his gaze.

"I am so frightened of him, Lieutenant. He will kill you. You have no idea how violent he can be."

"Christ, Helena, Jesus, what are we going to do? I must talk to him; tell him that he is entirely mistaken, that we are just friends."

"No, it is too late. I already told him that I have feelings for you." She looked pathetically at him.

"What? How …?"

She could see he was totally confounded.

"But, Helena, I like you. I admire you. But you are a married woman – a wealthy woman. I am not in a

277

position to support a wife, let alone a –"

"Mistress – is that what think of me? You are as bad as my husband. I do not want your devotion. I want your protection." She looked at him scathingly, suddenly transformed by anger. Her tear-filled eyes were furious.

"But Helena …" he said, nervously looking around, to see were there any witnesses to this embarrassing emotional scene.

Gretta had, deliberately it seemed, turned her back on them and was now some distance away. It was too cold for promenaders, and the park was eerily quiet.

"You have to take me away."

"Away? Where?"

"To Paris, maybe."

"But the scandal?"

"You would rather be dead?"

"He might challenge me to a duel?"

"*Tsch*, a duel! You think you are dealing with a gentleman here, Lieutenant? He will simply call to your billet and kill you!"

Lewinsky's face had turned a waxy white and he looked like he was going to get sick.

"Surely, if I –"

"No, there is only one way out of this. We must both leave the city."

"But, Helena, my dear. I have little money."

"Don't worry about money. I will sort that out. All I need for you is to get me to Paris. To safety."

"Helena, I am an officer, I can't just up and leave. I will be court-martialled for desertion."

"Surely you can get compassionate leave? Say your father is dying!"

"But ..."

"We have no choice, Lieutenant!" She threw herself at him, sobbing loudly."

Lewinsky, suddenly feeling lightheaded, looked at Gretta's stiff back and prayed that he wouldn't pass out.

Chapter 17

Daisy felt the warmth of the winter sun on her face and could feel its energy seeping through her body. Although it was early December, and cold, the outdoor heaters and sunshine made it feel like a warm spring day. Fairy lights were strung across shop fronts, and the windows were filled with seasonal decorations.

"I had forgotten how much I love this city. And what nicer time could there be – to be here – than on the run up to Christmas."

They were sitting outside Café Frauenhuber on Himmelpfortgasse – one of the oldest coffee houses in Vienna.

"It's magnificent alright. The Hapsburgs certainly left their mark," said Ben, looking through the guidebook. "The building of the Ringstrasse was inspirational, preserving the medieval centre and building a ring of elegant buildings and parks around it. As opposed to the military-inspired layout of Paris, with its long boulevards and vast triumphal public spaces."

He looked up from the guidebook.

"I am trying to imagine what it must have been like when my great-great-grandfather lived here. The building works started around then. It would have been such a vibrant place – a cultural melting pot, where the East met the West – teeming with an eclectic mix of people: Hungarian Magyars, swash-buckling Austrian military men, and elegant courtesans."

"But what would it have been like for Jews?" asked Daisy.

"Well, from what I have read about it, the 1848 revolution was considered disappointing for the Jews, as entitlements promised by the revolutionaries were subsequently revoked. But, although the revolution was quashed, it still brought progress. At least from then on, their community was recognised. And in 1860, the young emperor Franz Joseph granted them rights to own property. His tolerance towards the Jews and other minority religions was considered liberal for the time."

"This is all very highbrow, Ben."

"Well, you can't be chit-chatting in a Vienna coffee house – it requires a more intellectual level of conversation," he said, putting down the guidebook and eating a generous forkful of Sachertorte.

"I thought we were supposed to be sharing that," Daisy said, amused.

"Sorry," he said sheepishly, pushing the plate over to her.

"So how hard was it to persuade Julie to allow you to come?" Daisy watched him as she savoured a mouthful of chocolate cake.

"Wasn't easy, to be honest. As you may have gathered, she sees this as a complete waste of money. But I explained that if we are to sell the painting at a reasonable price, there was no other way."

Daisy suspected that money wasn't Julie's only concern.

"How's your mum?" Ben asked.

"She's fine, hanging in there. She's charmed by our adventure. She rings me every day for news. Usually, she has forgotten what I told her the previous day, so I have to start all over again."

"You are lucky to still have her," he said.

"I know," Daisy looked across the bustling street so he wouldn't see the tears in her eyes.

"Are you nearly finished?" A small chubby girl of about five was peering up at them through round, pink-rimmed glasses.

"Yes, I think we are, actually. Aren't we, Ben?"

"Can I have the west of your cake," she lisped.

"Hannah, leave those people alone!" An English woman, obviously pregnant, with a small toddler in tow, attempted to pull the child away.

"Don't worry," said Daisy, already getting up. "We were just leaving."

"Hannah, I'm going to get you a cookie to share with your brother. I'm so sorry. She's very chatty."

"Have you twied Mozart balls?" the child persisted.

"Hannah!"

"I'm just telling them, Mummy. They're chocolates," she said conspiratorially to Daisy. "But I got weally sick, I ate so many."

"Really?" said Daisy.

"*Hannah!*" admonished the mother again.

"It was wurf it," said the child.

"Well, we had better go and buy some immediately!" Daisy said, trying not to laugh – then turning, smiling, to the mother. "Enjoy your coffee, if you can!"

As they left the coffee shop, Ben took Daisy's arm to guide her through the crowds gathered at the entrance and they set off down the narrow street in the bright winter sunshine.

"She was so adorable," said Daisy. "I loved her pink glasses."

"I thought you didn't like kids?"

"I never said that. I just said we weren't planning to have any."

Ben raised one eyebrow, looking at her quizzically. "Really."

"Come on, we are going to be late for our meeting," she said, changing the subject.

***

283

When they arrived at the Jewish Museum, Barbara Selig was already waiting for them in the foyer. The genealogist had been recommended by the museum when Daisy had contacted them ahead of their visit. Daisy had hoped that she would do some groundwork before they came and guide them between the various archives. The Dublin Jewish Museum had advised her that because no census had been undertaken in Vienna during the nineteenth century, carrying out this type of research was not straightforward. Daisy figured it would also be helpful to have someone who could negotiate the bureaucratic red tape and act as a translator.

Barbara shook hands with them both in a business-like manner. She was a small, thin, woman, stylishly dressed in a short black coat with a turquoise and gold silk scarf, artfully arranged around her neck, and gold hoop earrings. She was carrying a neat, expensive-looking briefcase.

"Let's sit down over here," she said after the introductions had been made.

She led them to backless modern chairs and a low table near the reception desk where they all sat down.

Opening the briefcase, Barbara pulled out a sheaf of papers.

"I looked up the records at the synagogue. Quite interesting as it turns out. The Tarrant family lived on Spiegelgasse from around 1851 until 1917. In 1853 Meyer, his mother Miriam, his wife Jessica, his son Isaac and his wife Lena are listed as living there."

284

"Isaac was married to Lena?" said Ben, confused.

"Yes, here are photocopies of community records in Yiddish from 1853 showing names and addresses. It is the first record of them I found here, it states the family's origins as Kornyn."

Barbara showed them a map of Eastern Europe as it was during the 1850s indicating Kornyn.

"It's now in modern day Ukraine," Barbara explained. "Before 1792, it was part of Poland."

"I was told by an uncle that the family were originally from Poland."

"So they were, but by the time the Tarrants left to come to Vienna, the area was part of the Russian Empire. Here, you can see ..." she said, indicating on the map. "Kornyn lies west of Kiev, in an area that the Russians designated as the Jewish Pale of Settlement. Jews could only live in this area. They were not allowed to own land, so farming was not an option. Nor were they allowed enter most professions. So, most Jews were forced to live in small market towns such as Kornyn where they eked out a living as traders. I should warn you, although the Russians were better record-keepers, the records of the Jewish community are often unreliable. Many families falsified information, didn't register births, or changed their names, to avoid their sons' conscription to the Tsar's army. So, I am afraid I have had no luck tracing your ancestors in Kornyn. But a document has come to light here in the museum that might be of interest to you. It's from a shadchan."

"What's a shadchan?"

"They were the traditional Jewish matchmakers who arranged marriages on behalf of the community. This letter was written by Constantin Edelman who operated here in Vienna during the 1850s and 60s. It's addressed to Meyer Tarrant who lived on Spiegelgasse."

She handed Daisy a page of yellowed paper. The black ink had faded but was still eligible. On the top left-hand corner of the page was a typed address, with Edelman's name in a professional-style letterhead. It was dated 1854 and written in German.

"I'll translate. The first section of the letter covers merely the formalities. Constantin is telling Meyer that he is recovering from a bad chest infection that he caught from a long walk in the Prater. But then it gets interesting. *'It was unfortunate that the engagement did not work out with Rosa Rabinovitch. It must be a heavy burden for her family to carry that shame. But I hear on the grapevine that Isaac subsequently married her younger sister. Under the circumstances, and because of the expenses incurred in finding the girl in the first place, I think it fair that you pay me the remainder of my fee.'"*

"So, Rosa must have been Lena's sister!" exclaimed Daisy. "Rosa was to marry Isaac but, because some shameful event occurred, he married her younger sister instead."

"Goodness, I wasn't expecting that," said Ben. "I wonder what happened?"

"Possibly, she was pregnant, or was found guilty of

some petty crime. It sounds as if, whatever it was, it was sorted out within the family."

"Did Isaac and Lena have children?"

"No, they didn't. In 1865 they were divorced, and in 1866 Isaac married again. And now it gets even more interesting. This time it was to Rosa."

"So, she got him in the end."

"Apparently. They had a son Anton. Rosa died in 1915 and Isaac died two years later. They are both buried here in the Jewish cemetery. There are no more records of the family after that date. Anton must have moved away from the city."

***

That evening, walking over to Isaac Tarrant's house on Spiegelgasse, on their way out to dinner, Christmas lights were everywhere. The city was glittering, like an elaborate stage set. They passed a street hawker selling hot chestnuts and carol singers on a street corner singing "Silent Night" in German.

"If only it would snow, then it would be like we were caught in one of those glass globes that they were selling today in the market."

"It's magical alright," said Ben pensively. "Do you know, Daisy, after all we learned today, I still don't understand why our family – Rosa's descendants – would have Lena's portrait."

"Yes, I was thinking that too. Under the circumstances, you would imagine that there wasn't a lot of love lost between them."

"That reminds me, Daisy, in all the excitement coming here, I forgot to tell you. Doctor Nolan rang me yesterday and said to arrange that slot in the Radiology department in Bons Secours Hospital."

"Did he say he'd found anything? He said he'd only do an X-ray if he believed it was warranted."

"Yeah, I asked him. But he was very mysterious. He said he'd tell us all after he had seen the X-ray."

"*Mm*, the plot thickens," said Daisy intrigued.

When they reached Spiegelgasse they stood across the street, looking at Ben's great-great-grandfather's home.

"Impressive residence," said Ben. "The family has obviously gone rapidly downhill over the last hundred and fifty years."

Daisy gazed up at the four-storey townhouse. "It's so elegant. I love the ornate plasterwork, and the little balcony. It's a pity we don't have time to see can we contact whoever lives here and see what it is like inside."

"We'll just have to come back again," said Ben cheerfully.

"Maybe you could come back on your honeymoon?" said Daisy, looking up at him.

But he didn't meet her eyes.

"Maybe," he said vaguely.

Earlier, Daisy had booked Do & Co for dinner. A rather

fancy restaurant on the edge of Stephansplatz . It was in a modern building, on the top floor, with full height glazing and dramatic night-views across the city. As the maître d' took their coats, Daisy noticed Ben looking admiringly at her. She was wearing a simple black dress, well cut, that she knew showed off her figure, with a long silver chain and hooped earrings.

"You look great," he whispered.

"You scrub up rather well yourself," she said with a smile.

"Can we afford this on our budget?" he asked, looking guiltily around the crowded restaurant.

"Well, seeing as I twisted your arm to come in the first place, and I have just received my annual bonus, this meal is on me."

"Absolutely not," he said adamantly.

"Ben," she said, putting her hand on his arm, smiling, "I never took you for the old-fashioned type. Surely you can be man enough to let a woman buy you dinner."

"Well ... if you insist," he said reluctantly. "What can I say? Thank you."

Once they had been shown to their table, a waiter appeared instantly and handed them both large leather-bound menus.

"The food here is amazing. The lobster is really good."

"You were here before – in this restaurant?"

"*Mm*. I thought I told you. I was here before with Fintan."

After the waiter had brought wine, Daisy relaxed back into her chair.

"That was an eye-opener earlier today. The more I think about it, the sorrier I am for poor old Rosa. I wonder what she did that was so shameful that Isaac wouldn't marry her."

"As Barbara suggested, maybe she got pregnant with someone else and he dumped her."

"Possibly." Daisy swilled the wine in her glass thoughtfully.

"Well, it was an arranged marriage. Maybe he just decided he fancied the younger sister instead. I suppose we'll never know."

"It such a big decision, isn't it?" said Daisy.

"Yes, it's a great menu, I am torn myself. Between the lobster and the steak."

"No, Ben, I meant marriage, the whole works."

"Oh! Are you and Fintan planning on tying the knot anytime soon?"

"Maybe in a few years' time when his contract in London is finished. How are the wedding plans going? Did you book the hotel?"

"Ah, I ran into a bit of a problem."

He told Daisy about Sal, how Fergal was harassing her, and how the solicitor had advised that she should pay him his share of the equity of the house.

"Poor Sal. She is such a lovely, feisty woman. It's hard to think of her being bullied like that."

"Well, hopefully it's sorted. The solicitor is going to settle with him rather than have a lengthy court case. I lent Sal ten grand and she is borrowing the rest from the Credit Union. I also visited Fergal last week and told him I'd beat the shite out of him if he ever tried to contact her directly again."

Daisy looked alarmed.

"I am not normally one to advocate violence but, in this instance, it is the only language he understands."

"Do you think it will work?"

"I expect so – I am much bigger than he is." He smiled ruefully. "The problem is, I haven't been able to pay the hotel deposit for the wedding."

"Does Julie know that?"

"No." He shrugged. "I decided to wait to tell her when I got back from here."

"Wise move." She paused. "I can lend you the money if you like – until we sell the paintings. As I said, I just got a bonus."

He looked at her quizzically. "You hardly know me, Daisy."

"Actually, I think I do. Anyway, money isn't everything. If it is what you want, go for it."

"That's the trouble," he said ruefully. "I am not so sure what I want anymore. With the wedding, I mean." He filled up her glass and poured himself another. Then, changing the subject, "So, tell me what exciting project are you working on now? Whose minds are you messing with?"

"It's with Dublin Transport Authority." She sensed his reluctance to talk about his relationship. "They are trying to alter the current dynamic whereby cyclists vote for more cycle-ways in the city, whereas non-cyclists usually vote against. So, they are trying to find means of changing the non-cyclists' mindsets to make them see that freeing up the city is good for everyone."

"That will be a challenge."

Following a pleasant meal, and mellow with wine, they headed across the now deserted Stephansplatz towards their hotel in Schulerstrasse behind the medieval cathedral.

"I have really enjoyed this evening, this whole trip in fact, Daisy. Much more than I expected to, to be honest."

"That's a bit of a back-handed compliment."

"Do you know, when we first met, I called you Frau Ffraw."

"Why?" She sounded hurt.

"Ffraw – meaning 'fine, fair and brisk', implying a coldness about you – do you remember? But you're not – cold, that is."

He stopped, facing her.

"Anything but, in fact." He took her face in his hands and bent down and kissed her firmly on the lips.

"I have been wanting to do that all evening."

Daisy knew, on so many levels, this was wrong, but she closed her eyes and savoured the moment anyway.

"Sorry," he said eventually, "I shouldn't have done that."

"No – but it was nice all the same."

He put his hands in the pockets of his overcoat and they returned in silence to the hotel, lost in their own thoughts.

"I'll see you in the morning, so. The flight is at ten. Meet you for breakfast at seven?" he said as they reached the lift.

Chapter 18

Vienna
March 1862

Helena had allowed Thomas to fondle her breasts, and to kiss her with his long tongue. She had tried not to gag, as she thought it was like having a live snake thrust into her mouth. Initially this act of defiance had been satisfying. It served Isaac right that she allowed another man to enjoy her body, after he had treated her so cruelly.

The thought of him sleeping with her sister made her feel sick – now, lying on the chaise longue, she moved her hand instinctively to soothe her belly.

"Helena, my darling, can you please try to stay still?"

She threw her eyes up to heaven, shuffled, then resumed the pose, lengthening her long neck and looking slightly to one side. Thomas was in a frenzy as usual. To him, she was only an object of desire to satisfy his male gaze. But at least he loved her – only her – so he said.

She had been confused at the strength of her reaction

294

to Isaac's unfaithfulness. Up until then, she would have been relieved that he had found someone else to pester, to satisfy his needs. But taking her sister brought up feelings that were complicated, old sibling rivalries and feelings of her own unworthiness. But more than that, was the knowledge that what had happened threatened everything she had strived so hard to achieve.

Her life in the shtetl was still a recent memory – the pain of hunger during long winters – and the agony of chilblains on her blistered feet as she walked on frozen rutted roads in ill-fitting boots. But it was memories of the smells that brought her right back there, of sweat from unwashed bodies, and the sickly scent of boiling cabbage.

There was no doubt in her mind that life had been good in Vienna. She had insisted on her freedom from the start. And – she reluctantly had to concede – Isaac had gone along with most of what she wanted. He had even tolerated her friendships with other men. But sometimes she caught him looking at her, his eyes filled with a desire that filled her with disgust. If only she enjoyed the sexual act. At least if she had satisfied his lust, he might not have strayed with the one person that she could not bear to lose him to – Rosa – Saint Rosa. Rosa the good daughter, the good wife. No doubt she was even a good lover, Helena thought bitterly.

Her mind drifted back to her visit to the doctor the previous week. She had tried to explain to the old fogey that she felt no desire – no feelings stirred within her at the sight of a man's cock. The self-righteous idiot had given her a lecture that the Lord expected women to support men spiritually and physically, to satisfy their bodily needs. He had advised her to try to arouse herself, and to eat more meat.

But sitting here now, half naked, she didn't feel aroused – she felt unguarded, not in control. The grim prospect once more played out in her head of Rosa lording over her, having breakfast with them both, her sister still warm from her husband's bed. She would send a note to Moishe to tell him of his wife's duplicity, that might satisfy her need for revenge. But she knew the problem was deeper than that. Isaac no longer wanted her – she had lost her status in his affections – she had lost her power in the household, and that would be unbearable.

She tried to concentrate on the plan she had formed. Following the day, they had met at the Prater, Lieutenant Lewinsky had agreed to lie low, terrified of Isaac's retribution, until the appointed time. But he had assured her that he would play his part. Now she had to convince Thomas. She felt he would be an easier target. At least now she had a plan. It would be hard at first. She knew she had to act swiftly.

"Thomas, may I take a break?"

"Oh, if you must. Sorry, Helena – of course, my darling. I'll make you some tea."

"Not tea, would you get me cocoa from the café across the road. I feel chilled today. I don't know what's wrong with me."

"Of course."

She knew he was irritated at wasting his precious time with her, but too polite to refuse her. She wrapped a fine-wool shawl around her shoulders.

Thomas put on his coat and bounded down the stairs. She looked at the clock on the mantelpiece – she had ten minutes. It would be another half an hour before Mim returned from Frau Lipsky.

When he returned, he poured the hot drink into her cup. As he placed it on the table beside her, she stood up, letting the shawl fall to the floor.

"Thomas, do you love me?"

He knelt in front of her and pulled her to him, pressing his face into her breasts.

"Of course, I love you. I spend every waking moment thinking about you. How can you ask me this when you know how besotted I am with you?"

"Do you love me enough to live with me as man and wife?"

Thomas's head jerked up.

"What I would give for that honour!"

"Well, what if I were to leave Isaac and run away with you?"

"I would die a happy man. But your husband?"

The dramatic delivery of his devotion suggested that he was not taking her seriously – he thought she was play-acting.

She touched her cheek, her eyes wide and frightened.

"He has started again, Thomas."

"He's beating you!"

That wiped the smile off his face.

"Constantly. I live in a permanent state of fear."

"*The bastard, I will kill him!*" Thomas shouted.

"No, Thomas, unfortunately violence will serve no purpose. With his knowledge of the law, it is you who would end up being arrested, and I would lose you. There is only one solution – I must leave."

"Leave?" he said, confused.

"Yes, leave Vienna, as soon as possible. I am in fear of my life." Tears ran down her beautiful face as she thought of Isaac with Rosa. "Please, Thomas, please, I beg you – take me away from all of this, help me escape from him. We could travel to London, start a new life. There are plenty of wealthy patrons in London, with beautiful wives and daughters for you to paint. You would be such a success, I know it for sure." She dried her eyes delicately with the edge of her fine linen handkerchief, careful not to rub away the smudged kohl that she used underneath her eyes.

"But money, my darling, how would we live? There would be expenses!"

He rubbed the back of his neck, and she could see the fear in his eyes as the enormity of what she was suggesting dawned on him.

"I have thought of that. I will sell my jewels. I have the sapphire necklace and earrings that Isaac gave me, and the emerald brooch and other bits and pieces. They should make at least fifty florins. I have some money as well."

"Ironically, I have just been paid by your husband," said Thomas thoughtfully. "There is also money in my chest from the portrait of Countess Alice. Look, if you are sure that this is the only way ... I cannot bear to think of him hurting you." He stroked the scar on her cheek, which as her face was flushed was now red and pronounced. "Yes, let's do it! Helena, you have made me the happiest man alive! When will we go?"

"As soon as possible. Every day I spend in that house, I risk my life."

"My darling, have no fear, I will protect you. It will take me a few days to wind things up here. Can you manage to survive until Friday?"

"Yes, I think so," she said in a frightened whisper. "Can you hire a carriage, and pick me up at the corner of Spiegelgasse at two o'clock on Saturday morning?"

"I will be there, have no fear, little one. I will not let you down."

***

It was fifteen minutes to the hour of two, and the city was asleep. Although, a gaggle of noisy stragglers could be heard a few streets away returning home from one of the city's many late-night taverns. A few hadn't quite made it and had collapsed in the gutters. Only the night-soil men were about, shadowy creatures wrapped up from head to foot in their filthy rags, quietly going about their business. A mangy dog was scavenging through discarded pigs' trotters in newspaper wrappings while rats gathered nearby, waiting to pounce on what was left.

No more snow had fallen. Thank God, Thomas thought. The streets in the city had been swept and had remained clear. Although, they would not travel tonight. They had agreed he would take her back to his studio and leave from there at first light.

Everything was ready for her. He had left the stove on, filled with smouldering wood. The bed linen was freshly changed, with a warming pan between the sheets. He had hidden all the mousetraps in a press and placed a vase of winter jasmine on the dresser. He wanted tonight to be special – this first night of the rest of their lives. He felt himself become momentarily aroused at the thought of it, but the cold soon dampened his ardour. Thomas looked at his pocket watch again. It was two o'clock – she would soon be with him. He wrapped his greatcoat tightly around his body. Although he was wearing several layers, he was still freezing.

The horses were getting skittish, whinnying, and scraping their hooves on the cobblestones and he could hear the driver trying to soothe them. "Whoa there, my beauties – easy does it."

Thomas looked over at the house on Spiegelgasse, the shutters were firmly closed, and the building was in total darkness. She had warned him under no circumstances to knock on the door.

Thomas was tired. He yawned and lay his head on the upholstered seat. The last few days had gone in a frenzy – there had been so much to arrange. He wrote notes to his suppliers, the colour-man, and the framer and to the few friends he had made in the city. He had visited Frau Lipsky and been obliged to drink vodka with her for several hours the night before. He told them all the same story. He had been offered an important commission to paint a society lady and was planning to travel to London where he would be staying indefinitely.

Frau Lipsky had insisted he pay her the rest of the month's rent, even though he had already lined up a tenant for her. "For my troubles," she had said. His last visit had been to his bank where he withdrew his savings. Two hundred florins, that and the one-hundred florins in his desk was a princely sum for a boy from Dublin. But how long would it last if he were to keep her in the style to which she was accustomed? It was enough to get them to London anyway, to set them up in a modest way. Then, hopefully after a month or two, he would get a few commissions.

He looked at his watch again. Half past two – she must have been delayed. Please God she hadn't been discovered in her attempts to leave. He wriggled uncomfortably in the seat.

The driver knocked on the panel at the back of the carriage and Thomas slid it open.

"Much longer, sir? The horses are cold," he said impatiently.

"Shouldn't be too long, hopefully."

At ten to three there was still no sign of her. The house was still in darkness. The driver knocked on the panel.

"Looks like the young lady's changed her mind, sir!"

Thomas, filled with despair, reluctantly had to admit that appeared to be the case.

He paid off the cab driver outside his lodgings. Once inside, he climbed the stairs, as quietly as he could, so as not to disturb any of the other tenants. With a heavy heart he opened the door to the studio which to his surprise wasn't locked. In his haste to leave, he must have forgotten to do so.

As he entered the studio, he sensed immediately something was wrong. Maybe she had somehow arrived here on her own and was waiting for him in his bed. His heart lifted momentarily. But dropped like a ton of bricks when he noticed in the corner of his studio that his bureau was open. The wooden cask where he kept his money was upturned on the desktop, empty. Looking wildly around the room he saw that her finished portrait, that he had left proudly displayed for her to see on the easel, had been cut roughly from the timber stretcher. It was gone. Shaking like a leaf, he checked the bedroom. It was as he left it. He returned to the studio and checked the small jug where he kept the key to the cask. As he had suspected, it was missing. He looked carefully around the room, nothing else had been disturbed. But on the card table he noticed a single sheet of bone-coloured paper. With shaking hands, he picked it up, fresh with the smell of her scent, and read.

Sorry, Thomas, it was the only way.

Thomas fell back on the chaise longue, head in hands, sobs racking his body, and wept like a baby. He had been duped.

When he finally stopped crying, he poured himself a large glass of vodka. She must have taken the key the last time she was here while he was at the café. As the sudden realisation dawned on him that she might have discovered the other painting, he felt a cold sweat spread over his body. In a panic, he stumbled over to the stack of unfinished canvases in the corner of the room. But breathed a sigh of relief when he found it there untouched. Thomas drew it out, and, removing the vandalised stretcher, placed it on the easel. He sat there drinking the vodka, the alcohol warming his blood and the image of her filling him with an all-consuming anger and lust. Until the oil lamp was empty and the room in darkness, and he fell into a fitful and frustrated sleep.

***

"Rafferty, you bastard, open the door!"

Someone was pounding on his door. Thomas's head

felt as if his brain had been cleaved with an axe. As he rubbed his eyes, his eyes resting on the nude, memories of what had happened the previous evening flooded back. It was Tarrant, her husband. In a panic, he grabbed the painting from the easel and placed it with its face to the wall.

"Where's my wife? You won't get away with this!"

"Irish, what is happening!" Frau Lipsky's disembodied voice could be heard three flights of stairs below as he opened the door. *"Herr Tarrant, you will not shout like a costermonger in my house. I will call the police!"*

Isaac ignored her, as he pushed Thomas into the room, grabbing him by the throat and thrusting a pistol into his head.

"Where is my wife?"

Tarrant's eyes were black and his face cold and expressionless.

Thomas could feel his eyes bulging. He was finding it difficult to breathe.

"She was here earlier. She's gone – stolen all of my money."

"Helena!" Tarrant called, dragging Thomas to the door of the bedroom. He saw the bed, unslept in, and released Thomas violently so that he fell to the floor.

Still pointing the pistol at him, he sat down calmly on the chair.

"Now, tell me exactly what you were planning to do."

PART 3

Chapter 19

London,
April 1863
Brown's Hotel, Albemarle Street, Mayfair

Brown's Hotel was comfortable. It was better than staying in a lodging house. It had the advantage of having a private dining room and an afternoon tearoom where, with a little ingenuity, introductions could be made. The guests were upper class, mainly gentry from the countryside who didn't have the luxury of owning a town house. A few of the better-off clients had permanent rooms – like the tea-plantation owner from the Bahamas who liked to spend the spring and summer in England's cooler climate.

Their suite of three rooms was on the second floor with windows overlooking Albemarle Street. This morning, Helen was sitting in her bedroom, a woollen shawl over her nightgown. The peal of bells from the city's churches signalling that it had just gone seven o'clock. She was cold and tired, having found it difficult to sleep, and was feeling sorry for herself. Every time she had closed her eyes the previous night, images of Rosa and Isaac together filled her mind. As a result, she had spent the night tossing and turning and had woken up in in the morning with her bedlinen wrapped around her body in a twisted rope. To make things worse, she could hear Gretta snoring in the room next door.

Helena poured lemonade from the carafe on the side table and sipped the drink. The chambermaid was due to arrive shortly to set the fire. She had found the last few weeks unbelievably stressful. Money was running low. She was also weary of her peripatetic existence and painfully aware that in a few weeks, if her circumstances hadn't radically improved, she would have to sell the sapphire necklace. They would be forced to move to cheaper accommodation.

Since arriving in London a year ago, she had only managed to operate on the edges of polite society, wrangling a few invitations here and there from the other guests. She usually targeted older women who tended to be more gullible and were grateful for the small errands she offered to run for them. Middle-aged, married women avoided her like the plague, wary of their husband's admiring glances. She'd received plenty of attention alright. A few men had even indicated an interest, although it was of an unwelcome kind. Unlike her sister, she thought bitterly, she wouldn't settle for being anyone's mistress. She knew that the physical aspect to such a relationship would be non-negotiable – she simply couldn't do it. No, marriage to some undemanding gentleman was still the only option. So far, however, she had not met any suitable candidates, and she was beginning to think that it wouldn't be such a bad idea to move on. Maybe to one of the fashionable spa towns on the coast where it might be easier to make the right sort of social connections.

When they first left Vienna, they had travelled to Paris, but after a few weeks she realised that the city was expensive, and the risks of bumping into friends and acquaintances from home was high. London was a better bet. So, after an emotional scene with Lieutenant Lewinsky, where she had threatened to contact Isaac and tell him that he had abducted her, the lieutenant had reluctantly agreed to escort her and Gretta on to London. But as soon as she was settled in Browns, he had scuttled off like a scalded cat to make the following morning's steamboat back to Calais. His time was running out, he had told her. As she had suggested, he had got a month's furlough from his commanding officer on the grounds that his father was dying. What a weak and pathetic man the lieutenant had turned out to be! She was glad to see the back of him.

On the other hand, she was sorry she had hurt Thomas – he hadn't deserved it. But Isaac had broken her heart and had left her with no other choice – this was all his fault. If only he had accepted things the way that they were. They had enjoyed a good life – until Rosa came along.

Since leaving Vienna, she had changed her name to Helen Schmitt. She had also orchestrated the transformation of her German maid, the older, sensible Gretta, into a lady's companion. Gretta, presenting a satisfactorily drab appearance, now wore Helen's more subdued cast-offs, under a serviceable dark-brown coat and bonnet that Helen had instructed her to buy in a Paddington second-hand clothes shop. Fortunately, Gretta had one of those faces, desirable in a lady's companion, that one instantly forgot – or thought you had seen before on someone else. Helen found her personality soothing – she was intelligent, quiet, and resourceful. It helped that she adored her mistress and had the sense never to voice a contradictory opinion. Helen generally introduced her to people they met as a second cousin. But Gretta rarely spoke. She was under strict instructions to avoid talking to people whenever possible, and then to speak only in French.

In the mornings, Helen took singing lessons with Monsieur Badeaux in Regent Street. She had read an advertisement in *The Ladies Monthly Magazine* that it was an invaluable way of improving one's elocution, which was currently one of her primary concerns. The cadence of Yiddish, where sentences commonly ended in a lyrical uplift, so that they sounded like questions, clearly identified her Jewishness. In Vienna, within the established Jewish community, and enjoying the security of Isaac's wealth, this was not a problem. But here in London, trying to fend for herself, being Jewish was a distinct disadvantage. Fortunately, her fair colouring was a distraction, and singing English popular ballads had certainly helped her pronunciation. So, although her speech was still heavily accented, her origins were no longer quite so obvious.

Helen got up from her chair, opened the window slightly and looked out at the street below. It was still early. Only a few delivery boys were about, with handcarts stacked high with groceries, and the odd businessman walking briskly on his way to work.

It had been unseasonably warm for April. But despite the good weather, the maître d' explained to them that the hotel was still quiet, the season hadn't yet started.

On fine days, carrying umbrellas to protect themselves from the odd shower and the precarious English weather, Gretta and herself would stroll through Hyde Park. They would walk along Rotten Row (a corruption of the French *Route du Roi*) 'taking the air,' as the English called it, and gawping surreptitiously at the fashionable ladies and gentlemen, who passed by.

However, compared to Vienna, Helen found London dull and lacklustre. At first, she thought the whole city was in mourning following Prince Albert's death two years previously. But she had been advised that this was not the case – the English were by their very nature subdued and restrained. Helen had hoped to catch a glimpse of Queen Victoria, but since the funeral she hadn't been seen in public. The other guests whispered that the Queen had gone mad, inconsolable with grief, and after all this time she was still languishing at Balmoral.

If the weather was inclement, the two women would browse in the nearby Burlington Shopping Arcade or visit Fortnum and Mason's to buy a few delicacies – Turkish delight or peppermint creams – to keep in their rooms. And in the late afternoon they rested before dressing for dinner – a formal affair which was served at half past seven on the dot in the hotel dining room.

***

Helen and Gretta had just finished a light breakfast when, out of the corner of her eye, Helen saw a distinguished-looking gentleman sitting at a table near the window with two older women. She had noticed him arriving a few days ago in a handsome crested carriage with a liveried coachman. He had been accompanied by the two women, one of whom, Helen guessed by the plainness of her attire, was the other lady's companion. The other, older woman was tall, hatchet-faced and with a manly physique. She was elaborately dressed – English old-lady style, all fox-furs and folderols – with the kind of sensible boots a Frenchwoman would never wear.

Helen had hoped that they might meet at breakfast the

following morning, but there had been no sign of them. They must have been served in their rooms. She had to wait until now to get another look at him and eavesdrop on their conversation. On closer inspection, she decided that the young man was probably in his early twenties, of good build, a few years younger than she, with blonde curly hair and an amiable face. She surreptitiously watched them as he fussed over the hatchet-faced woman, pouring her tea, and passing her salt for her coddled eggs.

"Maybe a walk in an hour or two, Aunt – a short stroll in Hyde Park," he said. "I have some business I must attend to first."

"Fine, Georgie. Don't worry about me, I plan to sit with Constance in the residents' drawing room and read. Your mother sent me over Mrs Henry Wood's novel *East Lynne*, and I am very much looking forward to getting stuck into it."

Helen dabbed her napkin delicately on her rouged lips and smoothed down her navy taffeta skirt.

"I am just going up to the room," she said to Gretta who was still sipping her tea. "Don't get up. Follow me in a few minutes when you are finished."

Helen took her lace handkerchief from her pocket then stood up, coughing delicately into her fist. As she did so, he looked up, his eyes lingering on her beautiful face. Then, passing their table, she dropped her handkerchief on the floor.

He followed her out into the hall. "Excuse me, Miss!"

"Yes?"

"You dropped your handkerchief!"

"Oh, thank you so much. So kind of you."

"May I take the liberty of introducing myself to you? The Honourable George Frome, at your service."

"Delighted to meet you, Mr Frome." She smiled. "My name is Helen Schmitt."

"Helen, the Greek goddess of beauty. Have you been staying here for long, Miss Schmitt?"

"Oh, for several months now."

He seemed unable to take his eyes off her face.

"My aunt will be wondering where I have got to," he said, after a few seconds trying to collect himself. "Hopefully, I'll have the pleasure of meeting you again." He made an exaggerated bow.

Things were beginning to look more promising, she thought, her heart racing as she climbed the four flights of stairs to the second floor.

Later that morning, the Honourable Agnes Frome – prompted by her nephew, no doubt – introduced herself to Helen in the residents' drawing room. She gave Helen her card and invited her to take tea with her in her suite the following afternoon.

When Georgie came in later to collect his aunt to take her out for the promised walk, they exchanged further pleasantries. The Fromes, Helen learnt, were an old English aristocratic family from Bath. Georgie's father was a Baron. Agnes Frome lost no time in explaining that their presence in the hotel was only because their Cavendish Square townhouse was being decorated following a recent kitchen fire which had caused extensive damage.

As Georgie lead her away, the aunt said in a loud voice, "You didn't tell me she was forrin!"

***

"So where exactly are you from?" Mrs Frome asked the following afternoon when Helen descended the stairs to the Frome's suite on the first floor.

"Well, my parents were Bavarian," said Helen, reciting the carefully rehearsed version of her pedigree – loosely inspired by the Empress Elisabeth of Austria's idyllic accounts of her childhood growing up there. "Unfortunately, both of my parents were drowned tragically at sea during a freak summer storm while travelling between Venice and Trieste. I wasn't with them – I was only four years old at the time."

"How terribly sad for you, my dear." The older woman's beady eyes were cold and appraising. She gestured to her companion, Constance, to pour her more tea.

"Yes, it was awfully sad. You see, I had no other relatives, other than Gretta who is a distant cousin. Both of my parents were only children. Fortunately, money was not a problem. My solicitor, an elderly bachelor, was appointed my legal guardian. He packed me off to a boarding school in Lucerne, Switzerland, where they only spoke French. So, my English is not as good as it should be, I am ashamed to say."

"That explains the accent," said Agnes Frome. "I speak French myself, of course, but only when I absolutely have to. I find it such an imposition. I insist on speaking English, particularly when I am in France. What age are you, Miss Schmitt?"

"Twenty-three," said Helen, generously deducting three of her years.

"And not yet married?"

"No, as you can appreciate my circumstances are unusual. Although, I have had several offers." She blushed and lowered her gaze demurely. "But I am afraid that the gentlemen concerned were more interested in my fortune than holding any true affection for me. After finishing school in Lucerne, I spent a few years in Paris. I had never been to England, so I decided to come here to London to see the sights. Also, I had enough of France. I find the French a little ..."

"I know exactly what you are going to say: rude, and disrespectful."

"Exactly, Mrs Frome. It is one of the reasons why I extended my stay in London. I plan to rent a house for the next year or so, see if I could make a home here."

"Oh," she said, sounding unpleasantly surprised. "And what did your father do?"

"He dealt in ivory."

"Oh, elephants and such."

"Yes, a family business – we were the main suppliers to manufacturers of piano keys in Europe. My father himself was an educated man. A scholar of classical studies. Hence the name Helen."

"How interesting!"

Helen sensed that her father's academic credentials lessened some, but by no means all, of the social stigma of her family's involvement in trade.

From that day on they fell into a routine. Helen played cards with Agnes Frome in the morning, while Georgie conducted his business, and in the afternoon they all went for a stroll together in Hyde Park.

Usually, Gretta stayed at the hotel and Mrs Frome's companion, Constance, accompanied them, holding Mrs Frome's arm.

Georgie, with a little encouragement, took it upon himself to improve her English, teasing her gently when she mispronounced a word and helping her to increase her vocabulary. He talked about his father's estate, Somerville Hall, and his own plans to develop the land, to introduce modern farming techniques, and new breeds of livestock. His trip to London was to attend a month-long series of lectures organised by the Royal Agricultural Society about industrial-scale husbandry. His father had insisted that he bring his sister, Agnes, Georgie's aunt, to London as a holiday for her. But Georgie suggested it was also a break for him, to get her out of the house.

"She drives him mad," he said affectionately, "but she's not the worst in the world."

His father was quite intolerant, he told her, a stickler for the old ways, a very conventional man. He rarely came up to London as his health wasn't good. He suffered badly from gout.

Helen, on the other hand, amused Georgie with stories of her imaginary boarding school, and the life she had led there. Fortunately, she had borrowed a rather explicit romantic novel about an heiress who was sequestered at such a school from a private lending library on Regent Street.

The young couple's obvious delight in each other's company had been initially tolerated by Agnes Frome. But over the last week Helen had noticed a coolness develop and vain attempts by his aunt to convince Georgie to spend his free time engaged in activities that didn't include Helen. Fortunately, Georgie had ignored her.

This morning, as they strolled along the Serpentine River towards Hyde Park Corner, there was a gentle breeze, the temperature was rising, and the sky was a clear cobalt blue. The world and his wife were out enjoying the fine weather. Uniformed nannies pushed large black perambulators with gaggles of well-behaved children in tow – and elegant ladies with extravagant costumes and bonnets were accompanied by dashing military men. Helen and Georgie were enjoying the entertaining tableau. She was also flushed with pleasure at the admiring glances she had received from everyone they passed. She was wearing a fitted, short jacket over a new peach-coloured dress with cream frogging to the front of the jacket. And as she walked, the fabric, as light as a feather, clung to her figure.

"I have really enjoyed these last few weeks in your company, Helen," said Georgie. "I shall really miss you when I return to Bath." He stopped and faced her. His aunt and Constance were a good distance ahead.

"Oh, when are you planning on leaving?" Helen said with dismay, her pulse racing. She wasn't quite sure how enamoured he was of her. Although she knew he desired her.

"Well, I received a telegram from my father this morning. It's come as a bit of a shock. I must return to Sommerville Hall by the weekend. The lectures aren't even over. I had hoped to stay here longer – to spend more time with you and get to know you better."

He turned and smiled at her adoringly, and she thought of how much she had enjoyed being admired for the last few weeks.

"Why so suddenly?" she asked.

"A good friend of my father's, Lord Streatham, his wife and daughter are coming to visit us and plan to stay for a while. I think my father and her parents are trying to arrange a match for us."

"Arrange a match?" Helen asked, unfamiliar with the expression.

319

"Yes, hoping we will be attracted to each other and become romantically involved."

"And is she beautiful, this young woman?"

"Her name is Pamela. And she is pretty enough, in an English-rose sort of way. But she is nowhere near as beautiful as you."

"Georgie," said Helen, smiling sadly at him, "you are only being polite, and excessively amiable as usual."

"You have no idea how hopelessly in love with you I am, Helen," he blurted out.

He was looking miserable, she saw with great satisfaction.

"Your beauty, your wit and charm. No other woman I have ever met comes near. I must speak with you privately. I asked my aunt to obtain an invitation for you for Lady Wentworth's charity ball, tomorrow evening. Did you receive it?"

"Yes, I did. I am really looking forward to it." She smiled, looking away from him demurely, in an attempt to look flustered at his words. If he really knew quite how much she was anticipating the opportunity!

"I will try and find some time alone with you there so that we can speak privately."

***

The packed oval-shaped ballroom at Lady Wentworth's Belgravia house was decorated with swathes of a variety of white flowers. Chandeliers sparkled, and the light from oil lamps glinted off ornamental swords, and diamond necklaces. Couples waltzed to the music of Strauss, almost magically managing not to collide. As much as the constraints of her corset would allow, Helen breathed in the scent of gardenias which filled the room. Hopefully, he would make a move tonight, she thought. She could not bear it if she had wasted all this time with him – and time was running out.

Helen was wearing an ivory-silk ball gown cut low at the front with a single white rose at her breast. Around her neck was the sapphire necklace Isaac had given her and matching earrings. Gretta had dressed her hair elaborately with tiny curls that framed her face and had twisted a plaited knot on top of her head. The look was understated, classical, and accentuated her exotic beauty.

She had laughed as Georgie had filled her dance card at the beginning of the evening so that she had only two slots free. "For appearances' sake," he had said. But Aunt Agnes was giving him disapproving looks. Over the last few days the old crone had been trying to avoid her and made excuses when Helen offered to play cards or take tea with her. The older woman was obviously alarmed at how attached her nephew had become to the "forrin girl". For that was how Helen knew she still saw her. She was certain that Agnes Frome had warned her brother of the budding relationship and had orchestrated their sudden departure.

After the third dance in a row with Georgie, Helen was flushed and breathless. Drunk with exhilaration, she could sense the excitement he was feeling with the physical closeness of her. He got himself wine, and a glass of lemonade for her, and they wandered out to the terrace overlooking the landscaped gardens.

It was a fine clear evening. He guided her to the edge of the terrace. Helen pulled her shawl closely around her neck and looked up at the stars, praying that her luck was about to change.

They waited for several minutes, saying nothing, just gazing, companionably at the night sky, until another couple standing nearby eventually returned to the ball room. Then taking her glass and placing it on a table, Georgie turned to her where they stood in the shadows.

"I cannot leave you here, Helen, you have bewitched me with your beauty." He leant over and kissed her passionately on the lips."

She responded with as much enthusiasm as she could muster, then abruptly pulled away.

"You are laughing at me, Mr Frome. You are just like the others. Shame on you for taking advantage of me, unprotected as I am." She turned from him to lean on the balcony.

"No. No, my darling, I wish to protect you. For the rest of your life."

His face was flushed, and she could smell the sour taste of wine on his breath, as he turned her to him. She looked into his blue eyes heavy with desire, and firmly pressed into him, feeling his arousal.

"Ah, there you are, Georgie," said Constance. "Your aunt sent me to find you. She's come over all faint – she wishes to return to the hotel."

***

That night he came to her room. She knew he would. He knocked tentatively on the door.

"I must speak to you, before I leave."

She was waiting, her hair brushed into a golden veil that lay over her alabaster shoulders. She had taken a glass of cognac to calm her nerves, but she was still terrified. She tried to do the breathing exercises the doctor in Vienna had taught her. She knew she had to go through with this. It was her only chance. Just the once – she said, over, and over again – just the once.

"I love you, my darling."

"Be gentle," she whispered.

And, as he entered her, she winced with pain and thought of the future.

Chapter 20

Two years later
Paddington, London
March 1865

"Have we much longer to go, Thomas?"

"No, thirty minutes or so. Would you like to take a break, Mrs Appleby?"

"Please, my neck is so stiff, I am afraid that I shall never get full movement in it again." She rubbed the back of her neck with the fingers of both hands, bowing her head.

Thomas put down the palette on the side table and wiped his brush with a dirty rag before placing it in the brush holder on the table beside his easel.

"Can I get you a drink, some ginger-ale perhaps?"

"No, thank you, Thomas. Let me just stretch my legs for a minute." She stood up, releasing an anguished sigh as she did so. "Age is a terrible thing, Thomas."

He reckoned she was in her fifties, hardly ancient by any standards.

Mrs Appleby had a stout physique encased in an evening dress of maroon taffeta, which she had chosen to wear for the half-portrait. Thomas mused that her bosom was rather like a shelf that protruded from underneath her chin and formed a solid mass that tapered off at her elegant, buttoned boots. If he was honest, the boots were the only elegant thing about her. Her face was square-shaped, powdered and rouged with improbable purplish pouting lips. She had told him that the portrait was a 'present' for her husband. Thomas was using all his skill to make her look more attractive than she really was.

The truth was, she was damn ugly. For an artist to have to spend hours painting an ugly woman must surely be one of the worst penances on earth. Especially as Mrs Appleby's plainness made images of Helena's loveliness hard to get out of his mind.

He hadn't thought about her for a while. He tried not to – but sometimes, he just couldn't help himself, she continued to haunt him even after all this time. Where was she now? Was she somewhere in Europe torturing some other hapless idiot? How could she have done what she did – to deceive him so cruelly?

Mrs Appleby stood by the window, looking out over the roofs towards Paddington Station.

"How long have you been in London, Thomas?"

She'd asked him this before, but he responded politely.

"Three years now. I was in Vienna for two years before that."

"One of my favourite cities, you know. So elegant, the architecture I mean, not the women. Most Viennese women look like they have just stepped off the stage in Drury Lane. To be honest the men are not that much better. As for the food, it is simply awful, unless you are a fan of sausage, which I am not. Why did you leave?"

"I was there with friends, and they left," he said vaguely. "I had stayed longer than I intended anyway."

She resumed her pose, seated on the chaise longue and they both fell into a comfortable silence.

Prompted by her comments, his mind wandered back to the day after Helena had left. He hadn't stuck around once she had gone. The police had got rid of Isaac for a while, but Thomas had been afraid that he would return, and that he would kill him. Occasionally, he still woke up in the dead of night, particularly if he had drink taken, dreaming of Isaac's black eyes, filled with hate, glaring at him and his long, strong fingers crushing his windpipe. After Isaac had been escorted off the premises, Thomas had sent a boy around with a note to Rosa to tell her what had happened. The boy returned with a message to meet her at lunch hour in the little coffee house, in a side street off Kärntner Strasse, near the hat shop.

Rosa hadn't gone to work that day – the house had been in an uproar. When she had eventually arrived, she had been so nervous, constantly looking over her shoulder as if Isaac would come in, all guns blazing, through the coffee-shop door.

She told Thomas that the previous evening, while the family were out at the theatre, Helena had hired a carriage and told the servants she was going away for a few days to stay with friends in the spa town of Baden, thirty or so kilometres south of Vienna. Taking her maid Gretta, and a suspiciously large amount of luggage, they had left Vienna.

It was not until after breakfast the following morning that Isaac discovered his money had been stolen and most of his wife's possessions were gone. He had interrogated the servants. Rosa said he was like a bull, roaring and shouting. Helena had taken the key from the secret drawer in his desk and opened the safe in Isaac's study.

When Rosa had told him the amount of money involved, Thomas had been shocked. It seemed that a few days previously, Isaac had drawn down funds from the bank to make the final payment to the builders. She had taken all her husband's money, her jewellery, and she had even taken a bust by the sculptor Canova that she had recently bought for the alcove in the hall.

Rosa had suggested to Isaac that maybe she had run off with Lieutenant Lewinsky. Isaac had laughed at that, a demonic, desperate laugh. Rosa told him Isaac had replied, "She's no such fool. Apart from the fact that his father is almost bankrupt, he prefers men. And whereas his sexual preferences might suit her, his lack of a decent annual income certainly would not!" There was also the fact that as an army officer he could not just up and go.

No, it had to be someone else. But the only other man Helena had any prolonged social contact with, Jessica had suggested, was Thomas Rafferty. Initially Isaac had dismissed the idea. He thought it unlikely, he had said that the artist had even less money than Lewinsky. But he had admitted it was possible that one of them had abetted her escape. However, when he had found Thomas in such a state of despair at his studio, Rosa told him Isaac had concluded that they had been having an affair, which had then enraged him even further. The thought that she had given herself to another seemed to make him incandescent with rage.

No matter how much the tearful Thomas had protested, Isaac had refused to believe him that he had never slept with Helena, or that he had no part in the grand theft that she had orchestrated. But Rosa did not think he would go to the police. For a man as proud as Isaac, the shame would be too great. Isaac had told Rosa that he intended to deal with Thomas himself.

That morning in the café Rosa had urged Thomas that it was in everyone's interests that he left Vienna as soon as possible. He'd left that day – he was ready to go anyway. But, by doing so, he had confirmed his guilt to Isaac. Thomas had to sell the gold fob watch his father had given him, although doing so nearly broke his heart. But the watch wasn't that distinctive and, when he was able, he'd simply buy another. Papa would never know. He had also borrowed fifty gulden from Frau Lipsky, promising faithfully that he would pay her back. She had made him leave a few of his paintings behind as collateral, including the nude he had done of Helena, which she had found when she had entered his apartment while he was out. She knew immediately who it was – of course she did.

When he had arrived in London, Thomas had written to his old landlady and sent his forwarding address. He was expecting a final cheque for the portrait of the wealthy banker's wife. He would use this money to repay Frau Lipsky. When he finally heard back from his old landlady, almost three months later, she informed him that the banker had since died, and his wife was unable to honour his fee. Frau Lipsky demanded that Thomas immediately pay back the money he had borrowed. She had intimated that she might tell Isaac about the nude if he failed to do so. But, to her chagrin, after his journey and the initial costs of setting up in London, Thomas simply did not have the money. They had eventually agreed that he would send her instalments whenever he could.

So far, thank God, she hadn't sunk to blackmail. But Thomas was anxious to get the painting back. Hopefully, within the next few months he would have repaid Frau Lipsky in full.

As an aside to the debate about his debt, his old landlady had also informed him that Helena had disappeared completely without a trace.

Thomas still missed Vienna – the colourful sway and

swagger of the place, its swashbuckling soldiers and the theatrically costumed ladies of the Empress Elisabeth's court that Mrs Appleby had just so harshly dismissed.

London in contrast was damp, dull and grey, even on fair days. He found English men to be severe and unctuous, and the women in their dark-coloured costumes were generally strait-laced and humourless. And if they weren't demure, then they were vulgar – but without the flair of Frau Lipsky who, even with her improbable red wig, had a certain bohemian chic.

Compared to the Viennese, the British simply had no style. He blamed their dowdy queen, the dumpy Victoria – who, even though her husband died two years ago, was still dressed permanently in black. A pity, as she had shown a fondness for German Romanticism in the portraits she had commissioned as a young woman from Winterhalter. It was also said that she had bought the Prince an erotic painting for his private delectation. Maybe the late Prince Albert and himself had more in common than he thought.

That evening, after Mrs Appleby's departure, Thomas looked out of his attic window. The fog had descended, a thick, black sooty smog. Rubbing a circle in the misted glass, he could see the roof directly behind his – but that was all. The pigeons that normally congregated on the ledge outside the window had gone to roost elsewhere. With the limited visibility, sounds from the street below were accentuated: carriage horns, and street hawkers shouting their wares, and in the distance, he could hear steam pistons from trains coming and going to Paddington Station. Thomas wiped his forehead – the room was still warm from the fire that he had roaring for Mrs Appleby. It had been a long day.

He poured himself a glass of whiskey to perk himself up – he was due to go out that evening. The previous week, he had received an invitation to a musical recital from Lady Broughton, whom he had met at a church social. He mustn't look a gift horse in the mouth. He'd have a nap for an hour or so, before sprucing himself up to face the cohort of worthy, god-fearing, London matrons in the hopes that he might garner another lucrative portrait commission.

***

Several hours later in the cold comfort of Lady Broughton's Gothic-style ballroom, the string quartet was taking a break. Thank God, thought Thomas. His behind was sore from sitting in the rather hard gilt balloon-back chairs. You would think, with her obvious wealth, that Lady Broughton would at least have provided comfortable chairs for her guests. He was sipping stewed tea – which he had chosen rather than anything alcoholic, simply to warm himself up – and engaged in conversation with Lord Brocklewood and his charming daughter, Daphne.

She was telling him about a recent visit she had made to Rome where her likeness had been drawn by a local artist. As he dreamily admired Daphne's beauty, Thomas was distracted by the sight of a serving maid passing around a plate of plum cake. He had slept longer than he intended and hadn't time to buy food from a street vendor. Worried that his stomach would start to grumble, he placed one arm protectively in front of his belly.

"Haven't these photographers put you lot out of business, old chap?" asked Lord Brocklewood. He was an amiable man with watery, rabbit's eyes and a whiskey nose that was red and bulbous. Thomas wondered would his daughter's pert retroussé nose follow a similar fate.

"No, sir, a photographer's process is purely a mechanical one – it cannot reflect a man's spirit, or a woman's soul – or capture the essence of their character."

"The Queen and the late Prince Albert were very keen on it, all the same. It's amazing how the royal couple allowed family photographs to be so freely available. It used to be that only the middle classes could afford lithographic prints of royal portraits. Now every farm labourer and factory worker have a photograph of Her Royal Highness pinned to their wall. Doesn't seem right somehow."

"Maybe her popularity with the people is why she is still on her throne, sir, not like the *er* ... the ... the Bourbons."

"Good point, Rafferty, good point," said Brocklewood.

332

"You all right, old chap? You look like you have just seen a ghost."

Thomas felt like he had stopped breathing, his heart was beating so fast that he could feel it knocking against his ribcage. He was afraid he was going to swoon like a girl. At that moment, she turned – startled – and their eyes met. It *was* Helena. But she looked different, her appearance changed. Her hair was blonder, more elaborately styled, and she was heavily made-up.

"Please excuse me," he said to the gawping Daphne and her father. "I've just seen someone I haven't seen for a long time."

Helena had resumed talking to a couple she was with, her back to Thomas. But, as he approached, she turned her head.

"Thomas, how nice to see you again. Major Archibald Howard, Mrs Letitia Howard, this is an old acquaintance of mine, Mr Thomas Rafferty," she said quickly in a breathy, high-pitched voice. Before waiting for the couple to respond, she said, "Please excuse us – we haven't seen one another for years and have so much to catch up on."

She held his arm in a surprisingly steely grip and steered him away towards a window alcove.

"Say nothing, I beg you, or my life will be in danger." She looked around nervously. "My husband is here. It is too dangerous to speak. Call on me tomorrow, after two in the afternoon. Here is my card. But, Thomas, for your sake as well as mine, say nothing to anyone. *Please*," she whispered – her rouge lips parted to bare her small even teeth in a forced smile.

He could see she was terrified.

***

As the cab approached Cavendish Square the following morning, the cabbie slowed the horses, stopping outside number five. As Thomas paid him, the Londoner nodded towards the palatial house on the opposite side of the square.

"Harcourt House, the London residence of the Duke of Portland. The Duke is a queer cove, by all accounts. An eggcentric." He went on to explain how the duke had built an underground maze of rooms at his country residence in Welbeck Abbey in Nottinghamshire.

Thomas smiled absentmindedly and checked Helena's card once again. Number five was in similar baroque style, more modest in size, but still a substantial residence.

After paying the cabbie, Thomas climbed the steps and knocked three times firmly on the front door which was answered promptly by a footman. He showed him into a drawing room on the first floor.

The room was luxuriously furnished with damask-covered couches, chairs and two small marble-topped tables. But, as Thomas entered the salon, his eyes were drawn immediately to his portrait of her, on the opposite wall, in a handsome gilt frame. Anger suffused him. How could she be so brazen, to flaunt the painting she had stolen from him here in her new home? He crossed the room to examine it more closely. At least, whoever had framed it had done a good job.

He paced around the room, furious, his heart racing and – despite himself – feeling aroused in anticipation of seeing her.

Judging by these luxurious surroundings, she had certainly done well for herself, he thought, trying to calm down. Along one wall was a sideboard with large decorative chinoiserie urns and an ormolu clock. The almost floor-length window had a view across the square's ornamental gardens where neatly ordered circular beds of daffodils and bluebells presented a colourful vista. Thomas noticed a faint smell of lilies-of the valley in the room, but he could see no flowers. He stopped to examine his profile in a large, gilded mirror hanging on the end wall, pulling in his stomach and straightening his white cravat.

"Thomas," she appeared at the door, "can you ever forgive me? If you don't say you forgive me immediately, I shan't come in."

"Helena, we meet again," he said stiffly.

"Is that an 'I-forgive-you'?"

"I see you have at least made good the portrait."

"Sorry for taking it. I wanted to have something to remind me of the time we spent together." She hovered at the door.

"Why did you do it?" he said coldly. He wasn't going

to roll over and forget everything. He wanted her to know how much she had hurt and humiliated him.

"If you will allow me, I'll explain everything. But you mustn't be cross with me. And no shouting!" She looked back through the door as she closed it firmly behind her. "Please, Thomas. Sit down."

"So why? Please, do tell!" Once Thomas had got over the fleeting pleasure of seeing her, he felt the pent-up anger well up inside him once again. "Helena, I lost everything. Your husband Isaac nearly killed me. I had to flee Vienna in fear of my life with the police on my heels."

"Isaac was furious about the money, I presume?"

"That, and everything else. He refused to believe that we didn't have an affair."

"*Mm.*" She screwed up her mouth to one side, then adopted her previous inscrutable expression. "Well, that's good enough for him. Thomas, if you only knew the violence that man inflicted on me. I was in a state of constant fear. Then ... then when I discovered he was sleeping with Rosa, my sister ..."

"Rosa is your sister?" said Thomas, horrified. "But why –"

"It's a long story. Maybe some other time. But yes, Little Miss Goody-Two-Shoes is my sister."

"He's even more vile than I thought!" Thomas clenched his fists, jumped up from the chair and stood with his back to her, looking out of the window, so that she couldn't see the desperation on his face. "What I don't understand is, why did you go without me?"

"Thomas, I knew that Isaac would look for me, possibly even send the police after me. Lieutenant Lewinsky kindly agreed to escort us to London – to protect us, Gretta and me – just in case."

"Lewinsky!"

"We were friendly, as you know. He was aware of my situation. But we were never …"

Thomas turned his head slightly but still stood with his back to her.

She continued, "I had intended writing to you, asking you to join me once I got to London. But I got ill, and then I met Georgie, and all my plans changed. They had to."

"Who on earth is Georgie, and why did your plans change?" He turned abruptly to face her.

"Because … because I was pregnant."

$$\sim \!\!\curvearrowleft \!\!\curvearrowright \!\!\sim$$

Chapter 21

Vienna
March 1865

"Any news from Kornyn, Rosa?" asked Bubbe Mim, walking over to the samovar and refilling her cup with tea.

"Papa has been poorly, his chest is not good. He has not really recovered from the shame of Lena's flight – and my situation, of course. But Mama soldiers on," Rosa replied sadly, folding her napkin.

"Will you return this summer to visit?" asked Jessica.

"No, although I would dearly like to. But, as I am sure you know, I would be given short shrift in the community."

"Even after Moishe agreed to a get?"

"The divorce formalises – but does not forgive."

Isaac lowered his newspaper and looked at her sadly, taking her hand in his. Behind closed doors his mother and grandmother had accepted that Isaac and Rosa were now in a relationship. The joy of baby Anton's birth was

338

enough for the two older women to accept the unusual nature of their arrangement. But only on the tacit understanding that once Isaac obtained a divorce from Helena, they would marry. Outside the narrow confines of their home, Rosa was still introduced as a distant cousin.

"I have people looking for her in Paris, London, even New York, she cannot hide forever. The sighting of her in Paris by the Goldsteins at least tells us she is still somewhere in Europe and hasn't disappeared back to the wilds of Russia."

"Yes, but that was three years ago!" said Rosa in frustration.

"Infuriating, I know – but, eventually, she will turn up."

"Like a bad penny!" exclaimed Bubbe Mim.

"Yes, indeed, Grandmother." He squeezed Rosa's hand then released it. "But then at least our son can witness his father marrying the loveliest woman in Vienna."

"How is Frau Kauffman, Rosa?" asked Jessica to change the subject. She found any show of affection distasteful. "I don't know why you continue to work for that woman."

"Rosa is no longer an employee, Mama. They are partners now," Isaac said, smiling at Rosa. "Rosa is the modiste – *une première* – I think that is what they call them in Paris."

"It gives me an interest, Jessica, a financial interest, now that Isaac has bought half of the business."

"The commodity markets may rise and fall, but I reckon women will always buy hats," he said genially.

"I heard that the Empress Elisabeth brought twelve 'coiffures' – they are hair ornaments," Jessica explained to Bubbe Mim, "as well as sixteen hats from Bavaria as part of her trousseau. There were two white ones, one pink one made of feathers, one Florentine straw hat with blue plumes, several lace bonnets, and numerous riding hats. Even a garden hat with a garland of field flowers."

Rosa smiled to herself – Isaac's mother always had a weakness for hats.

Rosa remembered the first time she had met Jessica all those years ago in Kornyn, in the Tarrant's dining room with her ridiculously extravagant hat. And how her own poor mother had outshone her with her own elegant, homemade tichel. It was one of the reasons that Rosa had suggested that Isaac invest in the hat shop. Because Rosa dreamt that one day Mama could join her in Tissot's and that together they would run the business. But until they could find Lena and regularise her situation with Isaac, that day was still a long way off.

"The Empress must be married over ten years at this stage. Imagine how many hats she has now," said Jessica.

"Probably nearly as many as Helena had. What has happened to all of her hats by the way?" Isaac asked.

"Well, I took the liberty of taking them into Tissot's to be refashioned," said Rosa.

"*Mm*, a sensible solution no doubt – it doesn't look like

340

she will be coming back for them anytime soon," said Isaac, picking up his newspaper once again.

***

The conversation at breakfast prompted Isaac to call into Schneider on his way to work. Known in the city as Schneider the Snoop, Isaac had engaged the Prussian lawyer to act as an inquiry agent to find Helena. Without a divorce he could not remarry. He was confident, at this stage, that he would not need to mention to the Synagogue committee the humiliating details of their marriage. Her desertion was now sufficient cause. If only he could bloody well find her. The current situation was deeply upsetting.

Rosa's divorce had not been quite so difficult. Moishe's heartbreak had been painful to witness when he tried to get her to change her mind. But him learning of her infidelity had put the final nail in the coffin of their relationship.

Samuil, as Rosa had feared, was devastated that Rosa wished to leave his father and torn between his loyalty to them both. Ultimately, he had chosen to return to Kornyn to console and support Moishe in his time of need. However, he still wrote regularly to Rosa, and next year he planned to return to Vienna. Encouraged in his musical ambitions by Doctor Strauss, Samuil hoped to play the flute and to study Music at the Academy, now that his asthma was manageable. Perle had also finally forgiven her. Although that had taken longer. She was due to visit next spring, and Isaac suspected she too would eventually become part of his ever-extending family. There seemed to be only one-way traffic from Kornyn, he thought with resignation.

Isaac tried to focus his mind on more cheerful things. Rosa had brought him contentedness, and of course great joy with the son he had always longed for. Little Anton was now two years of age – a good-tempered boy with a head of light-brown hair, fair like his mother. But every now and again, he thought of her – Helena. He couldn't help himself, despite all that she had done to him. In the black of night, his tormented mind and body still yearned for her. However, the next morning when he drew the curtains and daylight illuminated Rosa's gentle face, he was filled with shame.

The lawyer's suite of rooms was on the top floor of a building in Stern Gasse, a narrow medieval street in the Jewish quarter. A pale-faced clerk, with legs as skinny as a cricket, met him at the top of the stairs and showed him into the office. Sitting in the anteroom was a rough-looking character improbably dressed in in an old army officer's coat (stripped of insignia). The coat looked like it had seen more military action than he had. Isaac wondered was he one of the ex-convicts that Schneider was known to employ to do work that the police were unable, or unwilling, to do.

Inside the Prussian-Jew's office all was neat and

orderly. The walls were book-lined, although they appeared to be mostly for show – they looked unused. Schneider, seated at his desk was smoking a cigar. He was balding and had wide, rubbery features, his eyes bulged slightly as if he was being permanently throttled, and he had a short, hairless upper lip.

"Herr Schneider, sorry for arriving without an appointment. I was passing and thought I would call in for an update. I was wondering had you anything to report on Frau Tarrant?"

"Well, your call is fortuitous, Herr Tarrant. Although I still have no news on her whereabouts. I was going to contact you today. There has been a development that might be of interest. A London art gallery in Mayfair, Pickering's, has a painting for sale. A nude portrait of an unknown lady." Schneider pursed his mouth, making his chin jut forward in a vain attempt to conceal his prurient interest.

"Why should that interest me, Herr Schneider?"

"Well, it so happens that it was painted by Herr Thomas Rafferty while he was in Vienna. One of my contacts in London was checking out Rafferty because of his, *eh* ... involvement with your wife. So, I took the liberty of writing to the gallery to establish the details of the work."

"And?"

"It seems the seller claims that the model is a wealthy Jewess. My associate in London wondered ..." he coughed delicately into his chubby fist, "could it be Frau Tarrant?"

343

"Rafferty did paint my wife, but fully clothed, I can assure you. I was told at the time that my wife cut the canvas from the frame and took the portrait with her when she bolted. The nude must be of someone else. I believe that Rafferty painted several society ladies during his time here. Maybe my wife wasn't the only woman who kept his bed warm." Isaac looked unconcerned. "And the seller?"

"A certain Frau Lipsky. Name mean anything to you?"

"*Mm*, rings a bell alright. She's an acquaintance of my grandmother's from Kornyn."

***

That evening, after dinner, Jessica and Bubbe Mim were out visiting friends. Rosa and Isaac were alone in the drawing room. Although the passion of the earlier days of their rekindled relationship had moderated, they still relished time alone together. For such a private man, Isaac was a tender lover, and on evenings such as this they would often just sit on the couch in front of the fire holding hands while they shared the details of the day's events. Tonight, however, Isaac was sitting in a high-back chair smoking a pipe which he had taken to doing occasionally, and Rosa was opposite him embroidering a pillowcase.

Isaac told her about Schneider's extraordinary information.

"I can't see Helena doing such a thing," he said

344

earnestly. "I mean having an affair is one thing. But exposing yourself for the predilection of every drooling punter is another matter entirely. If anything, she was surprisingly prudish about things like that. No, it just doesn't sound like her. I'll talk to Frau Lipsky anyway and see what the story is. I mentioned her name to my grandmother, but it seems she fell out with her. Said she drank too much and cheated at cards. In that regard, I would have thought they were both well matched. Anyway, she hasn't seen her for over a year and refuses to have anything to do with her."

Rosa put down her embroidery, giving him her full attention. "Yes, they had a row."

"Well anyway, maybe Rafferty was doing nudes as a side-line to earn extra money. I know amongst certain men, there is a market for such things. However, I suspect that it's just a red herring and nothing to do with Helena. But I had better talk to the old crone."

"Why not let me talk to her, Isaac? I'll probably get more out of her. You would only intimidate her. I'll call on her tomorrow, bring her some of my schnapps." Rosa looked down at her uneven stitches and tried to control her shaking fingers.

**

Two days later, after the older women had gone to bed, Rosa was alone with Isaac. He was due to travel on business the next day and the couple were catching up on household arrangements before he left.

"I visited Frau Lipsky today," she said calmly, although her heart was racing.

Isaac lowered the book he was reading and looked at her with interest.

"I told her that Simon Goldman, an English art expert that you were acquainted with – I made the name up – had questioned you about a painting that was for sale in London, by Thomas Rafferty, supposedly of a wealthy Jewish woman. The seller being Frau Lipsky. And that he was acting on behalf of an interested purchaser. Knowing of your connection with Rafferty, he wondered did you know who the woman could be? I told her that Herr Goldman had also asked you to check if Frau Lipsky was the rightful owner of the painting. He was concerned that it had been stolen. Frau Lipsky became quite defensive. She claimed that Rafferty left the painting behind as collateral for a loan she gave him when he left in such a hurry." Rosa spoke slowly and carefully. "But when he hadn't repaid his debt, a few months later she needed money and sold the painting to a dealer here in Vienna. She said that the portrait was of a model Rafferty often used, Dora Müller. I don't know whether you remember her, a nice girl, she used to work at the hat shop. She left when she got in the family way – by a young lad who sold coffee to the workers on the Ringstrasse. Anyway, to cut a long story short, Frau Lipsky thought that the painting was probably of Dora."

"Ah," said Isaac.

"Really, she had no right to sell it. It seems that Rafferty is unaware of this, thinks she still has it. She was clearly embarrassed. But she claimed her stove was broken, and she was desperate for money for a new one. She also talked about your two families' connection – asking after your grandmother."

"Good Lord, despite my … history with Rafferty, she has some cheek to suggest we would condone her actions." Isaac resumed reading his book.

"Yes, indeed she has." Rosa was relieved that he seemed satisfied with the explanation she had given. He appeared uninclined to take the matter further.

A few minutes later, Isaac looked up from the book and took a long drag from his pipe.

"I might extend my trip, Rosa, for a day or so. I received a letter today from a prospective business partner in Boulogne who is interested in developing a trading company between there and North America – silks, satin fabrics, and fancy goods mainly. I didn't mention him before because I thought it might come to nothing. We met at the club. Both of us had a fair amount of brandy consumed. But it seems he was serious after all. It could be in your interest also, my love."

"Sounds promising. Don't worry about me. As you will be away, I was thinking of accepting Frau Kauffman's invitation to go to Paris with her. She is visiting a modiste, a Madame Marchand who is making hats which are

347

creating quite a stir amongst the London fashionable set. She is holding a fashion salon next week. So, rest assured, I will be fully occupied in your absence."

Later that evening, as his manservant helped him disrobe in his dressing room, Isaac pulled a letter from his pocket that he had received from Schneider that afternoon. He had not wanted to alarm Rosa. He read it again.

12, Stern Gasse

6th March 1865

Dear Herr Tarrant,

It might interest you to know that today I received confirmation from my associate in London that Herr Rafferty visited a lady in 5 Cavendish Square. Servants from a neighbouring house later confirmed that the tenant of the house was a Mrs Helen Frome. From the description and the carte de visite of your wife that you gave me, I believe that Mrs Frome and your wife are one and the same person. I hope this information satisfies your initial enquiry. I now await further instructions from you.

Your humble servant,

Sylvester Schneider

Isaac hadn't lied to Rosa – he had intended to travel to Boulogne. But now with the knowledge of Helena's whereabouts he would spend a few days in London afterwards. He could feel his heart quicken at the thought of seeing her again, but fury soon replaced those foolish fantasies as he remembered how callously she had treated him.

Chapter 22

Dublin
9th December 2011

They had arranged to eat on Friday night in one of Ben's favourite restaurants, Il Caffe di Napoli on Westland Row. Julie had come in from Clontarf on the dart and emerged through the crowds outside the station. She was wearing a short fur coat he had never seen before, with a long black dress underneath it.

"Julie, good to see you," he said, giving her a peck on the cheek, then held her hand as they walked the short distance to the restaurant. Crowds of people were walking in the opposite direction, swathed in woollen scarves, jaunty hats, and Friday faces on their way home from work.

The restaurant entrance was through a tiny ground-floor café. His mood, which had been dire all day, lifted as they descended into the cavernous, converted cellar and inhaled the comforting smells of garlic and Parmesan cheese. But the sight of the Christmas tinsel, baubles and the overwhelming festive good cheer of the place made his heart sink again. He realised that this was not a good time to have a difficult conversation with Julie.

Even though it was still early, the place was packed. The head-waiter Nico, of the sad brown eyes and droopy moustache, nodded at Ben as they entered and showed him to a table in the corner of the room covered in a white linen cloth.

"Usual wine, Mr Ben?"

"Please, Nico."

Ben hadn't seen Julie since he had returned from Vienna on Sunday evening. He thought she looked tired. He wasn't looking forward to the prospect of dealing with her wrath – which he felt was inevitable when he told her about Sal and the money.

Nico appeared magically with a bottle of white wine and poured them both a glass.

Ben drank a mouthful of wine and took a piece of the crusty bread from the breadbasket on the table.

"So, you enjoyed Vienna?" Julie said with that smile that was not a smile, the way she did sometimes.

"Yeah, it's a very special place."

"Maybe we should go there on our honeymoon?"

"Yeah," he said unenthusiastically. "Funny, Daisy suggested that."

"*Mm*, did she now? I would probably find it dull – all those old buildings and shite food."

351

"Actually, we went to this lovely restaurant." Damn, wrong answer, he thought as soon as he said it. He winced, wishing he could bite off his tongue.

"I thought we were meant to be saving."

He noted her red mouth, pursed, and her black eyebrows arched like those Angry Bird cartoons.

"She paid for it," he replied defensively – knowing that this wasn't the right thing to say either. He thought she looked like she was going to say something but changed her mind. She gave him a tight little smile instead.

"I saw this house for rent in Sutton yesterday, it's got three bedrooms. We could use one for a nursery, and one for a study." It was as if she was goading him.

"Julie, you know I don't want to live in Sutton. I want to live in the city, near to the community where I teach."

"That's just not going to happen, Ben. I am not going to live in a place where I have to wear my handbag constantly strapped across my chest." She sat back in the chair and took a slug of her wine.

"That's really not fair, you know," he said, weary of the familiar conversation.

"Well, it's all very well for you. You have this romantic idea about poverty – like it's shabby chic or something. But me and Mam had to struggle to get where we are, to move from the inner city and live somewhere nice. And I have no intention of going back there. So yes, I do want a three-bed semi in a nice part of the city. One where the neighbour's kids don't do drugs and their parents don't know all of your business."

"Clontarf, I thought we agreed on Clontarf – did you see anything there?"

"No. Not within our price range." She paused and looked at him directly. "Did you put the deposit on the hotel?"

"Eh ... I need to talk to you about that. I had to lend Sal ten thousand euro to pay off Fergal."

"You did what? Without talking to me? What the fuck, Ben?" she said loudly.

"I thought you would understand," he said, rubbing the back of his neck anxiously and looking around the restaurant. "Look, Julie," he leant over the table, lowering his voice. The couple at the next table were staring at them. "That bastard roughed her up, she was terrified! She couldn't sleep – she was talking about getting an alarm fitted."

"Well, why didn't she get an alarm? Why do you always have to be the big guy? Did you pay the deposit for the hotel?"

"No, Julie. Look, can we talk about this later – people are staring at us."

"Watch my lips, lover boy! I don't give a shite. You had no right to do that without talking to me. I am sorry for Sal – but she's an adult. Why should I have to suffer because she wants some hippy-dippy life and can't afford to pay her bills?"

"Now you really are being unfair. You know Sal is like a mother to me."

"Shit, Ben, I really don't understand you sometimes." Her anger evaporated suddenly, and she looked confused and deflated.

He took both of her hands in his. "No, I don't think that you do." He looked sadly at her – all he could see before him was a frightened child. He steeled himself, and breathed in slowly, hating himself for what he was doing. "Look, I have had time to think while I was away, and this is not working out. *We* – are not working out. We just want different things. I cannot spend my life being the kind of man you want me to be. I am just a slob, Julie, and I am not going to change any time soon."

She choked back the tears. "You're not a slob. Well, maybe a little bit. Maybe we should just take a longer break, give each other some space?" she said desperately, clutching at straws.

"No, Julie," he said gently. "It would be putting off what we both already know to be true."

"Is it Daisy?"

"No, and ... yes. She made me see that you and I are not just different – I know that they say opposites attract – but you and I, fundamentally, want different things in life."

"Did you sleep with her?" she asked belligerently.

"No."

"So, this is it," she said, tears now running freely down her cheeks.

"I am afraid so."

"Your order, Mr Ben? Or will I come back?" Nico was standing beside the table in his long white apron, his sad brown eyes taking in the scene.

"I don't think we are that hungry after all, Nico. Sorry about that."

***

Ben hadn't been to the Bon Secours Hospital for years, not since he had been there with Sal as a small boy. On arrival, the sharp smell of bleach, and the institutional look of pea-green-coloured walls, brought him back to the time when his sister Katrina had recuperated there for months with tuberculosis. The hospital, built during the 1950s, unlike other modern hospitals, had a homely feel.

Sal's friend Madeleine had arranged everything. She had introduced the radiologist, Dr Carew, to Dermot Nolan. Then had rung Ben to tell him that they had been allocated a free slot to X-ray the paintings on Sunday morning.

Daisy was waiting for him in the entrance hall.

"Why the long face, Ben? Are you not excited about finding out the secret of the perfect copies?"

Despite her enthusiasm, there was an edge in her manner. Ben sensed an awkwardness – they hadn't met since Vienna.

"Daisy, good to see you," he said with a smile.

However, he didn't say what his mind shouted – *Julie*

and I have just split up. He hadn't told anyone yet, not even Sal. He just wanted to let it settle in his head, lick his wounds like a wounded animal. He was afraid that if he talked about it at all, he would end up blubbering – and he didn't want to inflict that prospect on anyone.

"Dr Nolan said he'd meet us here at ten o'clock," he said. "Ah, speak of the devil!"

The suave academic entered the reception area wearing a long woollen overcoat over neat blue jeans, and a crisp white shirt. He was carrying an old-fashioned leather briefcase. Ben stroked the two-day old stubble on his chin. Feeling embarrassed, he dug his hands deep into the pockets of his waxed jacket. He should have made more of an effort.

"Daisy, Ben, how are you?" Dermot Nolan slapped Ben's arm and then kissed Daisy on both cheeks. "You're looking very well this morning, Daisy."

Ben noticed she blushed when he said this. Ben mentally admonished himself for not complimenting her himself. She did look well this morning in a smart leather jacket and floaty skirt.

"Well, this is exciting, isn't it?" said Dermot. "I have been here for a while – I just slipped out to grab some breakfast. The two paintings have been X-rayed, and I have had a good look at them. I think you will be intrigued with what I have discovered." He turned to the receptionist. "Hello," he said, "could you call Doctor Carew, please? She is expecting us."

356

A few minutes later a diminutive grey-haired woman in a white coat appeared.

"Daisy, Ben, this is Dr Carew – she's a real doctor," Dermot said magnanimously.

"Pleased to meet you both. Come with me. This exercise has caused great excitement in the hospital amongst the staff. We are all dying to know Dr Nolan's diagnosis. Madeleine was most upset that she wasn't working today," she said impishly.

She led them to a white-walled examination room with a large radiography machine in the middle of a grey lino floor. On the wall was a lightbox onto which were fixed two X-rays.

Dermot took off his overcoat and put on the white surgical coat hanging from a coat stand.

"Before we look at these, I need to bring you up to speed about the investigations that I conducted in the gallery," he said. "Firstly, I carried out a detailed visual examination of the Tarrant painting and the Frome painting. Then, I arranged for a photographer to take infra-red photographs. These showed charcoal under drawings of the female form in both paintings. So far so good. But when I examined them both under ultraviolet light in the conservation workshop, I discovered something quite intriguing. You see, ultraviolet light agitates molecules in the animal-based resins used in old-fashioned varnishes. It causes them to effloresce which is picked up by the ultraviolet light, so that it looks like a blue-green sheen. Where there is overpainting, this efflorescence is missing. Overpainting is when an artist paints over the original varnished image. What I discovered was that on the Tarrant painting the efflorescence was absent from the woman's gown which would indicate that this was over-painted. So, to see what is under the overpainted clothes we needed to investigate further with an X-ray. Dr Carew, could you do the honours, please?"

Outside of the lab, an ambulance siren could be heard arriving at the hospital A and E, but inside the room you could hear a pin drop. No one said a word. Everyone's concentration was on the black radiographic images fixed to the light box.

Dr Carew switched the machine on.

"Now, these are the two figures," said Dermot, pointing to the now illuminated, blurry images. "How this works is that the X-rays pass through or are absorbed by the less dense materials. But they are reflected by the heavier ones, including certain paints with metallic contents. And some paints are denser than others. Skin tones are made from predominantly white paint with a small amount of ultramarine blue, cadmium red and burnt umber. White paint traditionally contained lead which reflects the X-ray and looks whiter than areas that have less metallic compound. You can see this quite clearly in the exposed area of flesh. But if you look at the Tarrant painting, you can see that there is an under-painting. This is not unusual. Most paintings, no matter what the subject, are built up in a series of layers. In oil painting artists traditionally use darker colours first and lighter ones afterwards. But as you can see here, the under-painting is in a lighter colour. In fact, it is not just an outline, it is a complete layer."

"You mean that there is another painting underneath?" Daisy asked.

"Yes. Look carefully. You can see – almost like a photographic negative – it's the model in the nude. The top layer was applied at a later date."

"Why would the artist do that?" asked Ben.

"I've no idea. For whatever reason, he was not happy with the nude and afterwards painted clothes over her naked form."

"Was this unusual?"

"Well, it is certainly the first time I have come across it. Although, I have heard of other examples before where this has happened. What struck me was that working-class women generally modelled for artists, not respectable women from the upper classes. In the nineteenth century, for a society lady – as I am assuming this lady was – to be painted in the nude would not be socially acceptable. For the artist to paint her like this suggests an intimacy above and beyond their relationship as artist and model."

"Well, we weren't expecting that," said Daisy, gob-smacked.

"No, we certainly were not," agreed Ben.

"My goodness! Wait till I tell Madeleine and the other staff," said, Doctor Carew. It's not often that we get to X-ray old masters, or maybe it's old mistresses in this case?"

After thanking Dermot Nolan and Dr Carew and agreeing to meet up in a week or two when Dermot had finalised his reports, Daisy and Ben went outside and stood in the carpark.

"Fancy a coffee?" asked Ben. "That's rather a lot to take in."

They strolled over to a local café. There was a Christmas buzz about the little shop with its tinsel and holly decorations. A waitress in a Santa jumper and brown felt reindeer's horns on her head served them cappuccinos and scones. The smell of mince pies made Ben briefly nauseous, and he remembered he hadn't eaten breakfast.

"Rough night, last night?" she asked, sipping her coffee and smiling at him.

"Yeah, sorry – slept it out. Didn't have time to shave."

"The rugged look suits you."

"*Uh*, thanks," he said embarrassed and not sure how to respond. "Well, what did you make of all that?"

"Fascinating, it makes it even more intriguing as to why she would have got herself painted twice in the first place. One fully dressed and one in the nude. It doesn't make any sense."

"Well, maybe the nude was for her husband's private consumption. They were a raunchy lot in those times by all accounts." Ben buttered his scone and covered it in a thick layer of jam. He realised he was starving.

"Yes, maybe," said Daisy. "Or maybe the nude was painted for her lover. I suppose we will never know. But where does that leave us with proving the provenance?" She was fidgeting with her phone and didn't seem too interested in her scone.

"Well, you are now in the clear. You have traced the ownership and can document your family connection. The painting is what you claim it to be. And, if necessary, you can use the photograph of Helen Frome wearing the sapphire necklace for further authentication. But this exercise seems to have given me new problems without solving any of the original ones. It's made things even more confusing." Ben looked forlorn.

"Oh, we'll just have to keep on digging."

"We? Now that you can … are you not just going to jump ship, flog it and run away with the money?"

"And not be involved in this adventure? No, I'd be afraid of what I might miss." She smiled at him.

"Really, you'll continue to help me?"

"Yes, of course."

"Well actually, there was something I wanted to tell you …" But before Ben had finished the sentence, Daisy's phone vibrated on the table.

"Oh! Sorry, it's Fintan," she said, picking it up. "Hi … No, don't worry, we were just finished. I'll ring you back in five minutes. Bye." She put down the phone. "Listen, Ben, I'm in a bit of a rush. I have a hair appointment in town. Fintan's due home this evening for Christmas. What was it you were you going to tell me?"

"Oh, nothing. It can wait. I'll call you after Christmas."

***

Christmas was, as Sal said, quoting the old saying, *"like the curate's egg, good in parts"*. Mostly it was sad. Ben missed Julie, missed her company anyway. It was hard to believe that this time last year they had just got engaged. But he had no regrets, he knew it had been the right thing to do.

Sal was in much better form now that things had been formalised with Fergal, and their solicitors had agreed a schedule of payments. She was also less anxious about borrowing money from Ben, now that she knew that it was all off with Julie and that the cost of the wedding wasn't hanging over him.

He had been surprised at her reaction to the news. He knew that Sal and Julie had never been best buddies, but he hadn't realised how little love was lost between them.

"All I can say is, I'm glad, Ben. She wasn't right for you. She's a nice girl but her values are all in the wrong place."

Sal always 'did' Christmas with great enthusiasm, and this year was no different. As Ben walked in the door, smells of oranges studded with cloves instantly evoked childhood memories. Sal had bought a real tree and arranged tasteful homemade Christmas decorations everywhere. The mantel over the fireplace with its roaring fire was covered in swathes of holly, and around the room strings of fairy lights decorated artfully arranged willow branches. While overhead, a cloud of lace-like paper snowflakes hung from the ceiling.

Christmas Day had been a quiet affair, as Katrina, Mick and the kids had gone to his family, so Sal had invited them all over on St Stephen's Day for the traditional turkey and ham left-overs dinner. Afterwards, Katrina's husband Mick and himself played charades with the kids. As he acted the eejit uncle, his sisters washed up and gossiped in the kitchen – probably about him. When the kids were fed up with playing games, they collapsed happy and exhausted in front of the telly to watch *Miracle on 34th Street*.

Ben sat down waiting for the others to join him. Sal had laid the table using the embroidered tablecloth from Kornyn. He had also noticed earlier the Russian silver cups with the wonky houses lined up on the sideboard. Both were nice touches. He knew that for his sister, family was everything. She would treasure these things from the past. They had also served as prompts to tell the kids a simplified version of the family's story to which they listened in awe. "We were Jews, *wow!*" little Rory who was eight had said in delight. The sisters had looked at one another, smiling sadly. Now wasn't the time to discuss the meaning of their Jewish heritage, its joys but also its terrible sorrows. That was for another day, thought Ben, when he had worked it all out himself.

Ben ran his fingers lightly over the linen cloth. Now clear of all the clutter, amazingly there were relatively few food stains. Those that were there, Sal had assured him, would wash out. The tiny stitches on the cloth were uneven and, in some places, even clumsy. Considering that everything today was so perfect, there was an innocence in the cloth's imperfections. Ben felt a shiver run down his spine. He thought of the women in his family who had embroidered this cloth, hundreds of years ago – maybe sitting around a fire on a winter's evening such as this. Was it intended for someone's trousseau, he wondered, possibly even Rosa's? Did Lena help her sew it? What tears were spilt in its making, what laughter rolled over its threads, and what tales they must have told. If only the cloth could talk.

"So, what is the story about the paintings?" Katrina asked, interrupting his thoughts, as the others sat down to join him at the table. "Have you found out anything more about them?" She refilled everyone's wine glass. Although she had heard about his recent trip to Vienna from Sal, with whom he had also discussed the X-rays, he hadn't had a chance to bring Katrina up to speed with recent developments.

"Well, although both paintings look identical to the naked eye, under X-ray Dr Nolan discovered that our painting of Lena Tarrant was originally a nude, and that her gown was painted on afterwards. Daisy's painting of Lady Helen Frome was painted when the woman was fully clothed. As both women look identical, we are assuming that they are one and the same person."

"But I thought that our great-great-granny's name was Rosa?"

"Yes, that's right, we always knew that the woman in the portrait was an aunt of some sort. Lena was Rosa's sister – remember the family tree I showed you?"

She nodded.

"OK, well, there are records of Lena Tarrant at the Jewish synagogue in Vienna up until 1862. Daisy has found records that her great-great-granny was Helen Schmitt. She was born in Bavaria and married the Honourable George Archibald Frome in 1863. He eventually became Lord Frome. The family had an estate outside Bath, Somerville Hall, and a townhouse in London, in Cavendish Square."

"Very pish-posh," said Katrina.

"Exactly, she did well for herself."

"Beauty meant something in those days," said Katrina, archly nudging her husband Mick.

"Because the women in the paintings are identical," continued Ben, "we are assuming that Helen and Lena are either one and the same person, or identical twins. And because the names Lena and Helen are so similar, we are assuming they are the same person."

"Why could Rosa not have been a twin?"

"It's possible, but then the painting would have been entitled *Rosa Tarrant*. What looks more likely, and because of the dates, is that Lena adopted a false identity."

"Why would she do that?" asked Sal, looking puzzled.

"Well, at that time being Jewish was a distinct disadvantage. Jews were only really tolerated in polite society if they were wealthy or particularly successful in a professional or artistic field, such as artists, writers, or musicians. In some parts of Europe there were still strict laws in place concerning travel, where Jews could live, what occupations that they could engage in. Vienna was quite tolerant of Jews at that time. But if Lena decided to leave Vienna – which she did, as there are no records there of her after 1862, then to change her identity was probably a smart move. Isaac subsequently divorced her in 1865, claiming that she had deserted him, and then married Rosa. Interestingly, Lena was still legally married to Isaac when she married Frome in 1863."

"No wonder Lena was considered a black sheep in our family. What more do we know about Rosa?" asked Katrina.

Ben paused, looking around the table. The women were all totally engrossed in what he was telling them. Even Mick, who up until then had been half looking at the television in the other room, was giving him his full attention.

"Only that she owned and managed Tissot's, a hat shop on Kärntner Strasse in Vienna, from 1862 until 1899.

Our great-great-grandfather, Isaac and Rosa's son Anton, moved to London in 1883 to work as a tailor and then subsequently to Dublin. There he changed his name to Antoine and married our great-great-grandmother Lilly Gorman in 1884."

"Jesus, Ben!" said Sal.

"You couldn't make this up!" exclaimed Katrina.

"But now you have a provenance," said Sal, "if a little sketchy in parts, so at least you can sell it."

"Well, Daisy can sell hers. She can trace the work's history now – she has a paper trail and can prove who the sitter was and that she was painted in 1862 by Rafferty. Done deal. But, unfortunately, I am even less sure of the painting's provenance than I was when I started out on this journey."

"Why is that?" said Katrina.

"Well, to recap. I have a painting of Lena Tarrant, who was my great-great-grandfather's wife's sister. It's a perfect copy of an accredited portrait of Lady Helen Frome, except it has a nude under-painting."

"Well, doesn't that make it more interesting?" asked Sal.

"Yes, it does to us and our family. But because of these irregularities and, importantly, the fact that it is not signed, there is still a serious question mark over the work."

The house phone rang, and Sal got up to answer it. A few seconds later she popped her head around the door.

"Your phone is switched off, Ben. It's Daisy, for you – she sounds ..." she looked at the kids in the other room and put her hand around her mouth, "she sounds pissed!"

***

Mick drove Ben into town and dropped him off at the Davenport Hotel entrance where Daisy was waiting for him. The uniformed guy behind the reception desk looked at Ben knowingly and threw his eyes up to heaven.

"God, Daisy, are you OK – what happened?" He rushed over to where she was sitting, rather forlornly, on one of the white leather couches and sat down beside her.

"Sorry, Ben, I am really sorry. I didn't know who else to call. Robert ..." she glanced over at the guy behind the desk, who was busily trying to ignore her, "Robert got Sal's number out of the phone book for me – I thought you would be there." She was wearing a rather low-cut cocktail dress and her mascara was smudged around her eyes. She looked very much worse for wear. "I was at a private party, up in Maribel's restaurant, with Fintan, with all of his phony friends – wanker-bankers." She spoke slowly, slightly slurring her words.

He winced – he had never heard her swear before. "I caught him in the ladies' toilets wearing the face off Sonya. She's a trader, you know. Trader-trash! *Ha!*" She laughed pathetically.

368

"Oh, Daisy, I am so sorry," Ben put his arm protectively around her bare shoulders and gave her a hug.

"Yep. You said it! Problem is, I was supposed to be staying here in this hotel with him. I left the restaurant in a bit of a state, and I seem to have lost my purse. I have no money – no keys. I don't want to ring my mother. She'd be too upset. Know-wad-I-mean?"

"Can I take you to one of your friends?" Ben asked.

"Not really – my friends are either gone home for Christmas or snuggled up with their boyfriends. Don't wanna spoil anyone's buzz!"

"Of course. Look, how about I get a taxi, and you can come home with me? My flatmates are both gone back to Cork for Christmas."

"What about the lovely Julie?"

"Oh, she's doing something else this evening."

"Could I? You are such a sweetheart, Ben, a real pet! A genuinely nice guy. Why do women always fall for the bastards? Your Julie doesn't know how lucky she is."

He smiled. Now was not the time to enlighten her, he thought.

"Come on then, let's get you sorted."

***

Daisy woke up about noon. She was still wearing the dress she had on the night before. She put her hands over her eyes to mask the glare. The window had no curtains, just a rather flimsy blind. Dazed, she looked around the room, wondering where she was. The only furniture apart from the built-in wardrobe was a bedside locker with a digital radio.

As the events of the previous evening slowly begin to dawn on her, her stomach sank as she remembered Fintan locked in a passionate embrace with Sonya. The absolute bastard, she fumed. But her anger was quickly superseded by humiliation and despair at what happened after that, being brought back here by Ben and thoughts of what he must think of her now. She got up slowly, wincing at the pain in her head, and walked over to the door. She could hear him moving about in the kitchen.

"Sleep well? I hope the bed was OK," he said as she entered the living space.

"It was grand. Ben … I am so embarrassed about last night."

"Don't be," he said. "Under the circumstances it was entirely understandable. Look why don't you have a shower – you'll feel much better. I've left a dressing gown and some towels in the bathroom for you."

She looked down at her black cocktail dress which was looking rather dishevelled at this stage.

Fifteen minutes later, she emerged, feeling a good deal better, rubbing her hair with a towel, and wearing his dressing gown, a soft fluffy grey one. She had cleaned off her make-up but was conscious that there were shadows under her eyes.

"Nice dressing gown."

"Yeah." He seemed embarrassed.

She guessed it had been a recent Christmas present, maybe from Julie.

"Are you hungry? I made you some breakfast. Well, orange juice and croissants. I got them earlier from the Spar down the road."

"Sounds like as much as I can manage. Nice apartment," she said, looking around.

It was open plan. At one end of the living area was a kitchen, fitted-out in shiny white melamine with stainless steel equipment, and a dining area with white tables and chairs. At the other end was a low grey couch with pale-blue cushions and two designer perforated steel-backed chairs. These were arranged around a low glass coffee table. The seating looked out onto a balcony. The apartment had a clean modernist look, thought Daisy, but lacked any personal bits and pieces.

"It's OK. I just use it as a base. I don't spend much time here. The lads I share with are IT techies – work long hours and go home most weekends. Plus, they are both very tidy. We literally pass each other in the lift lobby. Perfect roomies. I am the only messy one. I tidied up a bit when you were sleeping. Actually, I dumped all of my shite in the other bedroom," he said ruefully, rubbing his hand through his unruly hair.

He looked nice, she thought. He was wearing a pale-grey T-shirt and jeans.

371

"What a great view of the city," she said, moving over to the window. The vista was over the dock area, of high-rise offices and flats, and construction cranes were everywhere.

He moved over to stand beside her – she was conscious that she probably smelt like a brewery despite rubbing her mouth with toothpaste.

"Where is your school?"

"Over there, beyond the railway, that's Sheriff Street." He pointed proudly. "That's where I teach the little feckers."

***

When she had eaten and dressed, she rang her flatmate who agreed to drop back to the cottage to let her in and to give her spare keys. Ben gave her fifty euro to tide her over until the banks opened the following day.

"Are you sure that's enough?" he asked.

"Yes, I don't know how to thank you, Ben. Look, I'd better get the walk of shame over, and go home and sort my life out, ring the bank and report my lost cards."

"And Fintan?"

"He can go to hell! It's over. I should have done it ages ago. After Vienna I knew that he wasn't what I wanted anymore."

She turned and looked at Ben and caught him staring at her intently. He looked as though he was going to kiss her. But, horrified at the thoughts of her boozy breath, she pulled away.

"I'll ring you in a few days' time, after I have got my life back together," she said, embarrassed.

"Yes, we need to figure out where to next."

"Great," she said, not meeting his eyes.

"With the painting, I mean," he said awkwardly.

"Yes, the painting." She felt her heart sink, maybe she had just imagined he was interested in her.

～～～

Chapter 23

London
March 1865

Helen was relaxing, reading society gossip columns in the *Illustrated London News*. She was reclining on a chaise longue, drinking tea and eating sweet-almond biscuits. At her side was an embroidery frame, positioned there just in case any visitors called and she needed to look industrious.

She stretched her toes – her right foot was growing numb – and noticed a small hole in her silk stocking where her toenail stuck through. She would have to get her maid to mend it later – and cut the offending toenail, of course.

As she raised her head, her eyes were drawn to her portrait on the wall. The painting looked magnificent against the Wedgwood blue. The drawing room had been recently redecorated, and she had chosen the colour to highlight the sapphires on her necklace.

She thought back with relief to her recent meeting with Thomas. She'd been in a state of panic after she'd met him at the concert. But the next day they had eventually come to an understanding. He would keep her secret, she in return would recommend him to her wealthy friends and pay him back the money she had 'borrowed' from him. She had already discharged half of the debt by selling the diamond earings Georgie had bought her when Georgina was born. A helpful jeweller in Holborn had provided her with a passable paste copy so that her husband wouldn't notice. Since then, she had bumped into Thomas at several social events, and they had enjoyed polite exchanges. But she knew that he would never forgive her.

At least she had the portrait. She had convinced him that it would be the best possible advertisement for his wares. This was a relief. She felt the portrait gave her credibility. It reinforced the pedigree which she had so carefully constructed.

To her surprise, assimilating into London society had been easier than she had expected. Her foreignness lent her an exotic aura that the English seemed to find attractive. Fortunately, Georgie's hatchet-faced Aunt Agnes was always anxious to show Helen in a good light. Agnes was painfully aware that her brother blamed her for not protecting Georgie sufficiently from being ensnared in Helen's clutches. So now she went to great lengths to make her brother see that Helen wasn't so bad after all.

Still, Helen needed to be careful. A Bavarian diplomat she had been introduced to recently at the theatre couldn't quite place her family. But when she had explained her circumstances, her parents' tragic death at sea, the boarding school in Switzerland, he had seemed to accept it. After all, Schmitt was a common enough name.

Her father-in-law, Lord Frome, had been another matter entirely, an absolute nightmare to deal with. He had been in a towering rage with Georgie after they had arrived unannounced in Bath. Georgie had been intimidated, shaken even, but stood surprisingly firm. They had called in on their way back to London following two weeks' honeymoon in Scotland. They had married with a special license at Gretna Green, where they had fled on Helen's prompting. They both knew that Georgie's father would never have agreed to their marriage.

A few days later the Baron had visited her privately and tried to buy her off. She had handled it well, she thought, looking back with some satisfaction. Once she told him she was pregnant and that she had already attended a private doctor in Harley Street – whom he knew – he caved in. It helped that little Georgina, or Nina as she was known, was the image of Georgie, with fair skin and big blue eyes. But recently the old man had been tight with money, refusing to increase Georgie's allowance which was stretched now with a family to support. Still, he had given them the use of his London home, which he rarely used since his wife's death several years previously.

Although his sister, son Georgie, and now little Nina, were all the family Lord Frome had, Helen knew she couldn't afford to be complacent. He still did not trust her. She sensed that he was playing a long game, waiting for her to trip up. She felt her anxiety rise and she tried to put these thoughts out of her head.

She hoped she wouldn't have callers today. She loved this hour to herself in the afternoons to relax before Nanny brought Nina down from the nursery to spend half an hour with her before tea. Then she wouldn't get a minute's peace. It never ceased to amaze Helen how such a small person could be so tiring. Georgie, on the other hand, adored his daughter, but he had been hinting lately that they should try again for another baby. He never seemed to lose an opportunity to emphasise the need for an heir, telling her that it might soften his father's cough and free up the purse strings if she had a boy.

Gretta entered the room, in that sideways gait she had when she was nervous. She was looking a little flustered.

What's the problem now, Helen wondered.

"Helen."

"Yes, Gretta. What is it?" She tried to say it kindly.

Gretta was wearing a walking costume – she had obviously just come in and was flushed.

"I was just in Mayfair, meeting my acquaintance Daphne Montague, you know the one who –"

"Yes, Gretta, I know who Daphne is."

"Well, we passed Pickering's Art Gallery – and there was a painting in the window ..."

"And?" Helen wondered why Gretta was being so obtuse.

"Yes, a nude painting, of a woman – with no clothes on."

"Nudes usually are unclothed, Gretta."

"The only thing is, ma'am, I mean Helen ..."

"*Yes?*"

"It was you!"

***

Paris, near the Gare St Lazare

When Frieda Kauffman had suggested the visit a few weeks previously to Paris, Rosa had not realised how timely the opportunity would be.

The fashion salon itself had been quite an experience. Held in a townhouse in the second arrondissement, thirty or so wealthy Parisiennes sat sipping tea and nibbling macarons in the elegant first-floor drawing room overlooking Rue de la Paix, as Madame Jeanne Marchand introduced her 'mademoiselles'. Frau Kauffman whispered to Rosa that these girls had the celebrity status of actresses and were much in demand with the gentlemen of Paris.

Frau Kauffman and Rosa had been mesmerised by the fashionable modiste's elaborate creations. Exotic displays of hothouse flowers, ribbons and baubles decorated every type of hat a woman could possibly require. A few even incorporated stuffed birds perched on foliage and balanced on the heads of the elegant models. Rosa tried to memorise all the details of the hats, and to figure out their construction. She drew sketches of them in her small leather-bound notebook so that she could refer to them when they returned to Vienna.

Rosa had expected Frau Kauffman to resist her suggestion that they travel on to London to visit the shops on Regent Street and Oxford Street and extend their working holiday for a few more days. But the Austrian woman had agreed enthusiastically. As Rosa was not sure what lay ahead of her, on the long journey over she had reluctantly taken her into her confidence. Frieda Kauffman knew all about Isaac's wife running away, although they had never discussed it while working in the shop – Rosa never felt it was appropriate to do so. However, it was hard to disguise the fact of her sudden disappearance. Even the dogs in the street knew what had happened. She also suspected that Frau Kauffman realised her relationship with Isaac was more than that of a distant cousin and suspected that he was the father of her child. So that when Rosa told her she wished to try and find her sister, the older woman had not shown any surprise. In fact, she dropped her normally brusque and business-like manner and had been surprisingly kind and supportive.

"I had a sister myself once," she told Rosa, "but I lost her."

"Oh, I am so sorry to hear that," replied Rosa.

"Yes, typhoid. She was only sixteen. I still miss her dreadfully. So, of course I would be delighted to help you find your sister. Any clues?"

"Well, do you remember Thomas Rafferty who she was supposedly having an affair with before she ran away?"

"Of course. The Irish artist. He was a frequent customer in the shop – he used to buy hats for his models."

"Well, it seems he is now living in London and that one of his paintings is in Pickering's Art Gallery in Mayfair. But the thing is, Frieda, it is possibly a nude portrait of my sister."

"Oh, dear, the little minx!" Frieda laughed.

"Well, it's more serious than that. Firstly, if it is my sister, then its existence would be a cause of acute embarrassment to Isaac – it goes without saying that he never commissioned such a painting – and, secondly, I am afraid that Isaac will try and find Rafferty and kill him."

"*Mm*, understandable in the circumstances."

"Well, I think I have managed to put Isaac off the trail. I told him that the painting was of Dora."

"Our Dora?"

"Yes, an unfortunate lie. But one that is unlikely to affect Dora."

"No, probably not. So, how do you plan to find your sister?"

"Well, I figure Rafferty must know where she is. So, if I can get an address from the gallery for Rafferty then I might be able to find my sister."

"You also need her to divorce Isaac?"

"Precisely."

***

The steam-boat journey between Calais and Dover had been rough and the two women had stayed in the first-class cafeteria playing cards for the duration. When they arrived from Dover to Victoria Station, they were exhausted and took a cab straight to the hotel in South Kensington.

After a few hours' sleep they met for dinner in the hotel dining room where they spent an agreeable hour or so discussing all that they had seen in Paris and making plans for the future of their hat business. Then, as they were both still tired after their arduous journey, they retired early for the evening to their individual rooms.

The following morning, after a hearty English fry, the desk porter called a cab for them. They arrived at Pickering's in Mayfair at eleven o'clock. But as Frieda paid the cabbie, Rosa noticed a tall, sharply dressed and familiar figure walking towards her. How could this be? It was Isaac. Her heart raced, and she could feel her panic rising but she had no time to think. He had recognised her too and was fast approaching.

"Rosa, what on earth are you doing here?" he said, flabbergasted to see her.

"Probably the same as you," Rosa rallied. "I am trying to find my sister."

"Frau Kauffman." Isaac, not forgetting his manners, nodded at his wife's companion.

He gave a cursory look at the gallery window, a painting with a gilt frame on an easel formed the centrepiece. It was a landscape, a view of Cheddar Gorge.

"Well, let's not stand here discussing this on the street. Let's go inside."

He ushered the two women in through the door of the gallery. A doorbell chimed marking their entrance.

"Good morning, ladies and gentleman! Such a lovely morning. Welcome to my humble emporium! Archibald Pickering at your service."

The gallery walls were lined with paintings of all shapes and sizes and a distinct smell of varnish permeated the air.

Pickering was standing behind a mahogany desk with a leather writing mat and a small, green shaded desk lamp. He was tall and willow-thin with greying hair, pomaded, coiffed and shiny. He was wearing matching jacket and trousers in an elaborate yellow tartan material that was unusually garish for an Englishman. A monocle dangled from his waistcoat pocket.

"How do you do," he said, extending his hand to the ladies first and then to Isaac. "How can I help you, Mr ...?"

"Tarrant, Isaac Tarrant, and this is Mrs Rosa Cohen and Mrs Frieda Kauffman. I believe you had a nude portrait for sale by a Mr Thomas Rafferty, an Irish artist."

"Indeed, a rather fine nude."

"Do you still have the painting, Mr Pickering?"

"Oh, Good Lord!" Pickering exclaimed, his conciliatory smile disappearing. "The extraordinary thing is you have just missed them both. Mr Rafferty and the painting. He bought it back from me, said he wasn't happy with it and wanted to do some more work on it before it was put back on the market."

"That's disappointing," said Isaac, trying to conceal his astonishment. "Do you have his address by any chance? We were particularly keen to speak to him."

"I don't actually. But he wouldn't be hard to find. I am sure if you asked at the artists' suppliers down the street, they could tell you." Pickering chuckled. "He seems to be quite in demand this morning."

"What do you mean?"

"Well, a lady arrived before he did – sitting in her carriage outside the shop. I was waiting for a delivery of paintings from Stockport House – the old Earl died recently and his heir, a bit of a philistine, is selling off the lot. Anyway, this carriage was blocking my spot. So, I sent my boy out to talk to the driver."

"Who was it?" asked Isaac eagerly.

"Lady by the name of Helen Frome of Cavendish Square, the driver said. She was waiting for someone, a customer to my shop – Rafferty as it turns out."

"Cavendish Square? Is that far from here?"

"No, about five minutes."

"Thank you."

"Can I interest you in another nude? I have a very fine Italian –"

"Not this time. Could you call me a cab?"

"Certainly, sir," said Pickering, looking Isaac up and down, indicating he was not impressed at being so summarily treated.

Isaac turned to Rosa. "I will go there immediately."

"Are you sure it is wise, Isaac?" said Rosa, hands clasped nervously.

"You should go back to your hotel," he replied brusquely.

"No, I will go with you. But maybe, Frieda, you could leave us."

"Very well, Rosa," said the older woman reluctantly.

***

Half an hour or so earlier, Helen and Thomas had arrived in Cavendish Square after leaving the gallery. The footman relieved them of their coats and hats, then Helen directed Thomas to carry the painting into the drawing room on the first floor.

384

She marched on ahead of him, indicating that he should follow. But as he reached the door to the salon he stopped to rest. The painting was heavy.

"Thomas," Helen said, "don't dawdle, bring it in. Unwrap it and put it on that chair. I want to get a good look at it – before I have it destroyed."

Thomas carried it in and, fingers shaking, carefully unwrapped it, exposing its ornate gilt frame. He balanced it on the spoon-backed chair.

"I had forgotten how perfect it is," he said, his voice quivering, devouring the image with his eyes. "The best work I have ever done, even better than the commissioned portrait."

"Well, that's unfortunate for you," she said, looking in horror at the work. "Maybe next time make sure to get the lady's permission. If my husband saw this, he would never forgive me. My father-in-law, Lord Frome, would disown me. You absolute idiot!"

Thomas hardly heard her – he was in a daze. After all this time, it was as if he was seeing it anew. His heart seemed to slow down, so that he could feel it thumping in his chest. It was as if he was suspended on the cusp of consciousness. As he gazed upon the image, he was struck with the realisation that he had captured that elusive quality in her expression. The eyes that said, '*I am yours – take me – I also want you*'. But it was equally obvious that this was not true. It was a ruse – she was a siren – available to no one. It suddenly dawned on him that this was the secret of her allure. She was a sexual predator, a narcissist that fed upon the desire of others – no one could ever have her. He felt this cold chill of realisation dawn upon him.

"You will destroy the painting," she said, interrupting his trance, "and now it is you who owes me fifty guineas. Fortunately, it was less expensive than some of my more elaborate hats."

She stared at the image with knitted eyebrows, puzzled, her mouth turned up at one corner, while Thomas stood dazed, trying to process what she had just said.

A footman knocked and opened the door.

Helen rushed over before he could enter.

"Mrs Rosa Cohen and Mr Isaac Tarrant are here to see you, ma'am. She says she is your sister." The servant's face was impassive, but his eyes sparkled with barely concealed curiosity.

"*Damn!*" Helen turned to Thomas. "*You told them where I was!*" she said furiously.

"No, no. I promised you I would not," he said, horrified.

"Your loyalty to me is not something I rely on – as I am sure you can appreciate," she retorted sarcastically.

Isaac, dressed all in black, his hand on Rosa's shoulder as if he was steering a recalcitrant child, entered the room.

"Rosa, Isaac!" Helen said, trying to maintain a calm outward demeanour while inwardly aghast at seeing them. "What a surprise! The happy couple. What brings you to London?"

As Helen stood, arms crossed, Rosa and Isaac looked in horror at the painting on the chair, and then to the clothed portrait on the wall – before their eyes returned, as if by some magnetic force, to gaze, frozen – on the nude.

Helen's eyes sparkled with tears. "Shocking, sister – is it not?" Then to them both. "This appropriation of me for the casual satisfaction of any leery viewer. It is worse than actually being seen publicly naked." She turned to address a white-faced Isaac. "Well, what do you think, Isaac? Does it do me justice?"

"How could you do this to me?" said Isaac, eyes glinting, devastated at what he was seeing. "Lord save me, but I loved you, Lena! And, Rafferty, I will finish off what I should have done in Vienna! I will kill you!"

With that, Isaac launched his body with full force at Rafferty, grabbing him by the throat, forcing him to the ground. The sound of china ornaments shattering filled the room as a small side table was knocked over onto the hard parquet floor.

At sound of the fall, the door burst open, and two footmen ran into the room.

Helena shouted, "*Separate them!*" as Isaac and Thomas grunted and wrestled.

The footmen, not without difficulty, eventually dragged Isaac off Rafferty and pulled him to his feet.

"*Control yourself, Isaac!*" yelled Helen. "*Or I will call the police!*"

Isaac, now standing, straightened his shirt and cravat,

his expression furious as he glared with hatred at Rafferty. Rosa's face was ashen – she looked like she was about to faint.

Helen nodded at the footmen to leave the room. Her whole body was trembling, fuelled by the rush of adrenalin as she had watched them fight, and the dawning realisation of what he had just said. Isaac loved her – he had always loved her.

"Isaac," she said. "Look closely at the painting. Look at it!"

Isaac, still consumed with anger, reluctantly moved over towards the painting, and gazed at the image. Rafferty had captured her tantalising allure. His eyes swept over the fullness of her breasts, her brown nipples and the curves and hollows of her flesh, those secret places that only he should know. But there was something not quite right in the proportions, something jarred. And then he saw it – a small round brown birthmark at the top of her thigh.

"It isn't you," he whispered in disbelief to Helen. Then he looked at his wife. "It is ... you!"

"Yes, yes – it is my sister! Miss Goody-Two-Shoes," said Helen icily. "Well, Rosa what have you to say for yourself!"

Rosa's legs buckled – she sank to the floor so that her bustle stood up behind her and her satin skirt pooled in a stiff circle around her knees. She looked up at Isaac, tears spilling down her cheeks, her expression one of abject misery and supplication.

"I am so sorry, Isaac. I needed the money for Samuil – for the doctors. I was afraid to ask you, that you would send me back to Kornyn. He wanted to paint her naked, but she wouldn't let him." Tears ran down her face. "I didn't want to ask you for more money, Isaac. You have to believe me."

Isaac looked at Rosa in astonishment.

"You ... you have let me believe my wife was having an affair! While all the time it was you who were prostituting yourself for this man. How could you sink so low, Rosa!" He paused as the enormity of the situation sank in, then spat out, "You disgust me!"

"You have to believe me, Isaac! I modelled for money I desperately needed to pay Samuil's medical bills. – nothing more!"

Rosa, her head bent in her hands, started sobbing quietly. Isaac moved to the window and stared vacantly across the square. Thomas, rubbing his throat where Isaac had nearly strangled him, sat down on a chair.

"Oh, do get up and stop blubbering, Rosa," said Helen impatiently, as she sat down on the chaise longue opposite Thomas. She rubbed her temples with her long fingers. She had to think clearly.

Helen's harsh words seemed to bring Rosa to her senses. She got up awkwardly and dried her tears with her handkerchief, looking abjectly at Isaac's back.

After a few minutes' deliberation, Helen rose.

"Could you leave us, please, Rosa and Thomas," she

said. "I wish to talk privately with Isaac."

"No, Isaac, don't listen to her," Rosa implored. "I am so sorry. I –"

"Leave us, Rosa!" Isaac said coldly. "We will talk later! I can't even look at you. And, Rafferty, you will not get away with this!" He moved from the window, his face still contorted with rage. "Consider yourself a dead man."

At Isaac's words, Thomas's looked with renewed terror at Isaac, his eyes popping as he held his throat, still rattled after the assault.

Helen rang the bell and the footmen reappeared.

"Please show this lady and gentleman to my sitting room."

Rosa reluctantly and Thomas gratefully left the room.

When the door closed behind them, Isaac turned to Helen.

"Why did you do it? Leave me, steal all my money? I never showed you anything but kindness." His eyes were accusing. "I loved you, Lena. I always loved you."

"Because I knew, Isaac. I knew you were sleeping with Rosa. I couldn't bear it."

"But you didn't want me," he said simply, moving over to her, placing his hands tentatively on her waist.

"Oh, I wanted you," she said assuredly, looking into his eyes. "But not in the way you wanted me. I cannot ... I do not have the same desire as other women."

"What do you mean?" he said, confusion written over his face.

390

"I d-don't …" she stuttered. "Look, it is not you, it is me. I have problems in that regard. It is not uncommon, I believe – according to the doctors." She lowered her head – she could not meet his eyes.

"Doctors? You have a physical problem? You should have told me! Surely it can be treated?"

"No, it is not physical, it is who I am. I tried to tell you – once. But … I did not have the words. I understand things better now."

"And now?"

"I have a daughter."

"With Frome?"

"Yes."

"So, you can sleep with Frome, but not with me!" he said bitterly, releasing her abruptly, his face pained.

"I can – I always could – when necessary. Frome understands. He is very gentle. He is willing to accept me as I am. He is happy enough to live with me on these terms."

Isaac looked bewildered. "Like owning a painting."

"Maybe."

"And now?"

"I believe you and I need a divorce."

"But you married Frome."

"Yes, a necessity. I acquired a new identity using fake documentation in Paris which has stood me in good stead so far. But we should regularise things. Presumably you wish to marry Rosa?"

"Rosa. Yes, I do – or I did." He turned away, rubbing the back of his neck with his hand, pacing the room. "But she has deceived me, posing for Rafferty like that. It is not the act of a respectable woman."

Helen's initial fury at her sister had passed and she had already come to a decision regarding the unexpected turn of events. She realised that this was her nemesis – the past catching up on her. Unfortunately, at this stage, there was no turning back. But unwelcome as this situation was, it provided her with an opportunity to right a wrong that she would otherwise forever regret. It was a chance to make peace with Rosa.

Helen chose her words carefully. "Then you are a fool! Isaac, like all men your good sense was always clouded by desire. Such a fickle thing, as I have learned to my cost." She turned from him, drawing on some inner strength.

"What are you saying?" he said, his brows furled.

"Rosa loves you. She is a kind woman – a good woman. Posing for Rafferty was done out of love for her stepson, Samuil, to pay his medical fees. You know you were always intended for one another. All of those years ago, I did her a grave wrong."

"I must also accept some of the blame. But you are right, I do love her," he said sheepishly. "Not the intense longing I have for you, but she makes me happy. And you?"

"I have what I want," she said brusquely, disappointed that he had given her up so easily. "However, from now on, I am afraid that playing happy families is impossible.

I will give you your *get*. In return you and Rosa will return to Vienna, and I will not see either of you again – ever!"

Isaac paused briefly, then nodded his head in resignation and – Helen was not sure whether she imagined it – with relief.

"What about the painting?" he asked.

"Let me deal with that – and Rafferty, of course. You no longer have to worry about either of them."

Helen turned away from him, so he couldn't see the tears in her eyes as she walked over to the bell-cord to call the footman.

$\backsim\!\!\backsim\!\!\backsim$

Chapter 24

Dublin,
January 2012

Daisy had been so embarrassed about the events after Christmas that she had put off ringing Ben for a few days. He had been so sweet, looking after her, making her breakfast. He really was such a lovely guy. She had probably blown it, she thought, her heart sinking. He wouldn't be interested in her now after pulling that stunt.

At least, she had given Fintan, the bastard, short shrift when he had rung her the next day.

"Look, babe, it was nothing, you are overreacting."

But it was when he said, "It's all in your head," that she lost it with him.

"Fintan, you are a mind-fuck! It's over between us. And do you know, for your information, I actually *do* want children. I even like them. I don't want to spend my life wedded to whatever company is paying your salary, while you exist in a state of puerile suspended animation, living and playing life in the fast lane!"

She had slammed down the phone and sobbed, on and off, for the rest of the evening, feeling deeply sorry for herself.

A couple of days later, on her lunch break, she was walking along Nassau Street when she met Dermot Nolan.

"Daisy, good to see you. Looking fantastic as usual! Did you have a good Christmas?"

They chatted away amiably for several minutes. His Christmas had been a quiet one. He admitted he wasn't in a relationship, and she told him that neither was she. She didn't go into details.

"Have you time for a coffee? I have some news that I think you will be interested in about your paintings?"

"Shouldn't we wait till Ben is with us and tell him as well?"

"Well, it's no big deal – you can tell him if you like. I'll set up a formal meeting in a few days, once I've cleared my Christmas emails. So, coffee?"

It seemed churlish to refuse, and there was also the fact that he was attractive and good company. In the café on the first floor over the Kilkenny design shop he bought her coffee and a chocolate-chip cookie.

"It was great to bump into you like this. I was going to ring Ben anyway. Don't worry, I still will," he said reassuringly. "Ben must be disappointed that we are still unable to formally attribute his painting to Rafferty.

395

Obviously, it would make a significant difference to the painting's value. Unfortunately, Rafferty himself left no records. Most of what we know about him has been gleaned from secondary sources. So, as a last attempt, I rang Professor Jonathan Trimble in Trinity College, the expert in 19th century Irish painting I consulted initially. I told him about the underpainting of the nude and his interest was piqued. Remember at our first meeting I read an extract from Lady Fitzherbert's diaries during the 1860s where she suggested that Rafferty had left London under a cloud, following some sort of scandal. Well, the Proff told me that in Rafferty's later years he was a constant visitor to Lady Fitzherbert's house, and he remembered her writing about him during that time. Anyway, the Professor has promised to read through the diaries – and there are volumes of them, to see can he find these references that might shed light on the matter of the two portraits."

***

As promised, Dermot Nolan had arranged to meet Ben and Daisy the following Monday evening after the gallery was officially closed. Daisy, early as usual, was chatting to Dermot in his office when Ben arrived, slightly breathless. He apologised to them both.

"Don't worry, Daisy was entertaining me," said Dermot. "She was updating me about her attempts to sell the virtues of cycling to pensioners. She was telling me about it when we met up last week."

"Oh," said Ben, eyebrows raised, looking in surprise from Dermot to Daisy.

"But I have moved on to greater things now," she said ironically. "I am working on a programme to raise feelings of nationalism in Ireland's youth."

"Now why would anyone want to do that?" asked Dermot, smiling at her.

"Well, Dermot," she said archly, but with a steely tone, "the recent decline in religious practice and trust in our institutions has left society with no clear moral compass. So, my client feels that it's important to develop civic responsibility amongst young people to maintain social cohesion – and to prevent things happening like … like last year's London riots. In fact, the government in Britain is looking at a similar programme."

She could see Ben watching her intently, as she explained this to Dermot.

"That's really interesting, I'd love to hear more about it," Dermot said enthusiastically.

"You had something you wanted to tell us both about the painting," said Ben rather abruptly.

"Yes, as I told you on the phone, I met with Professor Jonathan Trimble in Trinity College, an expert on Nineteenth Century Irish art. He's a bit of a Rafferty buff. Remember, I read an excerpt to you and Ben from Lady Ellen Fitzherbert's diary when I first met you. Well,

Professor Trimble remembered reading in later volumes of the diary about visits Rafferty made when he was quite elderly to her family's estate in Leitrim. This was during the early 1900s – Rafferty would have been in his seventies then. From the details on Daisy's family tree, Helen Frome was dead at that stage. Anyway, Lady Fitzherbert had three granddaughters, and she got Rafferty to paint each of them. She dabbled in watercolours herself – flowers mainly – we have one of her works here in the gallery. Rafferty was a frequent guest at her country estate, Herbert Hall, and she referred to him many times in her diaries. Professor Trimble went through these volumes again for me, and on the 25th of November 1903 he found a rather interesting entry."

Dermot put on his round tortoiseshell reading-glasses and lifted a page from his desk.

"This is a transcript that the Prof kindly made for me: *'Rafferty here for the weekend. After dinner, having had a bit too much to drink, and after some probing from Freddy, he cleared up the mystery of his sudden departure from London and rumours of a scandal all those years ago. Rafferty claimed that as a young man, he had been commissioned to paint a wealthy Jewish woman in Vienna by her husband. She was incredibly beautiful, and he fell madly in love with her, obsessively so. He started to paint a second painting of her, intended only for himself, but in the nude. However, he found it too difficult to complete without a model. He was in the habit of using a young woman from a local hat shop, but she was the wrong build. But*

398

another woman, a poor relation of the wealthy Jewess who looked very like her, was also working in the hat shop learning the trade. At the time she needed money to pay medical bills for her sick son. Rafferty later discovered that this woman was the Jewess's sister. She was desperate for money, and Rafferty persuaded her to model in the nude for the second portrait.'"

"And the Jewess was?" asked Ben.

"Lady Fitzherbert never named her. Rafferty was probably still loyal to her, even after all those years."

"Or possibly afraid to," said Ben.

"Maybe. Lady Fitzherbert goes on: *'Rafferty was besotted with the Jewess, and he thought she was with him. They planned to leave Vienna and run away together. But at the appointed time, she didn't show. Instead, she robbed her husband, and some hours before she was due to meet Rafferty, she left with some Polish military man that she was also stringing along. When Rafferty eventually returned to his studio his safe had been opened and all his money was gone. She had also cut the canvas from the frame of his portrait of her. However, she was unaware of the existence of the nude which was left behind. A few years later the Jewess ended up marrying the son of an English Baron, under a new name as she had not been divorced yet. But one day the nude painting turned up in a London gallery and somehow the woman's Jewish husband got to hear about it. All hell was to pay because the Jewess knew nothing about the existence of the nude. When she found out, she wanted Rafferty to destroy it. But they were afraid that the gallery owner would tell the world of its existence, and its sudden disappearance would fuel the gossips. In the end, Rafferty was persuaded by her to paint over the portrait. Rafferty claimed he was told by the Jewess, and her ex-husband who were both furious with him, that if he wanted to stay alive, he would be advised to leave London and go back to Ireland. He claimed that after a brief sojourn in Brighton licking his wounds, that was exactly what he did. But the incident rankled with him. He told Freddy that it was a serious blow to his career as a portrait-painter in London, just as he was getting established.'* And then she goes on to describe new curtains she wanted for the drawing room."

"That's fascinating, Dermot," said Ben.

"Not exactly a happy-ever-after ending for any of them," said Daisy.

"Well, I suppose they all got what they thought they wanted. Lena, or Helen was quite the operator. She sounds like she was a tough cookie," said Ben thoughtfully.

"I'd say she had to be, in order to survive in those days," said Dermot. "Hopefully, as well as her good looks you will have inherited some of her resilience, Daisy."

"Thank you," said Daisy, smiling. "I would like to think so. My mother will be intrigued when I tell her. What a story! Dermot, we can't thank you enough. Please tell Professor Trimble that we are really grateful to him for all of his research."

"Of course. He was intrigued himself. He asked for permission to take some photographs of the paintings. He is planning to write an article about them."

"No problem," Daisy nodded.

"Yeah, fine," said Ben.

"An article from Professor Trimble will be extremely important to you, Ben. The fact that there is no signature no longer matters. This information, together with my analysis, are enough to authenticate it as one of Rafferty's works."

"Thanks, Dermot. As Daisy said, we are really grateful for all the work that you put into this. Can we pay you?"

"Absolutely not. I might even get to write an article myself about the conservation aspects. So, it looks like you are both good to go now with the sale."

"Looks like it," said Ben.

"Thanks so much," Daisy said gratefully.

"My pleasure. Hopefully, I'll see you again soon," Dermot replied, his eyes resting on Daisy.

"Yes, that would be nice."

When they got outside, Daisy was surprised at the glum expression on Ben's face.

"Aren't you delighted, Ben?"

"Yeah ... *mm*, that's great."

"I believe the next auction is taking place next week. With any luck, we can still get in the catalogue. I'll ring Bellamy's tomorrow."

"You met up with Dermot after Christmas? Like, last week after you stayed in mine?" Ben was standing his hands dug into his pockets, his face inscrutable.

"Yes, I bumped into him in Nassau Street."

"Had a good time?" he asked, eyebrows raised.

"Yes, he's a really nice guy."

"Well, looks like this is all wrapped up so." Ben gave her a lopsided grin.

"Yes, my mum will be pleased. She can finally stop worrying about money. Look, Ben, I'm afraid I'll have to rush off. I've got to work this evening. I have a presentation first thing in the morning on that project I was just talking about. Look, I'll give you a ring tomorrow and we can arrange about the auction. Maybe we could have a drink to celebrate afterwards?"

"Yeah. That would be great."

She was going to give him a peck on the cheek, but she thought he seemed uncomfortable in some way.

Despite the good news about finally being able to sell the paintings, after leaving him she felt suddenly dejected as she walked towards Merrion Square.

***

The auction room was busy enough. Daisy had kept him a seat at the back of the room so that they would have a good view of the proceedings. Bellamy's auctioneer was standing at the lectern waiting for the evening's proceedings to begin. True to form, he was wearing a pale-grey suit, yellow-and-blue-striped shirt, and a yellow dickie-bow tie.

Daisy looked anxiously at her watch, wondering what

was keeping Ben – the auction was due to start any minute. And their paintings were amongst the first batch to be sold, numbers twelve and thirteen in the auction catalogue. Daisy's painting was coming up first.

As the clock struck six o'clock, Ben sidled up beside her.

"Sorry, the principal called me to her office. She's like a dog – she has this sixth sense. I was afraid she was going to keep me in for detention."

"At least you're here now," she said, smiling. "Do you know, I was just thinking, although I am really excited about finally selling the painting, I am also quite sad about it."

"Why is that?"

"Well, these last few months have been such an adventure. I have really enjoyed spending time with you. I was hoping ... after this is all over, we could still be friends."

"I hope so too. But you have made another friend because of all of this – Dermot – and he seems to be quite an admirer," he said tentatively.

"Maybe." She laughed. "He's a nice guy, but he's not really my type."

"Ah." He paused. "And what is your type?"

"Well ... someone like you." Daisy held her breath.

Ben's heart soared but, before he had a chance to respond, the bidding started.

The auctioneer looked around the room and raised his gavel to quell the chatter, like an orchestra conductor with an unruly audience indicating that tonight's performance was about to commence.

"Ladies and gentlemen, without further ado, let us begin. We have several exciting works to bring to the market this evening. Lot number one is a rather fine water colour of College Green by the renowned American-born Irish artist Flora Mitchell."

The auction proceeded at a brisk pace, with some paintings reaching their reserve price while others were withdrawn if they failed to do so. Ben held Daisy's hand as they both sat electrified, in tense anticipation.

When it came to lot number nine, Ben whispered in her ear, "Forgot to agree a reserve price with Lamb. I'll be back in a minute."

As Daisy watched him sidle out of the row, she was momentarily exasperated. Jesus, after all that they had been through, she didn't want him to miss the bloody sale of the paintings.

But he got back a few minutes later, just as the auctioneer adjusted his pince-nez glasses at the end of his nose and announced with solemnity, "The next item tonight is one of two paintings that are the stars of this evening's show. Many of you will have read about them in an article in last week's *Sunday Independent*. Two paintings, perfect copies. Except one isn't quite what it appears to be on the surface."

Ben reached over and grabbed Daisy's hand. The audience was silent. You could hear a pin drop.

"The artist, the renowned Victorian portrait painter, Thomas Rafferty, was commissioned by a wealthy Viennese businessman to paint his wife Lena Tarrant. However, Rafferty fell in love with her, and was so besotted that he painted her in the nude – a second painting intended for his eyes only. She refused to model nude for him. But he persuaded her sister to model for him instead. The wife subsequently remarried, becoming Lady Helen Frome. When she discovered the existence of the second painting, she forced Rafferty to paint over it. A most unusual case. This is a unique opportunity to invest in this artist. So, can I have offers for the first and original portrait of Lady Helen Frome? I'll start the bidding at ten thousand. How about fifteen? I am offering this beautiful portrait for fifteen thousand euros." He surveyed the room.

A gentleman in front of Daisy and Ben raised a wooden paddle.

"Thank you, sir. I have fifteen. Twenty, anyone. Twenty, from the lady in the front. Twenty-five?" He nodded again at the back of the room. "Thirty, do I have thirty. Thirty from the lady at the back of the house. Do I have forty?" He nodded. "And ... fifty thousand ... I have fifty thousand from the gentleman to my left."

Daisy squeezed his hand. "I don't believe it! Fifty thousand!"

"James Lamb told me the story would drive up the prices."

"I have just received a telephone bid of sixty thousand. How about seventy thousand? In the room for seventy thousand. A particularly important work by Rafferty. Madam, can I raise you to seventy-five. No?" The woman shook her head. "So, seventy thousand, I have an offer in the room of seventy thousand. If I have no other bidders, I am going to accept seventy thousand. Fair warning. Sold for – seventy thousand!"

Ben put his arm around her.

She could barely contain her excitement. "We did it, Ben. We did it!"

"Now, the next painting is the over-painted nude," continued the auctioneer. "Although unsigned, in its own way it is even more interesting than the original. I already have a telephone bid for this, for sixty thousand."

A gentleman in a suit approached the dais and whispered in James Lamb's ear, then left.

"Oh, how disappointing," said Lamb. "The painting, unfortunately, has been withdrawn at the last minute." Then, as he looked witheringly at Ben at the back of the room, he said under his breath, but it could just about be heard with the microphone, "Seems like a case of déjà vu." Straightening up, he continued in a booming voice, "Never mind, we have lots more on offer this evening for discerning buyers. The next item is a lovely little oil painting by Letitia Hamilton RHA, entitled *A Fair Day in Ballinasloe* ..."

Daisy looked at Ben, shocked. "What the ...? Did you withdraw it?"

406

"How could I sell it, Daisy? It's part of our history. Yours and mine, it's who we are – complicated."

"*Shhh*," said the fat lady beside him.

"*Shhh* yourself," Ben said, and leaned over and kissed Daisy gently on the lips.

Epilogue

Spiegelgasse, Vienna
1883

Rosa, her mother Zipporah, and the two girls were examining the cloth.

"Careful, Miriam," said Rosa to her youngest daughter. "This cloth was made for me when I was a young girl, only a year older than you, and betrothed to your father – many years ago."

Rosa looked at Isaac who was sitting by the fire reading the paper. He lifted his head and smiled at her. Her son Anton was sitting on the couch, his head in a book, as usual.

"Tata said it was the finest cloth in all of Zhytomyr," she said, stroking the cloth gently, feeling the raised silk stitches with the tips of her fingers. "All those long, candlelit, winter evenings we spent sewing, gossiping, and telling stories. If this cloth could talk! You would blush at the stories it would tell."

"Old Bubbe Sadie's were the best!" said Zipporah.

"And now, after Pesach," Rosa continued, "Jessica will take it when she marries Adam." She smiled at her elder daughter with tears of happiness and sadness in her eyes. "The Lord willing, they will start their own family. A new generation to pray and share challah bread on this cloth."

Jessica smiled back at her mother.

"Tell us the old Bible tale, Mama – about Jacob marrying the wrong sister," said Miriam.

Rosa looked at Zipporah and smiled nervously. Of all the Bible stories they knew, why did this one fascinate them? Rosa cringed each time she heard it and the memories it evoked.

Images of her sister and herself as young girls floated through her mind. She had not seen or heard from her for years. Sadly, that was the price they had both agreed to pay. Occasionally Rosa bought the London papers to read news of her in the society gossip columns. Lena was always at some charity ball or other.

She had two children – both grown up now, a girl and a boy. One of each – for Georgie. And what had happened to that fool Rafferty, she wondered. She had heard that Lena had banished him back to Ireland. After he had painted over the portrait, of course. Lena had been terrified that one day their secret would be discovered and had insisted that Isaac and she take it back with them to Vienna. Rosa shouldn't have agreed. She shivered at the thought of it sitting above them gathering dust in their attic. She had asked Isaac several times to destroy it, afraid it would bring them bad luck. But she knew he was unable to bring himself to do it. She couldn't bear to even look at it. Although she suspected that Isaac did – the odd time.

"Mama, the story!" said Jessica impatiently.

"Why don't you just change the ending," said Zipporah, looking knowingly at her.

"I suppose, in the end, that's what I did. In my case the ugly sister won out in the end." Rosa smiled, looking over conspiratorially at her husband. But he, inscrutable as ever, was concentrating intently on reading his newspaper.

THE END

Further Reading

For readers interested in learning more about life for the Jews in Nineteenth Century Eastern Europe, the authors of the following works – to whom I am indebted – informed *A Perfect Copy*.

Non-Fiction:

Yohanan Petrovsky-Shtern, *The Golden Age Shtetl – A New History of Jewish Life in East Europe* (New Jersey: Princeton University Press, 2014).

Nicholas T. Parsons, *Vienna – A Cultural and Literary History* (Oxford: Signal Books Ltd.,2008).

Edmund De Waal, *The Hare with Amber Eyes* (London: Chatto and Windus, 2010).

Fiction:

Elana Dykewomon, *Beyond the Pale* (New York: Open Road Integrated Media Inc.,2013).